"A brilli... crime
partnership and sound forensic expertise." SUE BLACK, DBE,
FORENSIC ANTHROPOLOGIST

"[A] fantastic new crime novel…a gritty book with a surprisingly warm theme of female friendship." THE LIST

"MacL... ...d and engag... ...ursting with the liveliness of the Aberdonian vernacular… an impressive debut." RAVEN CRIME READS

"Proof that good things come to those who wait."
DUNDEE COURIER

"Crime fiction has a new stellar voice in Claire MacLeary. Cross Purpose is feisty, funny and darkly delicious."
MICHAEL J MALONE

"A terrific crime debut with an unlikely crime-fighting partnership that sets it apart from the rest. Takes the reader on an emotional roller coaster. Unsettling at times, even uncomfortable, but compelling to the end." THERESA TALBOT

"A surprising read with dialogue so salty and a plot so gritty that it could keep a Highland road clear all winter."
DOUGLAS SKELTON

"A dark devious delight, defi... ...one to watch."
NEIL BROADFOOT

# Cross Purpose

**Claire MacLeary**

CONTRABAND 🔒

Contraband is an imprint of Saraband

Published by Saraband,
Suite 202, 98 Woodlands Road
Glasgow, G3 6HB

www.saraband.net

ISBN: 9781910192641
ebook: 9781910192658


10 9 8 7 6 5 4 3 2


Printed and bound in Great Britain by Clays Ltd, St Ives plc.

MIX
Paper from
responsible sources
FSC® C018072

Following a career in business, Claire MacLeary gained an MLitt with Distinction from the University of Dundee. Her short stories have been published in various magazines and anthologies. She lived for some years in Aberdeen, and subsequently in Fife, before returning to her native Glasgow. *Cross Purpose* is her first book and will be followed by a sequel, *Burnout*.

# I

# Maggie

They stood, side by side, not speaking, Maggie barely breathing.

'When you're ready.' Detective Inspector Allan Chisolm indicated the floor-length curtains.

Maggie watched, her stare unwavering, as the DI drew the curtains apart. Through the glass of the viewing window, she could see the body. It lay on a metal gurney. Maggie had expected a marble slab. A plinth, perhaps. Something more solid, anyhow. She looked down at the uncovered face of the body that lay there. Nothing could have prepared her for that face. It was black and blue all over, mottled here and there with blotches of yellow. The thick, dark hair she loved was combed in a parting she didn't recognise, the sharp blue eyes blinkered by ink-stained lids. The facial expression was bland. Not tortured in its death throes, as she'd expected, but flattened somehow, all its humanity stripped out.

She stood there for some minutes, rigid, her breath gradually misting the glass. Then, 'George!'

Maggie splayed her fingers across the window, let her head fall forward until she could feel her forehead come into contact with the glass. She longed to drum her fists upon its unyielding surface, butt it with her head until it shattered, battle her way through the opening until she could be with him once more. If only she could come up close. Hold his hand in hers. Please, God. Just one last time.

'Mrs Laird, can you confirm this is your husband?'

She turned. 'Yes.'

Silently, the man standing alongside acknowledged her response.

'Can you give me a moment?'

'I'm sorry. I'm not permitted…'

She fixed him with a furious glare.

Maggie Laird had been to Queen Street many times, but never to the morgue. That morning, she'd expected Bob Duffy to receive her. The DS was, after all, the one who'd responded to the shout. But this guy Chisolm was a complete stranger. She'd heard he'd been drafted in. New broom and all that. Maggie seethed. A day like today and they couldn't even send a kent face.

'Is Alec Gourlay about?'

The inspector raised an enquiring eyebrow.

'He said he'd have a word once…'

The DI nodded. 'I'll ring through.' He retreated down the room.

Maggie slid onto the nearest chair. She squeezed her eyes tight shut, trying to blank out the images that were fighting for space in her head. She'd heard George describe in graphic detail the layout of the mortuary: the stark little viewing room. Beyond that, the investigation room. The post-mortem room with its grey walls, its impermeable flooring, the two stainless-steel cutting tables in the centre. She shuddered as she pictured her husband laid out naked in the dissection room.

She sat, mouth agape, lungs working overtime in the airless space. Maggie spread her knees, then let her head drop between them, clasped clammy hands at the nape of her neck. It couldn't have been more than a few minutes before she raised her head. The small space was sparsely furnished. Two charcoal upholstered chairs. Against the far wall, a teak-effect trolley was laid with an embroidered tray-cloth. On it sat a box of paper tissues and a bunch of artificial pink roses in a bulb vase. Somebody had made a bit of an effort.

She heard muffled footsteps approach. Was aware of the door opening quietly, then closing again.

A familiar voice. 'Give us some time, will you?'

Then Chisolm. 'I'll be upstairs.'

Maggie felt a light touch at her elbow.

The pathologist bent over her. 'Are you all right?'

She raised her head. 'Alec,' she summoned a feeble grin. 'I can't honestly say I'm pleased to see you.'

He was a small man, not more than five foot seven or eight. And wiry, with sharp cheekbones, a hooked nose and dark, darting eyes. Like a little bird, Maggie thought, that first time they were introduced. Alec dressed, always, in the same outfit: ancient, baggy sports jacket with patches on the elbows, Tattersall check shirt and threadbare cords. More like an out-of-work academic than a surgeon. His light brown hair was thinning at the temples, his haircuts erratic and never good. But looks belied, for he had a rigorous mind and a fearsome reputation for working to exacting standards. Maggie had been intimidated when they met first but, over time, she had warmed to him. For, behind the brusque manner, she had come to realise that Alec Gourlay was a thoughtful and sensitive man.

Now she was grateful for his presence.

'I'm sorry,' he took hold of her hand. 'I'd have come earlier, only...'

Brusquely, she cut in. 'Why is George here?'

'The death was sudden, and the attending GP wasn't too keen to sign it off.'

'Will there have to be a post-mortem?'

Gourlay let go of her hand. 'Depends. But seeing as George was already on heart medication, I'll probably get away with a visual examination.'

'Who decides?'

'I do.'

'A favour, then, Alec – a few minutes alone with him.'

He shook his head. 'Can't be done.'

'Why not?'

'The mortuary operates under Council jurisdiction.'

'Still, you must carry some clout.'

He regarded her warily. 'I suppose.'

'Then please?'

'No, Maggie.'

'*Please?*'

'I can't.'

She clutched at his sleeve. 'For me?'

'Not even for you.'

'For George, then?'

Gourlay brushed the back of his hand across his forehead. 'That's a cheap one.'

'I know.' She turned away.

There was a long silence, then, 'Let me see what I can do.'

## X

Maggie leaned against the door frame. She blinked hard. Squared her shoulders. Moved forward. By the side of the trolley, she stopped.

She reached out. With the flat of her hand, she gently smoothed his chilled brow. With one forefinger, she traced the outlines of that strong face: nose, cheeks, jaw. She pressed trembling fingertips to chapped lips. Cupped small palms over bruised eyelids.

For a few moments she stood, immobile, striving to summon in her mind the warmth, the vigour, the musky man scent of the George she had known. Then she clambered onto the metal gurney and covered with the length of her body her husband's corpse.

# Wilma

Wilma eyed Ian's plate of egg and beans. 'Sorry about the dinner.'

'Nae bother,' he grinned, shovelling in another forkful.

'I've had some day.'

'Oh? Why's that?'

'Me an' Maggie Laird had to go into town first thing. Husband dropped dead yesterday.'

Ian's hand hung half-way to his mouth. 'George Laird next door?'

'Aye. Police came knocking. Did you not hear them?'

'No. Must have been out for the count. But,' he frowned, 'how did you manage to get involved?'

'She'd to identify the body.'

'Didn't they offer to send a car?'

'Doesn't look like it. And the garage had just rung to say her own needed work.' Wilma's bright blue eyes stood out like gobstoppers. 'Woman came running round here in a right paddy.' She paused for effect. 'I was near as bad. Grabbed my keys and was out of here. By the time I got to Queen Street I was fair wrung out.'

'Still, you'd have got parked at the door.'

'At Police HQ? You're joking. There's no bloody way I was going to sit out front under those bastards' noses. I'd to go round the block I don't know how many times. It's all double yellows round there.'

'So where did you end up?'

'Nipped up a wee ramp round the back.'

'Wil-ma,' Ian tutted, 'isn't that where they keep the CID pool cars?'

'Could be. It was all big Vauxhalls, right enough. But I never saw a soul the whole time. Just as well. Maggie was in there for ages.'

'You didn't go in with her, then?'

'I did offer. Not that I was keen, mind. I've seen enough of that sort of thing up at the infirmary. But Maggie was having none of it. Poor-looking wee soul she was, too. Most I could manage was see her back home, make her a cup of tea. You should have seen the house an all. It's not as if she's even been left comfortable. That kitchen, must have been years since it was fitted. And the suite in her sitting room…like something your granny would have brought in.' She rolled her eyes. 'Not even your granny.' Wilma sighed. 'Wish I could do more for the woman.'

'She's got family, hasn't she?'

'Lot of use them kids will be. Daughter's away at uni. And that boy of hers, he's at thon glaikit stage, nae use to man nor beast.'

Ian set down his knife and fork. 'You've a big heart, Wilma, but you've enough on your plate without nosing into other people's business.'

'Nosing? Is that what they call it round here?'

'Who?'

'The toffs.'

'Toffs?' Ian spluttered. 'In Mannofield? Now, if it was Rubislaw we were living in, or Bieldside, or…'

'You know what I mean. They're stand-offish around here. Keep themselves to themselves. Not like in Torry, where you'd get a news on the stair, meet a body the street…' Her words tailed off.

'It's mebbe a wee bit quieter,' he conceded.

'Quieter? It's bloody dead.'

'Well, isn't that a good thing?'

Wilma's back stiffened. 'Don't you start, Ian Harcus.'

'Anyhow,' he changed tack, 'Maggie Laird's got family. And George was a copper, wasn't he, until all that business?'

'So?'

'Well, isn't it true what they say – that coppers look after their own?'

'Not in this case,' she countered. 'By the looks of it, anyhow.'

'Wil-ma,' Ian's face darkened, 'I don't think it's a good idea, you involving yourself in Maggie Laird's problems. End of.'

'Why not?'

'I just told you why not. And besides, you've your work to go to, and there's this house to run.'

'What about the house?' Wilma regarded her husband with hostile eyes. 'Is it your dinner that's bothering you?'

'Dinner?' Ian looked down at his congealing plate of food. 'No, the dinner's braw.'

'Now you're being sarcastic.'

'And you're being daft.'

'Daft now, is it?'

'Wil-ma...'

'Don't you "Wil-ma" me.'

'Och,' Ian came back, 'there's no arguing with you when you've got a drink in you.'

*Bugger! So he'd smelled it on her. And she'd only had a swallow to steady her nerves.* Wilma jumped up from the table. 'A couple of beers and I've got a drink problem?'

Wearily, Ian met her eye. 'That's not what I said.'

'Isn't it?'

'No.'

'Whatever. I'm away to my bed.'

## X

Wilma lay in the dark. Her thoughts turned to Maggie Laird, lying on the other side of the party wall. *End of* – Ian's words resounded in her head. That wasn't like him. He was such a pussycat, her new husband: ran her to Asda to do the big weekly shop, carried the stuff in for her. He was handy round the house an all. Not that they could afford to do much. Not yet, what with the mortgage payments. Wilma could set anything down in front of him, too, and he'd eat it without a murmur. Mind you, he'd dug his heels in over drawing the bedroom curtains. She'd always preferred them open, ever since she was a small child. But of course that was because... Forget it, she rebuked herself sharply. She wasn't sure whether her husband's preference arose out of modesty – Ian was a bit funny about showing his "bits" – or whether he really did sleep better in the dark. Wilma thought it a bit weird, a man being coy like that about his privates, for she knew from experience that fellas were forever whipping their dicks out: seeing how far they could pee up against the wall of the bike sheds at school, jumping in the showers together after football fixtures, lining up the way they did in men's urinals. And when it came to women, how they couldn't wait to wave their willies about. Still… In the dark, Wilma chuckled. Ian might be old-fashioned when it came to stripping off, but once *she* got him going he was brand new.

She heard the toilet flush. Heard the bedroom door open and close. Heard her husband undress, the mattress springs yield as he got into bed. Decisively, she turned her back and slid down further under the duvet.

For a few minutes she lay still, then Wilma felt Ian's arm creep around her waist. She'd already decided he wouldn't be up for it, what with his six o'clock start and the row they'd had at dinner time. Now, she felt his body mould to hers, his hard-on worm its way up the back of her nightie. She uttered a little grunt of satisfaction. No call for Viagra there.

Wilma felt a surge of warmth between her thighs.

She wouldn't make waves about Maggie Laird.

Not yet, anyhow.

She'd bide her time.

# Fatboy

Fatboy stood on the corner of the Castlegate. His runner was late. Fatboy scowled. He got royally pissed off when his runner didn't show up on time. Rain started to spit. He stamped his feet. Pulled his hat down over his eyes. Retreated further into the shadow of the close mouth. He'd have one more fag. Fatboy fumbled in his jacket pocket. On days like these, he wondered what he was doing there when he could be sitting in comfort at home.

Situated at the east end of Union Street, the Castlegate encompasses an expansive square containing the castellated Citadel, built on the site of the medieval Aberdeen Castle, the Mercat Cross and the Gallowgate, where the city's public hangings were once held. Fatboy rued the day he'd picked the place for a rendezvous. It was way too open, for one thing. Next to the courts. Within spitting distance of police HQ. And getting far too crowded, these past few months. Too many other dodgy trades going on.

Fatboy lit up. Took a long drag. Exhaled slowly. He watched as the smoke drifted upwards, savouring its acrid smell. He shifted from one foot to the other. Maybe it was time to move on, find some other kind of deal. After all, it *had* been almost a couple of years.

He'd rolled his first stick at school. There was no problem getting hold of the stuff. It came from a van at the school gates along with the Coke and the crisps and the other junk food. Fatboy had kept up the connection. Started to deal in a small way: friends, friends of friends, a bit of weed, a few poppers. And it had grown from there. As sales rose, he'd been passed up the supply chain, managed to squeeze costs. The profits funded Fatboy's lifestyle: the amusement arcades and the online gambling and the rest. It was easy money. He curled his lip. Easy, that is, if your runners were reliable. And this one wasn't. Not any more. In fact – Fatboy inhaled deeply, blew out a stream of smoke – he was becoming a bit of a pain. He wondered if maybe the guy had developed a habit. A real habit. Happened to so many of the stupid fuckers. Fatboy didn't want to know about any of that. Had enough savvy to realise that if he stuck to the recreational stuff, kept to the one small patch, he'd be safe enough. Wouldn't encroach on anybody else's territory. Wouldn't step on any toes. Because you wouldn't want to do that. Fatboy shuddered. Not in Aberdeen. He'd had one frightener already. Scared the shit out of him. That's when he'd taken up with Mad Mike. Kept Fatboy out of sight, his trades below the radar.

'You Fatboy?'

'Who's asking?' He glowered down at the small boy.

'Ah'm askin', Willie Meston shot back, undeterred.

Fatboy looked him up and down. He was a scrawny kid: sandy hair cut in a No.2, pallid skin, blue eyes below an eyebrow piercing.

'What the fuck's it to you?'

'Ah wis telt tae find Fatboy.' Willie Meston craned his neck at the big lad standing up the close.

'Who by?'

'Ah'll tell ye that once…'

Fatboy grabbed the kid by the shoulders of his denim jacket. He hauled him upwards until Willie's feet were dangling in mid-air. 'Don't you fuck with me, you mingin wee bastard,' he spat, 'or I'll flatten your face so fast even your mammy won't recognise you.' He set Willie down on the pavement again.

The boy made a show of straightening his jacket, then he spoke. 'Ma da sent me.' The voice didn't carry quite so much conviction this time.

'Your da?' Fatboy leered. 'And who would that be?'

'Michael Meston.'

Fatboy shrugged. 'Don't know anybody called Meston. Now fuck off.'

Willie scratched his shaven head.

'I said…' Fatboy curled his hands into fists. The lad jumped back several paces. 'Fuck off.'

From his safe distance, Willie stood for a moment, deliberating, then he cocked his head to one side.

'Mad Mike?' he ventured.

'Mad Mike?' Fatboy laughed. 'Why didn't you fucking say that in the first place?' The boy laughed too, but uncertainly.

Fatboy wiped the grin from his face. 'Where *is* your da, then? He's fucking late.'

'That's what...'

'Come over here, where I can hear you.' Willie stayed put. 'I said...come here.' Fatboy's arm snaked out. He yanked Willie towards him. 'Now tell me where your dad is.'

Willie gulped a breath. 'He's in the jail.'

'What jail?'

'Peterhead.'

'Since when?'

'Last week.'

'What for?' Fatboy's mouth was set in a grim line. 'No. Never mind what for.'

Fuck.

Fuck.

Fuck.

Fuck.

What the shite was he going to do now? He had a stash of stuff to shift, a load of punters waiting in line, and no effing runner. He clenched his teeth. Fuck Mike Meston, if that really was his name. The knob-head must have known he was about to be banged up. Hadn't breathed a word. And now the fucker was in jail. Fatboy wondered if you could still do a trade or two with the new HMP Grampian. Just as quickly he dismissed the thought. It was some-one with a lot more muscle than him that was sending packages over that particular wall.

Fatboy folded his arms across his chest. He'd need to have a re-think. And fast. He looked down. The kid was still standing there like a spare prick.

'Well,' Fatboy eyed Willie, 'now you've done what you came for, you can bugger off.'

The boy didn't budge.

'I said,' there was menace now in Fatboy's voice, 'fuck off.'

'Ma da says...'

'I don't want to hear what your dad says,' Fatboy hissed. 'That's me and him finished, d'you hear? The next time you speak to him...' a smirk creased his face, 'whenever that's likely to be, you can tell him that from me.'

'But...'

'And when he gets out of Peterhead, he'd better not come looking – you can tell him that, too. Otherwise that'll be another face your mammy won't recognise.'

Willie half-turned. He looked back over his shoulder. 'Ma da telt me...'

Fatboy started forward. 'Fuck off, ya wee bastard.'

'You again?' The voice came out of nowhere. 'Did ah no tell ye no tae show yer face here?'

'I was just...' Fatboy eyed the man sideways. Didn't dare meet his gaze.

'Or ye mebbe fancy yer chances?'

'N-n-n-no,' Fatboy stuttered. Wildly, he cast around. The charity shop facades looked hostile, all of a sudden. On the cobbled expanse of the Castlegate there was hardly a soul to be seen.

'Well?' The man came up close, thrust a scarred face into Fatboy's own. 'What are ye sayin?'

'I was just...meeting my...' his brain churned, 'wee brother.'

'Wee brother, is it?' the man leered.

'Y-yes.' Fatboy swallowed a mouthful of air. 'Willie?' he shouted at the receding figure. And again, 'Willie?'

Willie turned.

The man backed off a fraction.

Fatboy made a run for it. He grasped the boy by the sleeve. 'You wouldn't like to do a few wee jobs for me?'

'What kind of jobs?'

'Oh,' Fatboy improvised, 'bit of this, bit of that.'

'No way,' Willie shook himself free. 'End up in Peterhead like ma da?' He swivelled on his heel. Marched off down Justice Street.

'Hang on,' Fatboy kept pace. 'It's nothing heavy. Honest.'

Willie shrugged. 'Forget it.'

'You'd be covering your dad's back.'

For a moment, the boy hesitated.

'Keeping his bed warm, so to speak. I might even…' Fatboy played for time, 'reconsider my position. If you agree, that is.'

'Ye mean take him back on?' Willie's eyes were out on his sunken cheeks.

Fatboy almost felt sorry for him. A whore in all likelihood for a mother, and that wee runt of a father banged up in jail. 'What are you saying, then?'

'When would ah be needin tae…?'

'We can talk about that later. Got a mobile on you?'

'Aye.'

'Give me your number.' Willie pulled a phone from his pocket, flashed it at Fatboy.

Fatboy thumbed his own. 'I'll be in touch.'

Willie legged it down the street.

Fatboy watched as he vanished round a corner.

He grinned. Maybe his morning wouldn't be wasted after all.

# Something to Tell You

Kirsty lay stretched out on the settee. 'What are we going to do?'

'I don't know.' Maggie was curled up in George's big chair. She turned her head away. Burrowed her nose in the soft fabric, trying to summon some sense of him.

'Have you seen him? Dad, I mean?'

Maggie turned back. 'This morning. In the mortuary.'

'Couldn't you have waited? I'd have come with you.'

'Thanks, pet,' Maggie summoned a smile, 'but the police needed me there first thing.'

Stricken face. 'You didn't go there on your own, did you?'

'No. I begged a lift off Wilma next door.'

'*Her*?'

'What d'you mean "her"?'

'Well, she's not exactly…'

'Don't be so quick to judge. You hardly know the woman.'

Kirsty's lip jutted. 'Neither do you.'

From beneath lowered lids, Maggie gazed across at her daughter. Kirsty looked a bit peaky, she thought. There were violet shadows under the girl's eyes, a scatter of pimples on her cheeks. I wonder if she's eating well enough, was Maggie's first thought.

Kirsty sat up. 'Where's the car, anyway?'

'In the garage.' Maggie made a face. 'Failed its MOT.'

'And Colin, where's he?'

'Round at a friend's house. They're going to feed him and drop him back after tea.'

'Is he OK?'

'In shock, I suppose. A bit like me.'

'Me too. I couldn't take it in when they told me. It happened at Dad's office, did you say?'

'That's right. A heart attack, they reckon.'

'But that doesn't have to kill you, Mum, not these days. A girl in my class at school, her dad got one of those pacemakers and...'

'I haven't got the details, pet, but I gather there was nobody around and it sounds like the ambulance crew weren't in time.'

'But, Mum,' Kirsty protested, 'that's so unfair.'

'I know, pet. All we can be thankful for is that your dad didn't suffer.'

'How would *you* know?' Kirsty was sobbing now. 'He was all alone in that office. Without anybody to help. Hold his hand, even.'

Maggie crossed to comfort her daughter. 'It's hard, but life can turn in an instant. Your dad saw that in his job. It's just...you never think it will happen to you.' She could scarcely believe that the God she'd put her trust in all her life had struck her husband down with such casual cruelty.

The two sat for some moments in a close embrace, then Kirsty broke free.

'What about the funeral? Do you know when that's going to be?'

'Not yet. I'll have to ring the undertaker. Make an appointment. A solicitor, too.' Maggie ran a distracted hand through her hair. 'Just as well your dad made a will when we took out the mortgage. Then there's his savings plan. That will ease things a bit.'

Kirsty scrubbed the tears from her face. 'Maybe I could help with some of that?'

'Will you, pet? That would be a Godsend. Tell you what *would* help – why don't you fish the deed box out of the sideboard and we can sort through the papers together? Give us something to occupy our minds till your brother gets back.'

## X

'Hi.' Colin came in the back door, slunk through the kitchen, headed down the hall.

'Colin?' Maggie's head whipped round. She and Kirsty were

sitting at the dining table, a couple of empty mugs and a sprawl of papers between them.

He turned. 'What?'

'Are you alright?'

Small shrug.

'Have you eaten?'

He nodded.

'Can I get you anything? Cup of tea? Glass of milk?'

'I'm fine.' His back receded down the hallway.

'Do you think I should go up?' Maggie fretted.

'No, Mum. Leave him. The last thing Col needs right now is to be fussed over.'

'I suppose.'

'And tomorrow, *if* I can get the lazy sod out of his bed, we'll both be able to give you a hand.'

'Thanks, pet,' Maggie smothered a yawn. She rose from the table. 'I'm worn out. You must be too. Why don't you get changed into your jammies? I'll make you a snack before you turn in.'

Kirsty got to her feet. 'I couldn't eat anything. You head for bed. I'll nip up and check on Colin.'

'Would you? That will put my mind at rest.'

**X**

Maggie turned the key in the back door. She thought at once of George. Her husband was such a stickler for safety. She crossed the hall to the ground-floor bedroom they'd shared. As the door closed behind her, George's dressing gown swung on its hook, silent and empty. She fingered the soft towelling, then leaned to bury her face in its depths. The robe smelled of spice: aftershave, deodorant, some sort of man smell. Swiftly she let go, stripped off her clothes, pulled her nightie over her head.

She walked through to the bathroom and bent to the basin to splash her face. As she straightened, Maggie caught her reflection in the bathroom cabinet. A spectre stared back at her, the halo of red curls only serving to accentuate her pallor, green eyes huge in a drawn face. And that left pupil, floating in the outside corner of her eye socket. It did that sometimes when she was stressed. The impediment had bugged her since her early teens. *Skelly,* the kids called her at school. *A lazy eye,* the GP pronounced. *Be content with what God gave you,* she could hear her mother's voice, even now. Meeting Maggie for the first time, folk didn't know where to look. Would zero in on one eye, then the other, then quickly glance away. Hadn't she encountered it that very day: the split second's hesitation on Chisolm's face? The fellow had covered it well, but she'd caught it, that quizzical look.

She opened the cabinet and reached for the toothpaste. George's razor, his toothbrush and dental floss stood in an orderly row. And a bottle of Grecian 2000. She'd bought it before he went for that last interview. Maggie slammed the cabinet shut.

Back in the bedroom, the double bed they'd shared looked vast, all of a sudden. She turned back the covers and crept underneath. The sheets were cold, colder than ever she remembered. George's pillow, where his dark head should have nestled, sat plump and unyielding. In that moment Maggie saw once again the mortuary gurney; felt once more her husband's body, cold and unyielding beneath her own.

She screwed her eyes shut and turned away, saying a silent prayer that sleep would swallow her. But sleep wouldn't come. Restless, she rolled over onto her back. Adjusted her limbs this way and that. Flexed her fingers, wiggled her toes, willing herself to drift from consciousness. Then, still wide awake, she replayed in her head the night her orderly life started to fall apart.

George had just got into bed, when,

*I've something to tell you, Maggie. You know that big drugs case I was telling you about?*

*What of it?*

*Well, the Procurator Fiscal reckoned we had it sewn up, but that wee runt Brannigan has got himself some smart-ass defence counsel from Glasgow. He's already insinuating Jimmy offered inducements to the informant.*

*But, George, don't you think you'd be the first person to know if your partner was up to something?*

*That's what I thought. But since Louis Valentine started on him, I don't know what to think. That guy could make anyone believe their old granny was Gina bloody Lollobrigida. And you know our Jimmy. Sails close to the wind.*

*That's as may be, but everybody knows you're straight as a die.*

*They did, but that was before that devious little bastard Valentine got on the Aberdeen train. I'm worried that if he manages to take Jimmy down, he'll drag me into it.*

And that was just the beginning. Her mind churned with conflicting images: the trial, the fallout, the agonising wait. Then the formal letter of suspension. And afterwards, the sleepless nights, the violent rows, George's ultimate resignation.

She tried to think straight. How would they manage for money? Maggie ran through the long list of outgoings: mortgage payments, energy bills, insurances, school fees, uniform, books, Kirsty's uni accommodation. There were scant few assets: the joint bank account she'd held with George, her own savings account, with what was left from her last salary cheque. And the house. It was safe, surely. After that month's mortgage payment, the residual funds should tide them over for a few weeks. Except…there would be a funeral to pay for. Clammy beads of sweat prickled her brow. She'd no idea how much that was going to cost. She resolved to write to their mortgage provider, try to buy herself some time.

For a long time Maggie lay, too exhausted for sleep, too drained to contemplate anything but the void inside her. In desperation, she threw back the bed covers and swung her feet onto the floor. She crossed to the linen basket that sat in a corner by the window, stooped to fish out one of George's soiled shirts and held it to her face. For some minutes she stood, savouring – still – some sense of him. Then she shrugged into the sleeves, wrapped the shirt tight around her and slipped back into bed.

# A Miscarriage of Justice

'I'm glad you rang, Maggie,' Brian Burnett shifted in his seat. They were in her front room, a tray with a china teapot, two rose-sprigged cups and saucers and a plate of shortbread on the coffee table between them. 'I'd have called round sooner, only I've been away on a course.'

'For nine months?' she shot back.

'No,' a flush rose in Brian's face. 'I…'

'Forget it.'

'I'm sorry I couldn't have been there when…'

She cut him short. 'I phoned Alec Gourlay the minute I heard. He came in. It was your new DI did the honours – met me at Force Reception, took me downstairs, saw to my statement. Chisolm wanted to take me upstairs afterwards for a chat. But I was having none of it.' Her lip curled. 'He'd have been briefed on the background. Thought he was dealing with a bent copper. No way was I going anywhere near those bastards on the fifth floor.'

'Wouldn't blame you.'

'What I don't understand is why you haven't been in touch. All these months and not a word, not a phone call.'

'It wasn't on my part,' Brian looked at his feet. 'It was George. After that stuff blew up, he wouldn't answer my calls.' He raised his head. 'To tell the truth, Maggie, he's been avoiding me for months.'

Her face flushed. 'That comes as a surprise. I thought it was you had backed off. You'll know the trial collapsed.'

'Of course.' Brian had first-hand experience of the repercussions. Weren't the shockwaves still reverberating round Force HQ?

Maggie grimaced. 'Forgot you had a front-row seat.'

'Never got the whole story, mind you. Queen Street was awash with rumours, most of them manufactured. What I *do* know is the defence shot holes in our case.'

'*I'll* tell you why. The informant was a guy called Bobby Brannigan. Lied his head off in the witness box. Alleged both George and Jimmy offered inducements. Then Valentine demanded more papers. There was an interview and, according to George, the recording was stopped halfway through. Brannigan admitted his guilt shortly after.'

'Who stopped the tape?'

She brushed the tears away. 'George wouldn't say.'

'So it could have been either of them.'

'I suppose.'

'But surely George would have said if it wasn't him?'

'I doubt it. Loyal to the last,' Maggie gave a hopeless shrug. 'Anyhow, I don't know the facts. And now,' her chin wobbled. 'I never will.'

'Well, Jimmy Craigmyle might have sailed close to the wind, but George was as sound a guy as I've ever known.'

'Didn't help him, did it?' she spat. 'After the trial collapsed, the powers that be decided to disband the entire unit.' *A clean sweep… necessary to restore public confidence in the police service.* The words rankled still.

'Bloody politics. Wouldn't have happened if the press hadn't got their teeth into it.'

'What I never understood,' her brow creased into a frown, 'is why Craigmyle and George were singled out when the rest of them got away with a transfer?'

Brian wondered how much to let on. There had been a major miscarriage of justice, no two ways about it: a knee-jerk reaction from the fifth floor in the face of a barrage of bad press.

'That's the way it works,' he responded. 'The case rested on their evidence. They were partners, the pair of them.'

'I guess. Anyhow, you'll know the rest.'

'What I don't get,' he mused, 'is why George didn't appeal? That's not like him. He was a stubborn git.'

'Oh, Brian,' Maggie turned a stricken face, 'that was all my fault.'

'How come?'

'As I saw it, George was faced with two choices: face a disciplinary hearing and risk dismissal, or resign before he was pushed. He wanted to take it to a hearing, get the chance to clear his name. But I talked him out of it.'

'But why, Maggie? I mean, was there anything concrete to set against him?'

'The tape, I suppose.' She twisted the wedding ring on her finger. 'I'm not sure. Anyhow, what if he'd gone to a hearing and lost?'

'He wouldn't have lost, at least as far as I can judge. George was well thought of. I'm sure he'd have acquitted himself...'

'But what if he didn't? Perform well in front of the panel, I mean. He'd been under such stress. Was taking medication for it. What if he had an off day, what then?'

'All the same...'

'I was terrified they would find against him, Brian. George could have lost his pension. We might have had to sell the house,' Maggie's voice wavered. 'Everything we've worked so hard for. I decided it was too big a gamble. We had a blazing row about it at the time.'

'You can't blame yourself for that. God knows what any of us would have done in his shoes.'

'Yes, well, there *was* the small matter of a family to provide for. Oh,' she clapped a hand to her mouth, 'I didn't mean it like that.' She'd heard that Brian's wife had left him, and they'd never had any children. 'I was thinking of myself, me and the kids. I wanted to put the pair of them through private school, you see. Give them the advantages we never had. And George was happy enough to go along with me. But it's been a strain, all these years, keeping it up in the air. And when it came to it, that's what I was worried about. Not George. How *he* felt. What *his* future would be.'

'George would have done anything for you, Maggie.'

23

'Do you think I don't know that?' A muscle worked in her jaw. 'And I took advantage. Didn't trust my own husband to fight his corner. It was the biggest mistake of my life, Brian, and it's taken a trip to the morgue to make me see it.'

Maggie was sobbing now.

Brian stood. He wrapped his arms around her small frame.

'Is there anything I can do to help?'

'Oh,' she shook herself free. Brusquely she brushed the tears from her cheeks. 'Kirsty's going to give me a hand.'

'Where are they, the kids?'

'In bed, still – both of them. I looked in just before you arrived. Thought I'd leave them be.'

'Best thing, in the circumstances. Have you any idea when the funeral's likely to be? It's just some of the guys have been asking.'

'Next Tuesday, as far as I know. I saw the undertaker yesterday.' Maggie's thoughts strayed to the previous day's appointment: the undertaker's airless office with its bland furnishings and vertical blinds, the stiff silk flower arrangement on the desk, the funeral director with his soft hands and his unctuous manner. Her mind backtracked then to her visit to the mortuary. Coming so soon after that ordeal, the thought of George's lifeblood being drained out of him was too much to bear. Time was, she mused, you'd have had your loved one at home. Maggie could remember her grandfather's body lying in the front room at the farm: the drawn curtains, the family assembled. There was a closeness to it, a solidity, somehow.

With an effort she brought herself back to the present. 'They'll put an announcement in the *Press and Journal*.'

'I'll tell folk to look out for it.' Brian made to leave. 'I'm really sorry that you had to get in touch, Maggie. You know I'd have come to see how you were. I care about you.' He looked down, met her gaze. 'You know that, don't you?'

'Yes,' she responded softly. Now *she* felt sorry. The man looked to be on the verge of tears.

'I'd better be heading, though. I'm sure you've plenty to do.'

'Before you go,' Maggie's voice was uncertain, 'I wasn't going to bring it up, not since I haven't seen you for such a long while. But if it's not an imposition…' she coloured slightly. 'The funeral…could I ask… Will you say a few words?'

# A Daft Idea

The doorbell chimed.

Not that damn thing *again*. Maggie was demented by the stream of callers: old colleagues of George, parishioners from the church, neighbours bearing trays of home baking and Tupperware tubs of soup. Grateful as she was for the many small acts of kindness shown in the wake of her husband's sudden death, she longed for some quiet. Time to gather herself, hold her children close.

Ding, dong, it chimed once more. The ugly cream-coloured box with its dangling brass tubes had been in place when they bought the bungalow. They'd always meant to replace it. Now the thing was so old it was back in fashion.

Balefully, Maggie eyed it. 'Com-ing,' she bawled.

She stomped down the hall. Yanked open the door.

Wilma Harcus stood on the doorstep.

Wilma was a big girl: a size 16, at the very least, to her own size 8. Maggie took in the fake tan, the low-cut top, the sprayed-on leggings. She sighed inwardly. Although she owed her new neighbour a debt of gratitude, they didn't have a single thing in common.

'You OK?'

'Y-yes,' Maggie stuttered. Then, mindful of her manners, 'Come in, won't you?' She summoned a smile.

There were letters lying on the carpet. Heart sinking, she stooped to pick them up. She couldn't face another flurry of condolence cards, digest more carefully chosen words of sympathy. She shuffled the mail in her hands. There were a couple of cellophane-windowed white envelopes, a letter from Scottish Gas, another from the DVLA and an official-looking long envelope.

Wilma followed Maggie through to the dining room. 'I didn't want to call before. You've your kids to see to. Only I was worried about you. How you doing?'

'I'm…fine.'

They sat down at the table.

'Sure?'

'Yes. No,' a sob broke from Maggie's throat. 'You've no idea what it's like – getting through the day, climbing into a cold bed at night. And it's been no time since… I can't begin to contemplate what…'

'Oh, Maggie,' the big woman extended a comforting hand. 'You've still Colin for company, haven't you?'

Maggie's expression softened. 'Yes, but the poor boy's in bits.'

'How about your daughter?'

'Kirsty? She's a different kettle of fish. Been a big help already. Mind you,' she sighed, 'I'm sure a lot of it's for show. I've no idea what's going on in her head.'

'Your folks, are they still around?'

'Yes. They live out in Oldmeldrum. My dad's given up the farm, but they're getting on now. I wouldn't want to burden them.'

'Any brothers or sisters?'

'No, I'm an only child.'

'What about friends? Is there anyone close you could…?'

'Just the one.' Wry face. 'My school friend, Val. And she's in Kuwait.'

'If you ever need somebody to…'

'Let me get rid of these.' Abruptly Maggie changed the subject. She ripped open the first of the envelopes. 'Junk mail.' Slit open the second. 'More of the same.' Turned to the third. 'I'd no idea it cost that much to tax a car.'

'Bloody nightmare, the price of things.'

Maggie turned her attention to the missive from Scottish Gas. 'Oh,' her eyes widened, 'it says they're owed nearly £400.'

'Will you manage to find the money?'

'Yes, it's peanuts in the scheme of things. You wouldn't believe the cost of a funeral. Thank God I've George's pension to fall back on.'

She reached for the final envelope. Slid out the folded pages

27

inside. Brightened. 'It's from the SPPA.'

'Who?' Puzzled look.

'The police pension people.'

'Wow, that was quick.'

'Wasn't it? Still, I could fair use some good news, don't you think? I'm counting on the pension to keep things up in the air, Wilma. At least until Colin's finished school and Kirsty's got her degree.'

She started to read. Blanched. Clutched a hand to her chest.

The letter fluttered to her feet.

'What's the matter?' Wilma started from her seat.

'George's pension…' Maggie's voice was barely audible. 'They're saying he opted out. I'll be getting nothing at all until I can sort this out.'

## X

Maggie sat, head in hands. 'What am I going to do?'

'Don't you worry. Something'll turn up.'

She lifted her chin. 'I could sell the car.'

'But, Maggie, the MOT… You'd need to get that sorted first.'

'Oh,' her face fell. 'I forgot about that.'

'If it was any help,' Wilma ventured, 'my Ian could give it the once over for you.'

'Thanks. That would be a saving.' Maggie sat in silence for a few moments. She racked her brains. 'I suppose, if all else fails, I could sell the house.'

'You wouldn't want to leave it, surely.'

Her eyes welled with tears. 'No.'

'Oh, Maggie,' Wilma's open face was filled with concern, 'I hear you've had your troubles this while back, and now this.'

'You know about the trial, then?'

Although Wilma had moved in with Ian Harcus several months before, the only time Maggie had really engaged with the woman was the day she'd had to beg a lift to the mortuary.

'Aye. Could hardly have missed it, what with them red tops kickin up, and the telly and that. But don't you fret, it'll all come right.'

'How?' Maggie scrubbed the tears away. 'Tell me that.'

'Folk have short memories, you know. And even good coppers can be tempted.'

'*Tempted*?' Maggie turned on her neighbour. 'My husband wasn't corrupt, Wilma Harcus. And now he's dead.'

'Sorry I opened my big mouth.'

Maggie drew herself up, 'There's only one way I could possibly make things right, and that's by clearing George's name.'

The two sat, lost for words, then, 'Wasn't your husband running a wee business when he…?' Wilma asked.

Maggie brushed a drip from the end of her nose. 'Wee is the operative word.'

'But,' her neighbour persisted, 'it *is* still up and running?'

'It hasn't been wound up yet, if that's what you're getting at.'

'There you are, then – you've a ready-made business just waiting to be picked up.'

Maggie spluttered, 'I couldn't possibly do that.'

'Why not?'

'Because…' she groaned, 'it's a private investigation agency.'

Wilma grinned. 'All the better. You'll be able to kill two birds with one stone.'

'Don't get you.'

'Make a living and work to clear your husband's name at the same time.'

'But the business has barely got off the ground. As for clearing George's name, that wouldn't happen overnight. Before I could make a case, I'd have to establish the facts and…'

'No better training than working as a PI.'

'Wil-ma… ' Maggie got to her feet. 'Be serious. I couldn't possibly do a private investigator's job.'

'Why not?'

'Oh, come on. Solving crimes? All that cloak and dagger stuff?'

Gently, Wilma drew Maggie back down onto her chair. 'Private investigators don't solve crimes. That's a detective's job. They look into cases, that's all. And besides, PIs don't work like that any more. It's mostly desk stuff these days. Didn't your husband tell you that?'

'No.' Maggie hadn't dared speculate on what unsavoury activities her husband had got up to since he left the Force, and with whom. 'He was pretty cagey about the whole thing, if you must know.'

'Well, most of an investigator's work really *is* done on the telephone – either that or on the computer.'

'That's another thing, Wilma. I'm hopeless with technology: computers, tablets...'

'That boy of yours could help.'

'Maybe. But I'd need a SIA licence. That takes time, costs money. Plus a PI's job can't *just* be desk stuff. I'd have to be out and about some of the time.'

'So? Colin's seventeen, isn't he? You can leave him to it.'

'I don't want to leave him on his own. He's young yet. I'd worry about him.'

'I could keep an eye on him,' Wilma countered. 'My two lads are grown, and you kind of miss it sometimes – the hands-on stuff.' She paused. 'Well, what are you thinking?'

Maggie's head was swimming. 'I don't know.'

'Why don't you check it out?' Wilma pushed on, undeterred. 'There'll be computer equipment in your husband's office.'

'I suppose.'

'And George's mobile, where is it now?'

'Most likely with the personal effects the police brought the other day.'

'Well, then?'

'I'm not going into George's phone, Wilma, if that's what you're thinking. It would be too ghoulish for words.'

Sly look. 'It could be useful.'

'You make it sound so straightforward,' Maggie railed. 'Checking out the office. Downloading messages off George's phone. But then what am I supposed to do? I don't know the first thing about benefit fraud. Or divorce proceedings. Or whatever investigators do these days.'

'You're not telling me you've been married to a policeman all that time and not picked up a thing or two?'

She shrugged. 'I guess.'

'Plus you'll have contacts. In the police,' Wilma winked. 'Wherever.'

'I hope you're not suggesting...'

'Maggie...' Wilma's voice was stern all of a sudden. 'Do you want to clear George's name or don't you?'

Maggie's heart palpitated in her chest. 'There's nothing I want more in this world.'

'Then taking on the business seems to be the obvious solution.' Wilma's broad face was the picture of innocence. 'If it doesn't work out, there's no harm done now, is there?'

'If you say so.' Warily, Maggie eyed her neighbour. Wilma Harcus was well-meaning, she reckoned, but totally misguided.

She felt a wave of exhaustion wash over her. Wanted nothing more than for Wilma to leave so she could fall back into bed, lose herself in the darkness.

'What are you saying to it?' Wilma pressed.

Maggie slid down in her seat.

'No offence, Wilma. But I still think it's a daft idea.'

# No Job too Small

The heavy door that led from the pavement had come off its hinges. Maggie stepped around it and headed for the stairs. As her nostrils caught the sour reek of old piss, she cupped her fingers over her nose and mouth, averting her eyes from the jumble of takeaway cartons that lay heaped in the lee of the stairwell. She couldn't imagine why her husband would have chosen such a place, sandwiched between a bookmakers and an Indian restaurant, so close to Queen Street, with all its bitter memories. But it would have been handy for the Sheriff Court, she supposed. And cheap.

The first-floor landing was in shadow, a pair of brown varnished doors plastered with the sort of instant plastic signs they make up in shoe repair shops:

A1 DENTAL LABORATORY

ACE DOMESTICS

24HR TV SERVICES

'All right?' An old guy materialised from behind a door marked 'Same Day Jewellery Repairs'.

Maggie's nerves jangled. *Lord, what a fright you gave me!*

She drew a deep breath. 'Fine, thanks,' she murmured. Heart thudding, she darted past. Climbed on upwards towards the second floor.

She spotted it at once. The door had been mended recently, a ragged rectangle of bare hardboard tacked over one of the upper panels. Maggie took in the security features: the discreet spyhole, the heavy mortice lock set below the Yale. So typical of George.

The cheap name plate the door bore was, like the others on the stair, made up in plastic and black, the letters picked out in white.

She wondered where her husband had got the name from, who'd made up the poor little sign. She could picture him in some Timpson branch or other. He'd be fretting over the colour, the font, the cost.

Below the name plate, a piece of white card was secured with four brass thumb tacks. On the card was printed in careful capital letters:

NO JOB TOO SMALL

She grimaced. No wonder George had been so insistent she didn't come near his place of work.

She bent into her handbag and fumbled for the bunch of keys. As she drew them out of the bag, she could see that her hand was trembling.

The door swung open. Maggie found herself in a cramped hallway, punctuated by three cheap panelled doors. Gingerly, she turned the handle of the first. The room was devoid of furnishings. Beige Anaglypta wallpaper covered the walls, stained fawn carpet the floor. A dusty lightbulb hung overhead, suspended by a twisted, dark brown cord. At the far end of the room was a single grimy window. Quickly, she crossed to it, only to find it gave onto a bleak back court. In the window recess, a rust-ringed stone sink was littered with the carapaces of a myriad dead insects. On the bleached wooden draining board sat a cheap electric kettle and a solitary dark blue mug. Maggie recognised the mug as one she'd bought in a small gift shop in Ullapool. She'd wondered where it had gone. She picked the mug up. Pressed it to her lips. Ran her tongue round its rim. *Oh, George...* She put the mug down again with a clatter. She beat a hasty retreat, shutting the door firmly behind her.

The second door looked more promising, but turned out to be the bathroom of what must have been at one time a two-roomed flat. The avocado suite was dated but clean, hand wash and a fresh towel at the basin, a can of air freshener on the cistern. The toilet seat had been left up, the sight so poignant Maggie turned on her heel.

She stumbled towards the third and final door. It stood slightly ajar. Tentatively, she pushed against it. This room was larger than the other, its walls freshly painted in cream emulsion. A patterned rug covered the floor. In the centre of the room sat an oak desk. Not a good desk. *Utility*, her mum would have called it. Maggie wondered where her husband had found the thing. The Salvation Army depot, most like, round the corner on the Castlegate. Behind the desk sat a black swivel chair. An elbow chair stood in front. Her heart warmed. Against the odds, George had made his place of work look professional. Still, she speculated as to how many hours he'd spent in this room, sitting behind that poor wee desk, trying to make ends meet. How many days he'd had to trail round in all weathers, drumming up business. Looking into other people's business.

Maggie crossed to the desk and cast a cursory glance over the computer monitor and keyboard. She bent, slid open the drawers, one after another. They held nothing of interest: some scrap paper, a few chewed biros, a handful of paper clips. There was a box of business cards, a memo pad with some writing on it. She felt a stab of grief as her eye rested on the familiar hand.

A light was flashing on the telephone. Resolutely, she turned away. In the far corner of the room stood a dark green metal filing cabinet, its top drawer gaping. Swiftly, she crossed the intervening space, her pulse quickening as she moved towards it. It was only when she came up close that Maggie saw somebody had broken the lock.

'Anybody there?'

'Oh, it's you,' she whirled to face the man standing in the doorway. 'You did say to meet you here?'

'Yes. Sorry. I was distracted, that's all. Thanks for coming, Alec. I know you've always got such a lot on your plate.'

Alec Gourlay eyed her gravely. 'Not so much I can't make time for an old friend.'

'All the same, I really appreciate it. And I'm glad you got here first. I want to thank you for those few minutes alone with George. I know you were pushing the boat out.'

The pathologist cast his eyes to the ceiling. 'Lucky for you the Senior Mortuary Assistant was on leave that week. There's no way I'd have got you past him, post-mortem or no. And if there hadn't been a locum from ARI…and he hadn't owed me one…' He gave a small shrug. 'Best for both of us we forget it ever happened.'

'Whatever.' Maggie would never explain the primal urge that had propelled her onto that gurney.

'But I've arrived first, did you say?'

'I asked Brian Burnett along too. Before I bury George, I need to know about his final hours. Hoped between you, you'd fill in the gaps.'

Gourlay raised a questioning eyebrow. 'What precisely do you want to know?'

'How long George had been dead when the police found him. Whether anyone else might have had access before then. Anything at all you can tell me.' She hesitated. 'The Death Certificate stated the cause of death was a myocardial infarction?'

'Yes,' his voice was matter-of-fact. 'What happens is a blood clot occurs in the arteries of the heart and occludes it. The area supplied with blood by the blocked arteries loses its source of nutrition and oxygen and degenerates. If the block is severe, death can occur very quickly.'

'Hello?' Footsteps sounded in the hallway. 'Alec?' Brian Burnett strode through the door. 'You're a surprise.'

The pathologist threw him a curt nod. 'I was just about to tell Maggie that coronary thrombosis is the leading fatal affliction that strikes down otherwise healthy people.'

'But what could have caused it?'

'Genetic factors, obesity, heavy smoking, high cholesterol, diabetes, hypertension. I could go on.'

'But we all know that George was a fit man. He didn't drink heavily. Wasn't overweight. Well, not significantly.' She paused. 'You mentioned hypertension. Could the stress of the last couple of years have caused a blot clot to form?'

'Who knows?'

'Did you find anything else when you examined George? Anything out of the ordinary? Suspicious, is what I'm really trying to say.'

'No. That's why I didn't feel it necessary to do a post-mortem. In any event,' Gourlay gave Burnett the nod, 'that's one for your detective here.'

'Thanks for that.' Maggie turned to Brian. 'What can you tell me?'

'As I recall, George's body was discovered by Bob Duffy in the late afternoon. Duffy was responding to a call-out from another business at this address. He wasn't able to gain access to George's office and had to call for back-up,' Brian scratched his head. 'I'd need to go back to Duffy to check who exactly was in attendance.'

'What did they find when they got in there?'

'George was lying face down on the floor of the main office. There was no pulse and...'

Maggie broke in. 'Didn't anybody even try to save him?'

'Yes. Bob Duffy attempted immediate chest compression, and an ambulance with resuscitation equipment would have been summoned as a matter of course. If it's any consolation, the paramedics worked on George for long enough, but they were too late.'

'But why did the police feel the need to take him to the mortuary?'

'There have been a number of opportunistic thefts over the past few weeks. King Street,' Brian sighed, 'is not exactly salubrious.'

Maggie was painfully aware of that. She grimaced. 'So I gather.'

'Added to which,' Alec Gourlay chipped in, 'the doctor wanted a second opinion, and seeing as the mortuary is just across the street...'

'But aside from that,' Brian again, 'we'd want to do it by the book.

After all,' he pursed his lips, 'George *is* one of our own.'

'*Was*.'

'Was, then. But he was held in high regard.' Brian focused on Maggie's right eye. 'Nobody believes George bribed that wee bastard Brannigan.'

She pulled a face. 'Upstairs do.'

'Not all of them. You only have to look at the turnout to his presentation, the number of senior police officers who attended.'

'Not the Commander.'

'No. But I'd put that down to political expediency.' He rolled his eyes. 'It's all down to political expediency these days.'

'But none of this makes any difference to the reality of the situation,' Alec added. 'My external examination indicated no unusual features, and the police report suggested no extraneous involvement.'

Maggie turned to Brian. 'What about the damage to the front door?'

'Back-up would have done that to get in.'

'And that filing cabinet,' she waved her hand. 'Someone's broken into it.'

'Don't know anything about that.'

'So we'll never know,' she looked at each man in turn. 'Is that what you're saying?'

Brian Burnett answered. 'Pretty much.'

'Thank you, both of you. I'm grateful to you for coming along today.'

Gourlay threw her a sympathetic look. 'I hope I've reassured you, Maggie, at least as to the clinical aspects of George's death.'

'You have, yes, but only up to a point. You've been good friends, both of you. To George. And to me. And I have to accept your findings. My husband died of a heart attack. What I'm still not convinced of is...'

Both men eyed her warily.

'What brought it on.'

# Working on it

'How about this?' The salesman indicated another suit on the crowded rail. Seamlessly, he slid out the hanger and held it at arm's length.

Colin looked at his feet. 'Dunno.'

'You could try it on,' Maggie suggested.

The three of them were in Slaters, a vast menswear store upstairs from Oddbins in Bon-Accord Street.

'If I have to.' Colin shuffled sideways. He followed the salesman to a changing room.

'I don't know what's got into that boy.' There was a tremor in Maggie's voice. 'Your brother's changed, Kirsty. Just look at his hair. And he won't talk to me any more.'

Kirsty flapped her hands in front of her face. 'Calm down, Mum. He'll grow out of it.'

'And those clothes he wears. Things with studs. What are they supposed to...'

'I wouldn't worry about that. It's his Emo phase. Hardcore punk music,' she responded to Maggie's puzzled expression. 'Nightmare. Trust me, it'll be over before you know it.'

Maggie sighed. 'I hope so.' Already she regretted the idea of buying her son a suit for the funeral. She couldn't afford it. Not now, what with the pension letter. But it broke her heart to see her kids hurting, and she'd hoped it might prove a diversion, this shopping expedition. Get them all out of the house.

Colin emerged from behind a curtain. He stood, uncertain, eyes cast down.

'What do you think?' the salesman enquired.

The boy lifted his chin a fraction. 'Dunno.'

'Mum?' The salesman smiled at Maggie. Right eye, left eye, and away. She'd seen the reaction so often it barely registered. This time it wiped the smile from his face. Maggie experienced a sharp stab of hurt. Over the years she'd become inured to the sideways glances. But now, in her depleted state...

She rallied. 'The trousers are a bit baggy round the ankles.'

'Do you think so?' He concentrated on Maggie's 'good eye' this time.

'Mu-um,' Kirsty jabbed her mother in the ribs, 'that's how they're supposed to look, isn't that right, bro?'

Colin eyed his sister from beneath lowered lids. 'Dunno.'

'Oh, for God's sake.'

'Cut it out, Kirsty.'

'I was only...'

'I *said*...'

'Forget it,' Kirsty turned on her heel. 'See you downstairs.'

## X

'That looks nice.'

Colin had gone for the bus, suit carrier slung over one shoulder. Kirsty was in the White Stuff changing room, Maggie leaning against the wall outside.

'*Nice*?' Kirsty shrugged out of the garment and let it drop to the floor.

Maggie experienced a quick stab of envy, her daughter's firm, young body making a mockery of her own. 'What's that on your arm?' She caught a flash of white.

'Nothing.' Kirsty tugged at the sleeve of the dress she was stepping into.

'Here.' Maggie lunged forward, grabbed the girl by the wrist. 'Let me see.' With her free hand, she exposed her daughter's forearm. A line of raised white weals marked the fine, pale skin.

'It's not what you think,' Kirsty struggled to break free.

Maggie's grip tightened. 'What is it then?'

'I scalded myself,' she mumbled. 'Trying to make soup.'

'These aren't scald marks. They're cuts. Do you think I don't know the difference?'

No answer.

'I've seen it before.' That was a fib. Maggie had never come across such a thing, but she'd read about self-harm. She let go of the girl's wrist. 'Do you want to talk about it?' she asked in a gentle voice. 'You can tell me. I'll understand.'

'How can you?' Kirsty raised an anguished face.

Maggie took her daughter's hand in hers. 'Try me.'

'It's just…I feel so guilty, Mum, the way I ran off last year back to Dundee. I couldn't hack it: the press hammering on the door at all hours, the phone ringing off the hook. It was doing my head in.' She gulped for breath. 'I *abandoned* my dad,' her voice wavered. 'Just when he needed me most.' She turned a wretched face to her mother. 'I hated him. Can you understand that? Hated what he'd done to us. I couldn't bear to look him in the face. Couldn't stand to look at you either, if you must know – the way you carried on as if nothing had happened when our whole world was collapsing around us.'

Maggie struggled for a response. 'I… I was just trying to hold things together. Keep things normal at home.'

'*Normal*?' Is that what you call it?

'Listen to me, Kirsty Laird,' she cupped her daughter's face in her hands. That trial, it shook me to the core. Just because I didn't look distraught all those months doesn't mean I wasn't churning inside.'

Tears glistened on the girl's face. 'Oh, Mum.'

'But forget about me, pet. How do you feel now?'

'Now? I feel like some little kid who's got lost in a big department store. I just want to stand there and howl.'

Maggie could identify with that. Ever since the two police officers had come to her door, she'd felt a mounting sense of isolation and helplessness. A dislocation, almost, as if she were tumbling through space.

'That bad business,' she said softly, 'it wasn't your dad's fault.'

'I know. And now we'll never get the chance to tell him.'

Maggie spread her arms, pulled her daughter close.

'Love you, Mum.'

Her heart tugged. 'I love you too. Now...' She freed her daughter, took a backward step. 'Let me have a look. I think that one's perfect, don't you?'

Kirsty scrubbed her knuckles into her eyes. 'If you say so.'

She squinted at the label: £69.95. What with that and Colin's suit, she wouldn't have much change out of £200.

'Can I have it, then?'

For a moment Maggie hesitated. She'd planned to treat herself to some wee thing. Not a hat. She'd never wear it again. A scarf, maybe – something sumptuous in silk was what she saw in her mind's eye. It would perk up her black wool coat, the only thing she had that would do for the funeral. Never mind. She dismissed the thought. Her kids were more important. And George would want them to look smart.

'Of course. Hand it over,' she said decisively. 'I'll see you at the till.'

Kirsty wriggled out of the dress. 'Thanks, Mum.' She summoned a weak smile.

Maggie squared her shoulders. 'I'm going to make things right. For you. For Colin. For all of us.'

Kirsty raised a tear-stained face. 'How?'

Maggie looked into her daughter's eyes.

'I'm not sure, pet. Not yet... But I'm working on it.'

# Something Missing

Maggie stepped out of the big black car and stood on the curve of the pavement. The rain that had been forecast had held off, but dark clouds lowered and a sharp wind stirred into small eddies sand and grit and the occasional scrap of litter. Around her, dark-clad figures stood in small huddles: the men in sombre suits, the women in overcoats and scarves, a few of the older ladies sporting conservative felt hats. Oblivious to their pitying looks, Maggie was aware only of a blur of movement in her peripheral vision, of a dull throbbing behind her temples.

She felt a light touch at her elbow. It was only then she became aware of the other figures standing close by her – the sweet, sad sight of her lovely daughter and the stricken face of her only son.

'You all right, Mum?' Kirsty enquired.

'Yes,' she summoned a weak smile. 'You?'

'Mrs Laird?' Reverend Keith Whitehead took hold of her arm. 'Here, let me help you up the steps.'

The double oak doors of Mannofield Church stood open. Maggie stood, leaning slightly into the man who had been their minister ever since they'd moved to Mannofield. She closed her eyes, recalling Kirsty and Colin's christenings, the Sunday school the pair of them had attended, the events over the years in the church hall. She felt a gentle tug at her sleeve. Her eyes jolted open. She let herself be led from the familiar bustle of the street into the hushed calm of the church.

In front of the central bank of pews, the plain oak coffin rested on a folding metal trolley, the single sheaf of white lilies adorning its lid wafting its heavy scent into the chill air. Behind the coffin stood the solid bulk of the carved altar table. To the right of that a simple wooden lectern, its sloping surface empty yet of readings. There was the buzz of muffled conversation, a hand raised here or there in acknowledgement as someone caught sight of a kent face, a fleeting smile. The hum of voices swelled, floating upwards to the vaulted ceiling. A laugh escaped all of a sudden from a pair of lips. Then a guilty hush fell over the congregation as this nascent burst of jollity was quenched by a battalion of stern looks.

With faltering steps, Maggie followed the minister down the aisle. To either side of her, the figures of the congregation seemed to merge into one dark mass, the sonorous notes of the organ music to come from miles away. On her right, Kirsty kept pace, one arm threaded through her mother's, a small hand clasping Maggie's own. To her left towered Colin, chunkier than ever in his new dark suit. Her heart wrenched. For all their outward appearance, they were still kids, the pair of them.

Hastily, Maggie checked herself as she caught sight of the coffin. A lump rose in her throat. George always bought her lilies. *Had* always bought her lilies.

Her parents were already installed in the front pew. Ever fearful of having to make a late entry, they'd have arrived way too early for the service. As she sank down onto the seat flanked by her children, Maggie had an impression of her dad in his good suit, his cheeks sunken now behind his ruddy complexion, her mum shrunken and stooped. She turned her focus on her children. Colin's left knee jerked, a spasm in the soft darkness of the pew. Kirsty sat very still. Her new dress had ridden up to reveal shapely legs clad in opaque black tights. Maggie caught her mother throw a sharp look.

She glanced to her left. There were a good number of faces she recognised: friends from church, Wilma and Ian from next door, a teacher or two from Colin's school. No Val. She'd rung from Kuwait the minute she heard the news, offered to fly back. But to come all that way… And for what? Maggie had insisted she stay.

She wondered if Jimmy Craigmyle would have the brass neck to turn up. Scanned the pews, but failed to spot him. She turned her head to the right. Across the aisle, a row of police officers sat shoulder to shoulder, the silver buttons of their dress uniform glinting in the watery sunlight. Amongst them, Maggie spied Allan Chisolm. She cast a furious look in his direction. *Bastards, every last one of you.* Her hands clenched. Where were you when George was caught up in all that nonsense? What were you doing when the Investigation Team was rampaging through Force HQ, breaking into lockers, listening to whispers in the canteen, taking statements from every bit of lowlife from Torry to Tillydrone?

The organ struck up. The minister motioned to the congregation to stand. Maggie sleepwalked through the introductory hymn. The words made less sense to her than ever they had. The hymn ended. The congregation sat down. There were readings. A prayer. More readings.

A member of the congregation moved forward then and took the minister's place behind the lectern. She fought to focus. The man was tall but slight in appearance, gangly and rather boyish. His eyes were blue, his hair fair. It curled, cherubic, at the temples, adding to the impression of youth. Of course, it was Brian Burnett. Maggie's head felt woolly all of a sudden, as if she were swimming through soup. She cursed inwardly. She should never have taken that Temazepam tablet. The GP had prescribed them the year before, something to help her sleep. She'd come upon the packet when she was clearing out the bathroom cabinet. Put it in her bag. Swallowed one dry when she was in the limousine. She didn't want to let George down.

Burnett pulled a sheet of paper from his inside pocket and laid it on the lectern. He adjusted the microphone and began to speak.

'We come together today to pay our respects to our friend and colleague, George Laird.' He cleared his throat. 'What can I tell you about George Laird?' He looked around the assembled company. 'I can only tell you about the George I knew. The George I've known for over twenty years, ever since we started at Tulliallan together.' He swallowed hard. 'George was straight as a die.'

Did Maggie imagine that Brian was looking directly at the top brass across the aisle from her?

'In all the years we worked together, I never knew him do anyone down. He was the straightest, most decent, most hard-working guy you could come across.' He paused. 'George Laird loved the police.' He looked towards the front pew. 'And he loved his wife, Maggie. Loved her to bits from the day he first met her. He was forever talking about her: Maggie this, Maggie that. We all used to take the mick out of him about it.'

There was a ripple of subdued laughter. Maggie dug her nails into the palms of her hands.

'George was devoted to Maggie,' Brian's voice dropped, 'and to their children, Kirsty…' He glanced over to where she sat, alongside her mother. 'And Colin.'

Maggie extended a consoling hand to her son, who sat, head bowed, shoulders heaving.

'George Laird was a man's man,' he continued. 'A man I was proud to call a friend. The kind of man you would want to have at your back in a difficult situation. And believe me, there were plenty of those over the years we worked together.' There was a catch in his voice. 'George Laird was a good man: a good colleague, a good husband, a good father. Above all…' He fumbled in his top pocket for a folded white handkerchief. Shook it out. Blew his nose noisily. 'He was a good copper.'

There was absolute silence in the kirk. Brian Burnett picked up the piece of paper and stuffed it back in his inside pocket. He stepped down from the lectern. As he made his way back to his seat, Maggie glanced from beneath lowered lids across the aisle to where the top brass were seated. To a man, their eyes were fixed on their polished black boots.

She turned her gaze back to the coffin, appraised the sheaf of flowers. But there was something missing, she thought. Where was the dark blue police flag that should have draped the casket? The peaked cap with its distinctive Sillitoe check, the cap that George had worn with such pride for all those years? The leather gloves? *His* gloves. She clenched her teeth. Her husband deserved to be buried with full police honours. But those bastards sitting there had taken every last vestige of honour away from him. Taken it not only from George, but from his wife and children.

In that moment, Maggie's resolve hardened.
She'd get justice for George if it was the last thing she did.

# II

# The Decent Thing

There was a rap at the back door. Maggie looked up to see Wilma's face framed in the glass. She was wearing full make-up: green eyeshadow and deep magenta lipstick, in lurid contrast to her orange tan. Maggie's shoulders sagged. She wasn't feeling up to Wilma. The woman was too full-on. And besides, it was way too early in the day.

With a show of reluctance, she turned the key in the lock.

'OK?' Wilma barged in, a waft of cloying scent in her wake.

Smartly, Maggie stepped back. She'd never been one for heavy perfume. *Less is more*, her mother always said. Aside from which, there wasn't room for both of them in the doorway. She managed a thin smile. 'Getting by.'

'That right?' Wilma took in Maggie's state of undress, her wan face, the half-eaten slice of toast on the kitchen worktop. 'Aren't you going to finish your breakfast?'

'I'm not hungry.'

Wilma frowned. 'You have to eat. Proper food.'

Maggie dipped her chin. From the deliveries she'd observed, her neighbour seemed to exist on a diet of carry-outs and booze.

The two sat facing one another across the table. Although she'd not long got out of bed, Maggie felt wrung out. She wondered if this was how life was going to be from now on. This overwhelming feeling of fatigue took her back to when her children were tiny: when day ran into night into day into night again, with no glimmer of respite. If she could only clear the fog in her head, think straight. Then she could assess priorities. Start to make plans.

Her neighbour got straight to the point. 'Have you made any inroads in what we were talking about?'

'The agency?' Not really. The only thing I've done,' Maggie hugged her elbows, 'is check out George's office.'

'Turn up anything interesting?'

'Only a bunch of files.'

'Oh,' Wilma perked up. 'What was in them?'

'Don't know. Haven't looked.'

'Where are they now?'

'I brought them home with me.'

'Great stuff. Why don't we check them out?'

Maggie frowned. 'Now?'

'Good a time as any.'

Wearily, she rose and crossed to the sideboard. 'There you go, Sherlock.' She scooped an armful of brown manila folders out of a shopping bag and dumped them on the table.

'No need to be sarcastic, pal.'

'Sorry,' she turned a contrite face. 'It got to me, George's office, that's all.'

'Well, grab a bundle of these. That'll occupy your mind.'

For a few moments Maggie contemplated the files. Then she selected one at random and flicked through the papers inside: client details, dates, times, telephone calls, progress notes, invoice copies. It all looked so complicated. Angrily, she flipped the folder shut. She glanced across the table. Wilma's head was resolutely bowed.

Doggedly, she leafed through the remainder of the folders.

'Well?' Wilma looked up.

'Well, nothing. I've read through this lot.' Maggie brushed tired fingers through her hair. 'Read them and re-read them. There's nothing in those files, Wilma, that's the beginning and end of it.' She jumped to her feet. 'I'm going to dump the lot in the bin. There's got to be some other way of keeping a roof over our heads, me and the kids.'

'Hang on. Don't you want to see what I've got?'

She looked down. Saw that Wilma's folders had been divided into three neat piles.

'From what I can see, these...' Wilma indicated the first, 'look to be closed cases. These…' she pointed to the second, 'are works in progress. And these…' she stabbed a finger at the third, 'are corporate. The names of the same few firms keep cropping up, Maggie. Looks to me like your George was on their books.'

'Employed by them, d'you mean?'

'Not directly. What's the word again?' She scratched her head. 'Outsourced?'

'That's it. Anyhow, there are loads of searches, witness statements, stuff like that, relating to just those few law firms, so all you have to do is ring them up, say you've taken over the business.'

Maggie sank back onto her seat. 'But I've told you already, I'm not qualified to work as a private investigator.'

'Licence could be done and dusted in a few weeks. I checked it out. Plus you don't need to be licensed to consult public records or run credit checks, and you could use that time to bone up on…'

Maggie cut her short. 'Even assuming I were, there's no way I'd work up that filthy close.'

'No need. You could get the phone line transferred, work from here.'

'Then what? Say I had to set up a meeting, interview a witness?' She threw Wilma a warning look. 'I hope you're not suggesting I invite these…clients into my home.'

'Course not. You could meet them in a café, a pub, any old place, really.'

Maggie squeezed her eyes shut, her mind in overdrive. She'd always been strong-minded. *Wilful,* her mother would call her. Bucked against the constraints of home and school. Married George at twenty-one, against her parents' wishes. But this? Bringing up two kids on her own? Taking on a private investigation firm single-handed? No, this was a whole new ball game.

Her eyes snapped open. 'It's not even that. To tell the truth, Wilma, I don't have the confidence. Not any more. Put it down to all these years at home.' Her body sagged. 'It's knocked the stuffing out of me.'

'You've held down good jobs, have you no?'

'Before the children were born. Only bits and pieces after that.'

'But you went out and got yourself something, didn't you, once the kids were up?'

Maggie snorted. 'Yes, I did. As a classroom assistant in Seaton. Job's part-time. Brings in peanuts. And I only took that to get out of the house. Anyhow,' she fixed her companion with a steely look, 'now *I've* got an idea. If you're so convinced there's potential in it, why don't *you* go out and do the detective stuff and I'll do the admin?'

'Because,' Wilma sniffed, 'I've got Torry written all over me.'

Battling to smother her prejudices, Maggie turned her head away.

'Take a good look,' Wilma jabbed a finger at her ample cleavage.

Maggie took in the dark roots dissecting her neighbour's dyed blonde hair, the cellulite dimpling her upper arms, the love handles hanging over the waistband of her leggings.

'Now, look at you.'

She glanced down at her neat blouse, her boyfriend jeans, her Footglove loafers. Saw nothing unremarkable. 'What about this eye of mine?'

'What about it?' Dismissive voice.

'Oh, come on, Wilma, don't pretend you haven't noticed.'

'Well, it's mebbe a wee bit skelly.'

*Skelly!* One word took Maggie back to the playground: the taunts that had stung so. She wiped the image from her mind. 'That's an understatement.' She tried to make light of the matter. 'I've been meaning to get it fixed for years.'

'I wouldn't bloody bother, if I was you.'

Maggie touched a hand to her face. 'You reckon?'

'Aye. If anything, that skelly look gives you an advantage. Makes folk look twice.'

Maggie summoned a smile. 'I'd never have thought of it like that.'

'And you're so refined, Maggie Laird, you'd have those lawyers eating out of your hand.'

'That's rubbish. And even if you were right, it would all take time. And I haven't *got* time, not if I'm to pay the bills.'

'Agreed. But there's stuff here that we can get to work on right now. These...' Wilma indicated several fat folders, 'are cases that are almost complete. And this one...' she flicked open the topmost, 'looks to be wrapped up. All it's needing is an invoice sent out and Bob's your uncle, the dosh comes rolling in.'

Maggie snatched the folder and scanned the contents. 'It still needs the hours and expenses calculated.'

'Well,' her neighbour grinned, 'let me do that. I'm red hot on figures. We'll work together, you an me.'

*Perish the thought.* 'That's all very well,' Maggie countered. 'But have you shared this bright idea of yours with Ian? I mean, having your neighbour fix up your car is one thing, but taking on a detective agency is a major commitment.'

Coy look. 'I might have mentioned it.'

'And?'

'He said...the size of me and the size of you, we'd make a bonny pair.'

Despite herself, Maggie chuckled. 'Is that all?'

'No. As a matter of fact, he said it's not on.'

*Thank God for that.* 'That puts the lid on it then.'

'Och,' Wilma huffed, 'dinna you worry about Ian. I've ways of talking him round. The messages Colin downloaded off George's phone before the funeral...' She rushed on. 'The emails on his computer, and now these...' She waved an arm across the files. 'There's loose ends need tying up, just like I said.'

'I can see that. But the way I feel right now...' Maggie scrabbled for another line of defence. 'I'm just not up to it, Wilma, to tell the honest truth.'

'But these are folk that have gone to your husband for help. Shouldn't you give them a ring at least? That would only be decent.'

Maggie's conscience pricked. Isn't that what George would have done: the decent thing?

'And the earlier you do that, the quicker you learn the ropes, the sooner you can make a start on clearing that man o' yours.'

'Well…' Maggie swithered. 'I'm not convinced.'

'Come on,' Wilma's voice was insistent. 'What have you got to lose?'

*Oh, help!*

Small voice. 'Not a lot, I suppose.'

'Well, then. Deal?'

*Go for it!*

Decisively, Maggie drew herself up.

'Deal.'

# Do You Think I'm Fat?

'Do you think I'm fat?'

The sleeping form twitched, stirred, rolled over.

'I-an...' More urgent this time.

A face appeared from under the duvet. An eye blinked open. 'Wha-at?'

'Fat,' Wilma persisted.

'*What*?' The form jerked upright. Her husband ground his fists into his eyes, craned towards the luminous dial of the clock on the bedside table. 'It's the middle of the night, Wilma.'

'I know,' she let out a sigh. 'And I'm sorry, pet, waking you up like this. God knows, you've an early enough start. It's just...you know how I'm wanting to help Maggie out?'

'Ye-es.'

'Well, we were talking about it today. How she could make it work an that, the husband's wee business...' She broke off.

'And?' Patient voice.

'I offered to help. With the computer stuff, like, an mebbe other wee bitties o' things.'

'Did you?'

'Aye. But now I'm not so sure.'

'Why's that?'

'It was you.'

'Me?' Ian reached for the bedside light, switched it on. 'How?' He wondered what he'd done this time.

'What you said: *the size of me and the size of her...*'

'It was a joke, Wilma.'

'So you say. But...it's just, that Maggie Laird, she's such a neat wee thing. So...trim, I suppose is the word I'm looking for.'

Ian speculated as to what was coming, but kept his counsel.

'She makes me feel like a fuckin elephant.'

He burst out laughing.

'Don't you dare laugh.' Wilma's voice wobbled.

He adjusted his face into an expression of benign concern. 'What's brought this on?'

'I dunno.' She wiped a tear from one cheek. 'It's just the more I look at her, the more I realise I don't fit in.'

'How? Where?'

'Here. Mannofield.' She threw up her hands. 'It's a whole other world for me.'

'Come off it. Didn't you think Maggie Laird was like that – a bit snooty –when you first moved in? And now look at the two of you. You've been in and out of her house ever since...'

'Well, somebody has to. Woman doesn't seem to have anybody else.'

'All I'm saying is you seem to get on well, the pair of you. And if you're serious about going into business together...'

She turned on him. 'Thought you were dead against it.'

'I was.' He yawned. 'Am. If somebody as solid as George Laird couldn't make a go of it...'

'What can two middle-aged wifies...' She finished the sentence for him.

'Forty isn't middle-aged.' He landed a kiss on the tip of her nose. 'And that's not what I was going to say. But knowing you, Wilma, if you've set your mind to it, you'll do it regardless.'

'How can I? That's what I'm asking myself.'

'What's stopping you? If it's the money, I could...'

'It's not the money. I've a wee bit saved.'

'What, then?'

'It's...Maggie Laird's that well-educated, compared to me,' Wilma groaned. 'Makes me feel ignorant, the things she knows.'

'Well, look at you, the experience you've had.'

'Is that what you'd call it? Slopping out behind a bar, cleaning other folk's houses, emptying bedpans at Foresterhill?'

Ian laid a hand on her arm. 'It's all grist to the mill, Wilma. Look at the people you've had to deal with.'

She hooted. 'Drunks?'

'Not just drunks. You'd have to have social skills to manage all those patients in the hospital.'

'Dirty old men, d'you mean, flashing their willies at the old dears?'

'No. I mean people who are seriously ill, terminal, even. Their families, too. They all need delicate handling. And you're so caring, pet. Big-hearted. You can't deny that.'

'I guess.' Grudging voice.

'And the stuff you know: weights and measures, stocktaking, all those numbers...'

Wilma knitted her brow. 'I suppose.'

'Plus you have loads of drive. Self-confidence. You couldn't say you were exactly...' Ian chose his words with care, 'backwards in coming forwards.'

Wilma chuckled. 'That's true.'

'You'll be able to put all that to good use, you know, if you make a go of this detective thing.'

She bristled. 'What d'you mean *thing*?'

'Och, Wilma...' Ian was exasperated now. 'You know perfectly well what I mean.' He yawned again. 'Can I go back to sleep now?'

'No.' Petulant voice.

'Why not?'

'Because you haven't answered my question.'

'What was that again?' Puzzled look.

'Do you think I'm fat?'

He sighed. 'No, of course I don't think you're fat. I think you're beautiful.'

'Beautiful?' Wilma's voice was filled with disbelief. 'You don't think I need to lose weight?'

'Don't you dare. A fella needs a bit of flesh to hang onto.'

She hoiked up her nightie. 'Not this much.'

'Listen…' Ian leaned over her. 'I love you, ya daft quine.' And he buried his face in the folds of her belly.

# Playing Hooky

'Where have you been?' Maggie whirled from the sink when she heard the sound of the back door.

'Nowhere.' Colin slunk in sideways, his back to her.

'What d'you mean "nowhere"?' Her voice rose. 'Have you any idea what time it is? I've been worried sick.'

There was a muttered response.

'And turn round so I can hear what you're saying to me.'

The boy shifted from one foot to the other. Dropped one shoulder. Swivelled slightly, chin on chest.

'What's that on your face?'

'Nothing.'

'Let me see.' Maggie grabbed hold of her son's chin and yanked his face round towards her. She let out an involuntary gasp. A bloodied gash ran from Colin's left eyebrow up into his hairline. 'Oh, Col,' she reached up to gently brush the hair from his eyes. 'What on earth have you been up to?'

'Nothing.' The boy looked away.

She gazed into his young face. 'It can't have been nothing to leave you with an eye like that.'

Her son's mouth set in a stubborn line. Colin looked so like his father when he made that face.

Maggie took a deep breath. 'I want to know where you got that cut on your head.'

Colin shuffled his feet. 'Can't tell you.'

'You listen to me, Colin Laird, you'll tell me if we have to stand here all night.'

He studied the fingernails of one hand. Picked at a cuticle.

'Well? I asked you a question.'

Her son lifted his chin. 'Seaton Park.'

'But that's miles from school. What on earth were you doing down that end of town?'

'Hanging out.'

'Who with?'

'Other schoolkids. Students too. Didn't want to get caught uptown playing hooky.'

'And how often have you been "playing hooky", tell me?'

'Once or twice.'

'Right. So if I go to your guidance teacher and ask to see your attendance record...'

'A few times.' A flush crept up her son's neck.

'If that's the case, why hasn't the school been in touch?'

Colin tugged at the ragged cuticle until he drew blood. 'I put in sick notes,' he muttered.

'You have to be kidding me, Col,' Maggie cast her eyes up to the ceiling. 'This is an important year for you, I thought you understood that. And your school fees...' Swiftly, she checked herself.

The boy's eyes welled up. Fat tears spilled over and began to course down his cheeks.

Maggie spread her arms wide. 'There...' She clasped him to her breast. 'There.'

Her son was sobbing now. Maggie's heart ached. Colin might be a man, almost. She could feel the breadth of his shoulders, the muscles in his upper arms. But his forearms still bore a soft coating of down. She hugged him close, sensing the shudders run through his upper body, smelling the sharp tang of aftershave, feeling the brush of his soft hair on her neck and chin. With a sharp stab of nostalgia, she recalled the many times since Colin had been a tiny baby that she'd comforted him this way.

It was a good five minutes before his sobs subsided. Tenderly, Maggie wiped her son's tear-stained cheeks. 'I'm not angry with you, Col,' she began. 'I'm more concerned, really. If you've been skipping school for days on end, there must be a reason. A serious reason. And you didn't get that crack on the head just wandering around Seaton Park, now, did you?'

He turned away.

'You can tell your mum, you know,' she pressed on. 'We've all been young. Got ourselves in a bit of bother.'

He wheeled to face her, his eyes bright with anger. 'Is that what you'd call it, the shit we're in?'

'I don't want to hear you use that sort of language, Colin Laird.'

'I'm sorry, Mum,' his shoulders slumped. 'I didn't mean for it to come out like that.'

'Then take a deep breath and tell me. Right from the beginning.'

'It's about Dad. Ever since they ran those stories in the *P & J* – the ones about the drugs bust – I've been getting into fights at school.'

Maggie gave her son's hand a squeeze, 'But, Colin, that was all over months ago.'

'I know. Except there's this bunch of neds. Only they don't want to be there. They're just putting in time till they can leave. I've been getting a bit of aggro.'

'And that's why you've been missing school?'

He nodded.

She closed her eyes. Kirsty had looked so vulnerable when she set off back to Dundee. Maggie could still picture the ugly line of weals up and down her daughter's arms. And now this with Colin. She experienced a rush of guilt. She'd been concentrating her energies on George. Looking back, Maggie saw she hadn't involved her children enough, hadn't allowed them to share in the family's dilemma. And now…the reality of the situation hit her with brutal force: not only was her husband dead, her family – the family she'd nurtured and cherished – was shattered.

She blinked her eyes open. 'Isn't there someone you could speak to? Your guidance teacher, perhaps?'

'No,' her son's voice was vehement. 'I couldn't clipe, Mum. That would only make it worse.'

'What about your pals – don't they stick up for you?'

Colin shrugged. 'They do their best, but they can't be around the whole time.'

'Why don't I run you to school for the next week or two, see if that makes a difference?' Maggie regretted now her decision to send Colin back so soon after his father's death.

'No way, Mum,' Colin's face was aghast.

'Why not?'

'Because I don't want to look like a sissy, that's why.'

'A sissy? The size of you? Don't be daft.'

'I'm not being daft.' That look of George again.

'Fair enough,' she allowed. 'But make no mistake, I'm going to sort this nonsense out.'

# Get Creative

'You're down again,' Fatboy riffled through the roll of notes.

Willie fixed his eyes on the wet pavement.

Fatboy yanked up the boy's chin. 'Look at me when I'm speaking to you.'

The lad looked up, but didn't meet his eyes.

'Well, what have you got to say for yourself?'

Silence.

'I said...' Fatboy squeezed.

Willie's eyes rolled round in his head. 'It's no ma fault.'

'Whose fault is it, then?' Fatboy squeezed harder.

Willie wriggled free. 'Fuckin filth.'

Fatboy deliberated for a few moments, then, 'It's all down to the filth now, is it?'

Willie nodded.

'One day it's Paypoint,' Fatboy's voice dropped to a growl, 'the next it's something else.'

Willie shrugged. 'Canna help it.'

'Then how come you've never been down till now?'

The boy shrugged again. 'Dunno.'

Fatboy's eyes narrowed. 'You wouldn't be up to anything, would you, Willie?'

'Of course ah'm no up tae onythin.' Willie Meston's eyes were like saucers. 'Cross ma heart an hope tae die.'

'Talking of which, I wouldn't like to think what could happen to you, Willie, a wee lad like you.'

'Ye widna.'

Fatboy grinned. 'Of course not. We're pals, aren't we? But accidents *will* happen. You don't want to end up in ARI, do you?'

Willie grabbed hold of the bigger boy's sleeve. 'It wis the pigs.

Honest. They wis sittin ootside Northview Towers the whole mornin.'

Fatboy shook him off. 'So what?'

'So…naebody's gaun tae come lookin fur skunk wi a squad car sittin up their backside.'

'There *are* other places.'

'No in Seaton.'

'You're not looking hard enough, Willie. If we're to stay ahead of the filth, we'll just have to get more…' he struggled to find the right word, 'creative.'

'Ah telt ye, there's naewhere else.'

'There must be. Either you'll have to find somewhere else to do your deals or I'll have to find another runner.'

Willie's eyes brimmed. 'But, if ye got yersel a new runner, whit aboot ma da?'

'What about him? It was *him* left *me* in the lurch, remember?'

Willie scratched his No.2. 'It would need tae be aff the street.'

'Off the street?' Fatboy scoffed. 'Like where? You're already banned from most of the shops, and you're too young to go into a pub.'

'Ah'm no. Ma da sends me roon the pubs pickin up stuff.'

Fatboy smirked. 'Well, you'll not be doing that for a while. Besides, you'd be a kent face. And we can't have that, can we? Not in our line of business.'

Willie grinned. 'Richt enough.' He started on another fingernail. 'The high rises, mebbe?'

'Good idea,' Fatboy fingered his re-growth. There must be a dozen of those, he reckoned, within a quarter-mile radius. 'But how would you get in? Don't they have secure entry?'

'Aye, but ye can get in the hallway. Easy.'

'That wouldn't be out of sight. Not entirely.'

'Naw. But a hale lot better than staunin in the friggin rain.'

'And out of range of the filth.'

'Aye. Bastards.'

'But what if someone spotted you and called it in?'

Willie sniggered. 'One o' they immigrants? No fuckin likely.'

'Not an immigrant. Some old biddy, more like.'

'Then ah'd jist move on tae the next block.'

'Good thinking. But,' Fatboy deliberated, 'inside one of the flats would be better. Keep you right off the radar.' He gave the boy a nudge. 'I don't suppose you could cadge a favour off your mum, could you, Willie?'

The wee boy reeled back in alarm. 'Nae chance.'

'Just taking the piss. You couldn't wangle your way in anywhere else, could you?'

Willie stuck his pinkie in his nose. Wiggled it around for a few moments. Took it out again.

He inspected the glistening bogey on the end. Gave it a sook.

'Gie me a couple o' days.' He grinned. 'Ah'll think on it.'

# Cold Call

'Mrs Laird?'

There were two of them. The taller of the two had a chubby, pale face, fair hair, blue eyes. Like Tim Robbins on a bad day. The other was shorter, stockily built, dark hair slicked back with some sort of gel, brown eyes that were boring into her right now.

'Yes?' Maggie drew her dressing gown tighter around her.

'Can we come in?' The eyes were fixed on her forehead, the voice so low it was almost a growl.

'Are you police?'

A look flashed between the two. 'You could say that.'

She straightened, 'Then show me your warrant cards.'

Tim Robbins reached into his raincoat. Drew out a wallet. Waved it under her nose. She caught a glimpse of a blurred photograph, a badge, print that she'd be hard-pressed to decipher. The wallet snapped shut again.

She hesitated. The ID didn't look familiar. But it was Police Scotland now. She'd read about the new strap-line: *Semper Vigilo, Police Scotland, Keeping People Safe.* A sour thought crossed Maggie's mind. Who'd keep *her* safe now? She didn't recognise these men either. But then she wouldn't, would she? She hadn't been over the doorstep of Force HQ for a long time. Except for the day she'd climbed onto that gurney. In her thin housecoat, she shivered. George hadn't wanted her anywhere near when that bad business was blowing up in his face, and he'd said himself there had been many changes.

The dark man smiled at Maggie. The smile didn't reach his eyes. He took a step forward. Hugging the collar of her dressing gown under her chin, she stepped backwards into the porch. And they were on her, both of them, crowding her in the small space. So close she could smell their aftershave and an undercurrent of sweat.

'In here, is it?' The taller of the men jerked his head towards the door of the sitting room.

Maggie felt his breath on her face. 'If you like.' All she wanted was to put distance between them. For the pair of them to get on with it, whatever they'd come for, and get out of her house. She sank down onto a corner of the sofa, smoothing her dressing gown carefully over her knees.

The dark guy stood with his back to the window. The fair one folded himself into the big chair.

*That's my husband's chair*, Maggie wanted to scream. She felt wrong-footed, sitting in her nightclothes in her own front room, two complete strangers in possession. Decisively, she pulled herself together. 'Now, are you going to tell me what you've come for?'

'It's a small matter, Mrs Laird,' the short man flashed his mirthless smile again.

'Small, but important,' Tim Robbins chipped in.

'Well?' Maggie could feel her blood pressure rising.

'It's a matter of rent arrears,' the short man again. 'You'll have had our invoice.'

'Rent?' she exploded. 'I don't *owe* rent.'

'Not you, Mrs Laird,' the blond man's voice was curiously soothing, 'so much as your husband.'

'George, isn't it?' the dark chap added.

'*Was*,' Maggie spat. 'My husband is dead.'

'Yes. We know. Boss sends his condolences.'

'And who might he be?'

The blond man again. A Mr Gilruth. Not,' he added, 'that it will make any difference.'

She jumped up from the settee. 'So you're not policemen at all?'

'Didn't say we were,' the short chap smirked. 'But that doesn't take away from the fact that there's rent owing.'

'I don't owe anything. I've never owed anything in my life,' Maggie's voice trailed away. She knew that wasn't true. Not any more.

'Fact is…' Tim Robbins hoisted himself from the armchair. His huge frame blocked half the bay window, 'your husband owes us, and marital assets and all, it's you that has to pay.'

'Fact is,' she came straight back at him, '*I* don't *have* any assets.'

The blond man ran his eyes round the room. 'You've got this house, haven't you?'

'With a whacking great mortgage on it. So where does this rent come in, tell me that?'

'Oh, didn't we say?' The stocky chap's voice was silken. 'It's for your husband's serviced office accommodation on King Street.'

'And what sort of "services" were provided, tell me? None that I ever heard of.'

'Utilities, that sort of thing.'

Maggie's blood boiled. 'You've got a damn cheek, the pair of you, coming in here demanding money with menaces when my husband's hardly cold in his grave.'

'Menaces?' Tim Robbins again. 'We haven't made any threats.' Another look passed between the two. 'And anyhow,' his voice softened a smidgeon, 'we're only following instructions.'

'Well, I've never had sight of any invoice, and you can tell your boss from me that my husband paid upfront for his "serviced office". He told me so himself.'

'Then he was telling you porkies. The rent's in arrears. And if he wants to quit, he's obliged to give four weeks' notice.'

Maggie felt her knees give way. She sat down again. 'How can a man give notice when he's dead?'

'That's the way it works. Your husband signed a contract.' The blond man reached into his inside pocket. Drew out a piece of paper. Held it out to her.

She snatched it from him. Took in the heading – 'GDEVCO' – before she thrust it aside. Maggie let her head drop onto her chest. Her mind churned. All she wanted at that moment was to get these guys out of her house.

She looked up. 'How much?'

'Nine hundred.' The short man's face was devoid of expression.

Her eyes bulged. 'How on earth did you arrive at that sort of figure?'

'Arrears of rent, four weeks' notice and incidentals.'

'I haven't got £900.'

'I'm sure you'll manage to find it,' the man smiled his mirthless smile once more.

'How, exactly?'

'Not my problem.'

Maggie crossed her legs, uncrossed them again. She supposed she could borrow from her parents. Just as quickly, she dismissed the idea. She could go back to the solicitor, but that would incur more legal fees. She could go to the police. She was convinced it couldn't be legal, these men barging in on her like that. Except she hadn't actually refused them entry. And they hadn't threatened her, not in so many words.

She drew a breath. 'You'll need to give me some time.'

'Time?' Tim Robbins spread his hands. 'No problem. How about next Wednesday?'

'But…' Maggie stuttered, 'that's less than a week.'

'Missus,' the man hissed, 'I'm being generous here. Week's a long time in our business.'

She jumped to her feet. 'And what if I don't pay?'

Tim Robbins took a step towards her. 'What's the lad called?' He jerked his head towards his companion.

'Colin.'

'Your boy's still at school, isn't he? Gordon's, is it?'

Maggie's eyes narrowed. 'Don't you dare.'

'Your choice.'

Her mind churned. 'This boss of yours, whoever he is, will you set up a meeting with him?'

The blond man shrugged. 'Not going to happen.'

'That's for him to decide, surely.'

'Well, I don't know…'

She jutted her chin. 'Just do as I ask.'

'OK. But I wouldn't hold your hopes up.'

'We're going now.' The short man again. 'But believe me, we'll be back.'

# Somewhere Quiet

'There you go,' Brian deposited the tray on the table. His heart had flipped when Maggie rang, asked if they could meet. *Somewhere quiet*. His thoughts raced away: a glass or two of wine in some dark corner of a pub, dinner even, across a candlelit table...

Brian had fancied Maggie from the moment they first met, way back when he and George were rookies together. Not that she'd been such a looker. Not one of your dolly birds, as they called them then: big hair, false eyelashes, enough greasepaint to wax a car. No, Maggie McBain – as she was then – had been a different type altogether: petite, small-boned, delicate. Feminine, but not fragile, for there was steel behind that douce exterior. She'd been pretty enough though, with her soft red curls, that heart-shaped face. And those intriguing green eyes – one that looked right into you, while the other drifted dreamily away. Yes, Brian mused, Maggie McBain had been a pretty girl, right enough. Maggie Laird was a bonny woman, that's for sure.

*A café*, she said. *Up your end of town. Don't want to take up too much of your time.* The Art Gallery café seemed to fit the bill.

'Would you like me to pour?' He placed a teapot, cup and saucer in front of her.

'No,' Maggie smiled up at him. 'Let it brew for a minute or two.' She'd known for a long time that he found her attractive. And Brian Burnett was a fine-looking man, she had to admit, with his fair hair and slim figure. Maggie took note of the long lashes that framed his bright blue eyes. She'd never noticed until then what long eyelashes he had. Probably because she'd never fancied him. Had never fancied anybody much. Well, nobody except George. That was going to make it even more difficult when it came to asking Brian the favour she'd been framing in her mind. Difficult, that is, unless she turned Brian's fondness to advantage, the thought occurred to her now. *Don't you dare!* That would be a dreadful thing to do, for, in all the years she'd known him, Brian had never once stepped out of line. Plus he'd been a stalwart friend to them both. *Still, if you really want to clear George's name…*

Brian gave his cappuccino a stir. He looked up. 'How are things?'

'Oh,' Maggie gave a small shrug, 'so-so.'

'Anything I can do to help?'

'Not unless you win the Lottery. George has cashed in his life insurance.'

Brian's eyebrows shot up. 'Never.'

'I didn't find out until Kirsty and I went to see the solicitor. At first I thought there had been a mistake. But when he showed me the paperwork, Brian, the breath went out of me, I have to tell you.'

'But why would George do a thing like that? I mean, it's not as if he was ill-informed. He'd be well aware of the implications of cashing in a policy prematurely.'

'I know. He always read the small print. It just goes to show how…' Maggie's voice wavered, 'desperate he must have been.'

'How did he end up working as a PI?'

She grimaced. 'Don't even go there. You've no idea how many jobs he applied for – store detective, security guard, bouncer – before he went out on his own.'

'Still and all, cashing in his moneyspinner, it doesn't make sense. I mean, George was always so careful.'

'George was lots of things before our world came crashing down around our ears.'

'What are you going to do?' Brian's mind ran ahead. He'd offer to help, but things had been tight, one way and another, since Bev walked out.

'I've decided to take on the business.'

He drew back. 'I don't want to offend you, but a private investigation business – do you think that's wise?'

'It's necessary. My Seaton job doesn't bring in enough to feed us.'

'But, Maggie, you don't know the first thing about investigative work.'

Her eyes narrowed. 'Don't I? George tried not to bring his work home with him, I admit, but some of it must have rubbed off on me, don't you think?'

'I'm not trying to criticise. It's just…'

'I've got bills to pay, Brian. And I've picked up more about detective work than you give me credit for. I've already boned up on the files from his office. George was such a good copper. *You* know that, even if the rest of Aberdeen doesn't. And he kept scrupulous records. Once my SIA licence comes through, there are one or two cases I can wrap up with just a couple of phone calls.'

'Investigative work is about more than a few phone calls.'

'Don't you dare patronise me.'

Brian coloured. 'If it sounded like that, I apologise.'

'I'm sorry too. I didn't mean to bite your head off. I know perfectly well a private investigator does a lot more than just sit on the phone. But it's not rocket science either, is it?' Maggie looked into Brian's eyes. Saw that they were full of doubt. 'I've been on the internet,' she rushed on. 'You can get a lot of data off that: electoral rolls, company accounts, credit scores, court judgements. Plus I've spoken to the Association of British Investigators. The people in the office there were really helpful.'

'That's all well and good, but it's a big, bad world out there.'

'As if I don't know it.' There was bitterness in Maggie's voice. 'All the same, there are questions I need answers to.'

'Such as?'

'There were a couple of bruisers at my door the other day, chasing rent owing for George's office. Sent by some chap Gilruth.' She paused. 'Name ring any bells?'

'I'll say. Fella's got fingers in more pies than you'll find at Pittodrie. Story goes he started out with an ice-cream van. Built that up into a fleet. Then it was taxis, tanning salons, student flats, you name it.

Didn't George ever mention him?'

Maggie frowned. 'Not that I can remember.'

'Well,' Brian's voice was weary now, 'James Gilruth's a big wheel. You don't want to mess with him.'

'But those guys might have paid a visit to George first, don't you see? Tried to put the squeeze on him. Couldn't something like that have brought on his heart attack?'

'It could, but that's pure speculation.'

'Plus there was the damaged filing cabinet.'

'Was there anything missing?'

She eyed him bleakly. 'I don't know.'

'Maggie, I know how distressing these past few weeks must have been for you...'

'I'm not inventing a conspiracy, Brian, if that's what you're getting at. I just need some questions answered, to put my mind at rest.'

'But you're surely never going to take on George's business single-handed?'

'No, of course not. I've arranged some...' She struggled for the right word, 'back-up.'

'That was fast work. How did you manage that?'

'It's my next-door neighbour, if you must know.'

'Wilma Benzie?' He burst out laughing.

'You know Wilma?'

'Know of her. Let's just say her extended family are known to the police.'

Maggie glowered at him across the table. 'Well, for your information, she's not Wilma Benzie any more. She's Wilma Harcus now.'

'Leopard doesn't change its spots. Anyhow, what would the recently respectable Wilma Harcus know about private investigation agencies?'

She pursed her lips. 'Wilma knows loads of things.'

'I'll bet,' Brian gave her a steady look. 'And all from the wrong side of the law. Still, let's not fall out over this. I only want to help, you know that. And maybe your friend Wilma will be able to bring something to the table after all.'

'She's not my friend. She's my neighbour. And she's only going to help with the admin and...' Maggie's voice tailed off, 'stuff.'

'Well,' his tone was conciliatory, 'I'm sure she could be a big help with, you know, stuff.'

'That apart, I'm determined to clear George's name. For his sake, for my children's, and for my own peace of mind.'

'And how do you propose to do that?'

'Go back to the trial. Talk to people. I've mulled things over in my mind. Formulated a plan of action. Once I know the ropes, I'll have a better idea how to execute it.'

Grave face. 'I have to caution you against sticking your nose in where it's not wanted. These are dangerous people you're talking about.'

'I hear what you're saying, Brian. That's why I asked you to meet me today. I'm going to need your help.'

'Ask away.' He prayed that Maggie wasn't going to ask him for a loan.

'I have to find Jimmy Craigmyle.'

'George would have had his number, surely?'

'Of course. But it's no longer in service. Have you seen Jimmy about?'

'No. He seems to have dropped off the radar. I heard his marriage had broken up and he'd moved.'

'Any idea where?'

'Not a clue.'

'That's why I need someone on the inside, don't you see?'

'Inside?' Brian's face blanched. 'You mean inside the police force.'

She nodded.

'You can't be seriously suggesting...'

'Course not.' *That's a lie, Maggie Laird.*

'Because it isn't that long since one of our custody officers got done for copying crime files and police reports. He got banged up for a couple of years.'

'It's nothing like that.' *Two lies.* 'I only want to ask a tiny favour – just a wee snippet of information now and again.'

'Oh, well, in that case…'

*Get in there!*

She drew a deep breath. 'You could PNC Jimmy Craigmyle, for starters.'

Brian squirmed in his seat. 'That's a chargeable offence, Maggie.'

*Turn up the heat!*

She flashed a winning smile. 'You'll do that for me, won't you?'

Brian knew he was hooked.

Knew he'd been hooked long ago.

'Yes, Maggie,' he conceded. 'I'll do that.'

# A Filing Cabinet

The plastic name plate told her she'd come to the right door. Maggie turned the handle and went in. There was brown Lino on the floor, flock wallpaper on the walls. An old-fashioned shop counter ran the width of the room. Against the far wall stood a workbench, an old boy bent over it.

'Hello?' Tentative voice.

The old guy turned. He was in his sixties. Small. Thin. Bald. He was wearing gold-rimmed glasses and a brown cotton coat, the sort Maggie remembered grocers used to wear.

'Can ah help you?'

Her heart thundered in her chest. She'd have done anything to avoid a return visit to the scene of her husband's demise. Nonetheless, if she was going to be an investigator she'd have to start somewhere, and this seemed as good a place as any.

*Get on with it!* She squared her shoulders. 'I hope so.'

'Is it a repair yer needin?' The man rose to his feet.

'Not exactly.'

'What then?' The old guy crossed to the counter.

'I need some...' Maggie scrabbled for an anodyne word, 'information.'

'What sort of information?'

His face bore a wary expression. Well, it would, wouldn't it? She could imagine how she'd feel if she had to work in a run-down place like this. In her mind, she re-lived George's last moments. Her heart plummeted into her shoes.

He bent forward, his face in hers. 'Somethin up wi yer eye?'

'Oh,' her hand jumped defensively to her left temple. 'No. It's a bit lazy, that's all.'

The old man ignored this. 'Information, did you say?'

'About the office upstairs.'

'Him that drapped deid?'

She nodded.

'Why d'ye want to know?'

'He's...' Slowly, she raised her head. '*Was* my husband.'

'Aaah,' the old chap exhaled.

'Yes, and...'

'Ah *ken* you.' He pointed an accusing finger.

'Yes,' she moved to reassure him, 'I've been here before. We passed on the stairs.'

He scowled. 'Canna be too careful around here.'

'No, that's why...'

'Polisman, wasn't he?'

'*Ex*-police,' she stressed the first syllable.

The old man scratched his bald pate. 'That's what ah thought.'

'But...'

'Private eye, wis he?'

'Well, I don't know that...'

'Kept himself tae himself, onywye. Would nivver have kent he wis there. Except...'

'Yes?' She strained forward.

'That one time.'

'Was that the time you heard a noise and called the police?'

Subsequent to her meeting with Alec Gourlay and Brian Burnett, Maggie had grilled George Duffy on the call-out.

'Aye. Bit it wis naethin.'

'Oh,' she leaned back again.

'Him fallin doon, that's a.'

'My husband, you mean?'

'Aye. Ah've bin that jumpy, see, since thon burglary.'

'Burglary?' Her senses sprang to full alert. 'Is that right?'

'Aye.'

'In this building, was it?'

'Naw,' the old man's lip curled. 'Ither end o King Street.'

*Dammit!* Maggie felt suddenly deflated. That's what Duffy had said.

'Ah hiv tae get back tae work.' The wee man made to turn away. 'Ah've a rush job tae feenish, an…'

'Hang on,' she cut him off. 'I won't keep you a moment.'

'We-ell…'

'You couldn't tell me if George…' She broke off. 'If my late husband ever said anything about a filing cabinet?'

'A *filing cabinet*?' The old chap eyed her as if she were daft.

'The one upstairs.'

'Oh,' a wave of realisation came over his face, '*that* filing cabinet?'

*Yes. That bloody filing cabinet!* 'You see, I couldn't help noticing the lock seems to be broken.'

'Aye, George asked me about that.'

'He did?'

'Bought it second-hand. Bloody thing gied him naethin bit trouble frae the day he brocht it in here.'

'Oh? How come?'

'That's whit ye get fur buyin athing aff the Castlegate. Thing wis nivver richt.'

'In what way?'

'Key kept stickin. Ended up George locked the thing an couldna get it open. Came runnin doon tae ask a favour.' The wee man wrinkled his nose. 'Nae use haein a filin cabinet if ye canna get onything oot.'

'No,' she murmured, 'I quite agree.'

'No that ah minded, like, daein the man a favour.'

'No. Of course.'

'Onywye, ah went back up the stairs wi him an hud a richt look at it.'

'That was good of you.'

'Aye,' the wee man swelled visibly. 'Saved him the price o' a locksmith.'

'So did you manage to fix it, then?'

'Been in the trade comin on fifty year.'

'That's amazing, but…'

'Served ma apprenticeship at Jamieson & Carry. Ken who ah mean?'

Maggie tilted her head. The upmarket jeweller in Union Street would never be within her budget now.

'Worked wi aw sorts.' The old boy's eyes held a faraway look. 'Gold, silver, platinum, you name…'

'I was asking you,' she fixed the wee man with a level gaze, 'whether you fixed it?'

'Fixed what?'

'My husband's filing cabinet.'

'Oh,' the old chap's eyes swam back into focus, 'so ye were. Ma heid's fair frazzled these days.'

'So did you?' Maggie pressed.

'Eh?'

'Fix it?'

'Naw,' the old geezer frowned. 'Ah managed tae get the thing open, but by the time we'd both hud a go, the lock wis buggered.'

# Payment in Kind

The door was screaming for a lick of paint. Willie rang the bell.

'Fuck's sake!' On the seventh floor of Esplanade Court, Kym lay stretched out on the settee, six small children lined up on the rug by her feet. 'Can a woman no get a minute's peace?'

There was another ring at the door. Kym sighed. She'd had a bastard of a day. The weans wouldn't settle to anything for more than five minutes at a time, and to crown it all that wee Harvey had shat his pants. By the time she'd stripped him off and stuck another load in the washing machine, her youngest had sicked up his breakfast. She was that scunnered she'd topped up their lunchtime juice with a couple of tablespoons of Calpol. They were sitting quietly now, eyes fixed on the telly.

The doorbell rang again, one long ring this time.

'Shite,' she muttered under her breath. She'd been counting on an hour or so's kip before all hell was let loose again. She stifled a yawn. She was feeling a bit woozy. She'd had a wee snifter an all.

Kym wondered who it could be. It was way too early for the weans to be picked up, and she'd seen off that nosy cow of a social worker only the previous day. With the greatest reluctance, she hauled herself upright, scrunched fists into tired eyes and swung her legs off the settee. Slipping her toes into a worn pair of mules, she rose unsteadily to her feet, swayed out of the room and down the corridor, one hand clutching the waistband of her jeans. She'd lost that much weight this past while, and there was no way she could afford to buy new.

Kymberley Ewen – Kym, as she was known – couldn't have been much more than twenty, though she looked forty. She'd been a pretty girl once, back when she'd lived with her mum in Portlethen. Now she was stuck in a seventh-floor flat with three kids under five, all by different fathers. Kym didn't remember much about any of the men. These days Kym didn't remember much about anything.

'Who is it?' She glued one eye to the spyhole.

You couldn't be too careful around here, what with the filth and the Social and the housing inspectors and the rest. Seaton had always been a prime target for folk like that, but now the Council was packing the place out with fuckin immigrants, the high-rise flats were fairly hoatching with officials.

'Willie Meston.' The boy stood on Kym's doorstep. The big guy leaning against the wall behind him looked so laid-back, elbow crooked behind his head, one leg crossed over another, that she was caught off-guard.

'What d'you want?' She opened the door on its chain.

Willie grinned. 'Ah've come tae pick up Kyle.'

'Where's Ryan?' Ryan Brebner was Willie Meston's sidekick and Kyle's big brother.

'Awa fur messages.'

'Well, you're too early.'

'Can we come in and wait?'

'You can wait out there.'

'Aw...'

Kym eyed Fatboy. 'Who's yer pal?'

'Mate.'

'Does he have a name, yer mate?'

Willie shrugged. 'You can call him Fatboy.'

'And you must be Kym,' the guy called Fatboy threw her an engaging grin.

She sneaked a quick glance up and down the corridor. For a moment she swithered. Her visitor didn't look like the filth, more like a regular guy. A bit on the chunky side maybe, but these days she couldn't afford to be picky. Hell, she might even be able to cadge a bit of weed or a couple of fags off this big fella that called himself Fatboy.

Kym slid the chain off the door.

Fatboy pushed past her.

Willie brought up the rear.

'Nice wee set-up you've got here.' Fatboy swaggered down the hallway to the living room and settled himself on the settee. He sniffed. The air smelled fetid: an amalgam of unaired clothing, formula milk and smoke. 'How many of these are yours?' He cast an eye over the comatose row of kids sitting cross-legged on the floor.

'None of your business.' Kym was sorry now that she'd let the guy in.

'See,' Fatboy lowered his voice, 'from what I hear, you've three of your own. So the other three...' he jerked his head towards the floor, 'must belong to somebody else.'

Kym wrinkled her nose. 'Why would I have some other bugger's kids?'

'You tell me.'

She came out with her stock answer, 'They're just here to play.'

Fatboy smirked. 'That right? What's the most you ever have to "play" at the one time?'

Kym's neck stiffened. 'Depends.'

'Depends on what?'

'Depends how skint I am.'

'Skint, are you?' He fished in his jacket pocket. 'You should have said.' He dug out a twenty pack of cigarettes. 'Here,' he thrust the pack towards her, 'be my guest.' Fatboy turned to the boy. 'What you saying, Willie?'

Willie stood in the doorway. He shuffled his feet. 'Dunno.'

'Bit tight for space?"

'Mebbe.'

Fatboy screwed up his face. 'Yeah.'

'We could aye use the lobby,' Willie offered.

'Not too busy?'

'Sometimes. But there's the stairwell. That's out of sight.'

Fatboy rounded on the wee lad. 'I'm not hanging about some

shitty stairwell.'

'Not you,' Willie shook his head. 'Me. You'd be up here.'

'Oh,' Fatboy grinned, 'get you.' He turned to Kym. 'What do you say to me and Willie dropping by now and again?'

'Dropping by?' For a heady moment she wondered if the big lad fancied her.

'Once, mebbe twice a week. On a regular basis, like.'

'We-ell,' Kym eyed Fatboy from beneath demurely lowered lids, 'I don't know.'

'We wouldn't give you any trouble.'

'But the kids...'

'Them neither. We've a bit of business to do, you see.'

'Business?' Feverishly, she scratched her forearm. 'Here?'

'Well, not right here. Round the high rises.'

'What kind of business?'

Fatboy tapped the side of his nose. 'Never you mind.'

Kym deliberated. She was chancing her arm as it was. This big guy might attract unwelcome attention. Best be shot of him soonest.

'The answer's no.'

'Aw, come on,' Fatboy wheedled. 'Give me one good reason.'

She ran a furred tongue over her lips. She was gasping for another drink.

'I've things to do.'

'Things? What things?'

Kym's chin drooped. She didn't reply.

'I'd be able to give you a hand.'

'How?'

'Hold the fort. Give you a break now and again.'

'Out of here, you mean?'

'Yes,' Fatboy encouraged. 'Nothing like a breath of air, is there, when you've been stuck in all day?'

'You serious?'

'Totally.'

'The answer's still no.'

'That's *such* a shame,' Fatboy thrust his face into hers, ''cos a decision like that could land you in trouble.'

'Trouble?' She stopped scratching. 'How?'

'I don't suppose the Social know you're doing a bit of child-minding on the QT?'

Her eyes slid away. 'I'm only minding them for today.'

'That right?' Fatboy sneered. 'So they won't be here tomorrow, then?' He waved a hand over the half dozen heads that squatted cross-legged at his feet.

'Mebbe,' Kym could feel a flush creep up her neck. 'Mebbe not.'

'It's just…if someone from the Council should happen to call by, and you with all these kids in here…' Fatboy broke off. 'I'm pretty sure there are regulations concerning child minding.'

'I wouldn't know.'

Kym squeezed her eyes shut against this unpleasantness. She knew fine she was supposed to register with the Social, but there was no way Social Services would let her look after two or three kids on top of her own lot in a two-bed flat. Besides, she'd had a bellyful of social workers sticking their noses in, and never the same one twice. They'd be running background checks on her, nosing into her fridge and her kitchen cupboards, asking about play materials and sleeping arrangements and safety locks. Kym couldn't be arsed with any of that. She'd worked out a wee system all by herself: let the kids run around all morning until they wore themselves out, plonk them in a row in front of the telly, dish up juice and biscuits when they got hungry, sit them on the lav when they wanted to wee. And if they needed a nap, well, she just stuck them in her own bed. Kids liked to be cosy, didn't they? Anyhow, Kym reasoned, she must be doing things right, for she hadn't had a single complaint – not one in the entire eighteen months she'd been child minding. Not even the odd time she'd had a bevvy in her when the mums came to pick up their weans. Kym knew that was down to the fact that her services came cheap, far cheaper than if the women had to put their kids into a nursery. She knew that. And so did they. They didn't have a choice, not if they were to hang onto their benefit *and* hold down a wee job.

'What are you saying to it now – my wee proposition?'

Kym jolted back to reality. Warily, she eyed the big lad. She wished she'd never let him over her door.

'Well?'

Her voice faltered. 'I-I'm not sure.'

'There could be something in it for you.'

She brightened. 'Like what?'

'Let's just say...' Fatboy leered, 'a consideration.' He winked. 'Payment in kind. Get it?'

Kym did.

'That'll be OK, then,' her face broke into a grin.

# Big it up

'Before we start,' the solicitor cleared his throat, 'may I say how very sorry we at Kelman McRae were to hear of your sad loss.'

'Thank you.' Beneath the partners' desk, Maggie eased her feet from her shoes. The unaccustomed pair of heels were chafing already.

'Your husband was a fine man…'

Maggie bit down hard on her lip.

'And in his latter capacity provided our firm with a first-class service.'

She brightened. 'George was always very thorough.'

'Thorough, yes. Conscientious. Perceptive too. Saved us a considerable amount of man hours.' He lifted a piece of paper from the jumble on his desk. 'You say in your letter, Mrs Laird, that you've taken on the investigation business.'

'That is correct.'

'But from what I can establish, you have no experience in this line of work.' Michie eyed Maggie enquiringly. Right, left, right. Dropped his gaze.

'No, but I've a…legal background.'

'In what capacity, may I ask?'

'I was a secretary.'

'Ah!' He looked up. 'And when was that?'

She coloured. 'Some years ago.'

'I would advise you that the profession has undergone seismic changes since then.'

'Yes, I know, but…' Maggie fussed with her scarf. A bright wisp of silk, she'd pulled it from the drawer at the very last minute. Anything to help lift her spirits.

'So I can't quite see what you would bring to the table.'

'My administrative skills?'

'We've already touched on that.'

'My...' *Go on. Big it up!* She took a breath. 'It is my view that, in the private investigation industry, a woman can do many things that a man cannot. Be unobtrusive, for instance. Nobody would think twice about a woman sitting in a car or following them in the street. She can more readily gain people's trust, insinuate herself into situations...'

'Yes, yes...' Was that a smirk she saw playing on the young man's lips? 'I can see that.' Donald Michie was much younger than she'd anticipated. Tall, and skinny with it. *A long drink of water,* her mother would have called him. Dark hair, cut so as to stick up in a point. Bad skin. A callow youth. No matter, so long as the fellow had sufficient clout to put business her way.

'Plus my agency has significant resources. I've already taken on one operative. I have a solid client list, not least of which is your own firm, and I'm planning to expand.'

'Nonetheless, I thank you for your interest...' He dropped Maggie's letter back onto the desk. 'But I'm afraid we'll have to leave it there.'

Maggie felt her lip tremble. She'd made such an effort for this meeting: worn her best – indeed, her only – suit; brushed a sweep of blusher over her cheekbones, skooshed Kirsty's scent behind her ears. 'I've two kids to feed, Mr Michie,' she threw the young man a beseeching look. 'And a large mortgage. If you'd only give me a chance.'

'We-ell...' He picked up a pen, rolled it between finger and thumb. 'Tell you what, Mrs Laird, why don't I have a word with my partners, see if we can put some bits and pieces your way?' He rose. 'Leave it with me.'

'I'll wait to hear from you.' She stood, extended a hand.

Maggie dawdled back down Union Street. She'd taken the bus to her appointment, partly for reasons of economy – petrol was such a price these days – and partly for convenience. She'd have been hard pressed to find a parking space in the city centre. Her spirits ebbed. Despite her best efforts, she had scant confidence she'd hear from Kelman McRae anytime soon. And the bills were piling up. Taking on the agency was all very well, but she needed a fallback position. And fast. Still… *Think positive!* It was a lovely day, the pavements dry, the air crisp, with just a frisson of wind blowing from the direction of the Citadel, where Union Street terminates at the Castlegate and the road dips towards the Esplanade and the North Sea. Maggie looked up at the tall buildings on either side of her. Their granite fasciae sparkled in the sharp rays of the sun. Aberdeen wasn't called the Silver City for nothing.

George had explained it to her, once: how the material from which the city had been fashioned was, in fact, a coarse-grained grey rock composed mainly of feldspar and quartz; how it was the high mica content in its granite geological base that contrived to deceive the eye. *Looks belie.* Isn't that what Maggie's mum used to say? And she was right. Many of the retail shops had been converted to pubs and clubs, their shiny frontages concealing gey tawdry interiors.

Few things in life turned out as you expected. She breathed an involuntary sigh. Who'd ever have thought that she, Maggie Laird, would have come to this? Widowed, near penniless, taking tentative steps on an uncharted path. In the sunlight, she shivered. A path that might lead her into the very heart of darkness.

# A Small Favour

He wasn't what she expected: medium height, slight build, sandy hair combed into a careful side parting. Maggie had got into the habit lately of noting these sort of details. Behind the rimless glasses, the eyes were the palest of blue, so light they looked almost translucent. The man was dressed in a dark suit, well-cut. White shirt, double cuffs, discreet cufflinks. Plain blue tie that was probably silk. As he advanced across the carpet towards her, she could see that his feet were shod in black Oxfords, well-polished. Not a bruiser, then. James Gilruth looked to Maggie more like a corporate accountant than a criminal kingpin.

'Mrs Laird?'

'Yes.' She shivered with apprehension.

Subsequent to their visit, the debt collectors had, to Maggie's surprise, set up the meeting she'd requested. She'd had to psych herself up. Although the leafy enclave they called Rubislaw wasn't far as the crow flies from the quiet avenues and tidy bungalows of Mannofield, it seemed shrouded in secrecy, its mansions set back from the road behind dark thickets of shrubbery, the Rubislaw quarry – source of the granite from which they were constructed – now defunct and filled with water, lurking deep and dangerous beyond.

'What d'you want?' Gilruth stepped round a desk the size of a ship. His voice was surprisingly low. And rasping, as if he had something stuck in his throat.

Maggie fought for breath, her mouth suddenly bereft of saliva. She longed to clasp a palm to her diaphragm, feel it swell the way she'd been taught in her National Childbirth Trust classes all those years before. That always helped when she was in a tight corner.

*You can do this.* She drew in a lungful of air. 'I've come about the bill,' she croaked.

'Bill?'

'The rent my husband is supposed to owe you.'

'Not "supposed", the eyes glittered behind the glasses. 'Does owe.' Her voice sank to a whisper, 'But he paid his rent in advance.'

'*Some* rent,' the first word came out in a hiss. 'I understand he was in arrears.'

Maggie didn't know the facts of the matter. She changed tack. 'You do know my husband is dead?'

Gilruth's head inclined a fraction.

'Then it's iniquitous,' she started forward, 'trying to charge a dead man for an office he can't occupy, services he never received.'

'If you have a complaint,' James Gilruth didn't flinch, 'I suggest you pursue it through the proper channels.'

'And what might those be?'

'My credit control people. You'll find their details on the invoice.'

'Credit control? Is that what you call them?' Maggie drew herself up to her full five feet two. 'You do realise there were a couple of men at my door recently, threatening me?'

'Come now, Mrs Laird.'

'Don't you "come now" me,' she was in full flow. 'I bet it was you that sent them.'

'Mrs Laird,' the carefully modulated voice didn't alter, 'you have to understand I don't personally oversee every aspect of my business. However...' Behind the glasses, the fish-eyes shone. 'Credit follow-up procedures must take their course.'

'I understand that,' she adopted a more conciliatory tone. 'Which is why I asked to see you today.'

Gilruth's right eyebrow gave a marginal twitch.

'My husband's death, as you'll appreciate, has come as a great shock to me. I've teenage children to support, and...'

'You'll get by,' Gilruth cut her short. 'People do.'

'I believe you've a teenage son yourself?'

'What's that got to do with anything?'

*Keep going*! 'So you'll know how expensive...' She ad-libbed desperately.

'Mrs Laird,' Gilruth took a step towards her, 'I've said all I have to say on the matter.'

Maggie's shoulders slumped. 'Won't you even waive the notice period?'

'Your husband signed a binding contract.'

'Yes, I know, but…'

'Drawn up to protect the landlord from, among other things, loss of rent.'

'Yes, but…'

'Sadly, I now have a void to contend with.'

*Fight your corner!* She straightened. 'That's hardly my husband's fault.'

'Quite.' James Gilruth didn't move a muscle. 'But it doesn't alter the facts.'

Maggie stopped in her tracks. She knew she was defeated, that this mild-looking man had a core of steel. Still, she clung to straws. 'Then can I ask a favour?' The words hung suspended for what seemed an eternity.

'A favour?' Gilruth's bland expression didn't change.

'A…a small favour.'

The fish-eyes narrowed. 'There's no such thing as a *small* favour.' The rasp in the man's voice sounded more like a threat now than a cough.

**X**

Maggie sat in her car, hot tears of humiliation coursing down her cheeks as she played the encounter back in her head. It wasn't just that she'd been shown the door, decanted back into the street without decorum. It was that she'd failed so miserably – shown herself up as the stupid, naive little housewife she indubitably was. She made fists of her hands. Roughly, she scrubbed the tears from her cheeks. Her bravado had been born of rage, fury at the injustice meted out to her dead husband. But she'd failed at the first hurdle. Maggie had viewed the meeting with Gilruth as an initial assignment, a dummy run for the task ahead. Her remit was straightforward: make contact with the landlord, explain why his rent invoice was unfair, ask for its cancellation. It all sounded so simple when you put it like that. And it had started out so well. It was only when she came to face-to-face with the man himself that her resolve ebbed away. For James Gilruth may have been slight in stature, but he radiated power in a way she had never before encountered. Menace, too. She trembled in her seat as she pictured that expressionless face, those glittering eyes. Eyes that hadn't registered her own divergent pupils, the realisation hit Maggie now. Hadn't seen. Or been completely indifferent.

All of a sudden, she felt terribly tired. She let her head droop onto her chest, her eyelids drift shut. Maggie snuggled down, savouring the soft warmth of her old wool coat. She let out a sigh. If she'd learned anything that morning, it was that James Gilruth – sitting on his dark empire at the edge of the self-same quarry that built the silver city of Aberdeen – was devoid of any vestige of human kindness.

As disappointment turned to anger, a fat gobbet of bile rose in her throat. She snapped her eyes open. Coughed it into her open palm. Maggie eyed the pool of slime. She'd find out every last thing there was to know about the man and his business dealings, she resolved. More than that, if she could prove Gilruth had the least involvement in her husband's death, she'd find some way to make him pay.

# III

# Rock Bottom

'Would you like to come through?' A leggy brunette in a stretch miniskirt and ballet flats beckoned from an open doorway.

'Oh...' Maggie fumbled for her handbag, 'yes.' As she did so, the magazines she'd been leafing through slipped from her fingers and landed in a heap at her feet. 'I'm so sorry.' Pink in the face, she stooped to pick them up, then followed the girl into a small office.

'I'm Tracy,' the tall girl smiled as she settled herself behind the desk. 'Have a seat.'

Maggie dropped onto the chair on the other side. After her less-than-satisfactory meeting with Kelman McRae, she'd made an appointment with a recruitment agency in the West End. She'd been shaken by her encounter with James Gilruth, and hot on the heels of those two bruisers. But no matter how feeble she felt, she knew she'd have to put a brave face on things, earn a living, hold everything together for the sake of her kids.

'Now,' Tracy scanned the form that Maggie had filled in earlier, 'let's see what we can do for you.' She paused, pen poised. 'You're looking for a secretarial position, is that right?'

Maggie nodded.

'From what you've filled in here, you don't appear to have worked as a secretary since...let me see...1999?'

'Yes.'

'Mmm,' Tracy frowned. 'So what have you've been doing since then?'

'Nothing. I mean,' Maggie stuttered, 'I've been at home, bringing up my kids.'

'Oh, right. Haven't you worked at all?'

'On and off. Seasonal stuff. But I'm back in permanent employment now, part-time, as a Pupil Support Assistant in Seaton.'

'How long have you been doing that?'

'Just over a year.'

'And you're still employed in that capacity?'

'Yes. No,' Maggie felt herself getting flustered, 'I'm on leave at the moment.'

'I see,' Tracy scribbled some notes on the form in front of her. 'And your children, how old are they now?'

'Oh,' Maggie smiled, 'my daughter's in her second year at uni, my son's in fifth year at school.'

Tracy's pen hovered over the application form. 'So you're free to work full-time?'

'Well…' Maggie wondered how much time the agency might swallow up. 'I was really hoping for something that would fit in with school hours.'

'That will severely limit your options.'

'I suppose. But don't a lot of places offer flexitime these days?'

'Let's establish what you have to offer an employer first, shall we?' Tracy fixed Maggie with a steely look. 'Then we'll see what we have available.'

Maggie crossed her legs. Uncrossed them again. This wasn't going at all how she'd expected.

'Right,' Tracy flipped the form over, 'can we just run through what you've put down here? Six O-Levels. Secretarial Certificate. Five years as a secretary to a legal firm, followed by eighteen months as a personal assistant. Is that correct?'

Maggie inclined her head.

'And you can get references from both employers?'

'Yes, though they may be…' Maggie stopped mid-sentence.

'Not all that relevant at this juncture,' Tracy's intervention spared Maggie further embarrassment. 'What's more important is what skills you bring to the table. You are computer literate, I take it?'

'Yes,' Maggie brightened, 'I've taken a course.'

'Oh, which one?'

'PCs for the Terrified.'

Tracy raised an eyebrow. 'Yes, well, can I put down that you're familiar with Microsoft Office Suite.'

'Office Suite?'

'Word, Outlook and Excel?'

'I'm OK with Microsoft Word.'

'Good. What about the others?'

Maggie hesitated. 'I'm not sure.'

'Mmm,' Tracy made a series of small doodles on the form in front of her. 'To be honest with you, Mrs Laird, I don't know that I'd be able to put you forward for a secretarial position. Not with such a limited skill set and no recent experience.'

'But my qualifications...' Maggie had pinned her hopes on this interview.

'Yes, I know,' Tracy splayed her hands on the desktop. 'But what I'm saying is it's all computer-based nowadays, office work, and I can't see, quite frankly, that you'd be up to the mark.'

Not a hope in hell of picking up a PA job, then. Maggie felt a flush creep up her neck. Bit of temping, maybe, and that's if she was lucky.

'If you'd just give me a start.'

'I would if I could,' Tracy leaned towards the older woman. 'But given the current economic climate...' She offered a conspiratorial smile. 'And besides, the agency has its reputation to consider. We've worked hard to develop a good relationship with our clients, and we wouldn't want to jeopardise that in any way.'

'No. No, I understand. But,' Maggie was running out of options. 'If I could just get the chance to show you...'

'You'll have that opportunity when you complete our aptitude tests.'

'Aptitude tests?' Maggie had thought things couldn't get any worse, but this Tracy woman had reduced her to zero. Less than zero. She felt fit to faint.

'Yes,' Tracy continued smoothly. 'They fall into four categories: Microsoft Office Skills, Attention to Detail – that's filing, typing and so on – Language Skills and Customer Service.'

Maggie's stomach clenched. She covered her face with her hands.

'There's no need to be alarmed, Mrs Laird. You'll do them on the computer, and they're mostly multiple choice. Though I do have to warn you,' Tracy's voice dropped to a whisper, 'they'll be timed.'

'Timed?' Maggie's hands fell away.

'Yes.'

Tracy lifted the phone. She pressed a button. 'Ange, if you'd like to take Mrs Laird through.'

# Seaton School

'Classroom assistant my arse,' Maggie caught the snatch of conversation through the open door. 'How come Learning Support gets all the resources?'

There was a muttered response.

'Waste of space, some of those kids. Doomed from the day they were born.'

She squared her shoulders, breezed into the staff room. 'Morning, everyone.'

'Oh, hello.' Eyes averted all round. 'We were just talking about you.'

'Me?' She assumed an innocent face. 'Really?'

'It's not that you don't do a good job, Maggie,' the voice came from behind.

Needs must, Maggie thought. She hadn't intended to go back to her Seaton job so soon, but she still hadn't heard back from Kelman McRae, so her hopes for the agency remained in limbo. As to the prospect of more gainful employment, the recruitment agency debacle had been the final straw.

'We're so sorry about...' This from Julia.

Maggie looked at her feet. 'Yes, well...'

'There's nothing any of us can say, really. Still, you've done well to get back so soon. And the kids...'

Maggie looked up. 'I've missed them.' And she had.

She crossed the room. Switched on the kettle. Stood waiting for it to boil. For some moments, she reflected upon the things her pupils had brought to her life. Then she thought back to the bust-up she'd had with George.

*I saw a job in the paper today.*

*Who for?*

*Me.*

*But you don't have to work, Maggie.*

*No? A bit extra would save you putting in for so much overtime.*

*I don't mind, pet, you know that. But this job you saw – what is it?*

*A teaching assistant.*

*Don't be daft. Glorified skivvy, that's all they are. If you must get a job, why not get a nice job?*

*Such as?*

*A secretary, like you were before.*

*Don't think I haven't looked.*

*This teaching assistant post, where is it anyway?*

*Seaton.*

*You've got to be joking.*

*Why's that?*

*It's as rough as you get.*

*Oh, come on. There are a lot of decent people living in Seaton, George, you know that as well as I do – people who've lived there for years, who have extended family in the area, people who have a real will to make things better.*

*That's as may be. But it's not those poor sods I'm thinking about. It's the others – the ones who make their lives a misery with their drug dealing and their benefit fraud and their antisocial behaviour.*

*But some of those people just need a hand to pull themselves up. Their kids need someone to give them time, one-to-one attention. Kids who've never had the start in life our children have. Anyhow, you needn't worry. I'll hardly be there. The job's only for a few hours a week.*

*That won't bring in much.*

*It's not about the money.*

*But my overtime. I thought you just said…*

*I need to get out of the house, George. Rebuild my confidence.*

*Confidence? Is that what this is all about?*

*You've no idea, have you?*

*Men*! Maggie fumed. They hadn't the least notion how your children ground you down, sucked out the life force till there was nothing left but a shadow of what you'd once been.

The kettle switched itself off with a loud click. She dropped a teabag into a mug. Splashed water on. Seaton had been a revelation to Maggie. In that, at least, George had been right. Since she'd gone back to work, she viewed her life through fresh eyes. Critical eyes. Could hardly credit that she'd been content to sit at home all that time, striving to be the perfect wife and mother.

Too perfect. Fiercely, she squeezed the teabag against the side of the mug. She'd read somewhere you weren't meant to do that. Let out the bitter tannins, the article said. Bitter? With all her heart, Maggie wished she hadn't been quite so wilful when she was young. Kept her head down at school. Gone to college instead of settling for a secretarial course. Waited a few more years before she married George. Since then she'd determined no son or daughter of hers would miss out on any opportunity that was going. She let out a sigh. Then again, if she hadn't insisted Kirsty and Colin be educated at private schools, if George hadn't had to work all the hours to keep them there, she probably wouldn't be in the mess she was in now.

'These no-hopers,' she jolted back to reality, 'are you thinking of anyone in particular?'

'How about Willie Meston, for a start?'

A subdued titter ran round the room.

'I'll give you that one,' she capitulated, 'but only because the lad's hardly ever at school.'

'Too busy running after his da.'

'Not this week,' someone else chipped in. 'Meston senior's banged up. Read it in the *P & J*.'

'Hasn't made a whit of difference. Willie Meston's been in trouble twice this week already. Community bobby was round here. Couldn't raise anyone at home.'

'Bit of a soft target, don't you think?' Maggie crossed the room and sat down.

'How so?'

'Well,' she played devil's advocate, 'if I were a community police officer and my station was adjacent to the school, I might want to be seen as proactive.'

'I suppose...' Grudging voice. You have a point.'

'What sort of trouble was it anyway?'

'Bobby wouldn't say.'

'OK,' Maggie allowed, 'Willie Meston's been in trouble again. But Willie's just one pupil out of many.'

'Ryan Brebner, then.'

'Ryan? How come?' She stuck her nose in the steaming mug, took a tentative sip.

'Sees himself as Willie's lieutenant. Won't be long before he goes the same way.'

'Doesn't follow.' Maggie was pleased to be back at work, but she'd forgotten just how entrenched the attitudes of some of the older teachers were. Not that the atmosphere in the staff room was always so febrile. Maggie enjoyed the banter, normally. It was probably her enforced absence that had caused her to view her workplace in a more detached light.

'Oh, come on. There's no point defending him. That boy dogs Willie Meston's footsteps. His attendance is already dropping off.'

'I thought that was because he had his wee brother to...'

'Ah. Kyle, isn't it? In my opinion the wee chap's just a convenient excuse for Ryan to play truant.'

'Well,' Maggie took another sip, 'I'll keep a close eye on the pair of them.'

'Waste of time. Far better spend it on kids who want to learn.'

There was a general murmur of agreement.

'Like Lewis McHardy?' somebody suggested, quickly followed by, 'Joke.'

'Bad joke, in my opinion,' Maggie banged her mug down. 'Lewis can't help it if he's a bit...'

'Challenged?' A sarky voice offered.

'Yes, but look at the time you've spent in the classroom on that boy. And he hasn't improved one bit, you have to agree.'

'Fair point,' she retorted. 'But I do have other kids, you know.'

'Like who?'

Maggie retrieved her mug. 'Kieran Chalmers, for one.'

'Kieran? He's a different story altogether. Lovely lad. Not his fault they had to move here.'

'I know. Father died. Brain cancer. Killed him in weeks.' She breathed a sigh. Another woman suddenly widowed. Except Rose Chalmers had to up sticks. Move from a Wimpey chalet to a Seaton high rise. So why was Maggie feeling sorry for herself?

'How's Kieran coming along?'

She frowned. 'I'm not sure. We seemed to be making progress, but then…' She broke off. 'He became a bit difficult.'

'Difficult? How?'

'Hard to put a finger on. Introverted. Evasive. And he was always such a well-mannered boy.'

'It'll maybe pass. Just so long as he doesn't fall into bad company.'

Somebody sniffed. 'Chance would be a fine thing.'

'He's had a bit of bother with bullying lately,' another offered.

'Blast,' one of the older teachers. 'Thought we'd knocked that on the head.'

'Who is it this time?'

A new voice. 'That Wiseman lad.'

'I think you'll find Wiseman's been warned off.'

'That right?'

'Yes. And no marks for guessing who.'

'Meston again?'

'On the money. Saw Willie cornering Wiseman when I was on playground duty the other day. Come to think of it, your wee friend Kieran was with him.'

'Keiran?' she jumped, slopping tea onto the table.

'Yes.'

'With Willie Meston?'

'Yup.'

*Dammit.* Something was up. Something serious. Maggie would have to move fast if she didn't want to see a whole year of painstaking work go down the drain.

# Dug in

'Must do your head in.' Fatboy lounged on Kym's settee.

'What?' She raised a tousled head.

Fatboy eyed the row of kids on the rug. 'Looking after this lot.'

'I'm not bothered.'

Kym really *wasn't* bothered. She hadn't been bothered about too much these past few days, not since she'd managed to cadge a few Vals off Fatboy. This week, she hadn't needed to buy nearly so much booze down the shop to get high. The weans hadn't given her so much grief either, hers or the others. She sighed. She'd been that stressed this past while, ever since the Health Centre had said there were strict new rules on prescribing Temazepam. She gnawed at her cuticles. Maybe this new fella could get her a regular supply.

'See, you know what I think?' Fatboy leaned in towards her. 'You might not want to admit it, but I bet this lot would try the patience of a saint.'

Kym pulled a face. 'Some days.'

'Told you.'

They sat in silence for a few minutes, then, 'What do you do to unwind?'

'How d'you mean?'

'In the evenings,' Fatboy persisted. 'After you've got rid of them.'

'Make my own kids their dinner. Put them to bed.'

He frowned. 'I'd forgotten some of them are yours. But don't you ever get out? On the ran-dan,' he leered. 'You know – clubbing?'

Kym scowled. 'As if.'

'Not even the pub?'

She snorted. 'What d'you think I'd use for cash?'

'Oh, come on, you must be earning a fair bit off this lot.'

'Not as much as you'd think.'

Fatboy smirked. 'My heart bleeds.'

She drew herself up. 'I'm giving it to you straight.'

Kym wished Fatboy had never mentioned the pub. She was gasping for a drink. Any kind of drink. Fuck! These Valium tablets mustn't be the same strength as the last lot she'd had. Or maybe she was just getting used to them. She closed her eyes. Tried to visualise the shelves behind the corner shop counter. Zero in on the spirits. The last time she'd been in the shop, she'd got a warning. If she wasn't careful, she'd get banned altogether. Not that she wouldn't be in good company. Willie Meston had long been banned from the place, Ryan Brebner too. It was where both boys had served their apprenticeship in shoplifting. But Kym couldn't afford to be banned. The licensed grocer was handy for her flat, the only place within spitting distance she could get a bevvy.

'Penny for them?'

Kym's eyes opened.

'Penny for what?' she muttered.

'Aren't you the crosspatch today?' Fatboy responded cheerily.

Her head reeled. In front of her, Fatboy's face swam out of focus.

He rooted around his trouser pocket. 'Away and treat yourself.' In the blurred face there was a sudden flash of teeth.

Kym felt something being pressed into her palm.

She opened her hand. Looked down at the note. Looked at the children. Looked back at Fatboy. 'What d'you mean?'

'Away and get yourself something.'

Kym salivated. 'Out of here, is that what you're saying?' Feverishly, she tried to calculate what Fatboy's note would buy her.

He grinned. 'Why not?'

'But the kids...'

'Don't you worry about the kids.'

Her face lit up. 'Thanks a bunch.' She peeled herself off the settee. 'I'll away and get my coat.'

**X**

'Fatboy,' a pudgy girl with a pudding-bowl haircut piped up, 'what are we going to do now?'

He looked up. On the television screen, the *CBeebies* credits were rolling. 'Dunno.'

They'd been docile enough: four boys and two girls ranging in age from two to almost five years old. Fatboy glanced at his watch. It would be a while yet before he could expect to have sight of Willie Meston. 'What would you like to do?'

'Play a game?'

'What kind of game?' he asked cautiously.

Fatboy assumed Kym did some sort of activities with the kids – building bricks, finger painting, whatever it was you did with small children. First thing, probably. When the mothers dropped them off. Before Kym got herself tanked.

'Hide and Seek,' there was a yell from one of the boys.

'Oh, alright, then,' Fatboy hauled himself to his feet. He could remember that one. Somebody would go off and hide. The rest of them would go looking. He could stay put. Piece of cake.

'Who's going to hide?' he demanded.

'Me. Me. Me. Me. Me. Me.'

Six pairs of hands shot in the air.

Six pairs of eyes watched him expectantly.

'You can't all be the one to hide.' He did a quick head count. 'Kyle, you go first.' Ryan's wee brother was almost four and a favourite of Fatboy's, in part because Ryan's connection to Willie had facilitated an *entree* to the flat, but also because he was an engaging kid: blond, blue-eyed and bright as a button.

'Oh, but...'

'Shut it,' Fatboy's temper flared. 'Kyle's going first. The rest of you will get a turn when I tell you.'

# Maggie Practises Surveillance

Maggie took up position in a side street. She'd skipped out fifteen minutes before the bell. She was determined to get to the bottom of whatever was bothering Kieran Chalmers, had no intention of letting the classroom hours she'd put in with him go to waste. She might have drawn a blank for the moment with Jimmy Craigmyle, but she could use the intervening time to develop her skills as an investigator.

The previous evening she'd mugged up on surveillance techniques. The research would stand her in good stead. If Willie Meston was up to something with her star pupil, Maggie would nip it in the bud.

She'd procured the addresses of all four boys, Kieran and Ryan with relative ease, for it was straightforward enough to conduct a fishing exercise whilst the lads were attending Learning Support. Lewis had taken a little more time, for the boy's difficulties were such he became easily confused, and she had to winkle the information out of him. Willie Meston was a different matter – too streetwise by far to fall for a facile enquiry, so Maggie had resorted to the school office. Luckily, she was on good terms with the secretary, had managed to extract the information without invoking Data Protection.

It was a clear day, a watery sun bouncing its rays off the checkered windowpanes of the high flats, a soft sea breeze cooling Maggie's cheeks. On either side of her, the three-storey flats offered a blank facade. They were set back from the street behind low railings and dusty aprons of grass. She cursed the advent of security entry. Time was, you could stand in a lobby and nobody would think anything of it. Now, even if she were to find a main door wedged open or a security entry faulty, she'd most likely be challenged.

Maggie watched as the procession of mums and kids and buggies advanced up Seaton Road, pausing now and again to pick up a dropped toy, hitch up a schoolbag, light a fag. Kids on scooters were chided as they strayed off the pavement. There was the occasional cuff to the back of the head. She strained forward, trying to catch a glimpse of Kieran. Suddenly, there he was – a slight figure, the slick of dark hair flanked on either side by the shaved heads of Willie and Ryan, Lewis's awkward figure bringing up the rear. Maggie switched to full alert. Followed them with her eyes as they came towards her. At the junction with School Road they stopped, stood for a moment in huddled conversation, then scattered in four different directions. *Damn and blast!* Why hadn't she anticipated that? And she'd been hoping to nail at least two of them that afternoon. *Be decisive, woman!* She made a split-second decision. It would have to be Willie. She upped her pace and set off after him, shadowing the boy from a discreet distance on the opposite side of the road.

'Got a light?' A young lad blocked her path.

*Sod it!* She stepped smartly aside, trying to keep Willie Meston in sight.

The lad mirrored her action, cigarette waving in one hand.

Maggie watched as Willie turned a corner and disappeared from view.

Roughly, she pushed past. 'Sorry,' she called over her shoulder as she sprinted up School Road.

Maggie crouched between two parked cars. Mindful of the information she'd gleaned – keep changing your appearance, for one – she tugged on a black woollen hat over her red curls.

She was just in time to catch Willie Meston disappearing into one of the four-in-a-block flats. She breathed a sigh of satisfaction. Where Willie went, the rest would surely follow.

She shifted position. She'd only been outside the Meston home for a few minutes, and already her thighs were aching and she had pins and needles in her calves. She raised her head and peered through the dusty glass of the car windows.

'What are ye up tae?' A wee wifie pushing a shopping trolley stopped in her tracks.

'Oh…' Maggie ad-libbed. 'Managed to lock myself out of my car.' The old woman tsk-tsked, but continued on her way.

Now she'd been spotted, Maggie decided to change location. She cast around. Apart from the cars, there wasn't a thing on the street except for a clutch of giant black wheelie bins. She made a dash for them and squeezed into the narrow space in between. For just a moment, she wondered what George would make of this. Then she turned to speculating on what Willie Meston was doing – getting changed? Having his tea?

Maggie jumped when she heard the door to the close mouth click shut. She observed Willie wheel his bike down the path, mount, pedal off at a lick. *Oh, to hell!* When she'd planned that day's operation, she hadn't factored in bikes. She extracted herself from her hiding place and made a beeline for the school. She jogged down the road, her breath coming in shallow gasps, crossed the road and reached the safety of her car.

Maggie drove up School Road, eyes swivelling left and right. There was no sign of Willie or his bike. She pulled over. Was trying to formulate a plan of action when Kieran shot out of a side road. Keeping the boy's bicycle in sight, she hugged the kerb, letting the steady stream of traffic overtake her. She saw Kieran swing across the road and mount the pavement, watched him squeeze on his brakes and come to a halt outside the parade of shops on the corner of King Street. Maggie parked some way back. Her pulse quickened as Willie Meston emerged from the shadow of the local chippie. She craned her neck. Observed Kieran and Willie confer. It couldn't have been five minutes before Ryan Brebner appeared from the opposite direction, his wee brother Kyle riding pillion. A few minutes after that, Lewis McHardy pedalled laboriously into view.

The boys remounted their bicycles. At the traffic lights they crossed to the Spar shop then sprinted furiously up St Machar Drive. Maggie pulled out from the kerb. As she approached the junction, the lights changed from green to amber. She floored the accelerator. The car shot forward, narrowly missing a white van that was trying to make a right turn. The van's driver hit his horn. She spied one of the boys turn back. Helplessly, she watched as they disappeared from view.

Maggie sped up the hill and took a right into Dunbar Street. Nerve ends tingling, she nosed the car round the bend. On her left, one of Old Aberdeen's many historic houses proclaimed *Bishop's Gate*. Opposite, a pair of semi-detached bungalows presented a prim view. Of the boys there was no sign.

The car crawled forward, passing a small road on the right. At the top of a slight hill, she spied a jumble of bikes on their sides, wheels slowly spinning. Swiftly, she put the car into reverse. She was about to turn the wheel when she noticed the 'No Entry' signs. *Bugger!* She pulled into the kerb and leapt out of the car, not even bothering to activate the central locking.

Maggie crept stealthily up the Chanonry. Part-way, she stopped. She looked around. To her right, an ancient house sat blank-faced on the road. To her left, a high stone wall traced the contours of the incline. Her eyes darted from the bikes to the wall, to the house and back to the bikes. And then she saw it. The waste ground sloped from Seaton Park to the backs of the houses on Don Street. It was bounded by a pair of tall iron gates secured by a stout padlock and chain. They and the railings alongside must have been three metres high. Quite a challenge for those kids, for that piece of scrubland was the only place they could be. They'd have had to hoist the wee lad over, she reckoned. Maggie never ceased to wonder at the ingenuity of small boys.

*So that's all they were up to?* She smiled quietly to herself. Her eyes took in the knee-high rough grass, the dense canopy of trees. What could be more fun, she mused, than to seek adventure in such a place? More stimulating, surely, than the drab streets of Seaton or the wind-whipped forecourts of the high rises.

Maggie was retreating down the hill when a voice cried out. It sounded like Lewis, though she couldn't be sure. Anxious, she turned. There was silence then. For long moments she stood, ears pricked. Then, satisfied, she turned back and headed for her car.

# Keep Digging

'Have you got anything for me?' Brian had barely sat down when Maggie came out with it.

'Jimmy Craigmyle? Not a lot,' he shrugged an apology. 'But first, let me get you some tea.'

She made to rise. 'My turn.'

'Don't be daft.' He got to his feet, placed a hand on her shoulder.

Maggie felt a frisson of excitement. She turned her head, regarded the strong fingers as they pressed her back into her seat. Ever the gentleman. She watched as he made his way to the counter. That was something she'd always admired about Brian. Not that George didn't have good manners. It was just that he had a quieter way of showing his feelings.

Her pelvic muscles clenched. She let out a deep exhalation. Already she was losing all sensation of him, the husband who'd been her support and her consolation for all those years: the solid curve of his back, the way his fingers felt on her skin, that feeling when he...

'How have you been?' Brian set down a tray.

'Oh,' startled, she looked up. She was ashamed by her physical reaction. Wondered whether her body was telling her she reciprocated Brian's feelings, or if her response was simply some primal need for human contact. Like when she'd clambered onto that gurney. Maggie shuddered as she recalled once more the sensation of George's ice-cold body beneath her own. She'd wished herself dead that day. Like an Indian widow performing *suttee*, the thought occurred to her now. But she had to survive – for her children's sake, if not her own. And not just survive, but be resolute and fearless if she were to bring her plan to fruition and achieve justice for George.

Briskly, she brought her mind back to the present. 'I'm back at work, running around like a mad thing.'

'You're looking good on it.'

'Must be the kids. They always perk me up. But I didn't ask you here to talk about me, Brian. It's Jimmy Craigmyle who's my number-one priority. Once I've spoken to him, I can…'

'Let me stop you there.'

'You mean you haven't managed to run him down?'

'No. I asked around the Force. Folk confirmed what I'd heard – Jimmy's marriage broke up, right enough.'

'Oh.' Maggie couldn't mask her disappointment. Running down Craigmyle was crucial to her action plan. 'Has he moved away, then?'

'No, still in Aberdeen, from what I can gather.'

'Whereabouts?'

'Bedsit down Crown Street, I believe.'

'Great,' she sat up. 'Have you got an address?'

'Fraid not.'

'Oh, well, I'll probably manage to find him.'

'Somebody said they'd seen him down Windmill Brae. He's maybe working at that club. Used to be called Venue. God knows what they're calling it this week – changes its name that often.'

She brightened. 'I'll check it out.'

'No you will not.'

'Why's that?'

'Because for one, it belongs to our friend James Gilruth, and…'

'I went to see him.' It was out before she could stop herself. 'About that rent bill.'

'Gilruth? I thought I told you…'

'I don't dance to your tune, Brian Burnett.'

'No.' So much for thinking he might have a future with Maggie Laird. 'How did you get on?'

She looked away. 'Didn't.'

Brian stifled the urge to say I told you so. 'So the rent, have you paid it?' he asked instead.

'No, but Wilma…'

'Ah, yes,' he chuckled. 'Wilma. The answer to a woman's prayers.'

'It's not a laughing matter,' Maggie glowered. 'I'll have you know she cleared the rent arrears. *And* she sorted out the notice period.'

'They let you off?'

'Not exactly. Wilma told them we'd be out of there by noon the next day. I'd already had the phone transferred, you see, and there was nothing of value in the place.'

'But waiving a month's notice? Doesn't sound like Gilruth.'

'No,' Maggie gave a rueful smile. 'Fact of the matter is, Wilma told them they could sing for it.'

'Well,' Brian brought his hands together, 'that settles whatever lingering doubts you might have had in connection with George's death.'

'Does it?'

'Well, I mean, you haven't been able to turn up anything on Gilruth.' He grimaced. 'Not that you're alone there. Aberdeen's finest have been trying to nail the guy for I don't know how long.'

'What for?'

'Drugs. Who knows what else? Gilruth's into big property deals these days. From what we can gather, the other businesses are just a front now for laundering the money. But for all the time we've been on his tail, we've never pinned a thing on him, not so much as a parking ticket. Clever bastard. But back to George. The damaged door was easily enough explained. That only leaves the question of the filing cabinet.'

'Oh,' Maggie's pale face suffused with colour. 'I should have rung you, Brian. I'm really sorry. That filing cabinet – I did a bit of detective work.' She leaned towards him. 'Those burglaries in King Street, remember? Police took several statements from an old guy runs a jewellery workshop on the first floor. I went to see him. Slipped my mind, I've been that hard pressed. Apparently the keys were a bit iffy. George locked the cabinet, broke the key in the lock. He nipped downstairs and asked the jeweller to have a look.'

'Classic.'

'Anyhow, the old guy managed to get the thing unlocked and the key out, but by that time the lock was useless.'

'Well, Maggie Laird,' Brian grinned, 'aren't you the private eye?'

She glowed with satisfaction. Her visit to the jeweller had boosted her confidence.

'So...' The detective in Brian resurfaced. 'Now it's been established that there was nothing suspicious about George's death, all our focus should be on clearing his name.'

'Agreed. You were telling me about Jimmy Craigmyle.'

'Right. Apart from the fact that Gilruth owns that club, if – and it's a big if – Craigmyle is working there, he won't finish till three in the morning.'

'So?'

'I'd have thought it was obvious, Maggie. That part of town's no place for a woman.'

She sat upright. 'I can look after myself.'

'You can, can you? How is the PI business anyhow?'

'Coming away,' she smiled. 'Thanks for asking. Some aspects have been surprisingly easy to master, actually. Others...well, that's the reason I wanted to see you. I need some more information.' She turned her face up to his. 'That OK with you?'

'Depends.'

'You know I wouldn't ask you to do anything that would compromise your position.'

'No? Just PNC a few people and God knows what else.' He leaned in close. That tiny frisson again. 'Do you want to see me locked up?'

'Course not.'

There was a silence, then, 'Tell me what it is. I'll see what I can do.'

'Thanks, Brian. What I want is for you to keep on digging: Jimmy Craigmyle, first and foremost, plus anything you can find on Gilruth.'

'I thought that was settled.'

'It is. It's just...if you could float the name past a few more folk.

114

Run it through the computer, see what comes up.' You couldn't have too much information, she'd decided, if you were going to be a proper PI.

'Have you been listening to me, Maggie?' Brian's voice was heavy with exasperation. 'It's time to move on,' he reached for her hand. 'Put this Gilruth nonsense behind you.'

She resisted the temptation to pull away. If she was honest, she rather enjoyed the feeling. Except…she felt a twinge of remorse. Wasn't using Brian's attraction to her doing her dead husband a disservice? No. Maggie left her hand in place. She'd have to keep Brian Burnett onside if she were to clear George's name. And if the business took off, she'd no doubt have to call on Brian's services plenty more times.

'I know. All the same, will you do that?'

'I can't promise. To tell the truth, I…'

'You know I wouldn't ask unless…'

Brian looked down at the small fingers clasped in his. He sighed. 'I know.'

'Thanks, Brian,' she flashed a smile. 'I really appreciate…'

'Oh,' he let go of her hand, reached into an inside pocket, 'I almost forgot.' He drew out a scrap of paper. 'I've got a phone number.'

Maggie's heart beat faster. 'For Craigmyle?'

'Yup.' He handed her the paper. 'Might not be in service, but it's worth a try.'

# The Porn King

Kym sat comatose on the settee, the kids lolling at her feet. She'd had a fair old bevvy while she was out, and that on top of the pills she'd swallowed first thing. Her eyelids drooped. The doorbell jolted her back to reality. She looked at Fatboy. 'That'll be someone for Kyle.'

'Well,' he didn't budge, 'don't look at me.'

'Aw, come on. I've only just got in.'

'Your call, anything to do with these kids.'

Kym hauled herself upright. 'My call?' She engaged Fatboy through bloodshot eyes. 'Aye, it's my call right enough. But only when it suits you, pal. The rest of the time, Christ knows what you're doing up here with them.'

'Don't be daft,' Fatboy assumed an expression of supreme innocence. 'We've only been watching telly.'

'Telly, is it?' With that she staggered to her feet and lurched down the hall. There was the sound of the chain being slid off its housing, the front door opening and banging shut again.

'Cheers, big fella.' Willie swaggered in, Lewis at his heels.

Fatboy's face darkened. 'Who the fuck's this?'

Willie waved a hand. 'Fatboy, meet Lewis. Lewis,' he turned, 'say hello to Fatboy.'

Lewis looked at his feet. 'Hello.'

'What the hell's he doing here?'

'He wis jist...'

Lewis raised his head. 'Ah'm chummin Wullie the day.'

Fatboy threw Willie an evil look. 'Better not be getting in the way of business.'

'Naw,' Willie rushed to answer. 'Ah've hud a crackin day,' he grinned. 'Near ran oot o' gear. Nipped back here fur mair supplies. Ah bumped inta Lewis on ma way ower. We're in the same class,' he added by way of explanation.

Fatboy eyed the newcomer. He was big for his age. Limpid brown eyes under a dark buzz cut. Large hands and feet. A solid roll of fat where his waist should have been.

'What's *your* claim to fame, then?' he addressed Lewis.

The lad lowered his chin.

'Cat got your tongue?' Fatboy started forward. 'I asked you a question.'

'Loon's a ha'penny short o' a shilling.'

'You shut your mouth,' he barked at Willie. Fatboy swivelled back to Lewis. 'Well?'

Lewis kept his head down. He shuffled his feet. Finally, 'Naethin,' he muttered.

'Nothing?' Fatboy jeered. 'Oh, come on, you can do better than that.'

Willie jabbed an elbow in the boy's ribs. 'Lewis is the porn king, are ye no, pal?'

Lewis looked up, his face scarlet.

'Porn?' Fatboy grinned. 'You a fan, then?'

'Aye,' Lewis offered a vacant smile.

'Anything special?'

'Well…' Sideways look. 'There wis this video…'

'Dinna listen tae him,' Willie interjected. 'Fuck-wit's feal. Sits aw nicht watchin Goth movies.'

'That right?'

'Aye.' The boy's expression didn't alter.

'Shame,' Fatboy retorted. 'I know some cracking porn sites.'

'Ye dae?' Lewis regarded him with awe.

'Don't I just?' Fatboy made an expansive gesture. 'Something for every taste.' He grinned. 'You could swing past my place sometime, if you want. Take a look.'

'Ye kiddin me?' the boy's eyes popped.

'No.' The grin vanished from Fatboy's face. 'Here,' he pulled an envelope from an inside pocket. 'I'll write down the address.'

# Divvy up

'Maggie?' Wilma answered the door. 'You're a surprise. I thought you were in town today.'

'I was. But the meeting was off.'

'How come?'

Maggie hung her head. 'Got the wrong day.'

'Maggie Laird,' Wilma wagged a stubby finger.

She held up her hands in surrender. 'Don't know how I managed it. But I've been spread that thin lately, trying to beef up the business, keeping a weather eye on Colin. And now I'm back at work...'

'They weren't leaning on you, were they?'

'No, but it's early days yet. I need a fallback position. Especially after...'

'Your wee outing to Rubislaw Den. You should have told me, Maggie. That was a daft thing to do.'

'Don't I know it. And it's not as if I wasn't warned. It's just... I had it all worked out in my head, Wilma, and once I make my mind up to something...' It was her biggest failing, Maggie knew – the way she ran at things head-on. And hadn't that been responsible for the morass she found herself in now?

'At least your appointment wasn't yesterday.'

Maggie made a face. 'No. But I felt such a fool.'

'Never mind. In you come. I'll brew you a pot of tea.'

'Thanks.' She followed her friend through to the conservatory at the house and flopped into a capacious rattan chair.

Wilma puttered through to the kitchen. Maggie could hear the tap running, the clatter of crockery. She let her eyes droop shut. She could remember quite clearly the very first time she'd been invited round to her neighbour's house. Wilma had shown her into the sitting room. The space should have been the mirror of Maggie's own.

*Would* have been, were it not for the heavily patterned silver wallpaper, the over-sized leather sofas, the glitzy black glass chandelier. And the smell! Scented candles on every surface. Way over the top for a bungalow in Mannofield, she'd thought at the time. Maggie could hardly believe now what a judgmental bitch she'd been.

With a clatter, Wilma set down a tray on the coffee table.

Maggie's eyes shot open. 'Tell you what, though…'

'Oh, what's that?'

'Since we've been working together, one thing's become abundantly clear: if we're going to make this thing work – build up the agency and still hold our jobs down – we'll have to put it on a proper footing.'

Wilma poured tea into two mugs. 'Wotcha mean?'

'It's all been too…' Maggie struggled for the word. Settled for one of Kirsty's. '*Random* up till now: the way we've been setting about George's caseload, jumping at every prospective new client. Now that business is beginning to pick up, we really should adopt a more systematic approach.'

'I'm not sure where you're going with this, pal.'

'Well, it seems to me that a lot of the work that's coming in is routine: credit checks, traces, that sort of thing. Demands application, more than anything. Some of it, on the other hand, needs legal know-how, or computer savvy, or interpersonal skills. Instead of sitting down together like we've been doing, wouldn't it be more productive if we divided our workload, each worked on what we were best at?'

'How will we do that?"

'Make a list of our strengths and weaknesses: like me being careful – nit-picking, as you keep telling me. Having familiarity with legal jargon. Being able to frame a business letter, write a report, that sort of thing.'

'Oh,' a wave of recognition washed over Wilma, 'you mean a skill set?'

'Wil-ma!' Maggie burst out laughing. 'Where did you get that? Not from your pub in Torry.'

'I got it off *The Apprentice*, if you must know.'

'Oh, Wilma,' Maggie's voice was contrite, 'I'm not making fun of you.'

'Yes, you are. You and your legal knowledge, your command of English...' Wilma bit her bottom lip. 'Where does that leave me?'

'Well, there's your computer skills, for a start. I'd never have been able to run all that background stuff without you. Then there's your inside knowledge. The information you've been able to bring to the table about tenancy problems, the benefits system, fraud, petty crime – stuff you pick up in the pub, even. I wouldn't have known about any of that. And then divorce procedures, they've all changed since I worked in a lawyer's office.'

'So? You can get that off the internet.'

'Accepted. But there's the know-how you bring from working at the hospital: the folk who come through Accident and Emergency, the battered wives, the kids with suspect injuries, the druggies that have been duffed up. The drugs themselves,' Maggie paused. 'I don't know the first thing about anything like that – recreational drugs, Methadone programmes, even the number of folk that are addicted to prescription medicine.'

'Doesn't happen in Methlick,' Wilma teased.

'I know,' Maggie came back at her. 'I can't help it if I'm slow when it comes to these kind of things, but it just goes to show how savvy you are. Plus, on top of your practical know-how, you've got such a wide circle of contacts. Since we got up and running, you've been great at worming information out of folk.'

'Too much information, sometimes. I see what you're getting at, though. I suppose I do know a thing or two about life on the pointed end. When I was a kid, hardly a day went past there wasn't a squad car down our street.'

Maggie's eyes widened. 'Really?'

'You don't know you're born, Maggie Laird, sittin in that tidy wee bungalow of yours next door. Oh,' Wilma grimaced, 'I'm sorry. I didn't mean...'

'That's alright.'

'It's just, till I moved in with Ian, I'd never had a home, not a real home. Lived in nothing but rented stuff – cast-off furniture, outside toilets, electric meters that were forever running out. I was aye hungry, Maggie, when I was a kid, even with free school dinners. Had to leave school the minute I turned sixteen, go out to work at the fish processing. And once that Darren Fowlie got me in the family way...'

'Darren was your first husband?'

'Aye. Bastard. Lay around the house all day. Out half the night. Plus I'd get the back of his hand if I so much as looked at him sideways.'

Maggie stretched out a comforting hand. 'Oh, Wilma. Your boys – you mentioned you had two – are they around?'

'Aye. Still in Torry, God help them.'

'Torry can't be that bad, not these days.' Maggie couldn't remember when she'd last been there.

'It's not. I'll take you sometime, show you around.'

'Your lads, what are they doing now?'

Wilma tapped a finger to the side of her nose. 'Don't ask.' She changed the subject. 'I've landed lucky with Ian Harcus. And if we make a go of this wee business, you an me, I'll be luckier still.'

'There you are, then.' Maggie rubbed her hands together. 'Why don't we agree you'll do the computer research to start with? I can pick that up as we go along. You can be out and about on the divorce cases, the insurance fraud: working the locations you already know well and where I wouldn't fit in. I'll do the legal stuff: witness statements, business letters, reports. Concentrate on the corporate side: going into meetings with law firms, building the client list. How does that sound?'

'Fair enough.'

'You can finish off the billing if you're OK with that, and reconcile the accounts. You're quicker than I am, plus you've got a lot more nerve when it comes to asking for money.'

Wilma beamed with pleasure.

'Speaking of which, isn't it time we discussed how to apportion income?'

'Oh,' a grin spread across Wilma's face, 'divvy up, you mean?'

Maggie laughed. 'If you want to put it like that. Only, I was thinking…' Suddenly, she was serious again. 'It's time we talked about a salary for you.'

'I'll not be needing paid.'

'You *have* to be paid, Wilma. Especially if you're going to sit up half the night running credit checks.'

Wilma shrugged. 'What else would I be doing? The social life round this place isn't what I'd call dizzy. No discos. No rave-ups. Hell…' She jabbed an elbow painfully into Maggie's ribs. 'Ye canna even get yersel a quickie up a close. Oh,' she clocked Maggie's expression. '*Sorree.*'

'Yes, well…' Maggie clenched her teeth. Sex was something else that had gone downhill during and after the trial. Not that it had ever been earth-shaking, more an ease with one another, a corner of the comfort blanket George had thrown around her. Along with everything else, Maggie was getting used to not having a sex life. Those times she lay in the night aching for George, she'd masturbate sometimes, fingering herself furtively under the covers as a conduit to sleep.

'There you go again. Miss Prim.' Wilma jolted her back to reality. 'Do I no keep sayin? You can take the girl out of Methlick…'

'Don't remind me. It's weeks since I've taken a run out to visit my folks.'

Maggie grasped hold of her neighbour's hand. 'You've a big heart, Wilma, but you'll need to be paid for the hours you put in. When it comes down to it, you need the money as much as I do. Didn't you say just last week you were away to do a couple of cleaning jobs?'

Wilma coloured. 'It's the end of the month.'

Dammit. Maggie cursed herself for not having the wit to bring the subject up before. Not that Wilma Harcus was a special case.

There must be millions of working women in the world juggling their domestic responsibilities with more than one part-time job. And Wilma would be mortified if Maggie were to offer a loan. Not that she had much to offer.

She tried to think on her feet, only she was sitting down and she had a thumping headache. 'Why don't we compromise? Let's say your cleaning jobs pay £6 an hour.'

'£7.50,' Wilma came back, quick as a shot.

'Well, then, how about you give the cleaning jobs a miss and charge your time out at that? Would that work, do you think? Just to begin with,' she rushed on. 'Then if we make a go of things…'

'There's not enough coming in to pay either of us a wage.'

'Yes there is. Just about. We've had two invoices settle this week already and another due in.'

'That's as may be, but it all sounds so effin serious, this divvying up. It won't be the same, not sitting down together like this.'

'Wilma,' Maggie's voice was full of reassurance, 'every time we take on a new case, we'll have a briefing session, I promise. *And* regular progress meetings to share feedback. Plus we'll still sit down together to do the billing.' She paused. 'It'll be teamwork from now on. Agreed?'

'We-ell…'

'We'll have plenty opportunity to have a laugh, still, don't you worry.'

Wilma grinned. 'You're a good person, Maggie Laird.'

*Good person my ass.* Maggie was mortified now at how she'd misjudged her neighbour in those early days of their friendship.

'And you're a head banger, Wilma Harcus,' she responded with an affectionate smile.

# Bit o' Bother

In a dark alley down by the harbour, Wilma shivered. A snell wind whipped around her ankles, and it had started to rain. She shifted her weight from one foot to the other, wishing she'd worn boots instead of the six-inch stilettos she'd selected for the job. She checked the time on her phone. 10.27. Must be a slow night. Still… she hiked her PVC miniskirt further up her backside. If productive, that night's assignment – surveillance of a husband suspected of consorting with prostitutes – would net the agency sufficient to settle a couple more bills.

Wilma leaned back against the wall of a warehouse. She'd had a day of it, what with her shift at the hospital, a whizz round the house with the vacuum, preparing the dinner before Ian got in. Bugger all time to draw breath, far less apply all this slap. Then there was the long list of credit checks Maggie had pressed on her. *No hurry,* she'd insisted. But Wilma knew from long experience that if you didn't put your back into something… She had a vision of Darren, her ex-husband. *Useless fucker,* she muttered under her breath.

She raised a hand to her head. Rain or no rain, the heavily back-combed beehive, stiff with lacquer, was still in place. It was raining steadily now. Fat raindrops plopped onto Wilma's forehead, slid down her rouged cheeks, formed a drip at the tip of her nose. She wiped them away with the back of her hand. Wilma let out a long sigh. She was fit to drop. Her eyelids drooped. She'd give it another hour.

'Fuck off,' a voiced hissed in her ear.

Wilma's eyes shot open. So much for surveillance! 'Fuck off yersel,' she eyed the figure standing in front of her. In the rain-shrouded glow of a single street lamp she could make out an emaciated young woman. Seemingly impervious to the weather, she was clad in a skimpy vest top and sawn-off denim shorts.

'Ye're on ma pitch.' A flash of bad teeth.

Wilma squared up. 'Then how come ye're no on it yersel.'

'Ah've been…' The girl – who couldn't have been more than twenty but looked fifty – stuck one finger in her mouth and made vigorous sucking noises. 'Otherwise engaged. Now,' she leered, 'wull ye fuck off?'

'Sure thing,' Wilma tugged at the hem of her skirt. 'If ye'll give me twa meenits o yer valuable time.'

'Aye?' Suspicious look.

'Ye widna hae come across a guy doon here name o' John Cowie?'

'Ur ke kiddin me?' She struck a pose. '*My name's John Cowie. How do you do?* Punters dinna bother wi foreplay. Aside from which, they're all fuckin johns.'

'Fair dos.' Wilma could have swallowed her tongue whole. 'But this guy's a big bastard. Red hair. Drives a Beemer.'

'Half the buggers drive Beemers.'

'This one has an unusual ornament on the dash: a naked geisha that nods her head when the car's in motion.

The girl frowned. 'Might have.'

'And just say you did,' Wilma pressed her advantage, 'would you be able to pin down a date or a time?'

'Wha's askin?' The girl stepped back two paces. 'Ye're no the filth, are ye?'

'No,' Wilma rushed to reassure her. 'Nothing like that.' She palmed a £20 note. 'Would this jog your memory?'

The girl opened her fist. Held the note up to the light. 'Naw.'

Seeing her profit margin squeezed by the minute, Wilma proffered another note.

An arm shot out. A hand stuffed the notes down the front of a push-up bra. 'Fella comes doon most Thursdays.'

'What time?'

'Nineish, I'd say. But…'

'Bit o' bother, Savannah?' A male voice rang out from the end of

125

the alleyway.

'Naw. Ah'm done here.' Sharpish, Savannah turned away.

Wilma grabbed hold of her arm. 'You were about to say?'

The girl shrugged. 'Naethin.'

'Just one more thing. Would you be willing to put yer name to what you've just told me?'

Suspicious look. 'How, like?'

'Witness statement.'

'Thocht ye said ye were no the filth.'

'Ah'm no.' Hastily, Wilma crossed herself. 'Cross ma heart an hope tae die.'

'Then what are ye up tae?'

'Just makin a few enquiries. Discreet, like.'

'Aye…that'll be right.'

'So will ye?' Through the thickening rain, Wilma projected a full-on smile. 'Put yer name tae it?'

Savannah offered a lopsided grin. 'Nae fuckin chance.'

# The Beach Boulevard

Fatboy lay sprawled on the bed, his mind buzzing with what he'd just seen on the computer screen: images more graphic than anything he'd managed to source thus far. Every nerve end in his body tingled. He wished to Christ he could light up a fag, smoke some weed, swallow a couple of moggies, anything to help him relax. But the walls were paper thin and the smoke alarms would go mental. Fatboy had already got grief from upstairs for setting them off. He could get up, but he couldn't be arsed going outside. He diverted himself by totting up the spliffs he'd smoked. And after that the tablets he'd popped, the amyl nitrate and the wraps and... Fuck. He'd have to do something about those smoke alarms.

Fatboy propped himself up on his elbows. He looked around. The room was a tip: empty beer bottles, crushed Coke cans, socks and boxers and T-shirts strewn all over the floor. The air was thick, stale with the smell of sweat and spunk and unwashed bedclothes. Fuckin midden! Still, Fatboy smirked, it was *his* midden. He lay back again. It had been a good move, getting his folks to set him up in a place of his own. Fatboy was well fuckin out of it. He hardly knew his old man, these days. As for his mother, she was a slag. It hadn't always been so. He closed his eyes. Let his mind drift back to his childhood, that happy time when he could still command his mother's attention. He slipped a hand down the front of his trackie bottoms. For a few moments he fondled himself, then he began to rub.

Fatboy felt his dick stiffen and start to rise. With his free hand, he eased the elastic waistband of his tracksuit bottoms over his buttocks and down to his knees. He wriggled out of his underpants, freeing his erection. Cupping his balls in his left palm, he clasped the fingers of his right hand around his penis, easing the foreskin up and over. Up. And over. Pinching the tip with every stroke. As the tension began to seep from his limbs, he let out a long exhalation of breath.

The doorbell shattered the silence.

'Fuck.' Fatboy stopped mid-stroke. He pricked his ears. There wasn't a sound from the landing. He re-commenced his rhythmic stroke.

There was another ring at the door.

'Christ,' he exclaimed. He stopped again. Who in hell could it be? Wouldn't be his folks. Fatboy didn't encourage social calls at his flat on the Beach Boulevard, and he'd fucked it up big time that last occasion he went home. Wouldn't be a delivery. He snorted. He'd plenty supplies to see him through. He fondled himself for a few moments, but he'd lost momentum.

'Fatboy?' Thin voice. 'You there?'

'Shite,' Fatboy spat.

'Fatboy?' The voice again, louder this time.

'Fuck,' Fatboy muttered under his breath. Sounded like that wee kid from Seaton. He raised his head off the pillow. Felt for his manhood. It was completely flaccid.

Fatboy tugged up his pants. Rolled off the bed. Crossed the hallway. He squinted through the peephole. Lewis stood on the doorstep. Shit and fuck, he cursed inwardly. Served him right for playing the big man. It had been too tempting: Willie Meston serving him up a daftie on a plate. Who knows what sport the lumpen loon might afford? But the minute he'd extended the invitation, Fatboy regretted opening his big mouth. He'd got a frightener on the Castlegate that last time. Knew he'd need to duck out of sight. And it had been working out so well. Kym's flat might be a dump, but Fatboy wouldn't be fingered there. So what in fuck had possessed him to hand out his address? No, having some random kid come knocking at his door definitely hadn't been one of his better ideas. Christ, folk might even think he was a bum bandit. And besides, even if no harm came of it, when he'd said *swing by sometime* he hadn't meant the next fucking week.

Still, it's not as if he had anything on. And now the kid was here…

Fatboy unlocked the door. He grinned. 'It's yourself, wee man. Come away in.'

Fatboy sat in front of his computer, Lewis perched on a stool by his side. For a solid hour, he'd been clicking in and out of porn sites: men on women, women on women, twosomes, threesomes, orgies.

'What d'you think, then?' He turned to Lewis, a satisfied smile on his face.

The boy shrugged. 'Dunno.'

'What's up?'

Eyes averted. 'Naethin.'

'You can tell me. It's OK.'

Lewis fidgeted on his stool. 'They're a' the same, they things.'

Fatboy frowned. 'You're right enough, kid. Come to think on it, I'm sick of it an all. Same cocks. Same minges,' he rolled his eyes. 'Same moves, same fuckin set pieces. Let's see if I can find you something more interesting.' He typed a couple of words into Google. 'Oh, here's a good one,' he opened another link. On the screen, a huge African-American guy was humping a skinny blonde, doggy-style. As the man banged away at the bird, she moaned and sighed, silicone tits bobbing, curls jiggling like crazy around her head. Every few thrusts, the guy would pull his cock all the way out of her. He'd wave it around a bit, so the video camera could zoom in.

Fatboy felt his organ stiffen. 'Bet you've never seen such a ginormous dong?'

Lewis shrugged once more.

The black man changed position. He was lying on his back now, the woman straddling him, his giant pecker sticking up between her thighs. The blonde tossed her head. She shuffled backwards towards the video camera. Bent down. Wiggled her bum in the air so you could see the cleft between her cheeks. She straightened up, then, took hold of the dong, clasping her scarlet fingernails tight around it. Turned to look into the lens, then licked her lips. Like she was gagging for it.

The blonde bent again to take the thing in her...

Fatboy's cock started to rise. He threw Lewis a lascivious look. 'What are you saying to it?' he leered.

The lad stifled a yawn.

'That's nothing,' Fatboy clicked his mouse.

The two watched as a dozy-looking Labrador was licked into a frenzy by a fat brunette.

Fatboy turned to Lewis. 'That more to your taste, eh, kid?'

Lewis sat, blank-faced. 'Naw.'

Fatboy was hard now. He could feel his pants bunching uncomfortably. 'Fancy something to eat?'

'Such as?'

'Coke? Crisps?'

Lewis swung his legs. 'OK.'

Fatboy stood up. Rushed his erection out of the room.

'There you go,' he slapped two cans of Coke and a big bag of salt and vinegar crisps onto the desktop.

Lewis fell upon the crisps. 'Ta.'

For a few moments the two sat, glugging from the chilled cans, snatching handfuls of crisps from the open packet.

Fatboy winked. 'Fancy watching some more?'

Lewis drained the last of his Coke. Wiped his mouth with the back of his hand. 'Naw.'

Fatboy scrunched the cans and chucked them into a corner. The empty crisp packet followed. 'Didn't Willie mention Goth movies were more your scene?'

The boy brightened. 'Aye.'

'What?' Fatboy racked his brains. 'That Twilight stuff?' He'd heard that was what young teens were into these days.

'Naw,' Lewis scoffed. 'Twilight's fur quines.'

'Something a bit meatier, then?'

Lewis sat forward.

'Tell you what,' Fatboy bent to the boy's ear, 'let's see if I can find you something horny that's got blood-sucking as well.' He keyed in some search terms. 'Wait till you see this...' He opened a link.

The wee lad's eyes swivelled back to the screen. 'Holy moly,' Lewis breathed.

'That better?' Fatboy turned.

The boy nodded assent.

'You up for more?'

Vigorously, Lewis dipped his chin.

Fatboy typed another couple of words into Google. Scrolled down the page that popped up. Opened a link at random.

Lewis's eyes were out on stalks now, his mouth hanging open. A snail-trail of drool made slow progress down his chin.

'You OK?' Fatboy turned to him.

The boy sat, rigid, eyes locked on the flickering screen.

Suddenly, 'Ch-rist,' Lewis screamed at the top of his voice.

'Shhhh,' Fatboy pressed a finger to the boy's lips.

'Jes-us,' Lewis screeched again.

'*Lewis*,' Fatboy hissed. 'Shut it.'

Lewis started to sob, then: huge, wrenching sobs that shook his small frame. Fatboy could hear heavy footsteps cross the floor above his head. Shite! All he needed now was his fucking neighbour.

'*Be quiet*,' he put a restraining hand on the small boy's arm.

Lewis was hysterical now, his body shuddering, his voice shrill.

Above his head, Fatboy could hear a door open, slam shut again. Christ, what the hell was he going to do?

He squeezed the boy's arm. 'Did you hear me?' he threatened.

Lewis squirmed, but carried on sobbing.

Fatboy's grip tightened.

No reaction.

'Shut the fuck up,' he clamped a large hand over Lewis's nose and mouth.

# Baby Steps

'Good Lord,' Maggie looked up from the witness statements she was working through as Wilma staggered through the back door. 'What on earth have you been up to?'

'Chrissake, let me get shot of these heels first.' She kicked off her shoes, sank onto a chair. 'My feet are bloody killing me.'

'Where have you been?'

Sheepish look. 'Down the harbour.'

'Doing what?'

'Checking out that John Cowie. Like you asked me to.'

'For heaven's sake, Wilma, when I asked you to check out Cowie I didn't mean you to take me literally. Nor,' her lips formed a thin line, 'dress up like a...a...'

'Hoor?' Wilma shot back.

'You said it. In addition to which, we've only just got started. We're not equipped yet to be conducting clandestine operations.'

Guilty thought. Maggie hadn't yet told Wilma about her surveillance on the boys.

'Let's confine ourselves to the routine stuff for now. Take it in baby steps,' Brian's admonishments came back to her. 'If we don't do this right, we could get in serious trouble.'

'Right?' Wilma scoffed. 'Do ye no think we're in the wrong business for that?'

*God only knows.* 'I'm not arguing with you. All I'm saying is that we have to walk before we can run.'

'Och,' Wilma spluttered, 'Maggie Laird, ye're such a...a...country mouse.'

'I'm pragmatic, that's all.'

'What does that mean?'

Maggie yawned. 'Never mind. It's not important.'

'Are you no the one said we wis tae divvy up? Dae whit we wis best at?' Oot an aboot on the divorce cases, if ah mind right.'

'Well, yes.' Maggie had the grace to look abashed.

'An are we no strapped for cash? What d'ye think's the quickest way to get a result?'

Maggie lowered her head. 'So...did you?'

'Yes and no. I managed to establish that Cowie frequents the locus.'

'Oh,' she brightened. 'Good for you! Got evidence?'

'Not yet. Lassie I spoke to isn't willing to put her name to it.'

Maggie's shoulders sagged. 'So that's another case for the bin.'

'Not a bit. I'll put in another hour or two on Thursday.'

'You most certainly will not.'

'Oh, come on, I'm nearly there. It's just a matter of persevering.'

'Dressed like that?'

Wilma drew herself up. 'Don't be such a fuckin prude.'

'I am not. Well, not since I met you, Wilma Harcus.'

For some moments the two cast filthy looks at one another.

Wilma broke the silence. 'I see what you're saying, Maggie. But we're no gonna get results sittin on our arses.'

Grudging. 'No-o-o.'

'I was just tryin to be....what's the word? Proactive. An if ye're going to hang out down the docks, ye have to look the part. On a cheerier note... Before I went out, I managed to run some of those background checks you gave me.'

'Wow, that was quick. Don't know how you found the time.' Suspicious look. 'You didn't rope Ian in, did you?'

'You have to be joking. He's only just getting used to the idea.'

'Come on, then, open up. We'll need to share know-how. Otherwise, how are we going to learn?'

'Well...' Smug look. 'The first lesson I've learned is do your homework.'

'You don't need to tell *me* that.'

Wilma pouted. 'All right, Miss Pupil Support. But seriously, I've learned the hard way that the more research you put in beforehand, the quicker you get the case wrapped up when you go out in the field.'

'Yes, but how…?'

'Social media,' Wilma gave Maggie a triumphant grin. 'Facebook's my number-one friend these days, closely followed by Twitter and LinkedIn. You've no idea the amount of useful stuff I've found on that lot.'

'Like what, for example?'

'You know that employment tribunal case – guy claimed he was unfit for work?'

'Yes.'

'He posted pictures of himself playing footie,' Wilma beamed. 'Daft bugger.'

'I'd never have thought of that. Don't suppose you turned up anything on Jimmy Craigmyle while you were at it?'

'Sorry,' the smile vanished from Wilma's face. 'Facebook account's been disabled. Didn't you have any joy with that phone number you got from your pal Brian?'

'No.'

'Never mind. Between the three of us, we're bound to find him.'

Maggie's mouth turned down. 'I hope so.'

'I've managed a few trace enquiries an all this week,' Wilma rattled on. 'Passed them back to the letting agents. Helps that I know the area. Plus I've progressed some of the divorce cases. Including our pal Cowie,' she proffered a sly smile. 'So, yes, I reckon I'm getting on pretty well. How about you?'

'I'm working my way through George's client list,' Maggie eyed the bundle of folders in front of her. 'Cases look pretty straightforward now I've had time to get my teeth into them.' She toyed with a pencil. 'All except one.'

'Which one's that?'

'Client goes by the name of Argo.'

'Argo?' Wilma queried. 'That rings a bell.'

'Woman reckons her husband is trying to kill her.'

'Och, her? She's a bloody head banger, that one.'

'How d'you know?'

'Come across her at the hospital.'

'So what do we do?'

Wilma snorted. 'I know what *I'd* do.'

'What's that, then? No,' Maggie hesitated, 'on second thoughts, Wilma, I don't want to know. Anyhow,' she yawned again, 'it's time we were both in our beds. You've had a long night and I've to be up for Colin in the morning.'

'Before I go,' Wilma ventured, 'you were saying about me looking the part…' She tugged at the PVC skirt, trying in vain to cover her modesty. 'And it set me thinking.'

Maggie cast her eyes to the ceiling. 'What bright idea did you come up with this time?'

'Well, you know how you're the lead player? In the business, I mean.'

'Am I? Seems to me it's you that's been taking most of the initiative so far.'

'It's mebbe me that's been doing most of the talking,' Wilma offered a sly grin. 'But it's you that took the plunge, picked up the pieces, moved the agency forward.'

'It's not as if I had much choice.'

'Just because you were a bit low to begin with doesn't mean you're not the mainstay, the face of the business.'

'We-ell…'

'Oh, come on. You're the real deal, Maggie Laird. The one who's out there: talking to legal firms, prospective clients, doing presentations. And I'm the back-room assistant – doing undercover work, running checks, helping you with the billing.'

'With the notable exception of tonight's little outing.'

Wilma ignored this. 'If we're going to make a go of George's business, a *real* go, isn't it high time you had a makeover?'

'If you mean improve my appearance…' Loud sniff. 'I can't afford

135

to be buying new clothes. And, anyhow, George likes... *Liked* the way I look.'

'Mebbe so. But George wasn't exactly hip, was he?'

Maggie winced. 'Not exactly.'

'Well, I was thinking,' Wilma continued unabashed, 'you know how you've been trying to find out stuff about that James Gilruth?'

'Ye-es.' Guarded voice.

'Did you know he owns a hair salon in Thistle Street?'

'He does?' Wilma had Maggie's full attention now.

'You could have a restyle. Check him out at the same time.'

Maggie clapped a hand to her curls. 'But my hair's always been like this.'

'My point exactly. A decent cut would take years off you. I've made you an appointment, as a matter of fact.'

'You've *what*?'

'10.30 on Thursday.'

'But...'

'By way of cunning detective work,' Wilma countered with a smug grin, 'I managed to establish that the Gilruths are booked in Thursday morning – him and her. Sharon, the wife's called. She's a Torry quine, like me.'

'You know her, then?'

'Only by sight. Comes from a family of fish processors. Big bucks in that, so we've never exactly socialised,' Wilma sniffed. 'Plus she was one of Gilruth's hairdressers, and you know what they're like: only interested in two things – money and men. In that order.'

This was news to Maggie. 'Isn't that a bit of a generalisation?' She wondered if some unfortunate stylist had crossed Wilma in the past.

Wilma struggled to her feet. 'Anyhow, Thistle Street. 10.30 Thursday. My treat. It'll cheer you up, and...'

Maggie wondered what was coming.

'You can do some digging while you're there.'

# IV

# X Marks the Spot

The body lay spread-eagled on the slab. *X marks the spot* – the phrase leapt into Brian's mind. Just as quickly, he dismissed it. Still, the scene that faced him looked too contrived. Too tidy. Brian pictured the last corpse he'd come across: a teenage prostitute down the docks with her jeans round her ankles and her throat slit. In his experience, death wasn't tidy at all.

A veil of haar had drifted in off the North Sea, making the air smell raw. Threads of mist blurred the harsh, halogen edges of the arc lights which illuminated the scene. In the background a generator hummed. The SOCOs were already in place, bent silently on the process of collecting trace evidence. Inside the police tent, others were at work, garnering what intelligence they could. A flash-bulb popped. And another. And another still, as a photographer recorded graphic images of the scene.

'Where's the CSM?'

'Here, sir,' a dark figure clutching a clipboard appeared out of the gloom.

Gingerly, Brian stepped along the metal walkway laid by the IB team to preserve evidence. Behind him, the twin towers of the ancient St Machar cathedral pierced the sky. On either side, weathered gravestones cast weirdly shaped shadows. There were tombs, too: great slabs of stone manoeuvred by unknown hands into this, their final resting place. Some were level with the ground, bordered by a simple low kerb or a line of fancy rope edging, some raised on plinths, an unyielding replica of the soft, warm bed their occupant had long left behind. Below the hovering haar, he could make out small tributes: an open book fashioned from white marble, a heart-shaped granite stone, a curly-haired alabaster cherub, chin resting on one cupped palm. Those touching memorials would have been placed there for infants, he supposed: the countless wee mites who'd succumbed to the infections and the fevers of Victorian times. Brian Burnett wondered, as he picked his way through the mist, whose bairn he'd be looking at tonight.

He scribbled his signature. 'Who called it in?'

'Phone box. Wouldn't give a name.'

'Responding officers?'

'Souter and Elrick. Oh, and some community bobby from Tillydrone.'

'Where are Souter and Elrick now?'

'I sent them back to HQ. Told them to file a report.'

'Right,' Brian rubbed chilled hands together, 'what stage are we at here?'

'Death pronounced. Duty Doctor's not long away.'

'Any ID on the body?'

'Not as such.'

*Bugger!* For some years now, Brian had never come across a female who hadn't been joined at the hip by a giant handbag.

'I take it you've set up door-to-door?' He turned to look behind him at the high walls and dense greenery that lined the Chanonry. 'Though in a place like this, it's pretty unlikely anybody saw anything.'

'I have, sir.'

'Has anyone informed the minister?' Brian inclined his head towards the small opening in the graveyard wall that gave onto the entrance to the manse.

'She came looking for us not long after it happened, Sarge. Said she needed into the church – sorry, cathedral – to get some papers.'

'*She*?' The word jarred on Brian. He still hadn't got used to the idea of women ministers.

'Lady meenister. New, like. Said she'd stay put in the manse in case she was needed.'

'Very good. I take it the pathologist has already been called.'

'Just arrived at your back.' The CSM yanked his head in the direction of the tent.

'Fine. Well, I'll let you crack on.' He turned away.

Brian turned back to the tent and stuck his head inside. On the ground in front of him, a slight figure was kneeling, his back to him, head bowed as if in prayer.

'Evenin, Alec.' He tapped the figure on the shoulder. 'What have we got here?'

Alec Gourlay raised his head from the level of the huge tombstone. He half-turned.

'Young lassie.' There was no emotion in his voice.

'Age?' Brian could just make out light-coloured trainers, a pair of jeans, fair hair.

'Hard to tell.' The words were muffled. Gourlay had turned back to the job in hand.

'Guess?'

'Seventeen. Eighteen, maybe.'

'Cause of death?'

'Come on, Burnett,' Alec Gourlay turned to face him, 'you know better than that.'

Brian shrugged his shoulders. 'Got to give it a try.' His face broke into a sheepish grin. 'Give me something to go on.'

'Isn't a lot there.'

'Must be something,' the DS persisted. Gourlay could be a thwart bastard if you didn't catch him the right way.

'Blunt trauma to the head.' The police pathologist had already turned back to the body.

'Caused by?'

'A blunt object.'

Brian exhaled sharply. He'd as much chance of raising a cadaver as he had of getting information out of Alec Gourlay.

'Such as?'

'Can't tell at this stage.'

'Well, what *can* you tell me?'

'I *can* tell you,' the pathologist didn't look up, 'that when she was discovered, the lassie's jeans were pulled down.'

Brian whistled through his teeth. 'And?'

'There's penetration,' he continued, 'but not penile.'

'What are you saying?'

'I'm *saying*,' Alec Gourlay straightened, but didn't turn, 'there is an object lodged at the entrance to the vagina.' His head ducked forward again. 'Looks to me like a stick.' He paused. 'Correction. Two sticks.'

*Pompous little bastard.* Brian took a deep breath. No point in getting on the wrong side of the man.

'Can you elaborate on that?' he persisted, trying to keep his voice even.

'No. Not till I get back to the lab.'

'Thanks for that.' Brian decided there was little to be gained in asking the pathologist for a timeframe for lab results. He'd pushed his luck with Alec Gourlay as it was. 'I'll leave you to it, then.'

'Do that.'

Brian cringed inwardly at the heavy sarcasm in Gourlay's voice. He turned to go.

'One last thing.'

'Yes?' Brian threw a glance back over his shoulder.

The SOCOs were still moving around the tent, the pathologist still kneeling by the tombstone.

'The sticks…' Alec Gourlay's voice still carried no inflection, 'appear to have been fashioned in the shape of a cross.'

# Maggie Gets a Makeover

'Morning.' A pretty, dark-haired girl in a white tunic appeared at Maggie's side. 'Mrs Laird, is it?'

'That's right.'

'My name's Michelle.'

Their eyes locked. At least, Maggie's eyes locked onto Michelle's. The dark-haired girl looked right, left, right again, then swiftly averted her gaze.

'You're having a restyle today, is that right?'

Maggie nodded, uncertain. She'd been ill with nerves all the way to the salon. Managed to calm herself somewhat whilst sitting at the backwash basin. Now she studied her reflection in the mirror. God, she looked a fright. And that left eye was way out of order. No wonder the girl didn't know where to look.

'How about the colour? Wouldn't you like a change? A wee semi-permanent, maybe?'

Maggie had always hated her hair. Wished she'd been blonde, brunette, any darn colour but red. But change? That was one thing she'd always shrunk from. She'd been raised in the set patterns of farming life, married into gentle domesticity. She eyed Michelle's own barnet. It was a vibrant shade of aubergine. Not exactly subtle. She shook her head.

Michelle fingered one of Maggie's curls. 'How much are we taking off today?'

'Oh...' Maggie vacillated, 'I don't know.' Nor did it matter, she thought with some rancour. Colin would never notice. Kirsty wouldn't be home for ages. And George? George wasn't coming back. Not ever. She rallied. 'Do whatever you think.'

*Cut to the chase.* She plunged straight in. 'Have you worked here long?'

'Just a few months.'

*Quite new, then.* Maggie tried to keep the disappointment out of her voice. Another opportunity gone up in smoke. Still…a few months. You could pick up a lot in that length of time. 'Good place to work, is it?'

'Not bad. Would you mind keeping your head down?' Michelle clamped her hand to the back of Maggie's head and shoved it forward until her chin was embedded in her chest. Snip. Snip. She could feel the hair falling away.

'Mr Gilruth.'

Maggie's head shot up to see James Gilruth stride towards her. She panicked. *Oh, hell, what if he recognises me?* 'Sorry,' she addressed Michelle, 'think I'm going to sneeze.' She ducked into her handbag, extracted a tissue, spread it over her face.

Michelle turned from her side. 'You're early today, Mr Gilruth. But you might like to say hello to your wife. Mrs Gilruth is just over there,' she indicated a gowned figure. Then,' she flashed Gilruth a hundred watt smile, 'if you'd like to go through, I'll be with you shortly.'

*Sod it.* Covertly, Maggie observed James Gilruth and his wife conduct a brief exchange. She strained to catch their conversation, but all she could establish was that the body language was less than cordial. Then, with a turn of the heel, Gilruth vanished through to some hidden back room. Relieved as she was not to have been spotted, Maggie was stricken to have her hopes of gleaning information dashed.

She perked up when she saw that Sharon Gilruth was being escorted to a chair two down from her. Maggie gave the woman the once-over. Sharon was dark, her hair so black it had a bluish tinge to it. *Black Tulip*, the name sprang into Maggie's mind from some long-discarded magazine. She ventured another look. Sharon's makeup was heavy, her lips scarlet. Below the gown, Maggie could make out good legs, killer heels. On the floor by Sharon's side sat a handbag the size of a small car. Maggie sighed. Sharon Gilruth cut a striking figure, even with wet hair.

'How have you been since I saw you last?' Sharon's stylist sported a tight ponytail and a name badge that spelled 'Jackie'.

Maggie tilted sideways, ears flapping.

'Busy-busy,' Sharon's voice was raised over the hum of the hair-dryer. 'We've such a hectic social life I can barely keep up.'

In the mirror, the corners of Maggie's mouth turned down. Her social life was gone forever.

'How's your son these days?' Jackie again. 'I haven't seen him in ages.'

'Christopher? He's fine.'

'Still at Gordon's?'

Through a tangle of damp hair, Maggie strained to hear Sharon's response.

'No.'

*Dammit*. If the boy had been at Robert Gordon's, maybe Colin would have come across him.

'He at uni, then?'

'Not yet. He's taking some time out. Sort of a gap year.'

'Oh. Right.' Seamlessly, Jackie moved on to the next topic on her tick-list. 'You booked a holiday yet?'

Any conversation that followed was drowned by the hum of multiple hairdryers. Maggie sat sneaking surreptitious glances at Sharon Gilruth as Michelle worked methodically, smoothing sections in Maggie's newly-shorn locks. *Damn and blast!* She pursed her lips. She'd hoped to catch some other snippets of gossip, perhaps find the opportunity to engage the woman herself in conversation. She sighed. All that effort for nothing. Well, next to nothing. She could have sworn she caught a look pass between Gilruth and Michelle.

'That OK for you?' Michelle flashed a back-view mirror behind Maggie's head.

'Oh…' Her eyes widened. 'Amazing.' Maggie could barely recognise herself, so cleverly tamed were her unruly curls.

If her husband could only see her now. She caught a breath.

There was the eye, still.

But eye or no, she'd make George proud.

Use this glamorous new look to advance his cause.

# Cross Purpose

The first-floor conference room, like everything else in Force HQ, was institutional: white walls, dark brown paintwork, recessed lighting, bog-standard office furnishings that wouldn't have looked out of place in any council building up and down the country.

'When I told you to call a meeting,' Detective Inspector Chisolm strode through the door, 'it wasn't the fucking G8 I had in mind.'

Christ, Brian thought, he's on form. He'd heard the new DI had a short fuse, but this was pushing it. He ducked his chin. 'No, sir.'

'All I'm needing is a briefing from you and get the actions handed out.'

He squared his shoulders. 'Yes, sir.'

'Well,' the inspector threw a handful of files down onto the table, 'get this lot together, then.'

Brian looked round the room. A number of CID officers and a clutch of uniforms stood in small groups, heads bowed, absorbed in conversation or drinking out of waxed paper cups. Three people were already seated at the table: Dave Wood was a long-serving Detective Sergeant, a copper of the old school – a big man, with a bullet head and not that much in it. Dave's sidekick, Bob Duffy, sat alongside him. Across the table, Douglas Dunn sprawled, his chair tilted back at an angle. Douglas was a graduate recruit.

He tapped a water glass with his biro. 'Get your backsides over here, folks. Meeting was called for eight o'clock and it's almost ten past.'

The officers started to attention. They slid one by one onto the empty chairs.

'Let's get this started,' Chisolm cast his eyes round the table. 'Burnett,' he turned, 'give us the background to the St Machar incident.'

Brian looked down at the notes in front of him. He looked up. 'Sir. Incident was called in to emergency services at 19.07 last night. PCs Souter and Miller were first to respond, arriving on the scene at 19.16. They then commenced a search of the St Machar Cathedral precincts and were joined at 19.23 by PC Grassie, who...'

'Hang on,' Chisolm snapped, 'who the hell's Grassie?'

'Community bobby, sir. Picked up the shout from his beat in Tillydrone.'

'Continue.'

'PC Souter located the body of a young female in the kirkyard behind the cathedral, close to its boundary with Seaton Park. The victim was lying on a tombstone and appeared to be deceased. A check of her pulse by Souter confirmed this to be the case. Backup and ambulance were called in by PC Grassie. SOCOs and an incident van were in place by 20.00 hours and the crime scene secured...'

'What about forensics?' the DI interrupted. 'Are we confident at this stage that a crime has been committed?'

'Yes, sir.'

'Toxicology?'

'They're running tests as we speak.'

'Has Gourlay given us any leads?'

'Blunt trauma to the head.'

'Anything else?'

'When the girl was found, her lower clothing was disturbed. And there was this...' Brian hesitated. 'Cross was what it looked like. In the vagina.'

'Christ,' Douglas muttered. 'That's a first – a corpse with a cross up its cunt.'

'Don't be so crude,' Susan Strachan, the sole female DC retorted.

'Enough,' Chisolm threw a warning look. 'Tell us about the cross, Burnett.'

'It was a rough-looking thing, sir: couple of twigs fastened together with a rubber band. Place is surrounded by trees. And

147

then there's the park – Seaton Park, that is. It...'

Chisolm cut in. 'Let's move on. What about the rubber band?'

'It was pink, sir, like the ones the Post Office use.'

'Right. So you're telling me these twigs could have come from anywhere?'

'Yes, sir.'

'And the rubber band is one of thousands discarded at random by our beloved postal service?'

Brian lowered his head. 'Sir.'

'When will the pathologist be able to be more precise?'

'When he's good and ready.' The words were out before Brian could stop himself. 'Sorry, sir, but you know how he is.'

The inspector responded with a curt nod. 'How about ID?'

'Lassie didn't have a thing on her, except for a wee spiral note-book – the kind of thing you'd pick up in a supermarket or a corner shop – a stub of pencil and a Yale key.'

'Anything in the notebook?'

'A few doodles, that's all.'

'Clothing?'

'Converse trainers. Hollister jeans. Shirt had a label,' Brian looked down at his notes. 'Boden, it was. Waistcoat was one of those quilted jobs,' he looked up, 'like the nobs wear.'

'Our victim wasn't a schemie, then?'

'No, sir. More like someone from the Chanonry or the West End. A student, maybe, but a well-heeled one, I reckon.'

'I take it somebody has been in touch with the university?'

'Yes, sir. We've been on to the accommodation office and asked them to check with their halls of residence – whether anyone matching that description hasn't been seen in their room, has missed lectures. Though from what I can gather, neither of these would be that unusual.'

The DI pursed his mouth in disapproval. 'No.'

'I've also sent them a photo of the key, so we can check whether it's been issued for any of the university's accommodation.'

'Have we managed to establish anything else?'

'Not a lot, sir. The call was traced to a public phone box in Seaton. The caller, a young male, declined to give his name. Enquiries in the immediate vicinity haven't been especially fruitful. From what this lot,' Brian jerked his head in the direction of the uniformed officers, 'have managed to establish, nobody seems to have seen or heard anything unusual, and the only pedestrian we've managed to find is an elderly woman who was out walking her dog.'

'Anything useful from her?'

'Not really.' Brian ran a hand across his brow. 'Didn't see another soul the whole time she was out, not except for this one guy.'

'Description?'

'Forties. Dark-haired. Time was vague. But looked to be loitering, the witness said.'

'Has this information been verified?'

'No, but I've circulated a description.'

'Good. Well, brief all units, Burnett. The sooner we can trace, interview and eliminate this individual, that will give us one less thing to...'

'Yessir.' Dutifully he scribbled a note.

'Is that it?'

He felt the colour rise in his face. 'The Chanonry isn't exactly hoatching with activity at the best of times, never mind late evening on a weekday, but I can tell you I've briefed the Press Office and amended the scene boundaries to allow access to the cathedral.' Brian could feel the perspiration begin to seep from his underarms onto the polyester fabric of his shirt. He hadn't got the measure of this new man from Glasgow yet.

'Any questions at this stage?' The inspector scanned the faces round the table.

'What about a phone?' Duffy volunteered. 'Didn't the girl have a mobile on her?'

Brian shrugged. 'No sign of one.'

'Could have been nicked.'

'I guess.'

'Fuckin great!' Dunn stopped doodling. What next, *sir*?' he cast an insolent glance towards his superior officer.

'Next,' Allan Chisolm fixed him with a gimlet eye, 'we ask ourselves a number of questions: how did this girl arrive at the scene? On foot? By public transport? Or could she have been dropped off there by car? Where did she sustain her injury? At the scene? Elsewhere? What are the access points to the scene: roads, paths, gates, walls? Think of its proximity to Seaton Park, the High Street, King Street, St Machar Drive. What are our opportunities there: lines of sight, CCTV, cars, buses, houses, flats, university buildings? Who might have seen something?'

Douglas Dunn picked up his pen. He started doodling again.

'Are you hearing me, Dunn?'

'Loud and clear, sir.'

'Has anyone contacted the bus companies?'

'I've had uniform do that, sir,' Brian responded. 'And the taxi firms. They'll canvass their drivers. See who was in the area.'

'That brings me to the next thing.'

A dozen or so pairs of eyes focused on the inspector.

'We need to be looking at where this incident is pointing.' He paused. 'Which begs the question...Do we need to run the investigation on HOLMES 2 and if so, at what level?'

There were groans around the table. The massive analytical and research facility offered by the Police National Computer, they knew from experience, would also spew out a mountain of useless information.

'I see I have your commitment for that,' the inspector offered a tight smile. 'Remind me, who's on Disclosure?'

An auxiliary officer raised a hand.

'Well, make sure it's tight as a drum. Where I come from, investigations aren't completed on evidence, they're completed on paperwork.'

Chisolm changed tack. 'What's your take on the thing, Burnett?'

Brian felt beads of perspiration begin to prickle his brow.

'Well?'

'Judging by the contusion to the skull, the way the body was lying on the slab, the whole setup, it looked like the girl had been arranged. Staged, you might say.'

'That so?'

It wasn't a question, Brian decided. All the same, he felt the need to justify himself. 'It couldn't have happened by accident, sir. It was a conscious act.'

'So it wasn't a mugging?' a DC chipped in.

'Forensics have found no trace of a weapon.'

'Plus the victim was found flat on her back. When they've been hit on the back of the head, ladies...' Douglas threw a wink at Susan, 'tend to fall on their tits.'

'Quite.' Chisolm's face was a mask.

'So who would do a thing like that?'

'Goths?' one of the uniforms suggested.

'Possibly.'

'Some sort of religious freak?' One of the DCs. 'There does seem to be a ritual element.'

'Could it have been a tribute of some sort?' Susan offered.

'Tribute?' Duffy scoffed. 'You're bloody joking. What about the unzipped jeans, the knickers pulled down? And the thing was in her vagina, for God's sake.'

'More like some nasty wee perv.' Uniform again.

Chisolm's eyes swept the room. 'We'll need someone assigned to looking at who's got form for this sort of thing.'

'We've already checked out some of the usual suspects, sir,' Brian responded. 'They were all doing their dirty little deeds elsewhere.'

'And what sort of perv pays a tribute like that to some wee lassie, tell me that?' Duffy was fired up now, pen jabbing at his pad.

'Given what we already know, which is the most probable?' Chisolm cast his gaze around the room.

'Goth, sir.'

'Rubbish,' Duffy shot back. 'That cross holds the key to the whole thing. And it definitely wasn't some wee Goth that put it there.'

'Well,' the DI gathered his files together. 'Before you hand out the actions, Burnett, allow me to summarise.'

Brian glanced down at the table. The inspector's fingers were drumming an impatient beat.

'We have a dead female in a graveyard with a head injury and a makeshift cross up her...' Chisolm cleared his throat, 'vagina. No evidence as yet of other molestation. No ID and no suspects. Would that cover it, Sergeant?'

Brian's underarms were damp by this time. 'Pretty much.'

'Anything you'd care to add?'

'No, sir.'

Chisolm steepled his fingers. 'Well, Burnett, sort out your priorities. Right now I suggest you get some of this lot along to Old Aberdeen, turn the place over with a fine-tooth comb. Send a DC out to the university and see if we can get ID on that lassie ASAP. Grab yourself another couple of uniform if need be. Meantime,' the inspector raised his eyes to the ceiling, looked down again, 'I'll chase up those sluggish bastards in Forensics.'

Brian shifted in his seat. 'Sir.'

The DI gathered together his files, scraped back his chair, got to his feet.

'Oh, and one last thing. If we've got a major inquiry on our hands, we'd better give it a name. Any suggestions?' He studied the faces around the table.

Wood bit his nails.

Duffy ducked his head.

'*Murder in the Cathedral* springs to mind,' Dunn piped up. Douglas couldn't pass up an opportunity to remind everybody that he'd been to uni.

'We don't know that it *was* murder, ya wanker.'

'Plus, it wasn't actually *in* the cathedral.'

'And why the cross? We've no idea what that's all about.'

'Nothing, most like,' muttered the doodler. 'Some of those dirty pervs get their rocks off on stuff like that.'

'If we can't explain it,' Susan Strachan had been quiet up till then, 'why don't we call it Operation Cross Purpose?'

'Any advance on that?'

Chisolm's gaze was met by a circle of bent heads.

'Well, then,' the inspector stood. 'Go to it.'

# A First Time for Everything

'Comin up for a dance?' The man jerked his neck towards the jiggling mass of heads.

'Well...' Maggie hesitated.

After failing to make contact with Jimmy Craigmyle on the phone number Brian had given her, she'd spent an abortive afternoon checking out nameplates on bedsit doorways up and down Crown Street. She decided then that her only option was the nightclub.

The evening hadn't started well. She'd hoped to collar the doormen. There were two of them, built like barrels, hands like hams. Maggie tilted her face towards one of the shaven heads.

'Is Jimmy Craigmyle working tonight?' she asked.

'In you come, ladies.' The man either didn't hear or didn't want to.

Maggie felt a shove at her back. The pressure of the queue carried her forward in to the foyer.

Now Maggie's eyes darted to the sunken arena and back again. The guy was bordering on the repulsive. Still, she wasn't sure what the form was for refusing a dance these days, and besides, nothing ventured, nothing gained.

'Come on,' he grasped her by one bare elbow, propelled her down the stairs. He wasn't much taller than she, shirt flapping over skinny trousers. A gold chain gleamed at a hairy neck. Above it, a full mouth, flat nose, eyes so small as to be piggy. Maggie caught a whiff of aftershave, and behind that the rank odour of sweat. Time was she'd have been thankful for such manly excretions. She cast her mind back to those early days after George's death, when she'd nosed out every last trace of him, clung to it like a drowning person would a piece of flotsam.

She struggled to replicate the moves of the girls nearest to her, for women seemed to outnumber men by about four to one. Replete with tattoos and tangerine tans, they bopped up and down, but-tocks compressed in Lycra miniskirts, boobs spilling out of push-up bras. Surreptitiously, Maggie tugged down the frock she'd filched from Kirsty's wardrobe. She'd been shocked at how striking she looked with the new hairstyle and heavy makeup: *hot*, in today's parlance. Horrible word.

She caught the man's eye. He must have taken this as an invita-tion, for an arm snaked out, a hand closed around hers. The palm was damp, she registered, before it clamped around her waist, pulled her close. So close Maggie could feel shirt buttons make small indentations down her front.

'Come here often?' Strong fingers pressed into the small of her back.

'N-no.' Maggie stiffened. 'My first time.'

'There's a first time for everything,' he leered, his breath hot on her cheek.

She drew back. 'I daresay.' Then, *don't be so standoffish or you'll never get anywhere.* 'Can I ask you a question?'

'What?'

The music was deafening, the thump-thump of the bass notes pounding her head. 'A question,' Maggie leaned into the man's ear.

Wrong move. The hand pressed harder into her back.

'You haven't come across Jimmy Craigmyle?' she mouthed.

'Who?' A whiff of bad breath.

'Craigmyle. He works here, I believe.'

'Doing what?' A pelvis thrust into hers.

'Might be on the door some nights. I'm not really sure.'

'Naw.' So close were they she could feel bones grate, one against the other. So this was the sort of thing young women had to negoti-ate nowadays. For once, Maggie was grateful for her hitherto shel-tered life.

'I have to go to the bathroom,' she blurted as she broke free. She fought her way through the sea of bodies until she'd reached the relative safety of the ladies' loo.

Maggie sat on the toilet. Not that she needed. Anything to relieve the pain in her feet. She contemplated the graffiti-covered walls: *Danny has a massive dong* – this complete with graphic illustration – *Jason cums on my face*; *finger my bum hole*; *suck hot cock*. Her mind flew to her daughter down in Dundee. What sort of world had she brought her girl into?

'What the fuck are you doing in there?' Someone was hammering on the cubicle door.

She got to her feet and flipped the catch. She was met by hostile stares as two would-be WAGs tumbled past her into the toilet.

There were three girls at the basins. Well, perhaps 'girls' was stretching it. One of them at least was older than herself, a line of silver regrowth defining the parting in her dark hair, a ring of white concealer only serving to exaggerate the dark blue shadows beneath her eyes. The other two could have been twins: same blonde hair, bleached lifeless, same hair extensions, same kohl-rimmed eyes.

The three eyed Maggie in the mirror.

'Hi,' she did her best to look friendly.

Three heads ducked in unison.

'Do you come here often?' She pressed on, undeterred.

'What's it to you?' The older woman looked up.

'Just, you know, I wondered if you girls know any of the staff here?'

'Wouldn't touch the fuckers with a bargepole,' one of the women muttered. 'You never know where they've been.'

'Oh.' In the mirror, Maggie watched the colour rise in her face. 'I didn't mean it like that. It's just…I'm trying to get in touch with someone.'

'Aye? Like who?'

'Goes by the name of Craigmyle.'

'What does he do, like?' The older woman again.

Maggie shook the drips from her fingers. 'Security, from what I can gather.'

'A bouncer, like?'

She kneaded damp hands. 'I don't know.'

'You could ask Jason at the bar. He's been around a good while.'
She smiled. 'Thanks.'


Maggie threaded her way towards the bar. Around her, drinkers were squeezed shoulder-to-shoulder on buttoned, leather-look banquettes. Above them, a mezzanine floor was bordered by chrome railings. Spectators hung over, watching the goings-on below. The bar was six-deep. Behind it, a bank of optics was backlit in a lurid shade of pink. At least half a dozen barmen in fancy waistcoats were hard at it, twirling glasses, juggling bottles, moving at speed between the optics and the counter.

Maggie shouldered her way through.

'Fuck off,' an elbow jabbed her in the ribs.

'Sorry,' she kept on going.

Wilma would be proud of me, she thought. Not that Maggie had confided that night's outing to her neighbour. No, Windmill Brae would have to remain under the radar, at least until she had a result to show.

'What's it to be?'

She finally made it to the bar. 'You wouldn't be...' Someone pushed in front of her. 'Jason?' Just as roughly, she shoved back in.

'No,' the barman snapped. 'Don't hang about.'

'T-tonic water,' she stuttered.

'That all?' The young man didn't make eye contact.

'Yes.'

'Two pounds.' The barman squirted liquid from a hose. Banged a wet glass down on the shiny counter.

'Is Jason here?' She slid two coins across the bar.

The young man jerked his head. 'Down there.'

She followed his eyes. At the far end of the bar, one figure appeared slightly older than the others: plump, bald, shiny pate gleaming, diamond stud twinkling in each ear.

Maggie wormed her way down the length of the bar. 'Jason, is it?' After several fruitless attempts, she finally drew level.

'What if it is?' Jason cocked his head coquettishly. He made eye contact. Right. Left. Right again in quick-fire succession.

'Can I ask you a question?'

'If you make it quick.'

'Do you know a man called Craigmyle?'

'Jimmy? Aye.'

Maggie felt positively light-headed, 'Is he here?'

'No.'

'But he does work here?'

Jason homed in on Maggie's right eye. 'Didn't I say you'd to be quick?' The barman contemplated the outstretched hands all around.

'Does he, though?' she persisted.

'Aye. But he's off tonight.'

'Can you give me his phone number?'

'We don't give out confidential information.'

*Keep talking.* 'But, I'm a-a friend of his.'

'Then how come you haven't got his number?'

Maggie's mind worked overtime. 'He must have changed it.'

'That's your bad luck.'

'Jason,' she wheedled, 'I'm desperate.'

The man sniggered. 'He's no interested in sex.'

'It's not...'

His lip curled. 'They all say that.'

Maggie was being jostled back and forth, the drink in her hand slopping onto Kirsty's frock. 'Can you give him a message?'

Suspicious look. 'What sort of message?'

'Just...'

Jason made to turn away.

'Hang on,' her voice was pleading, 'have you got a pen?'

The barman rolled his eyes. Sighed theatrically. 'If you must,' he extracted a streamlined silver Sheaffer from an inside pocket.

'Thanks.'

Maggie scribbled her name and mobile number on a paper napkin. Pushed it with the pen across the counter.

'Please,' she produced her very best smile, 'will you give him this?'

# Baby Steps My Arse

The curtains were closed. Other than that it looked like any other house on the street: a six-in-the-block council flat, grey harled walls, slate roof, tidy enough garden out front. She climbed the steps. There would be nobody home. The wife was long gone, the bairns with her. And hadn't Wilma just left the fucker sitting bug-eyed in the sprawling estate's solitary pub?

She delved into her capacious handbag, a fake snake Gucci knock-off with tassels on the pockets and a plethora of shiny brass studs. She'd bought it at the Wednesday market on her honeymoon to Tenerife the previous winter. Her lips curled into a lascivious smile. They'd a rare time, she and Ian: no meals to cook, no dishes to wash, a good bevvy every evening, some lunchtimes too, no work to get up for in the morning. And night-time. Well… Wilma had another wee smile to herself. For a few moments she rummaged in its depths, fingers finding a well-used hairbrush, various items of makeup and – shite – a squashed cardboard Tampax tube. She groaned. Dirty bitch! Finally, she fished out an empty plastic milk container, its cap missing, most of its upper half cut away. Wilma eyed it approvingly. When she'd first hooked up with Maggie Laird on this wee venture of theirs, Wilma had gone online, invested in a range of gadgets to speed their investigations. Never mind she'd had to dip into her nest egg. Or that her meagre savings were meant for emergencies. Maggie Laird's situation was desperate, if ever anything was. And it would all pay off in the end, of that Wilma was convinced. She'd already employed a set of comb picks on the pad-lock of a lock-up out the back. But forget your jigglers and plastic cards, for a straightforward Yale Wilma found this cunning adaptation the most effective by far. Carefully she inserted the cut edge of the plastic bottle into the door jamb, worked it back and forth. She took a steadying breath. It had been a good while since she'd done this particular trick. Unlike when she was with that fuckwit Darren. The locks were aye getting changed on their rentals, he was that often falling behind.

The Yale slipped with a click. Wilma dug into her coat pocket, drew out a pair of hospital-issue blue Latex gloves. She eased them on. *Baby steps my arse*, she muttered under her breath. Casting a furtive glance over her shoulder, she slipped inside.

The heat hit her first, closely followed by the smell. Clasping a hand over her nose, Wilma followed the sweet, cloying aroma down the hall. The first door she opened revealed a grubby living room. The second, a kitchen so skanky she didn't linger. Ditto the third: a bathroom where the seat of the toilet pan was up, the bowl crusted with excrement. In the bedroom next door, the filthy unmade bed and strewn carpet further testified to a single lifestyle.

Wilma eyed the last door in the narrow corridor. Gingerly, she turned the handle, her Latex-clad fingers slipping on a film of moisture. The door inched open, meeting resistance from what she recognised as a wall of Polythene sheeting. With her free hand, Wilma hooked it aside and peered into the room. Behind its pink cotton curtains, the window was sealed with a second Polythene sheet. Against the primly patterned wallpaper, more plastic shrouded the walls. Two fans stood in opposite corners, their blades whirring softly. The atmosphere was humid, almost tropical, the smell sickly. Gagging, she reeled back, covering her nose with cupped hands. The plants stood in rows, their roots swaddled in heavy-duty black bin bags. Wilma eyed the distinctive pointed leaves. Christ, she marvelled, Duthie Park meets Mastrick, for the scene before her was Aberdeen's Winter Gardens in microcosm. Her lip curled. Give me a feckin Benson & Hedges any day.

It had been a bummer, this case. A fruitless slog trying to find evidence of another sort: the stash of contraband cigarettes she'd heard on the grapevine the fucker had been peddling. She groped for her camera. This little lot might serve the purpose instead. But how to explain? Just as quickly, her spirits sank. Maggie wouldn't take kindly to another breach of PI protocol. And there was no question of employing an anonymous tip-off. In Wilma's world, you didn't willingly engage with the police.

Grim-faced, she fired off a few shots. Just for insurance, she told herself, as she stowed the camera away. Carefully, she closed the door, retreated down the hall. Ah weel… She stood for a moment, checking neighbouring flats for nosey parkers. It's back to the lock-ups, then.

# Hotlips

268 Summer Street was a single-fronted shop. From the blacked-out window, a flashing pink neon mouth formed a perfect *moue*. Within its confines, fat lower-case lettering spelled "hotlips".

Maggie's heart raced as she pushed through the door. The interior was womb-like: red painted walls, deep Polyester shag-pile carpet, scarlet velvet chaise that had seen better days. To one side of the mirrored reception desk, a heavily padded doorway led to who knows what.

'I'm looking for Mr Imlay,' she addressed the black-clad bruiser behind the desk.

'Who?' The shaven head barely stirred from his red top.

'Your boss.'

No reaction.

Maggie approached the desk. 'Am I correct in saying Mr Imlay does own this operation?'

Flicks over a page. 'Might do.'

'Well, then…' She leaned over, thrust her face in his. 'Let's just say he does, when am I most likely to catch him?'

Shrugs. 'Dunno.'

'Doesn't he open up?'

'That's my job.'

'What about closing time?'

'We don't keep regular hours.' The man lumbered to his feet. 'What's it to you, anyhow?'

Maggie sized him up. He was a hulk, no doubt about it, but she was getting better at this. Knew the biggest guys often weren't the fastest on their feet.

She drew a breath. *Keep it vague, remember.* 'There's a business matter I need to discuss with him.'

'Well, he's no here.'

*Chip away at it.* 'He must come past sometime,' she insisted. 'Pick up the takings. After all, this place must rake in a fair bit, what with the...range I've heard you offer.'

'Don't know what you're talking about.'

'Personal services?'

'All we do is what it says on the door,' the man parroted a line she suspected was well-rehearsed. 'Plus, we've only got three girls. It's hard to get staff to work...' He smirked, 'unsocial hours.'

*Don't over-elaborate, you silly man.* Maggie realised by now it paid to keep your lies simple.

'Not unless they're illegals,' she shot back.

A flicker of recognition. He walked around the desk. Loomed over her.

In her mind Maggie ran through Wilma's strictures on self-defence: be quick, smart, go for the weak spots, then run. For the moment she opted to stand her ground. Big as he was, Maggie doubted the fellow would be looking for trouble.

For some moments the two squared up, albeit all Maggie could see was the black expanse of a barrel chest.

Tentatively, she raised her chin.

'Foxy wee thing, aren't you?' Two sharp eyes looked down from a great height. 'Wouldn't like a job, would you?' A sly grin crossed his face. 'Clientele likes them small. More...mobile, shall we say?'

Maggie could imagine. She didn't respond.

'It's a while since we had a redhead,' he persisted. 'Natural, is it?' The eyes travelled lasciviously from Maggie's head to her groin.

She shuddered, her cheeks aflame.

'Let me save us both time.' She struggled to regain her composure. 'My client is owed a substantial sum of money by your boss, who appears to have gone missing. My remit is to track him down.'

'Can't help you. He's out of the country.'

'Where?'

Pregnant pause, then, 'Spain.'

Maggie sighed. If it wasn't Europe or the USA, it was sodding Pakistan.

'On holiday, is he?' she fished.

'No, his auntie's sick.'

That was another one. The world was full of sick relatives, it seemed.

'Tell Mr Imlay I called,' she proffered a business card. 'But I'll be back,' she borrowed a line from James Gilruth's henchmen. 'As often as it takes,' she threw over her shoulder as she made for the door.

# Eeny Meeny

Eeeny meeny.

Willie loitered at the entrance to Kings Links Court. He eyed the battery of silver buzzers. Picked a name at random. Pressed the buzzer.

There was a crackle of static, then, 'Wha is it?' The woman's voice was heavy with suspicion.

Willie leaned into the speaker. 'Wull ye open the door fur me?'

More crackling, then, 'Wha's that?'

He ignored the question. 'The door. Wull ye let me in?'

'Whit fur?'

'Ah forgot ma key.'

'What?'

'Ma key. Ah forgot it,' louder this time.

'Wha is it?'

'A neebour.'

'How dae ah ken ye live here?'

'Ah dae. Trust me.'

There was a pause, then, 'Ye canna trust onybody. No these days. There's aw sorts gingin aboot.'

'Ma ma sent me oot fur messages,' Willie persisted, 'an ah canna get back in.'

Silence.

He hopped from one foot to the other.

More silence.

Ran a hand over his buzz cut. 'Please?'

'Well, ah'm nae...'

'She'll gie me the back o' her hand if ah'm no back soon.'

On the other end of the intercom, Willie heard a cough, a rustling, then, finally, a grudging 'OK'.

The catch on the door clicked loudly. Willie grinned. Worked a treat. Most times, anyway. And the odd occasion you didn't score, there were dozens more names to choose from. His bright idea of doing trades in the stairwells of the tower blocks was working well. Having gained entry, Willie's activities were rarely questioned by the residents, but he'd roped Ryan in just in case, to watch his back.

'Same routine?' Ryan followed him through the entry.

'Aye.' Willie headed for the stairwell. 'But gie me five meenits tae get set up.'

'Then ah let the fuckers in.'

Willie frowned. 'Aye. But wan at a time, mind.'

'Ye thinkin ye'll git worked ower?'

'Naw. The big fella gave me a pay-as-you-go. Any bother, ah've tae phone upstairs. An besides,' Willie smirked, 'there's aye ma da.'

'Thocht he wis in...'

Willie ignored this. 'Ah micht be feart o' ma faither, bit thon bunch o' wankers, they'd shit a brick if ma da sae much as clocked em.'

Ryan nodded vigorously. 'Richt enough.'

'Aw ye hiv tae dae is let them in an let them oot again. Got it?'

Ryan nodded again.

'Ye're the footman,' Willie grinned.

'The footman,' Ryan echoed.

'Ah dae the deals.'

'An ah keep tabs on the punters.'

'Spot on.'

'An the filth,' Ryan added.

'Christ, aye. It's nae the neebours we hiv tae worry aboot in this dump, it's that fuckin community bobby.

# Outside the Box

Communication Services International turned out to be a scruffy asphalt yard housing a single tatty Portakabin.

## NO UNAUTHORISED ENTRY

Maggie contemplated the padlocked gates. There was no sign of life. *Sod it,* she cursed under her breath. She'd spent the previous evening glued to the second-hand laptop she'd asked Colin to source for her, laboriously typing in search terms and cross-checking data. She'd hoped to gain entry before close of business but, in the maze of small roads that crisscrossed the vast industrial estate, it had taken a precious hour of her time to find the place.

The sky was streaked with grey. She pressed her face against the gates. To the rear of the Portakabin, a car was just visible. Maggie clocked it as an Audi A6. With Colin's input, she was becoming something of a car buff. Her spirits rose. Someone might be there after all. They sank again when she saw that the cabin was in darkness, its window obscured by a blind.

The assignment related to a claim for unfair dismissal by the manager of a mobile phone shop whose employment had been terminated on the grounds of gross misconduct. From its audit process, the company knew its employee was on the take: significant quantities of high-value goods had been vanishing into the ether. But without the phones themselves or a paper trail relating to their disposal, they couldn't prove it. When internal enquiries by the organisation's management proved fruitless, the agency had received a discreet approach.

Going by the demarcation lines she'd set, Maggie shouldn't have been involved in the case. She'd only stepped in because Wilma had been offered a lucrative double shift at the hospital. Her neighbour had already made significant progress: sussed out the interior of the man's home – Maggie hadn't dared ask how – produced a 2012 car registration number and a photograph of an orderly, nigh empty, garage. Only the previous day Wilma had turned up a suspect invoice and possible address. Now, Maggie eyed the stout mesh fence that surrounded the premises. Fat chance. That fence had to be eight-feet high. Not a hope in hell of getting over it. What would Wilma do, she wondered? Ram the gates, she thought wryly.

*Think outside the box!* She prowled the perimeter, looking for a way through. Finally she found it, a buckled section at ground level. For once in her life, Maggie gloried in her petite size. She crouched. Worked with both hands to ease the wire upwards. Slung her bag across her body and wriggled underneath. She was partway across the open ground when she spotted a gleam of light. Maggie stopped in her tracks. Narrowed her eyes, zooming in on the cabin window. Blinked. Might be just the waning sun reflecting off the glass. Gingerly, she crept forward. Another tiny flash. *Bingo!* She tiptoed towards it, wincing as her shoes crunched on the yard's rough surface.

Maggie was within twenty metres of her target when she heard the sound: a low growl at first, followed by a whine. She followed it to a space below the cabin. Stood stock still. Nothing happened. The animal must be chained up, she surmised, otherwise it would be out here, going for her. Heart thudding, she resumed her forward momentum. Two growls, louder this time. 'Shush,' she whispered, more in hope than expectation, as two large heads appeared, ears pricked. Two wet pointed snouts nosed the air. Two jaws gaped, tongues lolling.

Maggie made the lee of the Portakabin. The Alsatians were pawing the ground, now, straining at whatever tethered them. 'Shush,' she mouthed again. She wondered why they weren't barking. So much for keeping guard dogs. Perhaps they'd been sleeping. Or maybe – wry face – like her, they were new to the job. Crouching, she ran her eyes over the car's number plate, committing it to memory. She'd check it later against Wilma's notes, which were safely stowed in her bag. Maggie straightened, then pressed an eye to the exposed corner of the window. A man was seated at a desk, his back to her. With one swift glance, she filed a description. With another she memorised the scene. On the floor around the desk were stacked boxes – boxes of what looked very like mobile phones.

*Get the evidence!* She fumbled for the zip of her bag, extracted a small camera, held it up to the window. She'd only managed to fire off a couple of shots when her mobile trilled. *Idiot!* Maggie watched in horror as the man leapt up from the desk, knocking his chair over, and made for the door.

The Alsatians were barking in tandem now. She did a speedy about-turn, stowing the camera as she sprinted across the open yard. Halfway across she lost a shoe, stooped to retrieve it.

'Hey, you!'

She squinted over her shoulder. The Portakabin door was wide open, illuminating the scene: the man bent double, fingers working feverishly to loose the dogs. Maggie ran on, shoe in hand, the jagged ground sending stabs of pain into her stockinged foot. Her eyes raked the fence, trying desperately to relocate her entry point. She'd almost made it when the dogs came nipping at her heels.

# Go on then

Kym shrugged into her coat. 'That's me away.'

'No worries.' Fatboy looked up from his usual position on the settee.

In the doorway, she hesitated. Fatboy had proved generous this while back, slipping her a pack of fags, palming her the odd note, sometimes putting a few pills or a bit of weed her way. And now the big guy was holding the fort on a regular basis. Kym couldn't believe her luck. Still, she had a twinge of conscience. 'The bairn... You sure it'll be all right, me leaving him on his own?'

'He's not on his own. I'm here. And don't worry, I know what to do.' Over the weeks he'd been frequenting the flat, Fatboy had got the hang of what little routine there was: the plastic cups of watery juice halfway through the morning, the jam sandwiches at lunch, the biscuits in the afternoon. There were naps on Kym's bed for the wee ones, pink spoonfuls of Calpol for the gurny ones. The rest of the time the kids just seemed to sit there, bug-eyed in front of the telly. Idly, Fatboy wondered what else Kym dosed her charges with as well as Calpol. He dismissed the thought.

Kym grinned. 'Right enough.' She'd made up her wee one's feed. And it's not as if the bairn would know the difference. As for the other kids, it wasn't as if Fatboy was a complete stranger to them. Or under age or anything. Actually, Kym thought, as she pulled the front door behind her, *she* was doing *them* a favour. A bit of male company would do them good. For she knew fine that few of the children that darkened her door had a man in the household. Christ, Kym's own kids had never seen hide nor hair of their fathers. Yes, she reassured herself – a stint with Fatboy would be way better for them kids than sitting parked in front of the telly. A big fella like that, he'd be able to have a bit of rough and tumble with them. All to the good, Kym snickered to herself as she made her way towards the lifts. Tire the bastards out.

Fatboy half reclined on the settee. He'd been watchful at first, as he went back and forth to Kym's flat. He might pass the odd person in the entrance lobby, share the lift with someone. Or if the lift was broken – as it regularly was – he might have somebody try to chum him up the stairs. The beauty of it was, he had a wee chortle to himself, you rarely saw the same face twice. Even the kids that were dumped at Kym's for 'minding' seemed to turn over with some regularity. Now, Fatboy paid scant attention to the people he passed on the stair, or to the hire vans that often sat outside on the forecourt, for he suspected that the removals he witnessed day and daily would be supplemented by scores of moonlit flits.

He took a long toke on his spliff. Watched the sweet smoke-stack waft lazily towards the ceiling. He closed his eyes, a satisfied smile on his face. This new arrangement was going to work out just fine. Willie Meston's idea – taking his trades off the street – was ace. Who was going to finger Fatboy in a fucking high rise in Seaton? He smirked. The pigs were probably sitting down Queen Street on their fat arses right now, congratulating themselves that they'd run the dealers off the streets. Well, they'd done that right enough, and the change of venue hadn't harmed Fatboy's operation one bit. Quite the reverse. Willie was doing good trade, and takings had risen steadily since the new setup became known. Now they were no longer out in the open, the druggies were able to take time over their purchases. That in turn gave Willie the opportunity to up his sales. And it must surely be the icing on the cake that his business could be conducted out of the biting wind that whistled round the walls of the tower blocks and the rain that slashed across the tarmac in horizontal sheets.

Yes, he conceded, this new arrangement suited everybody. He and the girl had come to an understanding: he'd palm her enough to purchase a bevvy, she'd return the favour by giving Fatboy and

Willie the run of her place. They'd be safe enough there. For a while yet, anyway. Safe to cash up, to sort out stock, to plan for the next session.

A slow grin spread across Fatboy's face. Kymberley Ewen's setup might be shite, but he could sit in relative comfort and safety while the wee Meston bastard did his bidding elsewhere. And if things did turn sour, well, there were plenty more tower blocks in Seaton. Plenty more folk who'd be willing to give him the run of their place in exchange for a few bob.

'Gonna gie us a toke?'

Fatboy opened his eyes. One of the wee boys was perched alongside him. 'What did you say?'

The lad pointed to Fatboy's spliff. 'A toke?' he offered a gaptoothed grin.

Fatboy couldn't believe it. Still, he had to hand it to the wee fella, for cheek if nothing else.

He passed the spliff into a chubby hand.

'Go on, then,' he grinned.

# Don't Let it Be Him

A red light was winking angrily on the telephone as Maggie came through the front door. She stretched out a forefinger to the answering machine. Pressed 'play'. She hoped to hear a familiar voice, but all Maggie could hear was a long tone, disembodied, like a foghorn at half kilter, followed by a sharp beep. There was silence. She wondered if the caller had thought the better of it and hung up. She got a lot of that these days: callers whose courage deserted them at the very last minute, folk who decided they didn't want to deal with a woman. She could see that was going to be a problem, particularly in macho Aberdeen. She waited for a few moments, then bent over the machine and depressed the 'stop' button.

Maggie made her way down the hall. Behind the kitchen window, the sun sat low, casting tiger stripes across the sky. The garden was unkempt, the vegetable patch sprouting with shot cabbages, the grass ragged at the edges, the borders choked with old vegetation. She sighed. More expense. Dejected, she set her bag down on the worktop. Her spirits always soared when the agency got a new enquiry. Now, she felt a sharp stab of disappointment. With Wilma's help, she'd put in some serious groundwork since the day she'd picked up those files from George's office. And business *was* building steadily, but she couldn't afford to let up.

*Get on with it*. There was a pile of paperwork waiting to be tackled. And no Colin. He'd asked to stay over with a friend. Now she came to think on it, he'd been doing an awful lot of that lately.

'Hello-o?' Wilma turned her key in the back door. She no longer bothered to knock. 'I saw the light on. How's you?'

'Fine. I'm not long in.'

'Well, I won't hinder you. I just came round to see if you knew about that young lassie found dead at St Machar? Heard it on the news.'

Maggie gasped. 'Poor soul.'

'D'you reckon she was done in?'

'Doesn't follow.'

'Oh, but they said...'

'I've told you already,' there was real bitterness in Maggie's voice, 'you don't want to believe everything you hear.'

'But the telly...'

'Wilma, you have to stop jumping to conclusions. We need to be the embodiment of probity, especially now we're supposed to be private investigators.' Maggie felt herself flush. In the light of her recent escapades, that was rich.

'You an your fancy words.' Wilma experienced not the slightest twinge of conscience. 'Betcha it was some wanker from Seaton Park.'

'Seaton Park? What's that got to do with it?'

'Well, they're saying the quine was a student.'

*Dear God*! Alarm bells went off in Maggie's head. After years of showing contempt, Colin had lately taken an interest in the opposite sex. She'd even unearthed a men's magazine one morning when she was changing his bed. She'd been shocked at the time. Reassured herself that sort of thing was tame compared with what was available on the internet. The incident did make Maggie wonder, though: what else her son was keeping from her? If he was still skipping school, for instance? And if he was, what exactly did he do all day down the other end of town? Her mind ran away. What if this poor girl was one of the students he hung out with? What if he'd chatted her up? Gone into the graveyard? Made a clumsy overture? Been rebuffed? *Calm down, woman. You're tired, that's all.*

'You've got Hillhead here.' Wilma laid a pencil on the table. 'The University there.' She placed a second pencil parallel to the first. 'Seaton Park's the obvious shortcut between the two.' She whacked down a folder in between.

'Yes, I can see that. But what's the problem? I would have thought the fresh air...'

174

'Maggie Laird,' Wilma cut her off mid-sentence, 'are you honestly trying to tell me you've never heard of students being attacked in Seaton Park?'

'Well, I've maybe read the odd thing in the paper – somebody getting relieved of their mobile, that sort of thing, but I'd no idea…'

'As for Hillhead…'

'What's the matter with it?' The minute she opened her mouth, she regretted posing the question.

Wilma snorted. 'Just about everything – lousy accommodation, bugger-all facilities, expensive bus fares.' She harrumphed again. 'Wrong thing in the wrong place, if you ask me. As for them nobs at Aberdeen University… Bunch o' wankers. Couldn't put one foot in front of the other, some of them. Plus there's been nothing but bother since they built that place.' She paused for breath. 'Didn't your husband ever say anything about Seaton Park?'

'George didn't say much about anything lately.'

'Well, let me tell you, the place is hoatching with junkies, drop-outs, hoodies, you name it. And there's damn all in the way of lighting. It's bad enough in the daytime,' Wilma made a scary face, 'but I wouldn't go near the place after dark.'

Maggie threw a covert glance at her watch. 'I'm sure it can't be that bad.'

'You haven't seen what I've seen up at ARI: broken noses, fractured jaws, knife wounds.' Wilma was in full flow. 'I wouldn't want to go into detail on the sexual assaults.'

Despite herself, Maggie's curiosity was piqued. 'And these happened in Seaton Park?'

'Uh-huh. So if that poor lassie on the telly got done in taking a shortcut from Hillhead, I wouldn't be at all surprised.'

'I think you're exaggerating, Wilma.'

'That's you all over, Maggie Laird, looking to see the good in everything.'

*If you only knew*. In truth, the first thing Maggie looked to do on meeting someone for the first time was nose out the flaw. Like a

175

ferret after a rabbit. It wasn't something she was proud of.

Her lips formed a tight smile. 'If you say so.'

'Would you still be as charitable if it was *your* daughter lying dead? Oh,' Wilma bit her lip. 'Forget I said that.'

'That's all right. To be honest with you, I've had that much on my plate recently, I haven't had time to fret about Kirsty.' Maggie paused. 'Not till you reminded me, that is.'

'Sorry, pal.'

'Anyhow,' resolutely, she moved towards the door, 'I have to throw you out now because…'

Wilma cupped a hand to her ear. 'Do you hear that?'

'What?'

'Sounds like the polis.'

She pricked her ears. Sure enough, in the near distance there was the distinctive sound of a police siren.

'Wonder what's up? It's no often you hear them in this neck of the woods.'

'Oh…' Maggie's stomach lurched. Her first thought was the unfair dismissal case. She could hear, still, those Alsatians pounding after her, feel their hot breath at her back. *Breaking and entering!* She wondered if there were any further charges could be brought. *Don't be daft.* A thing like that wouldn't warrant a siren. She collected her thoughts. 'They're probably taking a shortcut.'

'Shortcut?' Wilma was already rehearsing in her head the yarn she would spin over her wee bit business in Mastrick. 'It's a fuckin cul-de-sac.'

'Well, maybe they don't know that.'

'You'd think they'd know, if anybody bloody would,' Wilma said. 'Tossers. Oh,' she pulled herself up, 'sorry, Maggie. I forgot.'

'Doesn't matter. If you've been married to a policeman for as long as I have…' She looked pointedly at Wilma, 'You get used to it.

The noise of the siren grew louder.

'Bet it's to do with that lassie at St Machar.'

*Could it be connected with Colin, then?* Maggie fought to still the

176

palpitations in her chest. *He couldn't have, surely.*

Louder, the siren wailed, and louder still.

Maggie's mind churned. She told herself it was irrational. Still, she said a silent prayer: *Don't let it be him.*

'Come on, chum, let's have a nosey.'

Wilma gripped Maggie by the elbow and steered her down the hall.

They were just in time to see the two dark uniforms framed in the door's glass panel.

# V

# Hillhead Student Village

Brian Burnett nosed the pool car into an empty parking space. Through a rain-spattered windscreen, he peered at the building in front of him. New Carnegie Court was a bland, four-storey block. The body at St Machar had been identified as student Lucy Simmons. The flat that Lucy shared with four other first-year students was located, he'd been advised by the Accommodation Office, on the second floor.

By his side sat DC Susan Strachan. She turned to her sergeant. 'What d'you reckon?'

Brian didn't know what the hell he was doing there. It was routine stuff, a job for the DCs. But he was still smarting from his run-in with Chisolm, and resources were spread so thin, all the foot soldiers were spoken for. His stomach rumbled. 'I reckon I could kill for a macaroni pie.'

Head bent against the driving rain, they ducked out of the car and made a dash for the entrance, negotiated the security entry and made a beeline for the stairs.

A girl answered Brian's knock.

'DS Burnett and DC Strachan, Aberdeen Police.' They showed their warrant cards. 'We buzzed from downstairs.'

'Oh...yes.' She didn't look too sure.

'It's about Lucy.' Brian added. 'We'd like to ask you a few questions.'

The girl nodded. 'You'd better come in.'

The two followed the girl down the hallway. She was tall and lissome: long legs in skinny jeans, Jack Wills printed sweatshirt, glossy hair swinging down her back. *Yahs*, Susan thought. You never used to get that many of them in Aberdeen. If they didn't get into Oxbridge, the public school kids tended to head for Edinburgh or St Andrews. She supposed the pressure on university places was sending them further north.

The living room was open-plan to the kitchen. The girl indicated a contemporary scarlet sofa. Susan sat down. Brian followed. The furnishings in the other halls he'd visited were pretty basic: narrow single bed, kitchens equipped with fridges, Baby Bellings, microwaves, but not much else. Contrast that with New Carnegie Court, where the soft furnishings were brightly coloured, the kitchens contemporary in stainless steel and blond wood. But this latter came at a price, Brian knew, being at the top end of the range of accommodation on offer. They do all right for themselves, this lot, he thought.

He spoke first. 'I understand there are five of you occupying this flat.'

'Yes. Well, there were, but one of the guys dropped out after the first semester.'

'And no one has taken his place?'

'No, like, there was supposed to be someone coming. But no one's appeared so far...' The girl's voice trailed off.

'And you are?' Brian fished out his notebook.

'Melissa. Melissa Harding.' She met Brian's gaze, bright-eyed.

His thoughts turned to Lucy Simmons. He knew that Lucy's body was lying now in a drawer in the Public Mortuary. She'd already lost her bloom of youth, her bright eyes become obscured by an opaque film. Hastily, he collected himself. 'The others, are they here at the moment?'

Melissa shrugged. 'No idea. I'll go and look.'

It must have been five minutes before the girl reappeared.

'There's no answer from Sally's room. I think she must be at lectures.'

'Can you give me her full name?'

'Sally Hay.'

He jotted this down. 'And she's studying what?'

'Linguistics. Dom's still in bed.'

'Dom?'

'Dominic. I've told him you're here.'

'Thanks. Now, can you tell me when you last saw Lucy?'

'Around 9.20 on Tuesday morning. I was sitting in my pyjamas at the breakfast bar, and she came into the kitchen and made herself a cup of coffee. Then I went back to my room to get dressed, and by the time I came out again she'd gone.'

'And you didn't see Lucy again that day?'

'No-o.' The girl burst into tears.

Susan patted her on the shoulder. 'Would you like me to fetch you something? Drink of water? Cup of tea?'

Melissa shook her head.

'If you could fill me in on Lucy's background,' Brian again. 'Does she have a boyfriend, for instance?'

'Did. They split up last year.'

'Know his name?'

'Edward something-or-other.'

Brian nodded. 'Do you happen to know where he is now, this Edward?'

'Up at Oxford. Somerville, I think.'

'And when would Lucy have seen him last? Any idea?'

The girl twisted her hands. 'Dunno.'

'Anything else you can think of?'

'Like?'

'Like what Lucy could have been doing in St Machar kirkyard? How would she normally get from halls to her lectures, for example?'

Melissa put head to one side. 'Catch the bus if it was bad weather. Mostly she'd walk through the park.'

'Just to recap,' Brian resumed, 'you said Sally had left the flat before you got up.'

Melissa pulled a face. 'She's a bundle of fun.'

'What do you mean by that?' Brian probed.

'Sally's a real swot. Spends all her days in the library. Evenings too.'

'So she's not likely to have seen Lucy Simmons at all that day?'

Melissa shook her head. 'No.'

'What about Dominic?'

'What about him?'

'You've told me Dominic didn't come out of his room that morning.'

Melissa sighed. 'Dom spends half his life in bed. He sits at the computer all night. Wakes me up sometimes, making coffee at four or five in the morning. Then he doesn't want to get up for lectures...' She broke off. 'Doesn't want to get up for anything, really. And there's another thing. Dom's always creeping about.'

'I thought you said he spent the whole time in bed.'

'I mean, like, when he isn't in bed, he just sort of creeps up on you. You'll turn round and he'll be, like, standing there.'

'And you find that annoying.'

'Not annoying so much as weird.'

'So,' Susan summarised. 'Correct me if I'm wrong, Melissa. You and Lucy were friends, but you didn't get on with the other two.'

The girl shrugged. 'It's not that we didn't get on. Just...well, like, we didn't have anything in common with them.'

'But you didn't fall out?'

'Fall out? No. Not except...'

'Except?'

Melissa pulled a face. 'The usual sort of things – nicking our stuff from the fridge, leaving dirty dishes lying around. It can be a real pain, you know.'

Susan thought of all those dirty bastards at Queen Street. She could identify with that.

'You said Lucy didn't have a boyfriend,' Brian again.

'That's right. After she broke up with Edward, she didn't want to commit to anything.'

'Could there have been anyone else?' he continued. 'Anyone Lucy had a particular attachment to?'

'I don't think so,' the girl wrinkled her brow. 'Not unless you count Guy.'

'And he'd be?'

'Lucy's Art History tutor. She had a bit of a pash for him. Oh,' colour flooded Melissa's face, 'I shouldn't have said.'

'Don't worry,' Brian's tone was reassuring, 'we'll use our discretion. Can you give me a surname?'

'No. Sorry.'

'Never mind. We'll check it out.'

Melissa glanced at her watch. 'Will that be all? I've got a lecture in an hour and I'll need time to get ready.'

'Just a couple more things,' he looked up from his notebook. 'Did your pal take a drink?'

'Take a drink?' Melissa puzzled.

'Did Lucy regularly imbibe alcohol?'

'Alcohol? No. Hardly at all.'

'What about drugs?'

'No.'

'Not even the odd E?' he prompted. 'When she was partying?'

'Lucy wasn't a party girl.'

He nodded. 'Leave me a mobile number in case I have to get back to you.'

The girl rattled off the number.

'Oh, and one last thing. Would Lucy have left her mobile here?'

'No.' Melissa eyed Brian as if he were mad.

'She'd have carried it with her?'

'Always.'

'Can you give me her number?'

Melissa thumbed through her contacts and flashed her phone at him.

'Thanks.' He scribbled a note. Flipped his notebook shut. 'That's all I wanted to know.'

Susan tapped on Dominic's door. There was no response. She knocked again.

'Wha-at?' Thick voice.

'Are you decent?'

There was silence, then, 'Just about.'

After a brief interval, the door opened a fraction.

She peered through the crack. 'Dominic, is it?'

The lad nodded.

Dominic Elwen was small, five foot four or so. Short legs encased in straight-legged jeans. Bare feet. A crumpled Nirvana T-shirt that could have been a collector's item. Sallow skin. Black hair brushed back off a high forehead. Dark eyes under brows that met in an untidy straggle over a wide, flat nose. The eyes blinked at Susan now.

'DC Strachan. I have some questions for you.'

Dominic stared, uncomprehending.

'In connection with Lucy Simmons.'

'Oh…right.' He rubbed sleep from his eyes and opened the door another fraction.

Susan caught a glimpse of a mouthful of bad teeth, smelled the sour reek of sweat. Behind Dominic, she could make out walls plastered with graphic posters, a computer desk piled high with papers, an unmade bed strewn with dirty clothes.

'When you're ready. I'll be in the lounge.'

# Doesn't Matter

'Have you seen this, folks?' In the staffroom of Seaton School, someone waved the local paper. 'They've named that girl we were talking about the other day.'

'The one at St Machar?'

'Yes. Listen up. I'll read it out to you.'

*The body of a young woman discovered on Tuesday evening in the grounds of St Machar Cathedral has now been formally identified as Lucy Simmons.*

*A student at Aberdeen University, Lucy, 17, was in her first year of a History of Art degree and shared a mixed flat in New Carnegie Court at Hillhead Student Village. Friends were said to be devastated by her death and are receiving counselling from the university.*

*Seventeen.* The blood drained from Maggie's face. *The same age as Colin.*

'What's up, Maggie? Is it someone you know?'

'N-no...' she stuttered. 'It's upsetting, that's all, when something like that happens so close to home.'

'Too true. All the same, let me read you the next bit.'

*Lucy's parents, Virginia and Michael Simmons, an executive in the financial sector, have flown to Aberdeen from their home in Surrey, but are unavailable for comment at this time. However, we understand Lucy to be their only child.*

'Poor souls,' there was a buzz of excited comments. 'Can you imagine what they'll be going through?'

'I know. They look such decent people, too.'

'Is there a picture? Let's see.'

Maggie sat, stunned, whilst the newspaper was passed round.

'What a lovely girl.'

'Can you imagine if it was one of yours?'

'Doesn't bear thinking about.'

'An only child as well. Don't know how you'd survive.'

'Who'd ever think there'd be a murder right on your doorstep?'

'I know. Seaton's one thing, but St Machar? And in the graveyard too.'

'Terrifying.'

'Wonder if the police have got anyone for it?'

'Not yet.' The words were out before Maggie could stop herself. She'd got a fright that day, when the uniforms had come knocking at her door. No matter it had been related to another matter altogether: an opportunist thief who'd been targeting the area. Nonetheless, she'd got straight on the phone to Brian.

All eyes turned to her.

'Are you still in touch with folk, then?' another of the teachers cut in. They all knew chapter and verse on George.

She fudged. 'One or two.'

'Come on, then. If you know something, you've got to let us in on it.'

Despite the shock, Maggie experienced a sudden flush of self-importance that was not altogether unwelcome, she was ashamed to admit. She'd always felt out of place in the staffroom. Pupil Support Assistants, she imagined, fell somewhere on the pecking order between the school secretary and the cleaners. And she knew full well the older teachers on the staff saw Learning Support as getting in the way of their teaching programmes. Hadn't she caught them moaning only recently?

'Well?'

'From what I've gathered, the girl had sustained a head injury.'

'There!' Triumphant voice. 'Told you it was murder.'

'She might have had an accident,' Maggie ventured.

'What sort of accident?'

'Not an accident as much as…she may have fallen over.' Maggie had made a hole and was digging herself further in.

'Fallen?' Somebody hooted. 'You don't fall over at seventeen.'

'Not unless you're tanked. You only have to look at the taxi ranks down Union Street every weekend.'

'Never mind that,' someone else chipped in. 'My newspaper said there was a sexual assault.'

'Ach,' scornful voice, 'there's red tops for you. Nothing sells better than a dollop of salacious sex.'

'Mebbe so, but it also said there was an object found at the…'

'An object? What? Where?'

'Paper didn't say.'

'See,' one of the older women said with some relish.

Maggie snapped, 'That's enough.'

Conversation switched to the pupils.

'How are the Famous Four doing?' someone enquired.

'Famous Four?'

'Willie Meston and his gang.'

'Didn't know he had a gang,' Maggie lied. 'The only person I've seen with him on a regular basis is Ryan Brebner.'

'Well,' a voice chipped in, 'he does now. Quite the wee posse – Willie, Ryan, Lewis and Kieran.'

'Kieran Chalmers?' she enquired guilelessly.

'Yes. And you thinking that boy had prospects,' one of the older teachers said with undisguised satisfaction. 'Thick as thieves, they are. They've been out of here after school like the proverbial bat out of hell.'

'That right?'

'You'd better keep a close eye, if Kieran's not to stray from the straight and narrow.'

'Yes, I'll do that.' Maggie wasn't going to let on the boys were only playing on a piece of waste ground.

'You still not going to tell us about that lassie up St Machar?' Cheeky voice.

She looked down at her watch. 'Sorry,' she fibbed, 'got to go. I'm on playground duty.'

Maggie scanned the playground. Beyond a mesh fence, a scrum of small boys kicked a ball about the Astroturf. Here and there on the tarmac, huddles of girls whispered behind their hands. In a far corner, a solitary figure stabbed his trainer with fierce concentration at a stone.

'You all right over there?' she called. Some of the staff balked at playground duty, but Maggie didn't mind it. Got her out of class and into the fresh air.

The lad carried on, worrying the stone with the toe of his trainer. Tugging her collar close against the wind, she crossed the tarmac.

'Is anything the matter, Kieran?' she asked in a soft voice.

The boy wouldn't meet her eyes. 'No.'

'Why aren't you playing with your pals, then?' She threw a glance over her shoulder. The other kids seemed oblivious. She took in their short sleeves, bare arms and legs, marvelled at their resilience.

For a moment, the boy paused. 'Just...' He carried on where he'd left off.

'Just what?'

No answer.

'If something's bothering you,' she persisted, 'don't you think you should tell someone?'

The boy stopped kicking. Started again. 'Dunno.'

For a few moments, Maggie speculated. Staff weren't encouraged to get too close to the children any more. Maybe she should leave the boy alone. She turned away.

'Miss?'

She swivelled on her heel.

'It's Lewis.' Kieran kept his head down.

'Lewis McHardy?' A furrow appeared between Maggie's brows. She'd seen the boy only that morning.

'Yes.'

'What about Lewis?' Her voice was filled with concern. 'Is there something you need to tell me, Kieran?' Over time, she'd gleaned a few choice facts about Lewis's home life. Couldn't begin to imagine what further crisis could have prompted Kieran to mention the boy.

'I... I'm not sure.'

She caught the doubt in Kieran's voice. 'He's not in trouble, is he?' If she didn't get to the nub of it right now, the bell would ring and the break be over.

'Sort of.'

'Serious trouble?'

Small silence, then, 'Mebbe.'

From the tremor in his voice, Maggie reckoned that Kieran was close to tears. She felt a sudden ache in the pit of her stomach. After all the hard work she'd put in, if Lewis was in trouble, then maybe Kieran was too. She could see his chances of going on to higher education disappearing like soapy water down a sink. Serves me right, she thought, for trying to get one over on them in the staff-room. She resolved there and then to re-commence surveillance on the four boys. But first she'd better get to the bottom of what was troubling Kieran.

'You think I might be able to help?' she asked gently.

Kieran raised his head, but didn't look at her. 'Willie says you're married to a policeman.'

'I *was* married to a policeman.'

'You divorced, then?'

The lad's tone was so matter-of-fact, Maggie felt a sharp pang of sadness. She remembered how shocked she'd been when she first started at Seaton to discover how few of its pupils actually lived with two parents.

'No, Kieran, I'm not divorced. My husband was in the police force, but he's dead now.'

'Oh.'

'Does that make a difference?' she prompted. 'I thought it was me you wanted to talk to.'

'It was, but...' For an instant, the boy's clear grey eyes met Maggie's own.

'What?'

In the background, a bell shrilled.

'Doesn't matter.' Kieran turned away.

# Craigmyle

The Hollywood Café in Holburn Street was seventy years past its sell-by-date. Maggie pushed the door and went in. The interior was cramped, the front shop bisected by a glass counter, behind which old-fashioned sweetie jars were arrayed on tall shelving, the seating area to the rear crammed with high-backed booths. She peered into the gloomy interior. Her spirits sank. There was nobody there.

She turned on her heel. Thought the better of it. Turned back. She rose on the balls of her feet and craned her neck. At the very rear, the top of a dark head was only just discernible. Maggie's heart skipped a beat. She should have realised. *See without being seen –* wasn't that what George always said?

'Jimmy?' She advanced down the aisle between the booths. Just as she'd given up hope of getting a result from her visit to the nightclub, Craigmyle had got in touch.

Keeping his head down, the man rose halfway to his feet. He wasn't as she remembered: leaner, shaven-headed, a rash of dark stubble on his jaw. 'Maggie?' He grasped her hand. 'Good to see you.' Jimmy Craigmyle slid back into a corner.

She dropped onto the banquette opposite. It was upholstered in scarlet leather, discoloured and torn, the rents crudely patched with curling strips of carpet tape. The place even smelled disconsolate, a sad amalgam of floor cleaner, stale chip fat and old smoke.

'Can't say the same,' she worked to keep her voice even.

'No, well. I'm really sorry. That business…'

'I looked for you at the funeral.'

'I was there,' Craigmyle said. 'How could I not? Nipped in at the back,' he continued. 'Ducked out before the crowd. Thought, in the circumstances…'

'I understand.'

'We were buddies, George and me. You know how it is in the Force.' He scrunched his face. 'I might not have been who he'd have picked. But you get stuck with someone, you learn to rub along.'

'I suppose.'

'Good turnout, wasn't there? Did George proud.'

Maggie's mouth turned down. She could picture, still, George's unadorned coffin. 'I'll come straight to the point. I left my number at the club because I need you to tell me about Brannigan.'

'That cunt?' Craigmyle put a hand to his mouth. 'Sorry. What about him?'

'Everything.'

'Why do you want to know?'

'Because I'm trying to clear George.'

'Why now? I mean, wasn't the time for action back when...'

Maggie sighed. 'I've myself to blame for that.'

'How come?'

'Oh,' she grimaced. 'That's ancient history. Let's just say I'm hell-bent on restoring my husband's good name.'

'And how d'you propose to do that?"

'I've taken on the agency, for a start.'

'You're kidding.'

'No. Deadly serious.'

'And how's that going to help?'

'Pay the bills, for one.' A tight smile played on her lips. 'Plus I hoped, if I'm honest with you, Jimmy, it might give me some ideas.'

'Like what, for instance?'

'How to conduct surveillance, investigate...'

'Listen, Maggie,' her companion leaned across the table. 'Leave that sort of stuff to the professionals.'

'Like who? I hope you don't mean the police force, Jimmy Craigmyle, because it didn't do a damn thing to vindicate George.'

'Like me,' Jimmy countered. 'Look, I know George was never that sold on me. Saw me as a bit of a fly man. As for you? I know fine well you never liked me.'

'That's not…'

'No need to deny it. Not now we're in the same boat, you and me.'

'Same boat?' Maggie's eyebrows shot up. 'Hardly.'

'Near as,' Craigmyle insisted. 'Wife threw me out. She's put up with me for years, but having to resign like that was the last straw.'

Maggie grimaced. 'At least you've got a wife.'

'Lot of use that is. She doesn't pick up my calls. Won't let me see my kids. Started off OK, but now it's any excuse.'

'Oh, Jimmy, I'm sorry.'

'Me too. Don't know if it's too late for the marriage, but I'd do anything to get my kids back. That's the reason I'm working in Windmill Brae.'

'I thought…'

'Thought I wouldn't be able to land anything better than a bouncer's job,' Craigmyle threw her a bitter look. 'That's what they all think. Down Queen Street, anyhow. And I'm happy for them to think that way. Lets me get on with the business in hand.'

'I don't understand.'

'I might not be the man George Laird was,' he flexed his arms, 'but I'm determined to nail that wee bastard that ran rings round the pair of us.'

'Bobby Brannigan?'

'Spot on.'

'But how?'

'The club…'

'I was gutted when the barman said it was your night off.'

'Belongs to a guy Gilruth.'

'Yes,' Maggie winced. 'His reputation precedes him.'

'I've managed to inveigle my way in,' Craigmyle lowered his voice. 'Been biding my time. Keeping my nose clean. I don't have the run of the place. Not yet. But there's this back room…' He met her gaze. 'Something's going on in there, that's for sure.'

'Drugs, you mean?'

'That, and the rest. I'm convinced if I can crack that, I can rubbish Brannigan's testimony.'

'But you're an ex-cop, Jimmy. Surely they're...'

'Suspicious?' he sneered. 'No feckin way. A cop? Yes. A bent cop? Come on in, the water's lovely. I could be useful to them, don't you see?'

'Mmm,' Maggie nodded.

'And if I can get that wee bastard to admit he perjured himself in the witness box, there's a chance we could get the case reopened.'

'Oh,' she felt light-headed all of a sudden. 'And both your names could be cleared, you and George.'

Craigmyle snorted. 'I don't give a flying fuck about that. My name was mud before any of this ever happened. No. All I want is to see my kids again.'

'But it's not just Brannigan's testimony that caused the case to collapse. There was the interview. George said...'

'The tape that got turned off?'

'Yes.'

There was a long silence, then, 'I'll hold my hands up to that.'

*Bingo*! Blood rushed to Maggie's head. Finally, she'd made a breakthrough. Still, she'd need more than a simple admission. 'You switched it off?' she probed.

'Yes.'

'But why?'

'Instinct. It's the only way, sometimes, to get these people to open up,' he offered a crooked grin. 'And the rest is history.'

'But why didn't George...'

Her companion grimaced. 'Loyalty, I suppose.'

Maggie's voice rose. 'Misguided loyalty, if you ask me.'

Craigmyle gripped her wrist. 'Pipe down. We don't want to be seen together.'

'I don't care.'

'Well, I do,' his voice was soft. 'Fair enough, Maggie, what you just said. Do you think I don't feel guilty, George taking it on the chin for me?'

'Guilty enough to stand up in court and testify to switching off that tape?'

'First things first,' he parried. 'There's a way to go before we get to that.'

*Can this man be trusted?* Maggie debated whether to go straight to Queen Street with his confession. But she needed more. And if he could be a conduit to Brannigan, uncover evidence on the drugs front…

'What did you tell me you wanted to achieve?' Craigmyle asked.

She drew a deep breath. 'Justice for George.'

'Well, if we're going to succeed, you and me, we'll have to stay on the same page. Agreed?'

*Play along.* With some reservation, Maggie nodded.

'So you'll keep me posted on any developments?'

'Yes. You?'

'Sure thing.' He paused. 'I'm making progress at the club.'

'You are?' Her heart skipped a beat.

'But it could take a while. Months. Years, even.'

Her spirits sank again. 'As long as that?' She collected her thoughts. 'What about Brannigan?'

Jimmy shook his head. 'Hasn't shown his face.'

'Do you know where he is?'

He shrugged. 'No bloody idea.'

# One More Thing

The Incident Room was alive with activity: people making and taking phone calls, a printer spewing out paper. On the far wall, whiteboards bore maps and diagrams and photographs.

'Right, folks,' Detective Inspector Allan Chisolm strode into the room. From under one arm, a bulging case file protruded. The DI drew out a chair at the head of the table. He threw the file down on the table with a thwack. 'Let's get this show on the road.' He called everyone to order.

'Sir,' Douglas Dunn slid smartly into a seat. Susan Strachan took in the artfully tousled dark hair, the hint of stubble showing on the weak chin. Smarmy little bastard, she thought, from her stance by the window. It was another grey day, heavy clouds lowering over the city's skyline. Fair matched her mood. Dunn was closely followed by Dave Wood, who licked the sugar off his fingers as he demolished the last of a breakfast doughnut. Brian Burnett unbuttoned his suit jacket and sat down. Susan picked up the sheets of paper that had fallen onto the floor by the printer. She stacked them in a neat pile and laid them on the big table, taking care to keep a comfortable distance between her own chair and that of Douglas Dunn.

'Where's Duffy?' The question came out like a bullet.

'Chasing up Forensics,' Brian replied.

'OK,' the inspector opened the folder in front of him. 'First, let me give you the good news.' He paused. 'We have formal ID. The bad news is we have damn all else. Let's start with an update from you, Burnett, on the victim's associates.'

'Sir. Strachan and I went out to Hillhead. Three flatmates: two girls, one boy. One swotty type, one yah and a weirdo.'

'Tell me about the weirdo.'

'That's one for Strachan, sir.'

'Dominic Elwen?' Susan pulled a face. 'Unproductive, I'm afraid. We checked the guy out thoroughly, and...' She shrugged. 'Agreed he's a complete geek, and he does look a bit odd. Plus...' She looked pointedly at Douglas Dunn. 'He doesn't seem to have a clue how to behave around the opposite sex. But, in my view, he's harmless. It's just hard luck on both sides he got billeted with Lucy and Melissa.'

'Boyfriends?'

'None currently.' Susan's mind turned to Lucy Simmons: a girl who had come to Aberdeen with high expectations, and whose life had ended. Ended on a cold, hard slab in a bleak, dark grave-yard. She focused her thoughts. 'Lucy had broken up with a long-term boyfriend in Surrey. Seems not to have formed any other attachments.'

'No surprises there,' Dunn sneered. 'Bet he gave her the heave.'

Susan pulled a face. 'You're a cynical bastard, Douglas. How did you come to that conclusion?'

'Obvious. Girl couldn't get far enough away.'

'She couldn't get much further then Aberdeen, I'll hand you that. You *do* realise it's on an even more northerly latitude than Moscow?"

Prissy voice. 'Little Miss Know-It-All, today, aren't we?'

Susan chose to ignore this. 'He seems to be out of the equation, anyhow – the ex-boyfriend, and there doesn't appear to be anyone else.'

'Classmates?' Chisolm enquired.

'No one in particular.'

'Anything else?'

'Yes, sir. We've established that Lucy did have a mobile. Latest model. Never went anywhere without it.'

'So where is the thing?' The DI's fingers drummed on the desk. 'Somebody must have taken it.' He turned to Brian. 'I assume, Sergeant, you've been in touch with the girl's service provider?'

'Yes, sir. Her flatmate provided the number.'

'And had uniform ask round the pubs?'

'As a matter of course.'

'Did door-to-door throw up anything, Elrick?'

'Young lad, late teens, seen close to the cathedral gates. Not much in the way of description: dark coloured anorak, grey trousers, black shoes.'

'Christ,' Wood came to life, 'can they no give us a break?'

'Yes, well,' Chisolm ran a weary hand through his hair. 'What does the description tell us?'

'Grey trousers?' Dave Wood scratched his head. 'Not a student?'

'Unlikely,' the DI concurred.

'Sounds like a uniform of some sort,' Susan offered.

'Check it out, Elrick. Anything from you on the park itself, Dunn?'

'Sweet FA from Seaton Park, I'm afraid, sir. The miscreants are understandably backward in coming forward.'

The inspector threw him a thin smile. He cast his eyes round the room.

'Do we have any idea what Lucy Simmons was doing in St. Machar graveyard in the first place? If she'd taken a short-cut from Hillhead through Seaton Park, she'd have come out the main park gates and gone straight down the Chanonry to St Machar Drive. So, given that her body was found at the far end of the kirkyard, my guess is she went in there on purpose.'

'I think it's connected to the notebook and pencil.' This from Susan. 'We know Lucy was artistic. Interested in history. Maybe she wanted to do some research. Write something down. Draw something, even,' she broke off. 'You know…like people do brass-rubbings and stuff.'

'Right…' Douglas jumped in. 'And then she took a turn…'

'At the tender age of seventeen. Dinna be daft, laddie,' Dave Wood interjected. 'More like some evil bastard duffed her up.'

'We don't have any hard evidence for that,' Chisolm intervened. 'Not until Forensics can find a match for the injury to her skull.'

'And how bloody long will that take?' Dunn this time.

'I'm afraid we'll all have to be patient on that front,' the DI responded. 'I'm leaning hard on Forensics as it is.'

'But what about the mobile, sir?' Wood protested. 'She could have been mugged for that. Followed out of Seaton Park and...'

'That doesn't square.' Susan said her piece. 'What about the jeans? And the cross in the vagina? What sort of mugger does that to a young girl?'

There was a bit of eye-rolling around the table.

'Where does that leave us, then?' Wood asked.

The inspector furrowed his brow. 'Waiting – still – for Sergeant Duffy to appear. In the meantime, Dunn, Elrick,' Chisolm closed the folder on the table in front of him, 'let's concentrate our efforts on finding that phone. Find out if anyone has acquired a fancy new mobile recently. All of you, check with your sources, ask around in the pubs. That phone may well hold the key to Lucy's death. Anything further?' The inspector looked round the table.

'There's just one more thing, sir,' Brian volunteered. 'Melissa, the flatmate from Hillhead, mentioned Lucy had a bit of a crush – "pash" was the word she used – on one of her tutors. Turns out the Art History tutor is dark-haired and fortyish, which loosely fits the description of the guy who was seen loitering in the Chanonry. I've established that he goes by the name of Guy Plumley. Married with four kids. Lives just around the corner in Don Street.'

'Christ Almighty,' Chisolm's complexion flushed from puce to pink and then purple. 'We've got a university student dead in St Machar graveyard, a tutor she had the hots for living round the corner, and a suspect fitting said tutor's description seen loitering in the Chanonry, am I correct, Burnett?'

'Yes, sir.'

'And it's taken you till now to flag up a fucking connection?'

Desperately, Brian cast around the table. The others sat slouched. Douglas ran his fingers through his carefully gelled hair. Susan wouldn't meet his eyes. 'I did try to get hold of him, sir...' Brian had delegated the job, but there was no way he was going to land her in it. 'But turns out he's a slippery character. Bit difficult to pin down.'

'I'll give you difficult,' the inspector seethed. 'Get someone's arse down there. Have them ask this lover boy tutor to come in for a chat. But Burnett...'

'Yes, sir?'

'Kid gloves, please. We wouldn't want to go rubbing up the university the wrong way. And Burnett...'

'Sir.'

'No leaks. And that goes for the rest of you. It's vital we keep control of the flow of information.'

# Maggie Has a Wobble

'What the blazes are they doing in there?' Maggie smothered a huge yawn. It had been over two hours since she'd snapped the man enter the house and there had been no sign of movement in the upstairs bedroom. She prayed they weren't dug in in front of the television or, God forbid, having a romantic supper.

And where was his car? He must have parked round the corner, she surmised. The new estate of swanky detached houses wasn't yet on any bus route. She cast a glance at the estate agency brochures which graced the car's front sill – her *raison d'etre*, should her prolonged presence on this quiet road be remarked.

Maggie sneaked a nibble of the cereal bar she kept in the glove compartment for such occasions. She didn't dare follow it up with a swig of water from the bottle in the central console. She'd been bursting for a wee for the past hour. She chewed resolutely, making the mouthful last, but the sticky slivers of cereal only stuck to her mouth. Maggie experienced a sudden twinge of conscience. It was the second time that week she'd had to leave Colin a microwave meal.

She'd clock the guy's car on the way home, she resolved. Maggie had noted the make, colour and registration number that last time, when the pair had met for a quick lunchtime smooch at Hazelhead. She sighed heavily. They were such a thankless slog, these divorce cases. Hours of dogged observation. And for what? Getting divorced was far too easy, in Maggie's opinion. Time was, you made your bed you lay on it. Then again – she thought of Wilma – there were no winners, she knew. Still, needs must. She reclined the seat a fraction, stretched her legs, rotated her ankles in turn.

The sky was fading to flannel grey and Maggie nodding off when a light snapped on in an upstairs room. She lunged for her camera, just in time to catch a female figure draw the curtains. She fancied she could make out the shape of a man standing behind, his arms encircling the woman's waist. Didn't matter, she thought, as she clicked furiously. If they were upstairs for long enough…

She settled down to wait.

## X

'You're not looking too hot.' Wilma sat in Maggie's dining room, a cup of black coffee on the table in front of her.

'Bittie tired,' she raised a pasty face. 'Didn't get to my bed till gone midnight.'

'Thought you were babysitting Colin.'

'I was.'

'What's he been doing until after midnight on a school day?'

'Homework.' Wilma shrugged. 'That's what he told me, anyhow.'

Maggie caught her breath. She'd no idea what her son got up to any more. 'If you *are* going to babysit, Wilma, you'll have to be firmer with him.'

'Well, thanks a bunch. *You* come swanning in at all hours and *I* get nothing but the third degree.' She offered a wan smile. 'You don't exactly look sparkling either.'

'Neither would you be if you'd been sitting in a car half the night.'

'And whose fault is that?'

'Yours. For hounding me into taking on the business.'

'No, pal, *yours* for letting the client talk you into it. You're a soft touch, Maggie Laird. I thought we'd agreed you'd steer clear of surveillance.'

'We did, only…he was such a poor soul.'

'I thought you said he was good-looking,' Wilma teased. 'Did you fancy him, like?'

'Don't be ridiculous. He was desperate, that's all.'

'If he was that desperate why didn't he go himself? Catch them in the act?'

'Because the guy was the wife's personal trainer. Built like a tank.'

'So you decided to take him on instead?' Wilma rolled her eyes. 'Maggie Laird, you're some woman.'

'I didn't know he'd be that size when I took the job on.'

'And when you said you were going on a wee job,' Wilma retorted, 'I didn't know you were going to come in at all hours.'

'That's as long as it took.'

'Well, aren't you going to tell me how it went?'

Maggie shrugged. 'I parked the car like you said, watched the guy go in, waited till the light went on upstairs.'

'And?'

'And nothing. I sat there for seven hours. Well, it felt like seven, but when I checked my watch it was only six and a bit. Then…' She slumped back onto the settee. 'I came home.'

'But that's great!'

'Great? Is that how you'd describe it? Sitting in a cold car for hours on end with damn all to eat or drink? I couldn't even go to the bathroom.'

'You'd have managed if you were desperate.'

'Managed? How?'

'Cooried doon behind the car.'

'Wil-ma,' Maggie shrilled. 'I'd never be so desperate I'd wee in the street.'

Wilma grinned. 'You might yet. Anyway, I could have given you a hand. Done a shift, like.'

'And how were you to know I was stuck there?'

'Simple. You could have phoned.'

Maggie turned her head away.

'Well?'

She turned back. 'I forgot my mobile,' she said in a sheepish voice.

'*Maggie*,' Wilma's eyes were wide. 'You daft sod.'

'I know.'

'You took some happy snaps?' Wilma hesitated. 'You did, didn't you?'

'As instructed,' Maggie summoned a smile.

'Good on you, kid. If we've got that in the bag, that's another case sorted.'

'But that's just it.'

'Christ,' Wilma rolled her eyes, 'you didn't forget to give the client our Terms of Business, did you?'

'No. He had them already. I checked. It's just…well…when I agreed to take on the agency, I never imagined it would be like this: creeping about like a criminal, hiding away like a…a…*voyeur*.'

'A what?' Puzzled look.

'A spy.'

'But isn't that what we are?'

'Up to a point. But it's so unsavoury, sharing people's most intimate moments. It's like we're in bed with them.'

Grins. 'We should be so lucky.'

'Don't be facetious.'

'But that's life, Maggie.' Wilma's voice was tender.

'Not *my* life. I just can't do it, Wilma. Spying on people. Taking sneaky photographs.' Her voice wavered. 'Not any more. I *thought* I'd be able to carry on George's business. I talked myself into it,' Maggie turned a miserable face to her neighbour. 'Let *you* talk me into it. I thought I could be strong. For George's sake. For our children.' Tears welled in her eyes. 'But, now,' she hiccuped, 'G-George has gone. And my kids…the problems they've had…the way I've neglected them this past while…I've been frantic with worry. Kirsty and Colin, they're all I've got.'

'Kids…' Wilma commiserated, 'they're a worry are they no?'

Maggie was weeping now, shuddering sobs that racked her entire body.

'Och, come here,' Wilma pulled her close, enveloped Maggie in her generous bosom.

'I used to be so positive,' Maggie struggled for air. 'But since George died, I'm not sure about anything any more. It's like, overnight, all my certainties have evaporated. And you're right, Wilma, what you said the other day: I *am* feeble, a weakling compared with you.'

'You're not weak, Maggie, just different. And such a wee scrap of a thing, mebbe the surveillance wisna such a great idea. Why don't we concentrate on the legals for the time being, pass on as much surveillance as we can? Once we're down the road a bit there will be no need to knock our pans out on divorce work. It's way too time-consuming for the return. Then we'll concentrate on the insurance fraud. That's where the big money is.'

'But, Wilma,' Maggie protested, 'we're not in a position to turn away business.'

'We can fob them off. Say all our operatives are fully engaged at the moment.'

'But that's a lie, Wilma. The last thing we want to be seen as is dodgy.'

'Dodgy's my middle name.' Wilma grinned broadly. 'Call it creative thinking, if you must.' She changed the subject. 'Has that cheque come in from Cowies?'

Maggie raised a weary head. 'Yesterday morning.'

'Talking of cheques, now we're up and running, we should mebbe jack our prices up.'

'Wil-ma. We can't do that.'

'Why not? "Don't ask, don't get," that's what I always say. You try getting a quote from another agency and see how much they charge.'

'I suppose. It's just…making money out of other people's misery…'

Wilma's face creased into a grin. 'If we don't do it, somebody else will. It'll all work out,' she extended a comforting hand. 'You wait and see, Maggie Laird, six months from now you'll be a new woman.'

'Don't know if I want to be a new woman.' Plaintive face. 'I used to be so clear-headed. Going back to my Seaton job…taking on the agency…seeking justice for George. I had it all mapped out.

And when I ran down Jimmy Craigmyle I thought I was doing so well. But, then, Brannigan. I've hit another brick wall. I don't know whether I'm coming or going, Wilma. What I *really* want, to be honest with you, is to go back to the way I was before...' There was a tremor in her voice. 'All this.'

'Oh, quine,' Wilma's face was heavy with concern. 'Ye ken fine that's no gonna happen.'

'I s'pose,' Maggie stifled a sob.

'And right now,' Wilma heaved herself to her feet, 'the best thing for the both of us is get some sleep.'

'I'm with you on with that one,' Maggie followed her neighbour to the front door. 'Night, Wilma. And thanks...for everything.'

Wilma turned. In the light from the street lamp she looked almost wistful. 'Night-night, Maggie.'

# See them Games

'How long have I got?' Kym stood at the door in her coat: a black quilted knee-length job with a scatter of stains down the front.

Fatboy eyed the dishevelled figure with distaste. 'As long as you like.' Hurriedly, he checked himself. It was critical to keep the slut onside.

'But…' she hesitated.

Fatboy smiled encouragement. 'Just as long as you're back before teatime.'

'Only…'

'If you're worried about leaving the kids…'

She shrugged. 'I'm not.'

'You've left out their dinner, haven't you?'

'Yes. On the worktop.'

Fatboy winced. He could imagine. 'Away you go, then, have a dander in the fresh air.'

'But…' Nervously, she gnawed on a fingernail.

'Go on,' he gave her an impatient shove. 'Trust me. Everything's under control up here, and Willie won't have finished his business for ages yet.'

Kym took her finger out of her mouth. 'You sure?'

'Positive.'

She flashed him a nicotine-stained smile. 'Thanks.'

'Off you go, then.' Exasperated voice.

Still she didn't budge.

'Kym, what's keeping you?' For a moment Fatboy wondered if Kym had heard about the spliff. His lip curled. So what. Who in hell would believe her?

Her face clouded over. 'I'm skint, to tell you the truth.'

'Skint? You're having me on.'

'I'm not.'

'But, didn't you just get paid for...?'

'Aye,' she coloured. 'But I'd stuff to get.'

'*Stuff?*' He could imagine the liquor she'd have slid down her scrawny throat, that and the dope.

'And my benefit's not due till the beginning of next week.'

Fuck. After that first day, when the kids had run amok in Kym's flat playing their riotous game of Hide and Seek, they demanded a game every time the girl went off on one of her expeditions and Fatboy was left in sole charge. Not that he minded. The time he spent waiting for Willie hung heavy on his hands, if all there was for him to do was sit watching *CBeebies* with the kids or fiddle with his iPhone. No, Fatboy had his afternoon all mapped out: feed the kids, hour of telly, game or two, bit of slap and tickle.

'If you could mebbe see your way,' she wheedled.

He cut her short. 'Don't you worry yourself about that.' He extracted a couple of notes from his wallet and slipped them into her coat pocket. Then he had a quiet smile to himself. Cheap at the price. 'Here, get yourself a snifter. Just to keep the cold out, understand?'

Happily, Kym patted her pocket. She didn't have to think twice these days about leaving her charges in the big lad's care. Why, he even played proper games with them, they told her excitedly – Pass the Parcel, Hide and Seek, Blind Man's Bluff. And other games. Ones she'd never heard of: games with funny names like Tickle-Tackle, Lolly-Sticks, Criss-Cross.

Kym asked Fatboy about those games, one time.

'*See them games...*'

'*What games?*'

'*The ones you play with the kids when I'm out.*'

'*What about them?*'

'*I've never heard of any of them.*'

'*Pass the Parcel?*' He raised an incredulous eyebrow. '*Blind Man's Bluff? Where the fuck were you dragged up?*'

'No,' she struggled to stand upright, 'not them. The other games. What d'you call them – Lolly something?'

He laughed. 'Don't you worry your head about those. They're just daft things I made up.'

Now, Kym tugged the collar of her coat up under her chin. She pulled the door behind her.

# A Pair o' Honeys

*Simply the best…*

Maggie sat on the bench, her knees drawn up. She looked around. The space was vast. Steel beams bridged the vaulted roof space. Suspended by chains from stout metal stanchions, black and scarlet leather punch bags proclaimed 'Lonsdale' beneath the logo of a prowling lion. On one side a range of fearsome-looking equipment was arrayed. On the other, exercise mats lined up along a mirrored wall. Here and there, huge barbells lay abandoned. A row of bumpy black weights with sturdy handles sat on a low shelf. Like kettles on a range, her mind flew back to the old farmhouse kitchen in Methlick. In the middle of the space, a boxing ring took centre stage. Raised a couple of feet off the carpeted floor, it was bounded by scarlet railings. Maggie wondered when they'd stopped using ropes. Then she wondered – and not for the first time since she'd teamed up with Wilma Harcus – what on earth she was doing there.

*Better than all the rest…*

Maggie's head pounded. In the oppressive heat, she wilted beneath her wool blazer. She closed her eyes.

'Bad as that?'

Her eyes batted open. Wilma was standing over her. True to her promise, she'd brought Maggie along to Torry to show her the boxing gym she trained in. After that they were planning a visit to the pub where her neighbour worked. Wilma's hair was tied up in a topknot, a few spiky ends sticking out. She was kitted out in a pair of knee-length black Lycra leggings and a fluorescent vest top, a rolled-up towel round her neck.

'Wow,' Maggie looked up admiringly. 'You look different. And haven't you lost weight?'

Wilma stuck out her tongue. 'Took you long enough to notice.'

'Oh, Wilma, I'm sorry. It's just we've been so busy this past while.'

'You can say that again.'

'So this is what you've been up to?'

'Too right. I reckoned if *you* needed a MOT, then *I* was in want of a full fucking service.' Wilma covered her mouth. 'Pardon my French.' She changed tack. 'What d'you reckon to this, then?'

'It's very…interesting.'

'Interesting? It's fuckin…' Wilma cast a toned arm around, '…amazin.'

'Agreed. I've never seen anything like it.' That was true, at any rate. 'And you can fairly do the moves.'

'D'you think?' Wilma swelled visibly. 'I've tried the lot – Bodypump, aerobics, kettlebells…'

'So they're kettles, right enough?'

'Aye,' pulling a face, 'bummers.'

'They'll be putting *you* in the ring next.'

'Not on your bloody life. You should see the young lads go at it, though. Knock hell out of one another. I'll stick to my punchbag, thank you.'

Maggie eyed the things. 'They look terrifying.'

'Challenging, the coach calls em. He's a fuckin challenge an aw'. Seriously, though, they're heavy going, them things. Good practice, mind you. Might even come in handy,' Wilma gave a stage wink, 'in our line of work.'

Maggie recoiled. 'I sincerely hope not.'

'Talk of the devil.' A man appeared at her elbow: thickset, shaven-headed, heavily tattooed. He was dressed in vest top, tracksuit bottoms and boxer's boots.

'Who's yer pal?' he enquired.

Wilma grinned. 'My neighbour, Joe – Maggie Laird.'

'Pleased to meet you.' He offered a wide smile, the handshake so firm Maggie could hear her knuckles crack.

'And you.' Covertly, she inspected the damage.

'Have ye come tae join up?'

'No. I mean, Wilma's obviously thriving on it, but...'

'Come on, hen,' Joe clamped Maggie's arm in an enthusiastic grip and positioned her in front of a punch bag. 'Show us what yer made of.'

She eyed the thing. Threw a feeble punch.

'Use both hands,' he encouraged. 'Like so.' She caught a whiff of sweat, as Joe's fists flew. 'Come on. Right, left. Right, left.'

Maggie tried to pretend it was Brannigan. She threw her weight into it.

'That's better. Can ah sign ye up, then?'

She turned. 'Another time, maybe.'

Over Joe's muscled shoulder, Wilma heaved with laughter. She caught Maggie's look and composed herself hastily. 'I'll away and get changed.'

## X

'I got the idea in here, as a matter of fact.'

The pair were sitting in the pub where Wilma worked, just around the corner from the boxing gym, two glasses of wine on the table in front of them.

'How so?'

'There's these lads come in, regular, like. They go to the gym two or three times a week.'

'So that's what you call work? Cosying up to fit young boxers?'

'Dinna fancy them. Most o' them, anyhow. There's this one fella, mind,' Wilma threw Maggie an evil grin. 'I'd chap the paint aff his door any day.'

Maggie giggled. 'Don't want to know. But you were about to tell me...'

'Never paid much attention to them, only a few months back they were chaffin awa, having a laugh over some new class that had started up. For quines, apparently. My nose was botherin me, so I asked them what it was all about.'

'And?'

'I ended up signing on.'

'You make it sound like joining the army.'

'S'not funny.'

'I'm sorry. It's just, well, until tonight I couldn't quite see you...'

'Neither could I.' Wilma adjusted her top. 'I tried Weight Watchers, way back. Couldna hack it. All that queuing up to get weighed. Havin to fess up to eating a fuckin Crunchie bar, for Chrissake. I mean,' Wilma cast her eyes to the heavens, 'get a life.'

Maggie suppressed a giggle.

'Plus them classes cost a bomb. Fiver a throw. You could buy yourself a bottle o' wine for that. Cheers!' She raised her glass, took a mouthful. 'And it's worked, hasn't it?'

'Absolutely.'

'Now you've seen the place, d'you fancy coming along sometime? Not that you need to lose weight or anything. But,' she hesitated, 'it fair gets stuff out your system.'

'You think I need to?'

'Mebbe. You have to admit, Maggie, you can be a bit...'

'What?'

'Oh,' Wilma puzzled, 'Canna mind the word. But you fair take a running jump at things.'

'Well, if I'm going to get justice for George – not that I'm getting anywhere fast on that front – I have to be proactive.'

'I know. And I'm not criticising.' She laid a consoling hand on Maggie's arm. 'Call it friendly concern.'

Maggie brightened. 'Thanks, Wilma.'

'Anyhow, back to the gym. Once I'd been going a few weeks, I wasn't so hungry, like, in the evenings. Cut back on the chocolate bars and the fizzy drinks. Mind you,' she rolled her eyes, 'I'd kill for a poke of chips and curry sauce right this minute.'

'Well it's certainly done the business.'

'Ta. And talking about business, don't look now,' she whispered, 'but see those two fellas over there?'

Maggie strained forward. 'Where?'

'Ssssh! Over there, at the bar.'

She followed Wilma's eyes.

'Pair o' honeys, are they no? Makes thon two that came round to you look like pin-ups.'

Maggie pulled a face. 'I'd almost forgotten about them.'

'Well, seems one o' that pair just got discharged. Been in here since having a bevvy.'

'So?'

'Blootered they are. Rabbiting on about Peterhead. Said the fella been sent down for doing drugs.'

'I'm not following you.'

'They're just the sort might be able to find yer man.'

'Brannigan, d'you mean?'

Wilma beamed. 'On the nail.'

'Oh, Wilma. I'd almost given up hope. So why didn't you...?'

'Maggie,' the smile vanished from Wilma's face, 'I work here. Remember?'

'Oh. I get it. You can't go snooping on the clientele.'

'Clientele? I've never seen the buggers before in my life. All the same, I'd better not chance it. But there's nothing to stop you.'

'Me?' Maggie shrank back. It was one thing bearding James Gilruth, but this was in a different category altogether.

'Go on,' Wilma elbowed her in the ribs.

*Oh, the hell with it!* Maggie squared her shoulders, rose to her feet. 'I'll get us a couple of bags of crisps,' she said in a voice that was far too loud.

### X

'Hiya,' Maggie sidled up to the two men propping up the bar. 'How ye doin?' She adopted what she hoped was a local accent.

The shorter of the two ran bloodshot eyes down Maggie's body and up again. 'Wha's askin?'

She scrambled for a name. Any name. 'Elaine,' she flashed a winning smile.

'Jockie.' He slithered off his bar stool. Drew himself up to his full five feet six. 'Buy ye a drink?'

'No…really…thanks all the same. I only came up for a packet of crisps.'

Jockie draped a sweaty arm around her shoulders. 'Come on, Elaine, let that bonny hair doon. Ah'm celebratin the day wi ma mate Wullie here.'

*Bingo!* Maggie's spirits lifted. This guy had to be the ex-con. 'Red wine, then?' Coy look. 'Don't mind if ye do.'

'Who's yer pal?' His drinking partner, who'd been morose till then, yanked a bullet head in Wilma's direction.

'Oh,' Maggie thought on her feet. 'You mean…Heather?'

'Come over an join us,' a large hand with tattooed knuckles waved in Wilma's general direction.

*Make an excuse.* 'She can't.' Loud voice. 'She's newly married.'

'Fine-lookin wumman.' Laboriously, Wullie moved to rise from his stool.

Maggie looked over at Wilma. Even slimmed down, she struck a commanding figure. 'And pregnant.' She saw Wilma's shoulders start to heave. Didn't dare catch her eye. 'Heather's not drinking. Sorry.'

The big man's eyes narrowed. 'There's twa glasses on thon table.'

'Yes,' Maggie lied. 'And they're both mine. I've had a lousy day.' Out of the corner of her eye she caught Wilma shaking with mirth, then making a dash for the ladies toilet.

For a long moment, Wullie's large frame hovered in mid-air, then he slumped comatose over the bar, head on crossed arms, the sleeves of his bomber jacket soaking up puddles of spilt beer.

'He OK?' Maggie would have felt more comfortable with Wilma at her back.

Jockie shrugged. 'Jist tired. We've been in here a fair while.'

'How about you?' Suggestive voice.

He raised his pint glass. 'Rarin tae go, doll. Fancy a change o' scene?'

*Help!* Maggie had a sudden urge to wee. There was still no sign of Wilma. She couldn't still be in the Ladies, surely. She took several deep breaths. 'There's this guy I went out with couple o' times. Took me to a great pub somewhere round here.' She batted her eyelashes. 'We could mebbe go there.'

'Aye? What's it called?'

'That's just it,' Maggie put a hand to her brow. 'I've a terrible memory for names.'

'Whereaboots is it, then?'

She rolled her eyes. 'And places.' *Keep pushing.* 'But the guy I was telling you about, you might have come across him. Brannigan was his name. Place I'm talking about was his local.'

'Bobby?' The wee man swayed on his feet, steadied himself against the bar. 'That wha ye mean?'

Her heart pounded. 'I guess. Can't be many o' those in Aberdeen.' She leaned in close. 'You in touch?'

'Huvna seen him this past while.' She was met by a mouthful of bad breath.

'Oh,' Maggie was gutted. So near and yet so far.

'Hud a wee bit o' bother, Bobby. Hud tae keep oot o' the public eye.' Jockie tapped the side of his nose. 'If ye ken whit ah mean. That wis a while back, mind. Could be he sorted the thing. Widna ken. Ah've been oot o' circulation an all.'

'Shame,' Maggie tried her best to look sincere. 'About his trouble, I mean.' Wullie was snoring softly now.

Over Jockie's right shoulder, she caught a movement in the gantry mirror.

She zeroed in. Wilma, hair re-lacquered, lip gloss replenished, was making frantic hand signals.

*One last try.* 'That pub, the one he used to drink in, what was the name of it again?'

Jockie's eyes glazed over. 'Canna pit ma finger on it. Ah mind it wis doon Saltmarket Lane.' He gripped Maggie by the arm, leered into her face. 'But there's plenty mair pubs in Torry, darlin.'

She loosed herself from his grip.

'Sorry, Jockie,' she drained her glass and turned to go. 'Another time.'

# You've Got it all Wrong

'Mr Plumley?'

'Doctor.' The man exuded casual affluence: sports jacket with elbow patches, needlecord trousers, Tattersall check shirt, spotted yellow bow tie. Talk about them and us! Brian looked down at his own washable navy two piece.

'Beg your pardon?'

'It's Doctor,' Guy Plumley cleared his throat, '*Dr* Plumley.'

Christ, these academics fair took themselves seriously. And them with all that leisure time, never mind the long holidays. 'Whatever,' Brian willed himself not to let his bias show. He'd put money down Guy Plumley had never done a proper day's work in his life, whereas he… Brian shook himself out of it, uttered a courteous, 'If you'd like to come this way.'

Plumley followed the detective through a security door, up some stairs and into a small reception room.

'Have a seat,' the DS indicated an upholstered chair.

The man sat down. He folded manicured hands in his lap. Brian registered that Guy's palms were perspiring. He sat down opposite.

'I understand you're a lecturer at the university.'

'*Reader*,' Plumley corrected, 'I'm *Reader* in Art History.'

'Right.' Brian couldn't think when he'd last read a book. 'Thank you for coming in, Dr Plumley.' He paused. 'The reason you're here is because we'd like to ask you a few questions in connection with the death of Lucy Simmons.'

'Yes?' Guy swallowed hard.

'I believe Lucy was a student of yours.'

'That is correct.'

'Was she a good student?'

'Oh, yes. Never missed a lecture. Took notes. Quiet, to begin

217

with. Didn't ask many questions.'

'That changed, then – her behaviour?' Brian prompted.

'Well, I wouldn't say *changed* exactly, so much as…' Guy wrung his hands. 'I wondered in the first semester if the girl was unhappy. Suffering from mild depression, perhaps. Then, after Christmas, she seemed to start taking an interest in things.'

'Like what?'

'Oh, let me see now. Medieval History, I seem to recall. Yes, the history of St Machar, that sort of stuff.'

'What else did Lucy take an interest in?'

'Oh, I really don't know…'

'You, perhaps?' Brian interrupted.

Plumley sat up straight. 'What on earth do you mean?'

'Exactly that. You see, Dr Plumley, we've been led to believe that Lucy Simmons had something of a crush on you.'

For a few moments, Guy Plumley sat in silence. 'I think you've been misinformed.'

'That's possible,' Brian's face was impassive. 'How long did you say you'd been a university teacher?'

'I didn't. But since you ask, about fifteen years.'

'Then I expect you'll have experience of that sort of thing.'

Guy snorted. 'It happens. I won't pretend that it doesn't. Not as often as you appear to infer. But yes, now and again.'

'And did Lucy Simmons have a crush?'

'Of course not.' Plumley studied his shoes.

'I'll ask you again,' Brian's voice was insistent, 'did Lucy Simmons have a crush on you?'

There was utter silence in the small room. Then, 'Yes,' the word was barely audible.

'Speak up.'

'Yes.' Plumley raised his head. He gazed, wild-eyed, at the detective. 'But it isn't…' He put his hands to his face. 'Wasn't…what you think.'

'How was it, then, Guy?' Brian flipped open the folder in front of him. 'You don't mind if I call you Guy?' He took out a notebook and pulled a pen from his inside pocket.

'Lucy was a lovely girl.'

'Fancy her, did you?'

'No,' Guy groaned. 'Not at all. Lucy Simmons was a serious girl. Studious, diligent – wanted to do well. During the first semester, she was so quiet you'd hardly know she was in class. But suddenly, after the Christmas break, she brightened up: started asking lots of questions. Too many questions, for my liking. Then she began to follow me around. It was at this point that I decided the girl was developing an unhealthy interest.'

'So,' Brian leaned in close, 'what did you do about it?'

Guy pulled a folded handkerchief from his top pocket. 'Nothing.' He mopped his brow. 'Lucy was very much her own person,' the academic looked up. 'Ambitious, determined. It would have been difficult to prevent her from doing something she really wanted to do.'

'Like following you?' Brian was fishing here.

Guy Plumley uttered a long sigh. 'I suppose so.'

'Following you home, even? Am I right in saying that you live at the foot of the Chanonry?'

'That is correct.'

'Which brings me to the question of your whereabouts on the day of Lucy Simmons' death. I understand you've already given a statement to one of our uniformed officers to the effect that you were at home that evening?'

Dumbly, Guy nodded assent.

'But just for the record, let me ask you again. Where were you, Plumley, on that Tuesday evening?'

'I-I was at home,' Guy stuttered. 'I told the constable that.'

'All evening?'

'Yes.'

Brian changed tack. 'Then let me ask you another question. You were going to tell me how it was with Lucy.'

'I was bored, I suppose.'

'Bored?' Brian eyed the man. The academic's face was the picture of misery.

'Yes. I've been in the job too long. No chance of a change,' Plumley rolled his eyes in mute appeal. 'Wife doesn't want another move, you see. The kids are settled in school, and not a hope in hell of promotion. Dead men's shoes and all that,' he uttered a bitter laugh.

'So...' Brian wished the bugger would get to the point.

'My wife...' Plumley went on.

Brian nodded once more. He reckoned he knew where this one was going.

'She... Well, she's not interested, if you know what I mean?'

The detective knew only too well.

'And besides, she's let herself go a bit, my wife. And...'

Coming from Plumley, that was rich, short-arsed little prick that he was. Brian drew a series of squiggles on his notepad.

'I know it was stupid, but...'

He stopped doodling, pen poised mid-air.

'When someone came on to me, I was up for it.'

'And that someone was Lucy Simmons?'

'No. No. You've got it all wrong.'

'Enlighten me, then.'

'It wasn't Lucy.' The man was clearly agitated now. 'Don't get me wrong, she was a beautiful girl, but we're well warned in our line of work,' Plumley broke off. 'It would be madness, don't you see?'

Brian nodded yet again. 'Go on.'

'It was the Dean's wife.'

'The Dean?' He reckoned he'd soon be an authority on all things academic.

'Professor Kowalski. He's Deputy Principal this year. Has to travel all over the place. So Marta...'

'Marta being the wife?'

'Yes, the Dean's second wife. A good bit younger than him. A bit of a girl, you might say,' Guy offered a sheepish grin. 'Been around a bit,' he eyed the detective. 'If you know where I'm coming from?'

Brian responded with a curt nod.

'I knew from the very start that I was fooling myself, that there was no future in it.' Once again, Plumley buried his face in his hands. 'But I just got caught up in the affair.' He lifted his head. 'It was fun. Did wonders for my ego. Made me feel a man again…at the beginning, anyhow. The clandestine meetings, the wild sex…'

Too much information, Brian decided.

'And then?'

'Then?' Guy bunched his hands into fists. 'I lost the plot, I suppose. Began to take stupid risks: dodging off work, ringing Marta at all hours, hanging around the Chanonry in the hope I might bump into her.' Guy's head dropped once more into his hands.

The silence hung heavy in the room.

Brian spoke first. 'And that's what you were doing on the evening Lucy Simmons met her death?'

Guy Plumley looked up. 'I'd been bathing the kids. I've got four,' he sighed. 'The mess, you wouldn't believe it. And then Lalage and I fell out. Something quite trivial. And my wife looked so bloody hideous, I took myself into my study for the evening. I've always got papers to mark, you see, or reading to do.'

'But you didn't stay there?'

'No. Kowalski was in Cambridge, giving a paper at some conference or other. I thought I'd just nip out for half an hour. I was hoping for a quickie. But I was out of luck.'

Brian returned a hard stare. 'I put it to you, *Dr* Plumley, that whilst you were loitering in the Chanonry, you might just as easily have happened across young Lucy Simmons.'

'No.'

'A young woman who, by your own admission, was beginning to make a nuisance of herself.'

'No.'

'A young woman who's continuing attentions might have cost you your job, your marriage,' Brian was in full flow, 'your affair, even.'

Guy was quietly sobbing now.

'You admit to lying to our officer?' Brian pressed on, remorseless.

Guy nodded.

'And earlier, to me.'

Plumley couldn't meet his eyes.

'I suppose this lady – Marta, did you say her name was? – can corroborate your version of events?'

Guy raised a tear-stained face. 'Do you have to? I mean...'

'We do. Yes. And your wife, of course.'

'My wife? Is that strictly necessary?'

'It is.' Brian felt a twinge of sympathy for the man. He'd seen this too many times before. 'Well, I think that will be all. *For now*,' he shut the folder in front of him with a snap. 'We may also ask you to take part in a line-up, Dr Plumley.'

Across the table, the academic slumped, face grey with fatigue.

# Northview Towers

Maggie slouched in the seat of her car. For the umpteenth time, she wished she drove something other than a large Volvo. It was way too big for her needs, a pain to park, and hardly inconspicuous. She'd debated asking Wilma for a loan of her Fiesta. But red? Maggie was thankful for small mercies. At least her vehicle was silver, one of the most common car colours, according to the surveillance websites.

She'd found a small car park ancillary to the low flats. The further away the better, according to the internet. She looked around. *Make sure your observation point is secure.* There were only two other cars in the car park, its exit clear. Maggie relaxed back into her seat. Didn't look likely she'd come under threat.

She glanced at the oversized watch on her wrist. She'd borrowed it from Colin. He'd handed it over without a murmur. Maggie's own was too dainty, and besides, if she was there for a while she might be thankful for its luminous dial. Don't be so stupid, woman, those kids will have to go home for their tea. Tea? She snorted. The looks of many of her pupils, they saw fair few nutritious meals for, Spar apart, the shops that catered to the residents of Seaton seemed to comprise nothing but takeaways. Not that Maggie could talk. Not these days. For weeks she'd been relying on ready meals to feed Colin. Bless! As long as his tea was on the table and his rugby strip in the wash, her son didn't complain. Col was so like his father in that respect. She sighed. George was easy-natured, even-tempered, not an unkind thought in his head. *If you're happy, I'm happy,* wasn't that what her husband always said? In such contrast to Maggie, whose mind worked overtime, who'd harboured during the years of their marriage so many angry, spiteful thoughts. *What a bitch!* Tears stung her eyes. Roughly, she wiped them away. Clocked the dial of Colin's watch. She'd only been there twenty minutes.

From where she sat, Maggie had a clear view of Northview Towers. She'd followed Willie Meston there by car on two previous occasions, and before that to another of the tower blocks. Although her initial surveillance exercise had proved unproductive, she'd determined to keep a weather eye on the boys. Willie's visits took place after school, sometime between four o'clock and four thirty. He always went on his bike. Rang the call system. Vanished inside, bicycle in tow. Seaton wasn't the sort of place where you left things lying around, especially something like that. Maggie was no expert, but the Meston boy's bike looked to her like an expensive bit of kit. Unlike poor Kieran's, a ramshackle old thing. She knew from her surveillance that the lad didn't live there. On both prior occasions she'd managed to sneak up close on foot, but all she saw when she peered inside was a bank of lifts. She'd had to scarper, then: once when she was waylaid by one of the school mums, the other time she'd spotted the community bobby from the school police office approaching from a distance.

*Cover the entry/exit point.* Maggie shook herself alert. Focused on the door of the high rise. Ryan Brebner had turned up that last time, shortly after Willie, no Kyle in tow. He too had wheeled his bike inside. She pulled a pad out of her handbag and consulted her notes. For a few moments, she ran back over the jottings she'd made on her previous sorties. Not that she really needed to. She'd been rehearsing the operation all night in her head.

Mindful of Wilma's instructions, for she'd finally confided her surveillance practice, Maggie picked up George's digital camera and fired off a couple of practice shots. She cupped the camera in her hand. It was lightweight, neat enough to slip into a pocket. But it had been expensive, she knew. She'd found the receipt with the other items the police had brought from George's office. She sighed. No wonder her husband had needed money to tide them over. She glanced at the dashboard clock. 3.55pm. She settled down to wait.

A small figure on a bicycle sped down Seaton Crescent and crossed the sea of concrete towards Northview Towers. Maggie craned her neck. The figure dismounted, removed a safety helmet. She watched as two fat pigtails dropped down the girl's back. The small figure depressed a call button, pushed the door open, wheeled her bike inside.

Ten minutes later, a huddle of boys rode across Maggie's line of vision. They didn't slow down, but pressed onwards towards the beach. She was beginning to despair when she spotted Willie. He rode up to Northview Towers and dismounted his bike. He propped it carefully to one side of the entrance.

Maggie wondered if it was a signal. She groped for the camera. Click.

Willie pressed the call button.

Click.

He went inside.

Not five minutes later, Ryan rolled up, alone once more.

Click. Click.

He too propped up his bicycle, this time on the other side of the main door.

Ryan reached for the call system. Maggie leaned forward in her seat. Craned her neck. Wished – not for the first time – that she owned a pair of binoculars.

Ryan slipped inside.

Click.

Maggie strained forward even further. She thought she could still see his small figure through the glass.

The boys had not long entered when a couple of lads in denim jackets sauntered across the forecourt. They tapped on the entrance then stepped through. Minutes later they re-emerged, joshing one another. Maggie fired off another couple of shots, just in case, her hands by now sticky with perspiration. *Stay cool.* She wiped them on her jeans. No point getting worked up over nothing. Those lads could have gone in on an errand, been laughing at a joke. Except she could have sworn she caught a glimpse of Ryan in the doorway.

Maggie was convinced that something was afoot. Her suspicions were confirmed when a steady stream of teenage lads, punctuated by the odd girl and a couple of underage mums pushing buggies, rolled up to the tower-block entrance. She'd seen enough of these young guys around Seaton. They tended to congregate at the heavily shuttered convenience store: lads not skilled enough to find work, not moneyed enough to own a car, not motivated enough to get involved in the Community Centre or play five-a-side football in the park. Poor sods, Maggie's heart went out to them. Compared with her own son, what chance did they have? They'd scant hope of finding a worthwhile job. Spent their days playing computer games or just hanging out. Small wonder they turned to dope. They might pick up a handful of poppers for the weekend, she'd divined. Didn't seem to touch the hard stuff, heroin and the like. Not yet. As for the girls, some of them would have had sex at fourteen, got in the family way at fifteen or sixteen, used their pregnancy to get on the housing list. They'd be stuck now in their high-rise flats, living on benefits. Maggie sighed. What a waste of young lives. Still…as she snapped furiously, she wondered how those young folk found the money to buy drugs when she could barely make ends meet.

The stream of callers slowed to a trickle. Maggie carried on taking photos. Every time the door swung open, she could have sworn she caught Ryan in frame. She was just lining up another shot when a figure loomed at the car window.

'What the fuck ye daein?'

Maggie's head whipped round. 'I was just…having a rest.' She slid the camera out of sight.

'Nae point daein that.' The woman's face was framed in the driver's window, the eyes darting right, left, right again in a sequence that was all too familiar. 'Ah've bin watchin ye.'

*Hell's bells!* Maggie swore under her breath.

'Open the windae, wull ye?' The woman rapped on the glass.

*No way.* Vigorously, Maggie shook her head.

'Ye fae the Social?' the woman spat.

'No.'

'Bailiffs?'

Maggie's eyes widened. 'No.'

'Ye're nae the filth?'

Maggie shook her head once more.

'Then the fuck ye sittin here fur?'

Maggie felt the car rock. *Hold your nerve.* 'I told you I was just...'

'Takkin photies o' wee weans.'

'No. Really.'

'Dinna gie me that. Ah seen ye fae up there.'

Maggie followed the woman's finger to a first-floor flat with neat net curtains.

'Ye can fuck off, d'ye hear me? Skelly bitch.'

Chastened, Maggie nodded. She turned the key in the ignition. Put the car into gear.

*Sod it!* She hadn't factored in twitchers. Not in Seaton.

# Tickle Tackle

Fatboy shuffled the kids into a circle. There were five of them today: three boys and two girls. They sat cross-legged on the floor.

'Fatboy,' one of the girls waved her hand in the air, 'what game are we going to play?'

'Dunno.' He assumed a fierce expression. 'You tell me.'

There was a chorus of: 'Pass the Parcel, Blind Man's Bluff, Hide and Seek!' The kids jumped up and down, joshing for attention.

'One at a time,' he shushed.

'Hide and Seek. We haven't played that for ages.'

After the chaos of the previous occasion, he knew the reason why.

'Pass the Parcel.'

'Naw. We done that last time.'

'Pin the Tail on the Donkey, then.'

That had been another disaster. The donkey Fatboy cut out of an old copy of *The Sun* was too floppy by far, and when it became obvious that the game wasn't going to be a goer, one of the wee boys decided to use the pin as a weapon instead. He lunged and jabbed at the others until he managed to draw blood. There were tears, and Fatboy had to bribe the lot of them with sweets to get them to calm down. After that debacle, he reverted to the old games, the tried and tested ones, sometimes a round or two of Snap to ring the changes. But after a few weeks, the children got fed up with all of those, so Fatboy was forced into making up games of his own.

He looked down at the expectant faces. 'How about one of *my* games?' he suggested with a sly grin.

Two of the boys nudged one another.

Fatboy wiped the grin off his face. 'What's up with you pair?'

'We don't want to play.'

'Why not?'

'Don't like your games,' one of the boys offered.

'Aw,' Fatboy wheedled. 'Come on.'

'Naw.' The other child's eyes slid away.

'Why can't we play Hide and Seek?' the wee girl again.

Fatboy's eyes narrowed to slits. 'Because you can't, that's why.'

'But...'

'Right, you lot,' he held up his hands, 'settle down now. We're going to play Tickle Tackle.'

'Aw...'

'OK,' Fatboy's jaw was set. 'Sit still, the lot of you. You remember the rules. Whoever wins gets a sweetie. Whoever loses gets duffed up next door.' He flexed his muscles. The wee girls sniggered behind their hands. They weren't quite sure what was involved in a duffing up. They knew it was something only boys did, but they weren't that bothered. On the odd occasion one of them lost, they'd get a goodie bag instead.

In Kym's bedroom, clothes were strewn over the stained carpet. Among them, empty cider bottles and crumpled beer cans kept company with discarded cigarette cartons and ancient crusts of bread. Thin curtains were drawn against the daylight, the air in the small room fetid with a cocktail of liquor and smoke and sweat. On the rumpled bed, Kyle Brebner lay curled, Fatboy stretched out alongside him. That day's game of Tickle Tackle had ended up with the wee lad losing out, and it had fallen to Kyle to be duffed up. Not that Kyle minded. Happily, he allowed himself to be led through to Kym's bedroom. The other four kids were settled now on the manky rug, *Cbeebies* belting out on the telly.

'Tickle, tickle,' Fatboy's fingers caught Kyle under his arms.

'Stop it,' the wee boy squirmed.

'Tickle, tickle,' the probing fingers wormed their way into the Kyle's ears.

'No... No!' The child squealed with laughter.

The fingers were behind his knees now. Kyle scrambled off the bed and made a dash for the door.

'Gotcha,' Fatboy grabbed him and wrestled him back onto the bedclothes. He tickled the soles of Kyle's feet. Wormed his fingers between the wee lad's toes.

Fatboy hadn't tried this on with any of the girls yet. It might only be a bit of slap and tickle, but even the littlest of the wee lassies that came in Kym's house looked old beyond her years, way too streetwise for him to engage with. Not that he was a pervert. He'd seen plenty of that sort of stuff online. Read the odd case reported in the papers: some guy getting banged up for interfering with wee girls. Sent not to Peterhead, but shunted down to Glasgow to keep company with the real head-bangers in Barlinnie. Fatboy shuddered. Nor was he a shirt-lifter. All he wanted was a bit of friendly contact. Still, he'd resolved to keep his recreational activities strictly to the boys.

Kyle was beginning to look bored, but Fatboy was having a whale of a time. 'Do you give in yet?' he demanded.

'Give in,' Kyle lay panting, for a few moments, trying to catch his breath. He rolled over towards Fatboy. 'My turn now.'

The wee lad's eyelids were beginning to droop. Fatboy drew the soiled bedcovers up. Gently, he tucked them around the little boy. Fatboy closed his eyes. Slid a hand down his trousers. Gave his cock a jerk or two. He lay there for some minutes, fondling himself. Then he inhaled deeply and let his breath out in a slow stream.

There was a clatter from the next room. Fuck it! The kids were getting bored. He'd better make a move. And besides… He took a squint at his watch. It wouldn't be long before Kym was back. And he wouldn't want to arouse the girl's suspicions. Wasn't the whole point of using the slag's place to keep him out of trouble?

Reluctantly, he extracted his hand. Gave it a cursory sniff.

Fatboy grinned. He didn't know what he was worrying about. Kym was usually well out of it by the time she got back.

All the same, even an alky like her must have the odd lucid moment. There was no point in pushing his luck.

# VI

# Brannigan

'Mind if I join you?'

The man looked up. He was small, hair slicked back off a bony face, shirt collar too big for his neck. 'Wha's askin?'

'Maggie Laird.' *Get yourself installed.* She dropped onto the seat opposite. Smiled politely. 'How do you do?'

The wee man regarded Maggie, eyes flicking back and forth between her own. They settled, finally, on her forehead. 'Nane o' your fuckin business how ah'm daein.'

*Make small talk.* 'They tell me you're a regular here.'

'They? Who's "they"?'

*Be circumspect.* 'Friends of yours.'

'What freends?'

*Establish a connection.* 'In the Drouthy Duck.' Oh, hell, you shouldn't have let that out.

'Ach,' the man spat, 'ye dinna want tae listen tae a load o' ex-cons.'

'No?' *In for a penny.* 'Aren't you one yourself?'

He threw her an evil look.

*Dammit!* Maggie cursed inwardly. This was her big opportunity, maybe her only opportunity, to beard the man. She'd been cock-a-hoop when, finally, she pinned down the pub that Brannigan habituated. And yet, in spite of all she'd read, the careful pre-planning that had preceded this meeting, there she went again, going for the jugular.

She regrouped. 'Mr Brannigan, isn't it?'

'Wha telt ye ma name? These freends again?'

Maggie nodded.

'So,' the wee man jeered. 'What if ah am?'

'The reason I'm here is...' she paused.

Brannigan eyed her warily.

*Keep it vague.* 'I wanted to ask you something.'

'An ah want tae drink ma pint in peace,' Brannigan drained his glass and set it down with a clatter.

'It won't take a minute.'

'Forget it.'

Maggie eyed the empty glass. 'Maybe I could get you another?'

'Pint of heavy. Don't mind if you do.'

X

'As I was saying…'

Brannigan took a deep slurp of his beer. 'Ye said ye wanted tae ask me somethin,' he rolled his eyes. 'Ask away.'

*Oh, well, too late now.* She took a deep breath. 'Do you remember a drugs trial?'

'Trial?' Brannigan studied his pint. 'Naw.'

'You sure?'

He shrugged. 'There's trials every day o' the week.'

'This one was special.'

'Special? How?'

'Judge threw it out.'

Brannigan cocked his head. 'That right?'

'You know it is.'

The man's lip curled. 'What if ah dae?'

'Thought you might,' Maggie continued. 'Seeing as you were the star witness.'

'Star?' Brannigan sneered. 'Aye, that'll be right.'

'In fact, it was your evidence, was it not, that brought the thing down?'

'Ye're talkin through a hole in yer heid,' Brannigan sneered. 'Case got thrown out fair an square.'

'Fair and square?' Maggie's hackles rose. 'Is that what you call it? Lying in the witness box? Wrecking people's lives?'

'Now, come oan. You accusin me o' perjury?'

'Yes,' she leaned across the table, 'that's precisely what I'm doing.'

Brannigan took a swill of his beer. 'What aboot thon tape?'

'The one that was turned off?'

'Aye. In the interview room.'

'I know all about that. It's you I'm asking.'

'Sae what if it wis ma test-i-mony?' He wiped his mouth with the back of his hand.

Maggie lowered her voice. 'I don't suppose you gave a moment's thought to the consequences?'

'Such as?'

'The repercussions for those two policemen: the effect the outcome of your testimony had on their careers, their families, their lives?'

'What's it tae you?'

'My husband was one of those officers.'

'Aye?'

'George Laird.'

'Thon sergeant?'

'Yes.'

'Fuckin filth. How wid ah give a shite fur ony o' them?'

'Because he's dead,' Maggie said softly.

'Dead? How?'

'Heart attack.'

'Naethin tae dae wi me, missus. It's no as if ah hit him ower the fuckin heid wi a hammer.'

Her eyes blazed. 'You might as well have.'

'How?'

'Because it was the stress of the whole thing that killed him.'

'Well, ye can fuck aff oot o' here,' Brannigan made to rise.

'Hold on.' Maggie changed tack. A confrontation was precisely what she'd been hoping to avoid.

Brannigan sat back in his seat.

'You got kids?'

'Four,' he fingered his glass.

'So you'll know...'

'Ah dinna see them. Ah'm divorced.'

'I've got two myself.'

'That right?' Disinterested voice.

'Yes. Their dad's death has affected them badly.'

Brannigan shrugged. 'Happens.'

'I was hoping you'd be able to help.' She gazed at the man in mute appeal.

'Me? How?'

'By owning up.'

Brannigan guffawed. 'Put ma hauns up tae fingerin the filth? Ye're aff yer fuckin heid.'

'A man's dead. And if you had any decency...'

'Decency is it now?' Bobby Brannigan bared a mouthful of bad teeth. 'Well, ah've a wee suggestion fur ye.'

'What's that?' Maggie leaned forward.

'Ye can dae the decent thing an fuck aff.'

# A New Development

Allan Chisolm pushed through the door of the Briefing Room. 'Listen up, you lot,' he addressed the detectives seated round the table, 'we have a new development in the Simmons case.'

'What's that, sir?' Douglas Dunn strained forward eagerly.

The inspector scowled. 'When I have everyone's attention I'll be happy to tell you.'

There was a scuffling of papers. Backs straightened in seats. Someone aimed an empty Polystyrene coffee cup at a waste paper basket.

Chisolm waved a folder in the air. 'Interim report has come back from the lab.'

'And?' Dave Wood queried.

The DI strode forward. 'Bad news, I'm afraid.' He pulled out a chair. 'It's inconclusive.'

An audible sigh ran round the room.

'Shit and fuck,' a male voice muttered.

'Tests indicate Lucy Simmons was a healthy young woman, other than – so the parents informed us – the girl had a minor heart defect at birth: one of her heart valves was narrower than normal.'

'So could that...?'

'Who knows? The doctors decided no treatment was necessary at the time, and according to the parents, Lucy has had no associated problems since – no shortness of breath, no high blood pressure, no abnormal heartbeat, nothing. That was one thing. Probably not enough to kill her on its own,' Chisolm paused, 'but could have been a contributing factor. The only apparent sign of injury on the girl was the contusion to the head.'

'But,' Susan Strachan interjected, 'haven't we already established that?'

'You might say so. But there's a problem: the samples Forensics have taken from that don't match up with anything at the scene, so they conclude Lucy's body was moved.'

'So she could have been attacked elsewhere and her body dumped?' Douglas threw in his tuppence-worth.

'Doesn't follow,' snapped George Duffy. Dunn was starting to get up his nose.

'By the same person who hit her over the head?' Douglas persisted.

'Same person,' Duffy qualified, 'or persons.'

'Pack it in, you two,' Chisolm intervened. 'Forensics haven't been able to establish yet whether Lucy was hit from behind or whether she fell and bumped her head on something.'

'There again, perhaps nobody moved her. Maybe Lucy Simmons climbed onto that tombstone all by herself,' Dave Wood volunteered from his seat in the back corner.

'That rules out the possibility of her having been bashed on the head, though,' Susan this time. 'And what about the arrangement of the body? Couldn't have happened by accident.'

'But we've no idea who laid her out like that.' This from Dave Wood.

'And the sexual assault?' Susan again.

Chisolm glanced at the folder. 'Gourlay has established that the lass was sexually active, but we know that. Minor abrasions to the vagina, but no genital bruising. No traces of semen present. No saliva. Not so much as a hair.'

'Christ,' Duffy again. 'Where does all that that leave us?'

Where, indeed? The inspector wondered about his team: whether they should have been deployed differently. That Duffy was a steady sort, a good man to have at your back. Wood? The DI had seen his type to often: the old brigade – plodding, resistant to change, they were being gradually pensioned off. Couldn't come quick enough, as far as Chisolm was concerned. Burnett, now there was a man keeping his cards close to his chest. Dunn, a bright spark. A bit full of himself, maybe, but he'd soon be taken down a peg or two. As for the wee girl, Strachan, she had the makings of a good detective.

'Whatever,' Chisolm's tone was resigned, 'Forensics have had to go back and take samples from other parts of the graveyard.'

'Don't tell me,' Douglas came back, undeterred, 'that will take another week.'

The inspector scowled. 'At least.'

'And that's before we factor in the cross.' Brian looked up from his paperwork. 'We don't know what the hell that's all about, sir. It's floored the lot of us, to tell you the truth.'

Chisolm's eyes surveyed the room. 'What's the story on the girl's phone?'

Brian straightened. 'No sign, sir.'

'And the tutor?'

'Waste of space. Plumley wasn't chasing Lucy Simmons. The twat was too busy fucking the Dean's wife. Plus he has a cast-iron alibi for our time-frame.'

'The young guy, then, any progress on him?'

'No, sir. Not a dickey bird.'

'Wasn't it a young guy called it in?' Duffy queried. 'Might tie up.'

'Or it could be coincidence,' Douglas put his oar in.

'Probably perfectly innocent,' Susan added. 'Some poor kid taking a shortcut. Plus the perp is more likely to be someone much closer to home: a family member, for instance, or someone Lucy was actually in a relationship with.'

'Whatever. Till Forensics get their finger out, this young guy is all we've got. So get yourselves out there and find him. If he's involved in this we'll nail the bastard.'

# Need a Wee

'Need a wee.'

'How can you need a wee?' Kym demanded. 'You just had a wee, no five minutes since.'

'Ah'm tellin ye,' the wee lad struggled up off the rug, 'Ah need a wee.'

'Well, you'll have to hold on.'

Kyle positioned himself alongside the settee, hopping from one foot to the other. 'Ah need. Honest.'

'You can't. I just told you.'

'But,' a small hand tugged at her sleeve.

'Bugger off. I'm away out in a minute.'

'Kym,' the tug was insistent now. 'Ah'm burstin.'

She cut the boy short. 'Well, away and do it yourself.'

Shame-faced, the lad looked down at the floor. 'Ah canna.'

She turned her head. 'Ye can fair pee yer pants.' For a moment she was tempted to rouse herself. Washing Kyle's trousers and underwear would be a damn sight more effort than taking him to the toilet, but still, she couldn't be arsed.

A flush crept up Kyle's neck.

'Away to the toilet like I told you.'

'Kym...' Tears brimmed in the child's eyes. 'Ah canna go masel.'

'How no?'

Choked voice. 'The lavvie's ower high.'

'It's no *that* high,' she snorted. 'Big loon like you.'

The wee boy cocked his head to one side. 'It's no that.'

'What the fuck is it, then?' Kym uttered a theatrical sigh.

'Ah need a jobbie.'

'So?'

'Ah'm feart ah'll fa in.' The boy was bouncing up and down now,

239

his crotch cupped in both hands.

'Here,' Fatboy rose from his seat. 'I'll take him.'

Fatboy headed down the hallway, Kyle trotting in his wake. He pushed open the bathroom door. Wrinkled his nose. The laminate flooring was blistered and cracked, the bath piled high with dirty laundry. A rust-coloured ring made a statement round the bowl of the lavatory. No change there, then. It obviously hadn't been cleaned since his last visit.

'Right, wee man,' he tugged Kyle's trousers down to his ankles. He eyed the wee boy's Y-fronts, unsure whether to pull them down or simply reach in and free Kyle's willie. Undecided, he stood for a moment.

'Canna keep it in.' The wee lad's high voice cut right through him.

Fatboy decided to go for it. He yanked Kyle's underpants down to his knees. He looked around for something the kid could stand on. Didn't they have plastic stools or something these days? Finding nothing, he grasped Kyle under his armpits, lifted him up and dangled him over the bowl.

'Naw,' Kyle bawled, 'no like that.'

'Like what, then?' He set the kid down again.

'Ye hiv tae sit me on the lav but,' Kyle gnawed his lower lip, 'see an no let me fa in.'

Fatboy grinned. 'Would I do that?'

The boy balanced on the back rim of the lavatory, pudgy legs akimbo. He hung onto the plastic toilet seat with both hands, his forehead knitted in concentration. Fatboy heard a couple of plops as small turds hit the water. He looked on with detached interest as Kyle's penis dribbled a few last drops into the bowl. 'Finished?' Hands still gripping the sides of the toilet seat, the child nodded. 'Give it a shake, then.'

Furiously, Kyle shook his head.

'What's the matter?'

'Dinna want tae let go.'

Fatboy reached down between Kyle's legs. Gingerly, his fingers closed around the child's penis. For some moments he held it in his hand. Christ, it felt weird. He closed his eyes. Light, almost weightless. And smooth, the skin so fine, like that grass snake he'd come upon once behind the beach at Balmedie. Fatboy could feel it still, the way it lay in his hand. Abruptly, he let go of Kyle's organ. He opened his eyes. Lifted the boy off the lavatory. Set him down on the bathroom floor.

Fatboy tore off a couple of sheets of lavatory paper. Gave Kyle's bottom a cursory wipe. He flushed the toilet. Tugged up Kyle's underpants and trousers. 'Gonna wash your hands?'

'Naw, Kym disna bother.'

'Oh, OK, then.' He eyed the basin. Ran his own hands under the tap. Shook them dry. There wasn't any soap.

Fatboy made his way back down the hallway, tugging Kyle by the hand. Kym had gone off without a backward glance. Fatboy knew the girl had managed to get herself banned, finally, from the corner shop. The hike up to Spar and back, together with the time the slag would spend knocking back her booze, would guarantee him an hour's playtime at the very least.

The television was belting out some jingle or other. Fatboy plonked Kyle back down with the others. He settled himself onto the settee.

'Fancy a game, you lot?'

Small heads turned, apathetic. 'Naw.'

He smirked. 'We'll play one later, then.'

The kids were half out of it, gently sedated by whatever it was Kym slipped into their juice. And Willie wouldn't be early. Not this week. The Social had been at his door again. Willie's ma had been pished, the boy said, so the fuckers hadn't got in, but it was only a matter of time before they managed to pin him down. Fatboy sighed. He wished Willie hadn't mentioned the Social. It would be ages yet before Mike Meston came out of jail, even if he *did* get remission for good behaviour. And Fatboy wouldn't want to lay a bet on Mad Mike behaving himself in Peterhead, not with the amount of dope that got slung over *that* wall. Now he came to think about it, he wondered if he shouldn't let Mad Mike go. Young Willie was shaping up to be a good wee runner. Just so long as he didn't get any grandiose ideas.

He cast a benevolent glance towards the kids gathered at his feet. There was something curiously appealing about them. Though the children in Kym's care were for the most part undersized and under-fed, they possessed the clear eyes and soft features of small children everywhere and a spontaneity that was infectious. Warmth suffused Fatboy's chest. He'd come to rely on the kids for company. A smile played on his lips. They were his wee posse. A family, almost. His family. He scowled. Well, as near a family as he'd ever had. He took a quick dekko at his watch. Did a quick mental calculation. If Willie wasn't due at Esplanade Court for an hour yet, then by the time he'd done his trades and cashed up… Fatboy took another look at the kids. Maybe he'd roll a spliff first. Help him relax.

Just then, Kyle turned. Gave Fatboy a look. The kid had such an old face in his head, it was hard to tell what exactly it signified.

The wee boy yawned.

Forget the spliff, Fatboy decided.

'Fancy a nap?' he enquired.

Kyle scrambled to his feet. 'If you like.'

# More Holes than a Colander

Maggie was installed in a quiet corner of The Wild Boar in Belmont Street. Now she'd run Bobby Brannigan to ground, she was desperate to build momentum. Despite the man's bluster, she was sure that, with Brian's help, she could get Brannigan to open up. Then there was the niggling question of Colin. Her son had been more withdrawn than ever this past few days and, in the lonely night hours, Maggie's imaginings had taken on even more lurid forms. If she could only dispel for good and all the feeling that her son was somehow caught up in Lucy Simmons' death, she could focus on her mission to vindicate George.

Chary of establishing a pattern to her meetings with Brian Burnett, she'd proposed a change of scene. The Art Gallery was near enough to the shops on Union Street that anyone might spot them. And it wouldn't do for Maggie's name to be linked with Brian's. Not in that way. She grimaced. Not in any way. Still, it was critical to keep him onside. He might yet prove an indispensable ally in her quest for justice. Hadn't he already gone out on a limb on her behalf? And, besides, the police had resources she couldn't match as a PI.

Brian jumped at her suggestion. He'd backed off lately. Maggie's persistent questioning over the past weeks had seemed to engender a growing sense of unease in him, but his suspicions were outweighed by the strength of his feelings for her. Unlike the bright Art Gallery café, the Wild Boar was dark and intimate. The change of venue might afford the opportunity for a fresh start.

*Soften him up first.* Maggie smiled up at Brian. 'How's your investigation going?'

He covered his face with his hands. 'Don't ask.'

'That bad?'

'Between you and me,' he muttered through splayed fingers, 'it's got more holes than a bloody colander.'

'But, your suspects…that tutor you mentioned when we spoke on the phone?'

'Out of the frame.' Brian regretted now that he'd shared intel with Maggie.

'How about the young guy, the teenager?'

'Oh,' he clasped a hand to his forehead. 'Nothing's come of it, as far as I know.' He wasn't going to give anything else away.

*Thank God!* 'What about Alec Gourlay? Hasn't he cracked it?'

'Not yet. But why do you keep on about the St Machar investigation, Maggie? I hope you're not using what you get out of me to titillate those teachers of yours. Because what I tell you in confidence…'

*Mollify him.* Maggie leaned forward. '*I* could tell *you* things.'

'Such as?'

'There are underage kids dealing drugs in the high rises.'

'And how did you come by this nugget of intelligence?'

'I saw them with my own eyes.'

'This was happening out in the open, then?'

'No,' Maggie corrected. 'In the high rises, I just told you.'

'So you were inside the high rises…'

'No,' she was becoming irritated now. 'The *kids* were inside the high rises. I was outside.'

'Then how do you know they were dealing drugs?'

'Because I saw these young lads – girls too – going in, one or two at a time and…'

Brian interrupted. 'Where exactly were you when this was going on?'

'Sitting in my car.'

'So you were some distance away?'

'Yes, but I took photographs: the kids going in, the junkies…'

'You don't know they *were* junkies.'

'Of course they were. What else d'you think they'd have been buying?'

'Contraband fags? Stolen mobiles? Pirated CDs?'

'Whatever.' Maggie reached for his hand. 'I wanted to ask…will you look into it for me, Brian?'

He snorted. 'No way.'

'Why not?'

'Because it's guesswork, that's all it amounts to. It's evidence the police need. Hard evidence that will stand up in a court of law. Besides which, if these kids are involved in drug dealing, it's none of your business.'

Maggie snatched her hand away. 'Then whose business is it, Brian Burnett?' She banged her fist down on the table so hard that the cups rattled in their saucers. 'Yours?'

'Maggie…' Reasoned voice. 'Conducting amateur surveillance into suspected drug dealing could be construed as obstructing the police in the course of their duties.'

Her eyes narrowed. 'And who's likely to co-operate with them? Tell me that. Not the druggies. Not the child. Especially when their only experience of our proud police force is having the cavalry roll up with their body armour and their big red door rams.'

Brian threw up his hands in exasperation. 'All that notwithstanding, the way you wanted me to look into this company of Gilruth's, the way you're going after Brannigan, and now these wee lads in Seaton. You can't go sticking your nose into things that don't concern you. There are rules to be followed, you know. Laws to be obeyed.'

'There's no point taking the moral high ground with me. You're forgetting that private investigators aren't governed by the same ethical code as the police.'

'Oh, yes they are. Anyhow, I've given away quite enough information for today. Any progress your end?'

*Cut to the chase.* 'That's why I wanted to see you. I've found Brannigan.'

Brian whistled through his teeth. 'There's a turn-up. How did you manage that?'

'Detective work.' Triumphant smile. 'First, I managed to narrow the field some.' Maggie made a face. 'I've been in that many pubs I reckon I could write a guidebook.'

Brian sat up. 'You didn't go on your own?'

'Who else would I go with?'

'Dare I suggest your pal Wilma?'

Maggie tutted. 'Wilma's too well known over there.'

'You can say that again.'

'Now, don't start.'

He shrugged. 'Didn't say a thing. So…Brannigan, have you actually spoken to him?'

'Yes.'

'What did he have to say?'

'He said,' she paused for dramatic effect, 'fuck off.' She grimaced. 'Doesn't that say it all? I reckoned I was halfway there when I nailed him, but my grand plan seems to be suffering one setback after another.'

'Mmm. I see what you mean.'

'So,' Maggie gave a small shrug, 'where do I go from here?'

'No bloody idea.'

'But, Brian,' she leaned in close, 'I've been counting on you to come up with the answer.'

He had a rush of blood. If ever there was a chance to redeem himself in Maggie Laird's eyes, it was now.

'The only thing I can think of…' He broke off, distracted, as he caught a waft of her scent: light and floral. Like lilacs. Or maybe hyacinths. Or there again…

'Well?'

He jolted back to his senses. 'What was I saying? Oh, yes, the only thing I can think of is you could mebbe do a trade. Long shot, mind, but…'

'A trade,' Maggie butted in. 'How d'you mean?'

'A plea bargain, if you like. Persuade the authorities to offer Brannigan immunity from prosecution or even a reduced jail sentence if he'll admit to perjury.'

Her spirits soared. 'Could you go to the fifth floor with that?'

Brian recoiled in horror. 'No way.'

Wilma's words *don't ask, don't get* echoed in Maggie's head.

'Chisolm...' she persisted. 'Would he take it upstairs?'

'The DI? Doubt it.'

'Somebody else, then.'

He held up his hands. 'Nobody I know.'

'There must be some other way, surely?' she pleaded.

'Not that I can think of.'

The corners of Brian's mouth twitched.

'*What*?' she demanded fiercely.

He made a show of straightening his face. 'Nothing.'

'*Tell* me,' she insisted.

'I said...' He tried and failed to smother a laugh. 'It's nothing.'

'Brian Burnett, if you don't tell me, I'll...'

He caved in. 'The only other way I can see to get Bobby Brannigan to admit to perjury is...'

'*Brian*,' Maggie hissed. 'Spit it out.'

'Put a gun to his head.'

# Bugger this for a Pantomime

A dark figure loomed across the tarmac. Slowly, Wilma slid down in her seat. Purposeful footsteps approached. She sat very still. The footfall drew nearer. Wilma stiffened, hands splayed, fingers pressed hard into her thighs. Christ, they were massive, the flesh squeezed solid into the legs of her jeans. Fuck's sake! Her shoulders sagged. For all she'd been working out and cutting down, she still had a way to go.

The footsteps came closer. Wilma froze. Closer they came, and closer still. She held her breath, trying to quell her racing heartbeat. The steps paused, then passed behind her. She heard a car door open, then slam shut again. There was the sound of an engine turning over, the low thrum of an exhaust. Tentatively, Wilma raised her head. Watched as the tail of a dark saloon started to reverse out of the space two down from her. Was forced to duck again, sharpish, as the vehicle slid past the rear of her Ford Fiesta and accelerated away.

Wilma turned the key in the ignition and threw the gearstick into reverse. She executed a rapid turn just in time to see the Mondeo exit the ramp and turn right out of the car park.

Eyes glued to its tail, she followed – along Riverside Drive, over Bridge of Dee, left onto Great Southern Road. Where the hell was the bastard going? She'd expected him to turn right towards Stonehaven. There was a chop shop at Nigg, she knew. Hell, wasn't that where her Darren used to offload thon fancy alloys, them and the other dodgy stuff? This guy, though, he was working the system big time: him and his cronies reporting their cars stolen and collecting the insurance, then selling the vehicles on to a suspect body shop to be cut up for parts. He'd chanced his arm tonight, though – Wilma had a wee, quiet chortle to herself – taking the Mondeo out of wherever he'd kept it hidden for what was surely its last spin.

Up ahead a right-hand indicator flashed orange. Wilma pulled into the outside lane. As she entered the roundabout at Provost Watt Drive, a silver Mondeo shot past her on the other side of the road. She caught a grinning face, two fat fingers raised in a V-sign. Teeth gritted, she spun the steering wheel, tyres screaming as she performed a speedy U-turn. She floored the accelerator and raced back along Great Southern Road, managing to keep the rear lights of the Mondeo in sight. At Brig o'Dee, the traffic lights stood at red. Bullseye! She'd mebbe manage to draw alongside, fire off a couple of shots of the bastard sitting at the wheel.

She was still a hundred metres short when the lights changed. Shite! The Mondeo moved forward. Made a right turn. Wilma watched as it crept over the narrow bridge. She'd almost made it when a siren screamed. Cursing under her breath, she pulled in. Impotent, she watched as an ambulance hurtled out of South Anderson Drive and over the bridge to where she sat, fingers still glued to the wheel. Then... *Sod it!* She took a quick shufti at the paralysed traffic and jumped a red light. On the far side of the bridge she retraced her earlier route and crawled along Riverside, scanning the streets on either side for any sign of her quarry. There was none.

*Bugger this for a pantomime!* Wilma was forced to admit defeat. Her clapped-out Fiesta was no match for some of these fraudsters' fancy motors. Spitting with frustration, she cut through to Holburn Street and drew up outside a Chinese takeaway. Best get back on the internet, she vowed, pick myself up one of them GPS things. Save the business a load of hassle. On second thoughts, Maggie wouldn't be best pleased. Wilma pushed through the door. Placed her order at the counter: sweet and sour chicken, a portion of chips on the side. She grinned. So bloody what? Maggie need never know.

# Brian Spills the Beans

'Sir?' Brian Burnett stuck his head round the door.

Chisolm's head jerked upwards from the desk. He'd snatched a quick five minutes. Spent it ruminating over the St Machar investigation. Operation Cross Purpose indeed. He snorted. Farcical bloody name. And talk about cross purposes? What a fucking dog's dinner! They were banging their heads off the proverbial brick wall. Added to which, he'd let far too much time run by already. If he didn't get a result soon, the Executive would start poking their noses in. Maybe send in the Review Team. And not just the Executive. The Press were already snapping at his heels. There was only so much *following a positive line of enquiry* they would take. It wouldn't be long before they were baying for blood.

The DI blinked hard. 'Burnett? You wanted to see me?'

Cautiously, Brian advanced across the carpet. 'I've come by some information, sir.'

'About?'

'Drug dealing.'

The inspector frowned. 'Why don't you take it to Drugs, then?'

'It concerns a minor, sir,' Brian rubbed his forehead. 'The child's from Seaton. Heads up some sort of gang.' He coughed nervously. 'We've also had a new witness come forward. Lady lives down Don Street. She's put a bunch of kids on bikes close to the St Machar scene.'

'Do we have a decent description?'

'Fraid not, sir. *Just kids*, she said, *four or five*. And *just bikes.*' All the same, I was wondering whether this might tie in with our investigation.'

'You did, did you? And has it occurred to you, Burnett, that Seaton Park is heaving with kids, many of whom access it on bicycles by way of the Chanonry?'

'Sir.'

'And if they're not from Seaton, they're from effing Tillydrone.' The DI fixed his sergeant with a gimlet eye. 'May I ask how you came by this information?'

For a moment Brian hesitated, then, 'I picked up the intel from an acquaintance, sir.'

'An acquaintance, is that right? And what precisely did this acquaintance have to tell you?'

Brian fished into his jacket and took out a notebook. 'William Meston. Age ten. Class Seven pupil at Seaton Primary. Father Michael – aka Mad Mike – Meston currently serving nine months in Peterhead. Two brothers, both with form, presently living in town. The child remains at the family home in Seaton with his mother. She has a minor dependency problem. William Meston has a long record of truancy and misdemeanors. Social Services have been involved.'

'All very informative,' the DI interrupted, 'but where do drugs come into this?'

'I was getting to that, sir. We think until he was banged up, Mad Mike acted as a runner for some guy supplying drugs to the Seaton area. We've known for years there's been dope changing hands down there. Not on an organised basis. Just the odd punter doing a trade or two on the street. The minute uniform pick up on them, they move on. But this pusher isn't one of our regulars. He's only just crossed the radar, in fact. Might be an incomer to the city. Confines his activities to Class B stuff. And to Seaton. But he seems to have the place sewn up.'

'The kid… Meston, did you say his name was? What's he got to do with all this?'

'We believe young Willie has been acting as a surrogate for his dad. Keeping the billet warm, so to speak, till Mad Mike does his time.'

'And the child is how old, did you say?'

'Ten, sir.'

'Any other minors involved?'

'Only one that we know of: Ryan Brebner, also age ten, also from Seaton.'

'OK. And I take it when you say "we", you're referring to your source.'

Brian nodded.

'This source – it's reliable, is it?'

He felt the colour rise in his neck. 'Absolutely.'

'A snout?'

He fiddled with the knot of his tie. 'No.'

'Who, then?'

Brian fidgeted in his seat.

'If…' His superior officer leaned across the desk. 'And it's a whopping if –I'm to give any credence to this fairytale, Sergeant, I'll need full disclosure of your source.'

Brian was so short of breath he reckoned he might be having a panic attack. 'It's someone I'm…c-close to,' he stuttered.

'*Close*? Like your wife, you mean?'

'No sir,' he uttered a grim laugh.

'Who, then?'

Brian sat in silence. After a few moments, he spoke. 'Can you give me your assurance, sir, that it will go no further than these four walls?'

The inspector nodded. 'For now, at least. Though neither of us can be sure where this will take us.'

'Understood.'

'Well?'

'It's a Mrs Laird, sir.'

The DI frowned. 'That policeman's widow?'

Brian blanched. 'Fraid so, sir.'

Chisolm raised his eyes to the ceiling. 'Christ almighty.' He'd heard rumblings about the woman taking up the reins of the husband's business. She looked such a timid wee thing, too. 'You have corroboration, I take it?'

'From two different sources. Plus I've asked the community bobby from Seaton police office to keep an ear to the ground.'

Chisolm sniffed. 'Wouldn't put any money on that.'

'With respect, sir, I don't agree. They can be a mine of information, these community bobbies.'

'*If* they remember to pass the information on.'

'Point taken.'

'What about the dealer? Do we have a description?'

'According to my snout...'

Chisolm's lip curled. If he had a pound for every skewed piece of intel.

'Late teens. Well built.'

'Hair colour?'

'Lad always wears a hat: one of those beanie jobs.'

Chisolm groaned. 'Covers half of Aberdeen.'

'Just about. My snout says he's not a kent face. Fairly new on the scene, but savvy enough, sir, to stay well clear of the big boys.'

'Where does he hand over the goods, this guy?'

'The Castlegate. At least it's been the Castlegate up until recently, but he seems to have gone to ground.'

'Any idea where?'

Brian shook his head.

'Well,' the inspector stood up to signal the end of the meeting, 'can't say I'm knocked out with what you've brought me, Burnett.'

Brian averted his eyes.

'Nonetheless, Sergeant, we're duty-bound to follow up every line of enquiry. No matter how tenuous.'

'Agreed.'

'But make no mistake,' the DI glowered, 'we're dealing with a girl's death here. All hell will rain down on your shoulders if you've got this wrong.'

'Sir.'

'However, in the absence of any other leads, I'll have a word with

Drugs Division and have the Seaton connection checked out.'

'Sir,' his sergeant stood up, 'thanks for your time.' He stood, awkward, waiting to be dismissed. Brian was uneasy. He wished he hadn't listened to Maggie. Hadn't rung the DI. Hadn't put himself in the firing line like this. Too many heads had rolled since the debacle of that bloody drugs trial. Plus it was never a good idea to get yourself noticed too soon.

'You'll let me know, Burnett, if you get any more intel that may be of use to us in our enquiries from your...' for a moment, the inspector hesitated. 'Acquaintance.'

'Yes sir.' Brian wondered if there was significance in Allan Chisolm's choice of words.

He headed for the door.

'Oh, and Burnett, before you go?'

'Sir?'

'This source of yours, how did she come by the information?'

Clever bastard, Brian thought.

'She didn't say.'

# We Need to Talk

'Willie?'

The boy turned from the entrance to Esplanade Court.

'Can I have a word?'

'Ah'm in a hurry,' Willie slipped through the opening.

*Move it*! As the heavy door swung shut, Maggie stuck out a foot and squeezed through the narrowing gap. She caught Willie jabbing at the lift buttons.

'Fuck.' He jabbed one, then another, and another still. Swivelled on his heel. Made for the door to the stairwell.

'Willie,' Maggie hurried after him, 'we need to talk.'

'Aboot?' the boy headed up the stairs.

*Remember – be circumspect.* 'You know what.'

Willie reached the first landing. 'Naw,' he didn't turn. 'Ah dinna.'

'It's about what you've been up to...' *Keep it vague.* The figure paused, mid-step. 'In the high rises.'

'Dinna ken what yer talkin aboot.'

Willie recommenced his upward trajectory.

*What the hell*! 'I know you're dealing drugs,' Maggie's breath began to labour as she reached the second floor.

'That right?'

'Yes.'

'Who telt ye that?' There was no let-up in Willie's step.

'Willie,' Maggie insisted, 'I saw you with my own eyes.'

Willie slowed. 'Spyin, wis ye?'

'If you like.'

He turned his head. 'Thocht ye wis on oor side, like?'

'I am.' The third floor came and went. 'Where are you heading, Willie?'

'Nane o' yer fuckin business.'

*Draw him out.* 'It's to meet your supplier, isn't that right?'

'Naw,' Willie snorted. 'Ah'm awa tae pick up Kyle.'

'Ryan's wee brother?'

'Aye. Ah've tae collect him fae the child-minder.'

'Why isn't Ryan picking him up?'

'He's messages tae dae.'

Maggie glanced at her watch, hoping to call Willie's bluff, 'But it's not five o'clock yet.' *Gotcha*! She knew from Ryan that his mum worked full-time. Reckoned it would be nearer six before she'd be home. Esplanade Court had to be where Willie's supplier was based – how else could a ten-year-old source the supplies, handle large sums of money?

Willie threw a sly glance over his shoulder. 'She's gettin aff early the nicht.' He resumed his climb.

'It's one thing you getting into trouble,' Maggie panted as she passed the fourth-floor landing, 'it's quite another involving other people.'

'Like who?'

'Like Ryan. He's been helping you, hasn't he?'

'Helping?' Willie's face was blank. 'What wi?'

'With the druggies.'

'Dinna ken what ye're talkin aboot.'

'Ryan's your runner, isn't he?' Maggie persisted.

'Runner?' Willie sneered.

'Lookout? Footman? Whatever you want to call him. He was on the door at Northview Towers,' Maggie fought for breath. 'I've seen him other places too.'

'Yer talkin through a hole in yer heid.'

'You sure?' Maggie stepped sideways as a woman struggled downwards with an infant in a buggy and a toddler by the hand.

'Aye.' Willie used the opportunity to lengthen the distance between them.

'And what about Lewis? He's been here too. I've seen him.'

Willie stopped in his tracks. 'Dae ye no get it?' He turned. 'We come tae pick up Kyle, whichever wan o' us can dae it.'

The sign for the fifth floor passed in a blur, a tangle of graffiti.

'Which floor did you say it was?'

'Ah didna. Now button it. Yer nippin ma heid.'

'I saw you go into Northview Towers, Willie. And the other tower blocks. And I saw the druggies go in after you.'

'What dis that prove?'

*Call his bluff.* 'I've got photographs.'

'So?'

'I could take them to the police.'

Willie stopped. Looked down on her. 'You dae that. Ah'm no feart o' thon community bobby. Fuckin do-gooder, ma da says, jist like them social workers.' He started up the stairs again.

'I'm not talking about the local police office, Willie, I'm talking about Queen Street.'

'Ah'm no feart o' them fuckers neither.'

'But if you were to get in trouble...'

Willie scoffed. 'Ah'm aye in trouble.'

'Serious trouble. What would your parents say?'

'Ma ma widna be bothered.'

Maggie seized her opportunity. 'Your dad, then?'

The boy blanched.

By the time they reached the sixth floor, Maggie was mesmerised by the bright green soles of Willie's trainers.

'The police would want to know the names of your...' her breathing was agonised, 'clients. Your supplier too. They'd investigate where he was getting the drugs from and...'

Willie stopped dead. 'Ye widna.'

'What?'

'Tak yer photies tae the filth?'

*Bargain hard.* 'Not if you're prepared to help me, Willie.'

'Help ye? How?'

'I want you to get hold of Ryan too. Meet me later. Somewhere quiet, so we can have a proper talk.'

'Bit ah've Kyle tae pick up, and git hame fur ma tea.'

'Tomorrow, then. How about I pick you up at Codona's at half past six?'

Willie shrugged. 'Dinna ken.'

They reached the seventh-floor landing.

Winded, Maggie bent over, splayed her hands on her knees. As she fought to regain her breath, she heard a door open. She jolted upright. Caught a glimpse of a figure in a sweatshirt and trackie bottoms. Strained forward.

'Hi, Kym,' she heard Willie say. 'Kyle here?'

*Dammit*! So the lad might be telling the truth after all. She watched as Willie's small figure disappeared through the door.

Desperate, Maggie summoned a breath.

'Willie,' she called out. 'Tomorrow. Six-thirty. Don't forget.'

# A Dead End

In the Briefing Room, the Major Incident Team sat round the table. The meeting had been timed for 7pm. Susan Strachan yawned. She was supposed to be on day shift that week. Should have finished at four. She rolled her head to the side, first one way, then the other. Her stomach rumbled. Bugger! She'd planned to nip round to Markies, pick up a ready meal in the food hall. Something tasty. She'd had a bastard of a day. Now it looked like it was going to be another shitty takeaway.

'Let's get on,' DI Alan Chisolm straightened his cuffs. 'What have we got on the kids. Dunn? Elrick?'

Douglas was first to jump in. 'Steady progress, sir. I've been into the schools, primary and secondary: Tillydrone, Linksfield. Had good co-operation...' He hesitated.

'Do I sense a "but" coming?

Dunn nodded. 'No feedback just yet.'

'What about you, Elrick?'

'I've been c-concentrating on S-seaton, sir.' Willie Elrick had a tendency to stutter when he was put on the spot.

'Turn up anything?'

'N-not y-yet. But there are three or four gangs of k-kids about the ages the d-door-to-doors have thrown up. They hang out round the high-r-rises. Mebbe when they get f-fed up, take their b-bikes up School Road to K-king Street and St Machar Drive.'

'Good stuff. Anything from you, Wood?"

'Well...' Dave Wood twiddled his pencil. 'I thought I was onto something with the arrangement of the body, but...'

The inspector raised a quizzical eyebrow.

'It turned out to be a dead end.'

There was a titter from the far end of the table.

'If you'll pardon the pun, sir.'

'This isn't a laughing matter,' Chisolm scowled. 'A young woman is...'

There was a hesitant tap on the door. A young WPC peeked in. 'I've got the final report back from Pathology, sir.'

The inspector wrinkled his brow. 'Not before sodding time.' He'd never known a department take so bloody long to produce a final report. Way before he'd come to Queen Street, Allan Chisolm had heard that Alec Gourlay was scrupulous, but shit-hot. Nonetheless, this was taking procedure too far. The inspector made a mental note to raise the matter with his superiors at some future date.

Still, the constable hung back.

'Well,' Chisolm rasped, 'bring it here.'

Gingerly, the young woman advanced across the room. She slid a large envelope across the desk.

The DI extracted the report from the envelope and skimmed through it, casting the sheets of paper aside one by one. From time to time he'd pause. Pick up one of the papers he'd discarded. Check something. Read on.

From beneath lowered lids, Brian observed his senior officer, trying to gauge the DI's reaction. Other than the occasional slight wrinkling of the brow, there was none.

After a few minutes, Chisolm raised his head. 'That's a turn-up. Well,' he addressed the constable, 'off you go.'

Head bowed, the uniform scuttled out of the room.

'What's Pathology saying, sir?' Brian ventured.

'Well, it's not good news, I have to tell you.' Chisolm leaned back in his chair. 'Gourlay's conclusions are that the girl collapsed, possibly due to her underlying medical condition: the heart valve defect that was identified at birth,' the DI looked down. 'Pulmonary Valve Stenosis is what it says here. Or maybe a blood clot on the brain.'

George Duffy broke in. 'When Gourlay says "collapsed" is he inferring the victim died of natural causes?'

'Sudden Death Syndrome. It's not unheard of.'

Duffy sat back. 'No sir, but...'

'If you'll allow me to continue?' Chisolm's voice was testy. 'She hit her head on a gravestone. In Gourlay's view, the blow to the head wasn't enough to kill Lucy, but may have exacerbated the pre-existing condition. However, it would have rendered her insensible for a time and, after that, confused and disorientated. Forensics managed to find an exact match to the injury with a memorial over by the dividing wall between St Machar kirkyard and Seaton Park. Then Lucy crawled. There are no indications that she dragged herself – or was dragged – close to where she was found.'

'That still doesn't explain how she got onto that tombstone,' Susan volunteered.

'She might have pulled herself up onto it,' Wood suggested. 'For comfort, if she was distressed, to get off the damp ground.'

'Some bloody comfort, if you don't mind me saying so,' Douglas scoffed. 'Sir.' He corrected himself hastily.

'And how do you explain the arms splayed over the head, the legs spread? 'Going back to the report,' Chisolm shuffled the pages in his hands, 'the Pathologist also states that...' the DI paused for dramatic effect, 'he found no evidence of ligature marks or manual choke holds on Lucy's neck, nor any enlargement of the tongue. Nor the bloodshot eyes one might associate with smothering. He did, however, find minute red spots in Lucy's eyes. Petechiae, he calls them: pinpoint traces, caused when capillaries near the surface burst. That's not something he would have expected to see, given the other evidence at the scene. There was also evidence of minor bruising around the nose and mouth.'

'Bruising?' Brian pounced. 'So Lucy Simmons was mugged after all?'

'Not according to Gourlay. In his view, the pattern could only have come from a woman.' Chisolm's tone was reflective. 'Or even a child.'

'A woman?' Duffy echoed.

'Yes, Sergeant. Doesn't seem likely, does it?'

'No, sir.'

'To summarise,' Chisolm held the report in front of his face, 'the Pathologist has concluded that Lucy Simmons died from asphyxiation.'

'But if Lucy was asphyxiated,' Douglas interjected, 'why wasn't Gourlay able to pick up on it earlier?'

'Petechial hemorrhages are tiny, Dunn. I've come across them before. Takes a good eye and a strong light source to spot the blighters. Anyhow, in short, someone – not necessarily the same someone who lifted Lucy onto that tombstone – also obstructed the girl's airways, albeit without undue force.'

'But, sir…' Duffy scratched his head in consternation. 'A woman?'

'It's not beyond the realms of possibilities,' Douglas pontificated. 'Lucy might have swung both ways.'

'Oh, come on,' Susan moved to silence him. 'She'd just ended a long heterosexual relationship, and Melissa said…'

'There you are,' Douglas smirked. 'Maybe we should be having another chat with Melissa, or the other flatmate. What was her name again?'

Brian stifled a yawn. 'Sally Hay.'

'Seems pretty far-fetched to me.' Duffy again.

'Let me throw this into this into the mix…' Brian felt it prudent to contribute. 'If, as Gourlay predicates, the pattern may have been caused by a woman, couldn't it equally have been made by a teenage boy?'

'Now, there's a thing.' Dave Wood came suddenly to life.

'Any progress with the young lad?' Chisolm's gaze focused on Brian.

'No, sir.' He felt like a rabbit caught in headlights. Wished fervently that he hadn't opened his mouth.

'And the cross?' Susan chipped in. 'We've still no idea…'

'Ah, yes,' Chisolm interrupted. 'The cross.'

For some moments, the assembled company sat in contemplation, their thoughts on the young girl who'd been found lying in the morbid shadow of St Machar.

The inspector leaned across the desk and fixed his team with a hard stare. He was a hardened copper and yet he never ceased to be amazed at the darkness of the human mind.

'We have to find that person. Or persons. The person who found Lucy Simmons dead – or dying – in that graveyard. The person who violated her body. The person who stole her mobile phone. One thing's clear. At the end of this protracted delay, we finally have confirmation that we're investigating a murder.'

# VII

# A Kiss, Maybe

Fatboy shouldered open the door of the close. He'd got the address off his phone: one of several listed, but this was the handiest by far. Christ, he wrinkled his nose, the smell of pish would knock you out. He was tempted to call it quits, turn round and try somewhere else. But he didn't want to waste time on this wee diversion. He made for the stairs and carried on upwards to the first floor.

It had been a lark to him at first, horsing about with children entrusted into Kymberley Ewen's care: a means of passing the time whilst he was stuck in that dump of a high-rise flat waiting for Willie Meston to finish his business. But as the weeks went by, Fatboy had developed something of a proprietorial interest. Now, he considered the youngsters 'his' kids as much as Kym's. Notionally, she might be in charge. But once she was gone – out on one of her sorties – the children morphed into Fatboy's own little family.

With the exception of Kym's own children and his favourite, wee Kyle, the charges entrusted to the child-minder's care turned over at a steady rate. This was due in part to the turnover in tenants of the tower block. Other times the mothers would be too skint – or too out of it – to make it as far as Kym's door. The downside to this was that the boys in particular, with their baldy heads and grey faces, were beginning to look all the same to him. The way that Kym Ewen was heading, Fatboy reckoned it wouldn't be long before he'd have to move on from Esplanade Court. And if he did that, wouldn't it be good idea to keep tabs on 'his' kids? After all, he never knew when he might have need of them again. He'd toyed with the idea of marking the children out in some way – cap, badge, T-shirt – something to show they belonged. Too obvious, he decided. Plus the little bastards would lose them. No, it would have to be something more subtle: a mark of some sort, a small one, just to show where he'd been. Fatboy flirted with the idea of a tattoo. The number of tattoos some of these kids were flashing already – the older ones, that is – another wee one would hardly be noticed. But this would present logistical problems. He couldn't just haul a bunch of kids down a tattoo parlour.

The idea had come to him when he was watching an old movie, Netflix being Fatboy's default position when he got hacked off with porn. Now he stood in front of the door. With narrowed eyes, he regarded the lettering on the plastic name plate. Then he turned the handle and went in. A counter ran the width of the room. Against the far wall stood a workbench. An old geezer was bent over it, an eyeglass lodged in his right socket.

The old man turned, the strip light on the ceiling bouncing a pattern on his baldy head. 'Can ah help you?'

Fatboy shrugged. 'I'm not sure.'

The man removed the jeweller's loupe and rose to his feet. 'Is it a repair ye're needin?'

'Not exactly.'

The old guy crossed to the counter, all the while keeping eye contact with Fatboy. He slid one hand underneath.

Fatboy suspected a panic button. He readied himself to turn and flee.

The hand re-appeared, clutching a well-thumbed duplicate book.

Fatboy relaxed. 'I was wanting something made.'

The man's face lit up. 'A ring, maybe, young fella like you? That's no a problem. Ah'd be delighted, to tell the truth. It's no often ah get the chance to make anything from scratch. It's aw repairs these days.'

'Ring?' Fatboy scoffed. 'No fucking chance. I'm far too cute to get cornered by some slag.' It wasn't that long since he'd seen off the last one. Emma was still texting him, stupid cow. 'No,' he lowered his voice. 'It's something much more...' He floundered till the word came to him. 'Artistic.'

'How d'ye mean?' Suspicious look.

'A one-off.'

The milky eyes flickered, uncertain. 'One-off what, exactly?'

'Don't you worry,' Fatboy's tone was reassuring, 'it's nothing illegal. More a special…' He hesitated. 'Tool.'

'A tool?' The man still didn't look too happy.

'Calm down, faither,' Fatboy flashed a smile, 'I'll be paying cash.'

He reached into his inside pocket and extracted a folded sheet of paper. He spread it on the counter. 'It's a very simple design,' he explained.

The jeweller studied the rough drawing. 'Ah can see that.'

'But it will have to be compact,' Fatboy continued. 'No bigger than a biro.'

'Mmm,' the old boy stroked his chin.

'With a good, solid handle. And…' he hesitated, 'the handle will have to be heatproof.'

'Heatproof?' The old geezer's eyebrows shot up into his nonexistent hairline.

'And the shaft should be slim, with…'

'Hang on.' Horror was written on the man's face. 'It looks to me like a branding iron.'

Fatboy grinned. 'Got it in one.'

'But what's it for, exactly?' the jeweller puzzled.

'A-a…project.'

'Hobby, like?'

A sly smile played on Fatboy's lips. 'Sort of.'

'Pokerwork, mebbe? Ah mind thon stuff in ma granny's hoose…'

'Not pokerwork,' Fatboy interrupted.

'What then?'

Fatboy wished he'd kept his big mouth shut. 'More like a…' He struggled for inspiration, then, 'tattoo.'

'We-ell,' the old geezer deliberated. 'Ah dinna ken.'

Fatboy rested his bulk on the counter. 'You just said yourself that the design isn't complicated.'

'Ah did, aye. But it won't be the easiest job, havin to keep it that small, but…' He cleared his throat. 'Robust.'

'Nothing like a challenge.' Fatboy leaned in close, his voice filled with menace. 'So can you make the thing up or not?'

The old man's voice was filled with uncertainty. 'Ah'm no sure.'

Fatboy straightened. He flexed his arms. 'What's the fucking problem?'

'N-n-naethin.' The old geezer eyed him from beneath lowered lids. 'What ah'm sayin is, naethin ah canna work ma way roon.'

'Well, then. There's only one thing left to do.'

'Wh-what's that?'

Fatboy smirked. 'Agree an effing price.'

'B-but, a b-branding iron…' The man's eyes were out on his cheeks. 'What did ye say ye were gaun tae dae wi it?'

'Never you mind.'

'We-ell, it's no the sort o' thing…'

Fatboy's arm shot out. He grabbed the jeweller by the shirt collar. 'Listen to me, Grandpa, you said yourself the design was straightforward.'

'Aye.'

'And it's not going to take much in the way of materials, don't you agree?'

The jeweller nodded, mute.

Fatboy tightened his grip on the man's neck. 'So what is it you're going to do for me?'

The old boy's face drained of colour. 'Mak somethin up.'

He squeezed harder. 'And that something is?'

'A-a-a tool. Nae bigger than a biro. Wi…' The jeweller struggled for breath. 'A heatproof handle.'

'And?' Fatboy prompted.

'A wee cross on the end.'

'Spot on,' he relaxed his hold. 'A cross…' A faraway look flitted across Fatboy's face. 'Or a kiss, maybe.'

# Bottom Line

'Six per cent, you said?' Maggie sat in Marks & Spencer's café.

'Bottom line.' The young man opposite flashed a set of artificially whitened teeth. 'Could go as high as twelve.'

He'd wanted to come to the house. Said his office was being refurbished and, anyhow, his clients felt more secure talking large sums of money in the privacy of their own homes. Maggie had been forced to invent a lodger, propose meeting on neutral ground. For she knew otherwise. 'Granville Securities' was one of many names adopted by the fraudster she'd been retained to track down. And time was running out: its registered office unmanned, telephone calls going unanswered.

Once Maggie gained entry through deceit to the serviced block where the company purported to be based, the poor receptionist – Norman, he was called – didn't stand a chance. He'd chuckled when she said she was looking for Jason. *You and the rest of the world*. Stood stoically as, in a halting voice, she'd recounted her tale of woe: how she'd put a cheque in the post, realised – too late – she'd added an extra zero, absolutely had to retrieve the envelope before the cheque could be cashed. Norman had taken her by the elbow. Steered her to a near-empty office on the third floor. Looked on as she rummaged through a hillock of unopened mail addressed to a plethora of different investment vehicles. Thrown sympathetic looks when she turned a teary face, only to concede she may not have posted the envelope after all. Norman had even succeeded in getting the elusive Jason on his cellphone, retreating to a discreet distance so Maggie could untangle her affairs in privacy.

Now she asked, 'And this return is guaranteed?'

'Rock solid. We've been investing in this product for going on five years and never had an unhappy client yet.'

Maggie struggled to maintain a neutral expression. Mrs Cowie, her own client, had been first tremulous, then tearful, ultimately despairing. By this stage in her nascent career as a private investigator, Maggie had encountered the scenario too often: a retired individual conned by some wide boy. At the lower end of the scale it was the opportunistic knock on the back door: the 'tradesmen' charging inordinate sums upfront to tarmac driveways or lop branches, disappearing with the work half done. But this case was in a different league. The 79-year-old widow had been introduced by a fellow parishioner to a *soi-disant* financial advisor, who in turn had persuaded Mrs Cowie to withdraw funds from her underperforming savings account and reinvest in what he described as a miracle investment vehicle.

When an unforeseen emergency had caused the widow to seek a withdrawal, she discovered her pension pot had been virtually wiped out. The distraught woman had pursued every avenue to seek redress, had come to the agency as a last resort.

'But,' Maggie countered, 'couldn't the stock market plunge without warning?'

Blank face.

'What I'm trying to say is…we live in such an uncertain world: acts of terror, the price of oil…'

'You're so right. But market volatility has been factored in, and anything more…dramatic – that's where your FSA guarantee kicks in. Protects your savings.'

*Draw him out.* 'Isn't that limited to a certain amount?' 'Well, yes – 85K.' Sideways look. 'But that's a fair whack.'

'But you're proposing I invest my entire pension…' Maggie well knew the FSA guarantee had fallen to 75K per financial institution, but had no intention of letting on.

'With any investment there's always a small element of risk. But with this product it's tiny. And you know what they say…' Sly look. 'Nothing ventured, nothing gained.'

She nibbled a fingernail. 'I'm not sure.'

'Let me reassure you.' Jason leaned across the table. 'Do you think

271

all these other clients – doctors, lawyers, well-informed people like yourself, if I may say so – would have rushed to participate if the infinitely small risk wasn't far outweighed by the return?'

'We-ell,' Maggie deliberated, 'I'd need time to think about it. Do you have a leaflet I could take away and have a look over?'

'No. Sorry. Things move so fast in this business, we'd have a new product on offer as soon as the last one went to print.'

*Get something in writing.* 'Then you won't mind if I make a few notes.'

Jason's eyebrows met in the middle. 'Who did you say you got my name from?'

'Oh dear...now, who was it?' Apologetic smile. 'My head's been all over the place since my husband died. Most likely someone from church. Now, if you'd let me have a piece of paper?'

With some reluctance, Jason reached into an inside pocket, tore a sheet from a diary.

'So, six per cent?'

'That's right.'

'You couldn't just write that down for me?' Maggie made her hand shake as she offered her pen. 'My nerves have been that bad...'

Frowning, Jason jotted a note.

'Guaranteed?'

'That's what I said.'

'Would you write that too?'

Jason scribbled the word.

'And you're sure 85K of that would be protected?'

'Totally.' Jason's fingers drummed nervously on the tabletop.

'If you'd add that?'

Jason eyed her, obviously rattled. 'Is there anything else?' he demanded.

Maggie sensed she was pushing her luck. She smiled sweetly. 'Not for the moment.'

'If I've answered your questions...' He pushed the piece of paper and pen across the table. 'All I need now is a cheque and I can get that money earning for you right away.'

She rummaged in her handbag. Deposited on the table a packet of Polo mints, a pink comb, a sleeve of Kleenex pocket tissues. 'Oh, dear,' her eyes widened in alarm, 'I can't seem to lay my hands on it.' She rummaged some more. 'Don't say I've left it at home. Do you know, Jason,' she leaned in confidentially, 'I know it won't go any further, what with you being in the business you're in, but I can't tell whether I'm coming or going since I've been on these anti-depressants. Short-term, you understand, but...' Stricken face. 'If you could just help me by writing down your bank details.'

'Actually,' Jason countered smoothly, 'a cheque in the post would suit me better.'

*Oh, no!*

'But that would take days. And didn't you just say I should get my money earning for me as soon as possible?'

Those teeth again. 'Sure did.'

'Well, if you'll put the details down there...' She turned the paper around, slid it towards him. 'Bank sort code, account number.' She thrust the pen into his hand. 'Oh, and the full name on the account.' She watched as, chewing his lip, Jason appended the information.

'You're so sweet,' she slipped the pen and paper into her bag. 'And...' Coy smile. 'Me such a silly woman too, forgetting to bring everything I needed with me.'

Not half as silly as poor Mrs Cowie. It was almost certainly too late to retrieve the poor woman's savings. Still, if Maggie had an account number and a sample of the sleazebag's handwriting, she could pass them to Brian. Fraud would follow the money trail, and maybe Maggie's input would save some other vulnerable soul the same fate.

She stood. 'Thanks for the coffee.'

Jason got to his feet. 'You'll be in touch, then?' He extended a limp hand.

'You've been such a help,' she smiled broadly, 'I'm going to put a friend onto you.' *With a bit of luck, he'll nail you, you bastard.* 'And I'll transfer the funds to your account the minute I get home.'

# A Formal Complaint

The doorbell chimed.

Maggie started in fright. She still hadn't recovered from that last occasion, when the squad car arrived at her door. She took a judicious peek down the hallway. A dark-suited figure was visible though the glazed panel. Not a uniform again? Her heart sank. She'd be mortified to have the police at her door a second time. In full view of the neighbours too. Not to mention Wilma. Maggie could still see the shocked expression on her friend's face.

Ding-dong. It chimed again.

Maggie took another look. It wasn't a uniform. Definitely. And it wouldn't be one of Gilruth's enforcers. Wilma was insistent Maggie had seen the last of them. And nobody would mess with Wilma. Of that Maggie was now quite sure.

Oh, well. What was it her mother used to say? *Better be hung for a sheep than a lamb?* She tiptoed down the hall. Ever so slowly, she opened the door. Detective Inspector Allan Chisolm stood on the doorstep. Over his customary dark suit, he wore a gabardine rain-coat, the collar turned up against the driving rain. Maggie could hear a rush of water from somewhere close at hand. She looked up. The gutter was overflowing at the corner of the house, something else she'd have to get seen to. She uttered a small sigh. What next?

'Mrs Laird?' His eyes travelled back and forth between Maggie's own and settled on the bridge of her nose.

'Yes?' she struggled to hide her surprise.

'DI Chisolm.' He threw her a curt nod.

'What do you want?'

'We met…'

'I'd hardly be likely to forget.' The sensation of George's body lying stiff and cold beneath her own sent an icy shiver down her spine.

'The reason I'm calling is...' The question hung in the air.

'If it's about...' Maggie started, then abruptly stopped. The rumour mill in Queen Street worked overtime, she knew. What if Chisolm had got wind of some of the stuff she and Wilma had been up to?

Grim face. 'It might be better if we spoke inside.'

She eyed the detective. 'I'm sure it's nothing that can't be said right here.' Bad enough that the bastard had intruded on her last intimate moments with George without invading her home.

The inspector looked to the right, then to the left of him. 'Mrs Laird, I must insist.'

'If it's my neighbours you're worried about...'

Allan Chisolm looked down. 'No.'

For a few moments the two stood in silence, then, 'May I come in?'

'I suppose.' Maggie stood to one side. She didn't offer to take his coat.

The inspector stepped into the hallway. He was an inch or two taller than George, but Chisolm was carrying less weight than her husband. Maybe he didn't have a good woman to look after him, Maggie speculated. There were a few grey flecks in the dark hair, a deadness in the blue eyes. Something of the dark about the man, Maggie couldn't quite put her finger on what. She'd already been filled in on the new DI's background, what little had filtered down on the grapevine: that Allan Chisolm's success rate at Strathclyde had been phenomenal, that he'd won many commendations, that he was a hard taskmaster – impatient, demanding, didn't suffer fools. But not much was known, apparently, of the man's private life. What Maggie did know for sure was that Inspector Allan Chisolm had inherited something of a poisoned chalice. She smiled bitterly. She hoped he was up to the job.

The pair stood, awkward, in the narrow hallway.

'I'll get straight to the point. I've received information concerning a minor involved in drug dealing in Seaton.'

Well, Maggie thought, there's a turn-up. So Brian decided to take her seriously after all.

'I understand you have some involvement there.'

She brightened. 'I work in Seaton, if that's what you mean.'

'In what capacity, may I ask?'

'As a Pupil Support Assistant at Seaton School.'

'You'll know a lot of the children, then?'

'I work with the pupils who need learning support.'

'Only those?'

'On a one-to-one basis, but I come into contact with most of the kids when I'm giving support in the classroom.'

'I see. So you talk to the children on a regular basis?'

'Yes. Though I was off for a few weeks. I'm sure you'll appreciate I've had other things to occupy my attention this past while.'

'May I ask whether you are on particularly close terms with any of these children?'

She felt a flush creep up the back of her neck. 'A few.'

'Mrs Laird, it is beholden on me to advise you that we have received a formal complaint from a member of the public.'

'A complaint?' Maggie's mind raced. 'What about?'

'Suspected paedophile activity.'

She had a sudden urge to evacuate her bowels. 'But that's…ridiculous!' she finished, lamely.

'So you haven't been sitting in your car taking covert photographs of small children?'

'Well, I…' Maggie studied her shoes.

'Can I take it that's a yes?'

For a moment her eyes flickered, then she turned her head away.

'Mrs Laird, you can't go around photographing children nowadays, not without parental permission.' The DI's lips set in a grim line. 'And while we're at it, skulking around in Seaton like you've been doing, you risk getting in the way of a police enquiry. And not just any inquiry – a full-blown investigation.' He paused for breath. One that was going nowhere fast, he was tempted to add.

Allan Chisolm wondered, and not for the first time, whether he'd been wise putting in for the transfer to Aberdeen, for the cultural divide wasn't confined to Glasgow and Edinburgh, he'd discovered. North-east folk were a different breed from what he was used to: civil enough to your face, but holding themselves close, not open like people in the west of Scotland. A bit like that granite the place was awash with: all glitter on the face of it, but just as murky underneath as any other city on the planet. And if ever there was an Aberdonian who typified that dichotomy it was the Laird woman.

'I was only trying to help,' she shot back. 'Prevent some of these poor, neglected kids get into even more trouble.'

'Spare me the justification,' he brushed her off. 'There's a Community Police Office in Seaton for precisely that purpose.'

*Pompous bastard!* Why did this man make her feel like a kid out of school?

'We'll leave that for now,' Chisolm changed tack. 'It has been brought to my notice that your husband...'

'*Late* husband.'

'Late husband, when he passed away, was conducting business as a private investigator.'

'That is correct.'

'And you have now picked up the threads of this business, I understand, along with another...' The inspector looked up to the ceiling. Looked down again. 'Person. A Mrs Wilma Harcus, I believe.'

'Right again.' Maggie squared up to the man. 'Not that it's got anything to do with you.'

Chisolm shifted from one foot to the other. 'And in the course of conducting this business, you wouldn't by any chance have made a connection between pupils at Seaton School and the drug dealing I've referred to?'

She didn't respond.

'Mrs Laird,' the inspector paused as if deciding how to frame his words, 'may I touch on an even more delicate matter?'

She looked up at Chisolm, a stubborn expression on her face.

'I need to ask you now about your relationship with DS Burnett.'

Maggie took a deep breath. 'There *is* no relationship.'

'None at all?'

'He was my husband's best friend, if that's what you're getting at. They were at Tulliallan together.'

'Yes,' the inspector threw her a superior smile, 'I already know that. What I'm asking you now,' he hesitated for a moment, 'is whether there is anything more?'

'Absolutely not.' Her voice was firm.

'Nothing personal?'

'No.' She paused. 'Not that it's any of your concern.'

'How about business?' Chisolm persisted.

'What do you mean?'

'I mean…' the inspector looked Maggie straight in the right eye. 'It might be useful for a private investigator to have a source within the police force.'

She bristled. 'I wouldn't do that – put somebody's job on the line.'

'Wouldn't you?' Chisolm's eyes bored into her.

Maggie's mind ran back to the series of favours she'd begged off Brian. *Lies and more lies.* She felt colour steal up the back of her neck.

'No.'

'So it's mere coincidence that DS Burnett brings me a tip-off on kids dealing drugs in Seaton and that you just happen to work there?'

'I suppose.'

'And in your reincarnation as a private eye that you've been drawing on sources inside Aberdeen Police?'

Maggie blanched. She wondered how much the inspector actually knew.

Another silence, then, 'It seems to me, Mrs Laird,' Chisolm's tone was measured, 'that you've jumped into this private investigation business with both feet.'

She drew herself up. 'That might be your opinion, but...'

'According to my information,' Chisolm cut her short, 'you've first questioned the circumstances of your husband's death. You then proceeded to implicate a well-known local businessman. And now, if my source is to be believed, you've managed to embroil yourself in this drugs business.'

Her mind raced. Where had Chisolm got this information from? It could only be Brian.

'Correct me if I'm wrong.'

'You're right. Up to a point.'

'And what point might that be?'

'Regarding the circumstances of my husband's death, for one. There was absolutely no reason for George to keel over like that,' Maggie's voice wavered, 'without any warning.'

'People do.' Chisolm's tone was surprisingly gentle.

'Yes, I know,' quickly she composed herself, 'but there were other things.'

'What things?'

'Things connected to James Gilruth.'

'James Gilruth, from what I've been led to believe, is well-regarded in this city.'

'He's a crook.'

'Mrs Laird...'

'You know bloody well that man has a finger in every dirty damn business in Aberdeen.' The DI turned his head away. 'Or if you don't know, you damn well should.'

'Mrs Laird,' the inspector turned back, let out a sigh of frustration. 'I understand your distress. From what I've heard, this past year or two can't have been easy for you, but that doesn't give you free rein to indulge in wild conspiracy theories.'

'They're not wild,' Maggie burst out.

'I appreciate that in the circumstances...'

Was that sympathy she saw, or something else altogether?

'You have to earn a living. Though I would strongly advise you against the investigations industry. Be that as it may, I must caution you... And that's why I've come here today, to speak to you in person, Mrs. Laird, rather than on the telephone,' Chisolm stood, feet apart. 'To *warn* you not to hinder the police in the course of conducting your business.'

Maggie took a step towards him. 'Hinder the police? That's the last thing I'd contemplate. What do you think I've been doing this past twenty years but supporting the police? And look where it's got me.'

Chisolm studied his feet. He couldn't believe he was letting a pint-size dame like her get the better of him. The bloody woman had managed to make waves all over the shop. Insinuate herself into matters that were none of her damned business. 'As I've already said, Mrs Laird,' he looked up again, 'I can understand the strength of your feelings.'

'*Can* you?' She drew herself up. 'What do you know about me? Or my feelings?'

'This whole business with Gilruth,' the inspector pressed on, 'and now this latest allegation about Seaton. I cannot allow you to interfere at any level with ongoing investigations. Do I make myself clear?'

Calmly, Maggie nodded an acknowledgement, though she was seething inside.

'Do I have your word on that?'

Saying a silent prayer that God would not strike her down on the spot, she drew a deep breath. 'You do.'

Chisolm raised the ghost of a smile.

'But now,' Maggie said, her voice firm, 'I have business to attend to.' And with that she showed him the door.

# Wanker o' the Week

'Bobby?'

The man turned in the shop doorway.

'Can we have a word?'

They were standing behind him, faces hidden in the depths of their hoodies, two dark figures blurring into one.

'A word?' He shook the drips from his dick. 'W-what about?'

'This and that.'

Brannigan eyed Wilma. 'What's that fat cow lookin at?'

'Never you mind,' she retorted. 'And put thon thing away, will you? It's givin me the boak.'

The idea had come to her that last time Maggie Laird broke down.

*I thought I'd done so well, Wilma. Tracking Brannigan to his local. Waiting till I got him on his own.*

*You done great, pal.*

*No, I didn't. My one big chance, and I blew it.*

*Well, leave it a while, then you can have another go.*

*I might not get the opportunity. Brannigan's already lying low. I'm worried my barging in there will make him duck out of sight completely. And then what will I do?*

*You could get your pal Brian to have a bash. Sounds affa like he's soft on you.*

*I've already asked Brian. He said there were only two ways he could see to get George's case reopened. He said to offer Brannigan immunity from prosecution if he fingers the big fish.*

*And who in hell's got the authority to do that?*

*Nobody we know, that's for sure.*

*What was the other thing?*

*Put a gun to Brannigan's head.*

*Now there's an idea.*

281

*Wil-ma. We can't go round threatening people.*
*Oh, I don't know. These days, I pack a fair punch.*
*Very funny.*
*We could get somebody else to put the squeeze on the guy.*
*Like who?*
*Dunno.*


Hands shaking, Brannigan zipped himself up. 'Ah've tae get hame,' he muttered into his chest.

'That right?'

'Aye,' the wee man trotted off.

'Nae problem,' the hoodies positioned themselves either side, Wilma bringing up the rear.

Silently, the four marched in step.

'Gie us a break, wull ye?' Brannigan darted across the street.

'A break, is it?' the hoodies caught up with him.

'Hiv onythin in mind, wee man?' The bigger one again. 'Couple o' baseball bats fur instance?'

Bobby looked up, eyes out on his cheeks. 'What dae ye want?'

'There's a wee matter needs cleared up.'

'Such as?'

'Tell you later.'

Brannigan knitted his brow. 'Tell me the noo. Ah've tae get hame.'

The big hoodie jeered. 'Ye wisna in such a hurry when ye were in the pub.'

'Naw, weel...'

'An it's no as if ye've got onybody waitin fur ye,' Wilma stepped in. 'That right?'

'Ye dinna ken that.'

'Aye, we dae. Richt, fellas?' The hoodies jerked their heads. 'No that it wis easy, ken? In fact,' Wilma stuck her face right up close, 'ye've bin lyin that low, there wis fuck all atween you an the grun.'

'Aye, weel,' Brannigan ducked his head again.

'But if ye feel ye've tae get hame, Bobby, we can chum ye.' She turned to the two lads. 'You up for a bit of action?'

The lads adjusted their hoodies. 'Bring it on.

Wilma grinned. 'Good stuff.'

X

Brannigan sat on a settee that had seen better days, the hoodies standing over him. Wilma occupied the only chair. She delved into her handbag, extracted a set of car keys and dropped them into her lap.

'This wee matter ye wis needin cleared up…' He put on a show of bravado. 'Tell me aboot it.'

'It wis tae dae wi thon trial,' the chunky lad towered over him, 'the wan far ye wis the prosecution's star witness.'

'The wan that accidentally had to be abandoned,' the smaller of the two chipped in.

'Aye,' Brannigan sneered. 'Hard lines, that.'

'Hard lines?' The chunky lad came back in. 'Is that aw it wis?'

'Aye. Aw doon tae police inefficiency.'

'How come?'

'Wanker turned the tape aff afore ah could pit ma hauns up tae it.'

'Oh,' big hoodie again. 'Nice one.'

'Nae half,' he grinned. 'Got me richt aff the hook. Only,' his voice dropped to a conspiratorial whisper, 'Ah've hud tae keep ma heid doon aye since.'

'Why's that?' the smaller of the hoodies enquired.

'Pigs'll do me fur the least wee thing.'

'That right?'

'Aye,' Brannigan rolled his eyes. 'Bastards.'

'There widna be onythin else?'

'Such as?'

The big lad bent over him, 'Any other reason that trial went up the swannee?'

He shrugged. 'How wid ah ken?'

'Any reason tae dae wi yer…' he leaned further, 'tes-ti-mony?'

The colour drained from Brannigan's face. 'Dinna ken what ye're talkin aboot.'

'No? And what if ah wis tae say that ye're kent tae hiv perjured yersel?'

'Aye? How? Tell me that.'

'By sayin two big polismen were takin backhanders tae turn a blind eye.'

'I-I-I...' Beads of sweat stood out now on the man's brow.

'That's why we've come along the nicht. So ye can tell us aboot it.'

Brannigan drew himself up. 'In yer dreams.'

'Ah said...' The hoodie repeated.

'An ah heard ye.'

'Well?'

'It's mair than ma life's worth tae...'

'Listen,' the big lad grabbed him by the throat, 'it's mair than yer life's worth tae no.'

Brannigan squared his thin shoulders. 'An who's gonna mak me?' He cast a glance towards Wilma. 'If they buggers lay a finger on me, ah'll dae them fur assault.'

'Assault?' Wilma's eyes widened. 'Who said anything about assault?'

'They mebbe no said it,' Brannigan muttered under his breath, 'but that's whit they meant.'

'Naethin tae dae wi me,' Wilma retorted. 'Ah'm jist an innocent bystander.'

'Bit now ye mention it,' the smaller of the two hoodies smirked, 'if oor wee man isna feelin up tae a chat...mebbe we could dae somethin tae persuade him.'

The big lad grinned. 'Ye carryin?'

'Naw. A thocht wi the polis an aw... You?'

'Same. So...' The bigger lad cast around. 'We'll jist hiv tae use oor imagination.'

'Aye,' the other threw in, 'lucky we got plenty o' that.' He crossed the swirly carpet. Picked up a poker from the hearth. 'This dae?' He waved the poker in Brannigan's face.

'Naw,' his companion snorted. 'Ower guid fur the likes o' him.' He ducked his head towards the kitchen. 'See if there's onythin useful in there.'

'Aw, come oan, boys,' Brannigan snivelled, 'there's nae need fur ony o' that.'

'Ye ready tae talk, then?'

'Naw,' his chin wobbled. 'Ah telt ye. Ma life widna be worth tuppence.'

The big lad grinned. 'That's mair than it'll be worth when ah'm done wi ye.' He turned. 'How ye doin in there?' The second hoodie appeared in the kitchen doorway. 'Knives are buggered.'

His companion pulled a face. 'Scissors?'

'Blunt as buggery.'

'Aw, shame – ah fair fancied a bit o' origami.'

Brannigan made to rise. 'Now, come oan, fellas...'

The chunky lad shoved him roughly back onto the settee.

'Cooker gas?' he called.

'Naw. Electric.'

'Shite,' the big lad screwed up his face. 'Don't suppose ye're a DIY man?' He addressed the question to Bobby.

'Naw. Why?'

'Could use a Black & Decker.'

Brannigan shrank back on the settee, face the colour of puce.

'There's a steam iron,' the voice came from the kitchen.

The big lad flexed his biceps. 'That'll dae.'

## X

'That wis guid o' ye,' the big hoodie sneered. 'Fillin us in on yer evidence, like.'

Brannigan contemplated the puddle on the carpet. 'Fat lot o' good it'll dae ye.'

The big lad cocked his head. 'An why d'ye think that?'

'Ah'll say it nivver happened.'

'That right?'

'Aye.'

Wilma rose from her chair. 'Know what these are?' She dangled the set of keys under Brannigan's nose.

He squinted. 'They're fuckin car keys.'

'Aye. And this,' she held up a small black box, 'is a *fuckin* key fob. A very special key fob. Procured for the very purpose of recording one Bobby Brannigan admitting to *fuckin* perjury.'

Brannigan snorted. 'Ye huvin me on?'

Wilma's big blue eyes opened wide. 'Would I do that?'

'Ye canna be serious.'

'Dead serious.' Wilma activated the tape. 'Dumb fucker that you are.'

As the tape played, Brannigan sat hunched, a stricken expression on his face.

'Need any more?' Wilma enquired.

'Naw.'

Wilma paused the tape. 'So you see, *Mister* Brannigan, I've got you on tape, owning up to lying in the witness box.'

'So? Widna be the first time.'

Wilma chuckled. 'Mebbe not. Except,' she threw a backward look at the bruisers, 'this time you're going to put your hands up to it.'

'And how are ye gonna mak me dae that?'

'I'm going to take this tape to the police. Hear what they're sayin to it.'

'The filth?' he scoffed. 'They'll throw ye oot.'

'They will? Why's that?'

'It canna be legal,' he eyed the key fob, 'that thing.'

Wilma grinned. 'You want to take your chance?'

'Aye.' Bobby jutted his chin. 'Fat cow.'

'What do you think, boys?' Wilma turned to the two hoodies.

'Dunno,' the smaller of the two shrugged.

'Fuckin heid bangers,' Brannigan eyed the two lads.

'Taks one tae ken one,' Wilma shot back.

'What if it wis tae fall intae the wrong hands, like?' the other lad

286

offered.

'Now, there's a thing,' Wilma cocked her head. 'Bet the big men wouldn't be amused. No the way ye bandied their names about.'

'Ye widna,' Brannigan shuffled his feet.

'Want tae bet?'

'Yer havin me oan,' Brannigan narrowed his eyes. 'Bet ye dinna even ken wha ye're talkin aboot.'

Wilma chuckled. 'You a bettin man, Bobby?'

'Aye, weel, no lately.'

'Keepin a low profile, ur ye? Canna show yer face doon the book-ies, like? Some life,' Wilma scoffed.

The wee man studied his shoes.

'So ye dinna rate ma chances wi the polis?'

Brannigan didn't answer.

'What ur we gaun tae dae, boys?' Wilma rolled her eyes.

'Bet it would fair raise a storm on YouTube,' the first lad again. He gnawed on a fingernail. 'Eh no?'

'YouTube?' Wilma raised an eyebrow. 'Now there's a thought.'

'Ah've got the movie an all.' The hoodie flicked on his phone. 'Fucker huvin a piss.' He waved the image under Brannigan's nose. 'Wanker o' the Week, how's that fur a strapline?'

'Ye'd nivver,' Brannigan jumped to his feet.

Wilma squared up. 'Try me.'

Brannigan took a step back. He caught his knees on the edge of the settee and sat down heavily. His head dropped into his hands.

'Are you ready now for that wee trip to the station?'

Wearily, Brannigan raised his head. 'Ah'll go the morn.'

'No time like the present,' Wilma said brightly. She turned. 'That right? Wayne? Kevin?'

'Yes, Mum,' the hoodies shuffled forward on their Nike high-tops.

Wayne and Kevin gripped Brannigan by the elbows. 'On ye come, pal.'

'Thanks, fellas,' Wilma grinned. She thrust the bunch of keys back in her handbag.

# A Woman's Touch

Maggie was browning mince in a pan. Behind her, she sensed George's bulk fill the kitchen doorway. She closed her eyes. Waited to hear his footsteps approach, feel his arms encircle her waist.

Her mobile rang.

Maggie started, turned. There was nobody there.

She fumbled for her phone.

'Mrs Laird?'

'Yes?'

'I'm calling on behalf of Innes Crombie. Are you free to speak?'

She turned the gas down to a peep. 'I am.' Colin would have to wait for his tea.

'You worked on a case for us some while back,' the caller continued. 'Do you remember?'

'Oh. Yes.' She wondered what was coming.

'Well,' the woman paused. 'When we received your report…'

Her heart sank. Wearily, she turned and leaned back against the worktop. 'We felt we had to pass it upstairs to our senior partner.'

Maggie's knees felt weak. What had they done now, her and Wilma? They'd made a mess of something, for sure.

'It was so professional.'

She slid down the kitchen units until she reached a sitting position and drew her knees up to her chin. She let her head fall forward to rest on them.

'Mrs Laird. Are you still there?'

'Oh…yes,' she fought for breath. She could barely believe what she'd just heard.

'You'll be aware, of course, that Innes Crombie is the largest firm of solicitors in the city.'

Maggie wasn't.

'And the longest established. And although we already use the services of several…. Ahem.' The caller cleared her throat. 'Several agencies like your own, Mr Crombie asked me to call you, Mrs Laird. He'd like to set up a meeting. At a mutually convenient time, of course.'

Maggie's heart thudded in her chest. She raised a hand to her brow. Wasn't surprised to find it filmed with perspiration.

'Please thank Mr Crombie,' she pulled herself together, '*so* much for his kind remarks. My staff are always pleased to receive positive feedback.'

'Mr Crombie also asked me to say that we have another case coming up.' The woman hesitated. 'A rather *particular* case that will require rather more than the standard treatment.'

'I see.' Maggie didn't.

'Mr Crombie feels this upcoming case demands a more oblique approach. Subtle, one might say. *Delicate,* even. What I think he was trying to say,' the caller adopted a conspiratorial tone, 'is it needs a woman's touch.'

'Oh,' Maggie responded. 'Quite.' With a jolt, she remembered Wilma's blandishments. 'And your terms? How do you propose…?'

The caller cut her short. 'Mr Crombie asked me to tell you that he is fully aware of your circumstances.'

'He is?' Small voice.

'Your firm's fee will, as usual, be open to negotiation. But our senior partner has asked me to assure you that it will be fully commensurate with the importance of the task, and settled by return on submission of your invoice.'

Maggie's mind ran back to the pile of bills that had kicked this whole thing off. 'I'd be more than happy to meet Mr Crombie,' she smiled inwardly. 'How about one day next week?'

## X

'Wilma?' Maggie hammered on the door to the conservatory.

'Hang on,' Wilma bustled through from the back kitchen. She

wiped her hands on an apron that sported what looked like the naked figure of a man.

*Lordy!* Maggie tried her best not to look too closely. That couldn't be a penis, surely. No, it looked more like a…

Wilma opened the door. 'God Almighty, you're in a right state.'

Maggie squinted at her reflection in the glass. 'Am I? That's because I've got the most incredible news.'

Wilma grasped her by the arm. 'Hold yer horses. I've something to tell you first.' She steered Maggie into the conservatory and lowered her into one of the capacious cane chairs. 'On second thoughts, hang on a mo. I'll open us a bottle.'

The two sat ensconced in their chairs, a bottle of wine open on the table between them.

'You know how you tried to out Brannigan?' Wilma demanded.

Maggie wrinkled her nose. 'You don't have to remind me.'

'And you know how Brian said the only way we'd nail the guy was to get a plea bargain?'

'Yes…' She threw Wilma a cautious look.

'Well, I thought and I thought for I don't know how long, and then I had a wee rush of blood. I decided the way forward was to put a wee bittie pressure on Brannigan.'

'If you mean violence, Wilma, haven't I told you a hundred times, private investigation isn't about strong-arm tactics, it's about…'

'I didn't say we'd actually do anything.'

'Who's "we"?'

'Me an a couple o' lads.'

'I don't believe it. You treat this business like some sort of Raymond Chandler novel.'

'Better that than fucking Miss Marple. Any roads, all we did was follow Brannigan home. Surveillance, as you would call it. And that, by the way, is no more than you've been doing in Seaton this past while.'

'Point taken.'

'Then we asked him to invite us in.' Wilma paused. 'Nicely, like. Then once the fellas got him to open up…'

'How exactly did they manage that?'

Wilma tapped the side of her nose. 'Don't ask. I recorded the bugger on a wee gadget I got off the net. Then we played him back the tape. Said we were going to take it to the police.'

Maggie sat up, suddenly alert. 'How did Brannigan react to that?'

'Told us to get lost.'

She slumped back in her seat. 'So all that effort was for nothing,' she mumbled in a defeated voice.

'Not entirely.' Wilma grinned. 'I had to think on my feet – literally. Brannigan sittin there like a piece o' shite. Me standin over him. The two fellas holdin up the doorposts like a pair o' spare pricks.'

Maggie resisted the urge to laugh.

'Anyhow,' Wilma continued, 'I threatened Brannigan with taking it to the big boys.'

'And what did he say?'

'Threw it back in my face. Knew I wouldn't know where to start,' she screwed up her face. 'Fair called my bluff. But then, just when I thought it was game over, didn't Kevin pipe up?'

'Kevin?'

'Aye, useless twat. Oh,' Wilma flushed beetroot, 'sorry, Maggie.'

'That's OK.'

'As I was saying, Kevin came away with he'd filmed Brannigan on his phone. Jist out the boozer he was, standin in a shop door takin a slash, both hands on his miserable wee dick. Kev said he'd stick it on YouTube, and that wee runt Brannigan went white as a sheet. Then Wayne…'

'Wayne?' Maggie queried.

Wilma ignored her. 'Wayne said they'd chum Brannigan to Queen Street, him and Kev.'

'So how did it end up?'

Wilma beamed. 'Fucker's in custody.'

'So…' Maggie could barely contain her elation. 'You did it.

Brought Bobby Brannigan to heel. I don't know how I'm ever going to thank you.'

Wilma blushed. 'Wisna me,' she mumbled. 'More of a joint effort.'

'You and your boys?'

'Naw. You an me. We're a team, remember?'

Maggie smiled broadly. 'So we are. And we're almost there, Wilma. A good way down the road towards getting justice for George.'

'I reckon. Now, will you tell me what got you in such a state? It's not money again, is it?' Wilma fiddled with her glass. 'I know some of those invoices I've sent out have been a bit on the slow side settling, but…'

'No, it's not about money,' Maggie rushed to reassure her friend. 'And yet it is, in a roundabout sort of way,' she reflected. 'Do you remember that fraud case we got from Innes Crombie?'

'Don't I just? Fucker claimed he'd lost the use o' his hands, an him playin the guitar at thon gig.'

'Well, apparently they sent our report up to the senior partner.'

'Christ, we didn't make a bog of it, did we?'

Maggie giggled. 'That's exactly what I thought when the woman rang up.'

'Well, if there isn't a problem, why was she ringing you?'

'Because…' For a moment, she hesitated.

Wilma picked up the half-empty wine bottle. Slammed it down on the table. 'If you don't come out with it, Maggie Laird, I'm going to pour the rest of this bottle right over your head.'

'You've got a nerve, Wilma Harcus. I come rushing round here to tell you and I can't get a word in edgeways. But as I was saying, they've got a big case coming up. The woman said their senior partner wants me to come in for a meeting because…'

'*Maggie.*'

'It needs a woman's touch.'

# It's a Surprise

*Chuggington* was going strong. Six kids – three boys and three girls – sat in a semi-circle on the floor in front of the television. Fatboy, sitting on the settee behind them, fished in his jacket pocket and pulled out a brown envelope.

'What is it? What is it?' There was a clamour of high-pitched voices.

'Never you mind.'

'Can I see? No, me.' The kids jostled one another.

He scowled. 'Calm down, the lot of you.'

There came a chorus of 'Aw-aw-aw-aw-aw.' The children resumed their places, but didn't settle.

Fatboy fingered the envelope. 'You lot fancy a game?'

'Yes, yes.' The girls jumped up. The boys held back.

'One of our old games,' he moved to reassure them. 'Hands up for Pass the Parcel.'

Five pairs of hands shot in the air. The last of the boys shunted up to Fatboy's knee.

'That parcel, what's in it?'

'Not telling.'

A small hand reached out.

'Don't touch.' He snatched the package away.

'Aw...'

'I said...don't touch.'

'Then gonna tell us what's in it?'

A huge grin split Fatboy's face. 'It's a surprise.'

**X**

The parcel was crumpled now, soft from clutching by small hands.

Fatboy crept through to the kitchen. He laid the brown envelope down on the cluttered work surface. Turned on the front ring of the gas stove.

He watched as the spark went tick...tick...tick...tick. But failed to ignite. Fuck! He twisted another dial.

Tick...tick...

Furious, he pulled a lighter from his trouser pocket. Cursed as clammy fingers slipped on the flywheel.

Finally, a flame. He watched as the spark leapt into life.

Fatboy slipped the implement from its paper sleeve. He held it up to the window. Twirled it between his fingers and thumb so the stainless-steel shaft caught the light. A satisfied smile played on his lips. The idea that had come to him was exquisite in its simplicity, and the jeweller in King Street had understood exactly what was needed. He'd fashioned the handle from wood, turned so as to fit snugly into the palm. Then he'd sealed it with varnish and fashioned a protective cuff to separate the handle from the shaft. Fatboy eyed the device on the end. He let out a little snort of pleasure. Wicked! The old geezer had executed his instructions to a T. Well, Fatboy exulted, not so much a T as... He eyed the small X on the end of the shaft.

There wasn't a sound from the living room save for the *CBeebies* voiceover. Fatboy smirked. The kids would be out of it for a good while, gently sedated by the liquid he'd slipped into their juice. They'd sit there, watching the endless circuit of children's programmes. He was familiar with them all by now: *Mister Maker, Small Potatoes, Waybuloo*. He reckoned he'd missed his calling. He'd get a job as a children's entertainer any day.

Fatboy held the implement over the flame. He watched as the X at the tip began to darken and glow. Every nerve end tingled. He'd lain awake for nights on end deliberating over the placement of the thing. The inside of a wrist? Too easily seen. The ankle, ditto. An armpit? Too ticklish. The locus would have to be easily accessed by Fatboy's device, but not apparent to the naked eye. Not that Kym was likely to catch on. As for the other mothers, more fool them for leaving their kids in her care. Nevertheless, the placement was critical. He didn't want some nosy social worker muscling in on his act. Somewhere hidden, then. Private, but not yielding. A trawl of the internet yielded the solution. Fatboy experienced a rush of adrenalin. It would be relatively easy to execute: a few minutes' preparation, the deed over in an instant. The kids would be too out of it to resist. And if they were a wee bit sore for a day or two, so bloody what. Back in their own homes, a wee scab wouldn't signify in the scheme of things. If the kids scratched, well, weren't wee boys always groping their privates? And if they did blab, who in hell was going to believe them? His lips curved into a malignant grin.

The tip of the implement glowed red.

Fatboy turned on the cold tap.

He flicked a few drops of water onto the device. It steamed and spat.

*Ev-il.* His lips curved into a smile.

He'd slipped a fair old dose into wee Kyle's juice. The kid would be fast asleep by now. Wouldn't feel a thing.

## X

Fatboy dropped his new toy into an empty mug and walked through to the bedroom. Kyle lay curled on Kym's disordered bed, one grubby thumb stuck in his mouth.

Fatboy's mouth filled with saliva.

It was time to try out his new toy.

The doorbell rang.

Christ! Fatboy jolted upright.

The bell rang again.

'Fatboy?' It sounded like Ryan's voice. 'Ah'm needin Kyle.'

Fatboy looked at the sleeping child. He looked at his watch.

'You're too early,' he shouted.

'Ah ken.'
'Come back later, then.'
'Ah canna.'
'Why not?'
'Ah'm in a hurry. We've tae be somewhere.'

# The Esplanade

'Far we gaun, Miss?'

Maggie sat in the front seat of her car, Willie Meston hunched beside her. Behind, four small figures were crammed into the back. She'd picked the boys up outside the entrance to Codona's for, much to her astonishment, Willie had turned up, gang in tow.

The funfair was in full swing, the illuminated metal archway over its entrance proclaiming 'Sunset Boulevard' in buttercup-yellow letters. In the background, the Big Wheel loomed. Beyond that, Maggie could make out the elegant silhouette of Marischal College and the stolid bulk of Police Scotland Aberdeen Headquarters. Music was belting out from the fairground, the cacophony punctuated by the occasional excited scream.

She looked around. There were knots of people sitting at the pavement tables outside The Washington Café and The Inversnecky, a sandwich board on the wide pavement proclaiming 'Hot Dogs to go'.

'Just looking for a place to park, Lewis,' she turned, smiling. She looked out to sea. The lighthouse at Nigg Point winked relentlessly. In the opposite direction, lumbering oil barges waited for berths.

Maggie started the engine. Sticking to a low gear, she crawled along the Esplanade in the direction of Seaton. After about a quarter of a mile, she pulled over and sat in plain sight by the sea.

'Right,' she said in a voice that carried real authority, 'who's going to go first?' She glanced in her rear-view mirror. In place of the usual show of eager hands, she was met by a row of bent heads.

Maggie turned her attention to Willie. 'Are you going to tell me what's been going on?'

The boy fixed his eyes on the windscreen. 'Naw.'

'Don't you think you'd better?'

'Fuck's sake,' Willie's head swung round, 'What's it tae you?'

Maggie took a deep breath. 'Nothing. Not directly. It's just, if you go on like this, dealing drugs in the tower blocks, you'll…'

'Ah wisna,' the words shot out of Willie' mouth.

'Willie, as I told you earlier, I've seen you with my own eyes, letting the druggies in and out then running over to Esplanade Court.'

Willie's mouth set. 'Ah wis pickin up Kyle.'

'That's where your supplier stays, isn't it?' Maggie was fishing now.

'Nane o' your business.' With a show of bravado, Willie turned to his back-seat audience. 'Skelly cow.'

From the rear there was a titter, swifty stifled.

*Skelly.* That word again. Maggie knew fine well they were only kids, but still, it stung. Resolutely, she pressed on. 'You'll end up in serious trouble, the pair of you.'

'Aye? Wi who?'

'The police, of course.'

Willie's chin jutted. 'Ah'm no feart o' the filth.'

'That,' she sighed, 'appears to be part of the problem. All the same, it's a bad thing to do.'

'Bad fur who? No the fuckin junkies. It's the only thing keeps them goin.'

Sad, but true, Maggie thought. She took another tack. 'You wouldn't want to get Ryan in trouble with the police, would you, Willie?'

The boy chewed on a finger nail.

'Especially when he's got wee Kyle to look after?'

Kyle sat squirming on his brother's lap.

'So tell me who your supplier is,' Maggie persisted, 'and I'll put in a good word.'

The boy whirled to face her. 'No way. Did ye no hear me?' Willie's face was aghast. 'Ma da'll kill me if he gets oot o' Peterhead an his wee bit steady income's doon the fuckin drain.'

The rain had come on. It puttered softly on the bonnet and

spotted the windscreen. Inside the car, there was complete silence.

Lewis spoke first. 'Miss, gonna get us an ice cream?'

'Shut yer mooth, ye retard, ye.' Willie silenced the boy.

'Well,' Maggie sighed. Alongside her tryst with Brannigan and pursuit of Willie up the Esplanade Court stairs, this had turned into yet another abortive exercise. 'If none of you will tell me what's going on, we'd better be heading home.'

She checked her rear-view mirror. Turned her key in the ignition.

Kyle's hand shot up. 'Did ye tell her aboot the lassie?'

Willie's head whipped round. 'Shut yer mooth.'

Maggie switched off the ignition. She turned to Kyle. 'What lassie?'

The wee boy's eyes were screwed tight shut.

'Willie?' She leaned into the passenger seat.

Willie Meston studied his lap.

'Ryan?' she turned once more.

Ryan Brebner looked out the side window.

'I asked you a question. I need an answer.'

Willie sat immobile. There wasn't a sound from the back.

'I'm waiting,' Maggie's voice was firm, 'and I'm prepared to go on waiting if we have to sit here all night.'

'But Kyle,' Ryan's voice. 'Ah'll git in bother if…'

'Then tell me what Kyle's referring to.'

Ryan shook his head.

'I'll tell you, Miss.' Kieran's voice.

'Fuck you,' Willie hissed. 'If ye hudna phoned the filth… Ah wish noo ah'd let Wiseman duff ye up, ya swotty wee bastard, instead o' lettin ye in ma gang.'

'Me an all,' echoed Lewis from his seat behind Willie.

'You shut yer gob, ya feal shite.'

'That's enough,' Maggie rounded on the two. 'I want to hear what Kieran's got to say.'

'We were in our den, Miss.'

'That piece of waste ground at the top of the Chanonry?'

'Yes. We go there to play, only...' Kieran's voice faltered. 'That night, the night the girl got killed, Kyle got upset. He started crying, and...'

'Naw ah nivver.'

'Yes, you did.'

'Didna.'

Maggie turned. 'Don't interrupt.'

'Then Lewis got hacked off. He climbed back over the gate. Next thing we heard was him screaming.'

'Ah wis no!' Lewis protested.

*Lord Almighty!* Maggie's heart thundered so hard she clasped a hand to her chest. That cry, the one she'd heard when she'd practised surveillance, could as easily have come from the graveyard as the waste ground. She waited in dread for what was coming next.

She tried to still the tremor in her voice. 'Go on.'

'We went over the fence. There was no sign of Lewis. Only his bike lying...'

'And?'

'We went into the kirkyard to look for him.'

'What happened then?'

'It was that girl, Miss.'

'The student?'

'Yes. Willie said she was dead.'

*Oh my God!* Maggie could scarcely credit what she'd just heard. Her mind shot into overdrive. 'And was she, d'you think?'

'Dunno,' Kieran puzzled. 'We tried to take her pulse but we didn't know how.'

'So,' she prompted, 'what did you do then?'

'We were scared. And Willie said...'

'Ah said,' Willie cut in, 'we should get the fuck outta there.'

'You ran away?' Maggie asked in a strangled voice. 'Why?'

'She wis deid,' Willie insisted. 'Or near as.'

'You didn't think to tell anyone?'

'There wis naebody tae tell.'

'I don't mean at the scene,' Maggie reasoned. 'I mean you could have contacted someone in authority: your mum, the Community Police Office...'

'Call the polis?' Willie snorted.

'An ambulance, then?'

'State o' thon quine, it widna be much use tae her neither.'

'So let me get this straight – you left the girl lying there and did a bunk?'

Kieran looked away.

'Well?'

There was silence, then, 'We moved her to a better place first.'

Maggie's blood ran cold. 'You moved what you thought was a corpse?'

'Aye.' Small voice.

'Where to?'

'No far,' Willie again. 'A gravestone. Wan o' thon big yins,' he added helpfully.

Maggie knew from Brian that the girl's body had been moved. But still, she couldn't believe her ears. 'Whose idea was that?'

Willie spoke up. 'Mine.'

'So...what happened after that?'

Kieran again. 'We went home.'

'Straight home?'

'No. We stopped at the shops to wait for Lewis.'

Maggie frowned. 'But I thought Lewis was with you.'

'He was, Miss, only...'

From the back seat, Lewis blurted out. 'Ah jist went back fur a keek.'

There was a long silence. Alongside Maggie, Willie stared straight ahead. She checked her rear-view mirror. Ryan and Kieran were looking out the side windows, though they couldn't have seen much, for the glass was streaked with rain. Kyle's head was back down. The wee boy had stopped wriggling. She supposed he was about ready for bed.

'A keek, you said?'

'Aye.'

Maggie's heart hammered in her chest. Her mind tumbled with terrible imaginings. 'And that's all you did, Lewis? ' She strove to keep her voice normal. 'Just look?'

From the rear, there was not a sound to be heard.

## X

It was raining harder now, water drumming on the roof of the car, running in rivulets down the windscreen. Every now and again, a huge wave hit the breakwater, sending a shower of spray through the railings. The water hit the vehicle like a whiplash: scattered and scratchy, as if someone had flung a handful of coarse sand.

'Did you go back then, Lewis?' Maggie prompted. 'Down to Seaton? Meet up with the others?'

A whispered, 'Aye.'

'And did you tell them? About looking at the girl?'

'Aye,' affronted tone. 'Ah telt them when ah met them at the shops.'

'Ye're fuckin lyin,' Willie spat from the passenger seat.

'Ah'm no.'

'Regardless,' Maggie stepped in, 'I can't believe that you lot came upon what you believed to be a dead body and didn't choose to tell anyone.'

'Clipe here called the polis,' Willie jeered.

'Somebody had to,' Kieran shot back.

'Willie said,' Lewis again, 'that we'd get in trouble if we telt onybody.'

'Trouble? You're already in trouble. Deep trouble. More trouble than you'll ever know.' Maggie turned to address the others. Come to think on it, she was in deep trouble as well. She recalled Brian's strictures about meddling in police business. After that last telling off, she wondered how she was going to explain this episode. And

302

never mind Brian. What about Chisolm? Her heart plummeted into the footwell.

It was still raining hard, a sharp east wind whipping off the North Sea. It rocked the old Volvo. Maggie fervently wished she hadn't parked somewhere quite so exposed.

'Fit ye gaun tae dae, Miss?'

'I'm going to take you straight down to Queen Street.'

'Naw,' Willie sprang to life, 'ye canna dae that.'

She turned. 'I thought you weren't afraid of the police, Willie?'

His lip jutted. 'Ah'm nae.'

'Well, then.'

'It's ma da.'

'I understand that.'

'Naw, ye dinna.'

'I do,' Maggie's voice softened. 'Believe me, Willie, I'm sorry about your dad.' She reached out a hand. Roughly, Willie shook her off. 'And I really do understand now why you're so reluctant to get involved with the police. But don't you see that you've already put yourself bang in the middle of a police investigation?'

'How?' The boy's face was the picture of misery.

'Lots of ways. What about tampering with a crime scene, for a start? Or maybe withholding evidence? I believe the police are still looking for that girl's mobile phone.'

There was a muffled sob from the back.

Willie Meston shrugged. 'Ah didna nick the quine's phone.'

'Somebody did.' Maggie looked at the lad. His face was even whiter than usual. And pinched, like a wee old man.

'Right,' she straightened in her seat. Reached again for the ignition key.

'Ah hiv tae git hame,' Lewis muttered.

'Me too,' this from Ryan. 'Ah'll get murdered if ah don't get the wean back.'

'Whatever, there are questions the police need answers to.'

'Nae way ah'm gaun tae the pigs,' Willie made to open the door.

'Not so fast,' she activated the central locking system. 'I'm taking you down there right now. All of you.'

'But...ma da, he'll...'

Maggie was overwhelmed by a wave of fatigue. She'd been buoyed by the prospect of nailing Willie's supplier. Of saving the boy – and the others, by association – from falling into a life of petty crime. But to discover that these five small boys, four of them her own pupils, had embroiled themselves in a murder investigation was too daunting to comprehend.

'Tell you what...' She had a sudden rush of blood. 'Why don't we do a deal? You lot come with me, but instead of going down Queen Street, I'll take you to a friend of mine. Then you can tell him the whole story.'

# James Goes AWOL

She was already there when he opened the door. She was wearing her work uniform: white tunic with a Nehru collar, short sleeves with a cuff, dark trousers – straight-legged – flat shoes. She looked, he thought, like a dental nurse. The notion appealed to him: the idea that this girl would minister to his hygiene. He felt a stirring in his groin.

'You managed to get away?'

'Yes,' she gave a small shrug. 'Said I had a hospital appointment.'

'Good girl.' James Gilruth rewarded her with a thin smile.

Some weeks back he'd taken out a lease on the apartment: six months with standard conditions. James wasn't at all sure he'd require six months. But the location was convenient: one of the quieter streets running down the hill off Justice Mill Lane. *The perfect bachelor pad.* That was how the estate agent's particulars had described it. Classic, James grimaced. When he'd made his cursory inspection visit, he was met by a cramped hallway, a narrow living area open to a minimalist kitchen, a bedroom just large enough to accommodate a bed and a tiny ensuite shower room. Hardly James Gilruth's idea of bachelor living. But the apartment was adequately kitted out: double bed, leather suite, flat-screen television, kettle and crockery in the kitchen. The agent had been willing to negotiate on the rental figure, and the underground garage was the clincher. There was no way James would want his Jaguar with its personal plate parked in plain sight. The set-up suited his purposes perfectly. For now.

The television was on. She must have been watching it whilst she was waiting for him to arrive. James caught a snatch of the STV lunchtime news:

*17-year-old Aberdeen University student Lucy Simmons was buried on Saturday in a private ceremony at her local church in Frimley Green, Surrey. The body of Lucy, pictured last summer on a family holiday in Sri Lanka, was discovered in the curtilage of St Machar Cathedral on 22nd May. Although the tragic death of the first-year History of Art student, initially suspected to be murder, was later attributed to natural causes, it has had far-reaching consequences: an investigation is currently underway into drug dealing involving children in the Seaton area of the city, and a petition to improve safety issues in Seaton Park has resulted in a consultation process involving...*

'Switch that thing off.'

The girl did as she was bid.

James took hold of her arm, steered her in the direction of the bedroom.

He didn't bother with the preliminaries. Time was money, after all. And the girl *was* on his payroll, whichever way you chose to look at it. He took his glasses off. Laid them carefully on the bedside table. Lay back, legs spread, eyes closed, as the girl removed the necessary clothing. He felt the tension in his spine begin to ease as she worked him over. God, she was good... Way better than that meat from Eastern Europe. Though there wasn't the same edge to sexual relations in the apartment, he'd discovered: the buzz he got when Michelle sucked him off in the salon. Nothing came close to that – the thought that his wife could be sitting just through the wall having her hair done, that at any moment someone could walk in on them, catch James Gilruth, king of cool, with his dick out. He pursed his lips. Partitioning off that back room had been a masterstroke. This place did have its compensations, though, James thought with a small grunt of pleasure: a bed to lie flat on, a shower to get cleaned up in. Above all, it was completely anonymous. In the handful of visits he'd made to the flat, James had never once encountered another soul. Not in the car park. Not in the lift. Not in the hallway. He ran his tongue over his lips in satisfaction.

She was sitting astride him now, her small butt slapping against his hip bones every time he thrust into her. James tugged at her nipples, his manicured nails digging into the soft, pink flesh. His eyes were open now. It amused him to watch the expressions on her face. The girl had spirit, he had to hand it to her. Never cried out. Never complained, not even when he was really giving it to her.

Emitting a loud groan, James ejaculated. He let his head fall back onto the pillow. God, that was terrific! He'd take a quick shower, he resolved. Have her give him a full body massage, maybe suck him off again. Then he'd send her packing.

It would be back to business.

James Gilruth had things to do.

# Urquhart Road

Brian sat in his bedsit. He was dog-tired. Operation Cross Purpose was stretching to infinity, and there was no end in sight. Chisolm had been tetchier than ever that evening. *If we don't get our finger out soon, the press are going to have our guts for garters. And then God help the lot of you.*

Brian saw his chances of making an impression on the new DI vanish faster than water down a plug-hole. He'd been so hacked he was tempted to join the rest of the team for a quick snifter in the Athenaeum. But since he'd split with Bev, he tended to shun company. And besides, that way ruin lay.

He stood up. Wandered through to the cubby hole that was optimistically called a kitchen. He opened the fridge and sighed. There was bugger-all to eat: a single egg, an end of mouldy cheese, a few limp vegetables in the salad compartment. He unscrewed the cap off the milk and took a cautious sniff. On the turn. Brian closed the fridge with a thump.

He looked around. There were dirty dishes in the sink, an untidy stack of carry-out containers on the draining board, an airing rack in one corner draped with damp shirts and socks and underpants. Christ, what a fucking way to live. And it was all down to Bev. Brian hadn't seen it coming. What a knob! And him a copper too. He'd been oblivious to the warning signs: the tarted-up appearance, the nights out with 'the girls'. Put the lengthy phone calls down to loneliness, the way she kept finding fault with him down to Bev's time of the month. Brian kicked himself. Wasn't the husband always the last to know? Oh, well... He made a beeline for the door. Looked like it was going to be another takeaway.

**x**

'Brian?'

He checked his caller display. 'Hi, Maggie.'

'Yes. Look, I'm sorry to be calling you in the evening like this.'

'That's OK. Wasn't doing anything critical.' Christ, Brian thought, as he stood waiting for his Indian meal, if she only knew.

'It's just…I need to ask for your help.'

'Oh?' Guarded voice. On the last couple of occasions he'd offered Maggie Laird his opinion, he'd been sent off with a flea in his ear. You never knew where you were with women. Brian had learned that the hard way. Still… His heart warmed. It was good to hear Maggie's voice.

'D'you remember last time we met, I told you about the young lad, Meston?'

'Ye-es.' He watched as his tinfoil trays were stacked in a carrier bag.

'And you weren't convinced?'

'Look, Maggie,' he slid a note across the counter, 'I'm sorry if I came over the wrong way. Only…'

'I know,' Maggie's voice softened. 'It's your training, that's all. Anyhow, I need to see you.'

His heart missed a beat. Then he steadied himself. She was only coming round to talk about the Meston kid. Still, that was better than nothing. 'When?' he asked.

'Now.'

'Oh,' Brian was torn between euphoria and desperation. On the one hand, he'd never willingly pass up the opportunity to see Maggie Laird. On the other… His stomach rumbled. He hadn't eaten since mid-morning.

'Where?'

'Would it be OK if I came to your flat?'

'We-ell…' There she goes again, he thought, putting me between a rock and a hard place. He didn't respond.

'Brian, are you still there?'

'Yes.' Weary voice.

'So…can I?'

The handles of the flimsy carrier bag were cutting into his fingers. Brian put a hand under the bag, burning his palm in the process. 'I'm not sure.'

'It's just…'

Maggie didn't seem to have heard. Brian wondered if he'd manage to clear the worst of the mess before she turned up. Otherwise… He was weighing his options, when:

'You see, I've uncovered something else.'

Brian couldn't believe this was happening to him. He decided to make light of it. 'Not more pub gossip?'

'Not this time.'

'Well, then?'

'You know how I wanted to help Willie Meston?'

'Yes.'

'Well, it's not just Willie.'

'You mean there are more kids involved in this drugs business?'

'Yes, it turns out there were five children…'

'From your school?'

'Four of them, yes. Willie Meston and Ryan Brebner you already know about. Lewis McHardy. He's a bit lacking…upstairs. Kieran Chalmers. Nice lad. Never been in any sort of trouble.'

'Didn't you say five?'

'Oh, yes. There's a little kid. Kyle, his name is. Ryan's wee brother. They take him along for the ride.'

Brian could just imagine. 'So, these kids…'

On the line there was silence, then, 'They moved the body of your murdered girl.'

'Christ almighty!' Brian didn't know whether to laugh or cry. 'You sure?'

'Sure as I can be.'

'What makes you…?'

'They hang out on a piece of waste ground that happens to be adjacent to St Machar kirkyard.'

His mind raced. 'Where are they now, these kids?'

'With me. I wanted your advice on how I should handle it.'

'*Handle* it?' Brian could contain himself no longer. 'It's a murder inquiry we're talking about here, Maggie, not some fucking Sunday school picnic.'

'I'm well aware of that.' Stony voice.

'Do you know where my place is?'

'I'm standing in the street outside right now. Kids are in my car. Didn't want to speak in front of them.'

Christ, Brian thought, so much for cleaning up. 'Well, then,' he admonished, 'you'll do nothing, Maggie Laird, except stay there. With the doors locked. I'm not at home right now, but I'll be with you in five minutes.'

## X

'What are you thinking?' Maggie asked in a whisper. They were standing face-to-face in Brian's cupboard of a kitchen, the kids sitting squashed up on the sofa bed next door.

'I'm thinking we don't do another thing until I've run this past the DI.'

'Chisolm? No way. I'll remind you, Brian Burnett, that those boys have shared this information with me in the strictest confidence.'

'*Confidence*? Christ, Maggie, we're talking about kids here.'

'And I don't suppose kids have rights?'

His voice rose. 'Give me a break. We've been through all that.'

'Keep your voice down,' she hissed.

'OK. OK. But to get back to what I was saying, I'll need to call this in to my superior officer.'

'We're back to the oh-so-charming Inspector Chisolm then, are we?'

Brian furrowed his brow. 'Quite.'

*God, they can be so pompous, these policemen.* 'But, couldn't you just...'

'Maggie, let me stop you right now. We're talking about a whole catalogue of crimes here.'

'But these children are minors.'

'Misdemeanours, then: their involvement in Lucy Simmons' murder, Willie's drug dealing. Then there's the activities of this Fatboy person – the pornographic material Lewis has just told us about...'

'Hold on a minute,' Maggie stuck her head through the doorway. Kyle was fast asleep.

'Not to mention this Kym, her role in the whole business.' Brian paused for breath. 'Need I go on?'

For a moment Maggie stood, chastened. When you heard it listed like that, it did seem like an awful lot. All the same, wasn't it her job to stand up for the kids in her care?

'Don't bother,' she backed off as far as the confined space would permit. 'It's obvious we're not going to agree, so...'

'You couldn't be more right,' Brian responded in an exasperated voice. 'Look,' his tone softened, 'it's not that I'm completely lacking in empathy. Of course I feel for those kids. Who wouldn't? For you too, come to that. You've landed yourself in an impossible position.'

She looked up. Met his gaze. 'Don't I know it.'

He grimaced. 'I think we both know.'

'What's to be done, then?'

'I need to get these kids along to Queen Street. Pronto.'

'But Chisolm...' Maggie countered. She had a mental vision of her last run in with the inspector.

'Tell you what...' Brian saw his opportunity to get back in her good books. 'Why don't I step outside for a minute? Give the DI a ring? Try to smooth the path, so to speak, before this lot,' he jerked his head at the huddle of small boys, 'have to be interviewed.' He cast his eyes heavenwards. 'You, too, Maggie Laird.'

# VIII

# You Listen to Me

'You come for a kid?' Fatboy's frame filled the doorway. He ran through the routine: right eye, left eye, right eye again. Focused somewhere in the middle.

'No,' Maggie wheezed. Knowing it would take time to launch a drugs raid, she'd doubled back from Brian's flat to Esplanade Court only to find the lifts were still out of order.

'What then?'

'I'm a...' *Play for time.* Her palms were sweaty, her face filmed with perspiration. 'I'm a friend of Kym's.'

'Friend?' Fatboy scoffed. 'Didn't know she had any friends.'

'You learn something every minute.' She offered an ingratiating smile. 'She here?'

'No. Only me. Kids have been picked up. Kym's gone walkies. Left me in the fucking lurch.'

*Get yourself established.* Maggie summoned her courage. 'I'll come in and wait, then.'

'Don't know about that,' Fatboy eyed her with suspicion. 'I've never laid eyes on you before.'

She shrugged. 'I could say the same about you.'

'Well, you can never tell who's on your doorstep in a place like this.' He cocked his head. 'How is it you know Kym?'

*Keep it vague.* 'Oh,' she responded airily, 'Kym and me, we've mucked about together for ages.' She took a decisive pace forward. 'I'm sure she won't be long.'

'Better not be. Fucker's left her keys and there's no way I'd leave the door on the latch.'

'I could hold the fort till she gets back,' she offered. 'Let you get on.'

'We-ell, I'm not sure.' Fatboy took a backwards step.

314

*Go for it.* Maggie slipped past him and marched down the hall.

She found herself in a living room dominated by a shabby sofa and an oversized TV set. Off this space, there was a small kitchen.

*Insinuate yourself.* 'Now I'm here,' she smiled, 'maybe we should introduce ourselves?'

Fatboy ducked his head. 'I'm just a mate.'

'Boyfriend?'

'Nae chance.'

'So,' Maggie persisted, 'if you're not Kym's boyfriend, what have you been doing up here this past while?' *Oh, hell, she was going head-on again.*

'Don't know what you mean.'

She spoke through clenched teeth. 'I think you do.'

'Nope.'

*Too late now.* 'These party games…'

Fatboy's head shot upright. 'Where did you get that from?'

'Never you mind.'

'Some kid, was it?'

Despite herself, Maggie blinked.

'Because you don't want to listen to little kids.'

Her hackles rose. She abandoned all pretence. 'Little defenceless kids. Little kids that have been billeted on some spaced-out child minder.'

Fatboy's eyes narrowed. 'I thought you said you and Kym were pals.'

'Yes, well…'

Fatboy thrust his face in Maggie's. 'You're not a friend of hers at all.'

'I'm…'

He gave her a rude shove. She reeled back. Caught her knees on the edge of the settee. Sat down with a dull thwack.

Fatboy loomed over her. 'What the fuck are you doing here?'

*Lord. I've done it again – jumped in without thinking.* She steeled herself. 'I've just told you. I want to know what's been going on in this flat.'

'Kym's been minding kids on the QT.'

'I'm well aware of that. What I want you to tell me is what you've been doing.'

Fatboy smirked. 'Watching *CBeebies*.'

Her fists clenched till the knuckles showed white. 'Don't give me that.'

He lunged at her.

Gripped her by the throat.

'Listen to me!' Maggie struggled to free herself. She fought for air, her breath coming in short gasps.

Fatboy kneed her, forcing her back onto the settee. His full weight was on her now, the pressure on her neck relentless.

Around her the room was whizzing.

Stars shone before her eyes.

The last thing she remembered was Fatboy's voice.

'No, you listen to me.'

## X

Kym wandered up St Machar Drive. She'd bought a half-bottle of vodka in the Spar. It was lying in her bag sending out 'drink me' signals. Now she was looking for some place to sit down. She frowned. She was sure there had been a bench at the top of Dunbar Street, but she must have got it wrong. She crossed the road and made her way down the High Street to Wrights and Coopers Close. The small memorial garden was protected by stout stone walls. It would make a braw corner for a bevvy.

She settled herself on a wooden seat, fished into her bag for the vodka bottle, took a satisfying slug. She could feel the liquid burn its way down her throat to warm her innards. *Whoa*, she settled back in her seat, *that's better*. She took another couple of swallows. Set the bottle down. Ferreted in her bag. Now she had a drink in her, a fag seemed like a good idea. She burrowed some more. No joy. Fuck! She must have left them in the kitchen that last time she'd had a smoke.

'Got a fag on you?' She accosted a student taking a shortcut through to the High Street.

'No. Sorry.'

Fuck. And double fuck.

'Cadge a fag?' She tried again.

'Sorry. Don't smoke.'

'What you lookin at?' She waved the vodka bottle at a young girl.

The girl ducked her chin and upped her pace.

Kym narrowed her eyes. 'Fuckin nobs.'

She screwed the cap on tight and stuck the bottle back in her bag. She'd better move. That last time Kym had used the place, she'd fallen asleep. Come close to being had up for drunk and disorderly by the community bobby. She hauled herself to her feet and retraced her steps in the direction of the Chanonry. It was a fine day. She'd be sure to find a quiet corner in Seaton Park.

Kym slumped on a park bench. She'd found a sheltered spot, not far from the gates and just over the wall from St Machar Cathedral. In the half-hour she'd been sitting there, she'd hardly seen a soul. It was a different world, she reflected, up here on the other side of King Street: the high stone walls, the muckle great houses wi their fancy curtains, the big gardens, not to mention the garages full of flash cars. So close to Seaton, and yet... She looked around. The park was quiet, green. Small birds chirped in the trees. Not like Seaton, where sodding great seagulls would nick the fish supper out your hand.

She'd polished off the half-bottle of vodka in no time. Kym wondered if she had enough left in her purse to buy a wee carry out on the way home. She had no idea what time it was. She'd been that chuffed to get out of the house, she hadn't thought to pick up her phone. She closed her eyes. Thought fleetingly of the kids – hers and the others – back in Esplanade Court. Smiled contentedly. They'd be fine with Fatboy. She could sit at peace. Her head fell forward onto her chest. As darkness descended on Seaton Park, Kym slept on, undisturbed.

X

Maggie's eyes fluttered open. She was slumped on a sofa in a strange room. She ran a furred tongue over her lips. They were cracked and dry. She tried to cough, moisten her mouth, but her throat was burning. She brought her hands to her neck. It felt sore, as if someone had... And then she remembered.

Painfully, she turned her head. Fatboy was sitting in a chair. He threw her the evils. Maggie's body quaked. Her brain worked overtime. She'd have to formulate a plan. And fast. Even so, she wondered if she'd get out of there alive.

Events overtook her.

'What's that smell?' she squeaked.

'Fuck,' Fatboy leapt up. Shot through to the kitchen.

Maggie struggled to her feet. *Fight or flight?* For a split second, she weighed whether to make a dash for the door or persevere in her mission. She walked unsteadily towards the kitchen.

Fatboy was standing by the cooker, his back to her. The big lad turned. In one pudgy hand, he held a tool. A screwdriver, she thought at first, then her eyes were drawn to the steel shaft. It ended not in a spatula shape or in a point. This object culminated in a tiny, glowing cross.

Fatboy extended his arm.

'What the hell is that?' Maggie's voice betrayed her fear.

'Good, innit?' Fatboy waved the implement under her nose.

She could smell the gas. See the glowing metal. Feel her facial hair singe. *Don't panic!* She drew a breath. Tried to lighten the moment.

'Interesting,' she responded with a feeble smile.

Fatboy advanced towards her.

A grin suffused his face.

'What *am* I going to do with you?' he asked in a deceptively pleasant voice.

'Police!' Someone was hammering on the door.

Fatboy started.

Maggie stood rooted to the spot, the hairs standing up on the back of her neck, Fatboy's hand with its seething cargo hovering inches from her face.

'Open up.' Urgent shout. 'Or we'll break the door down.'

Fatboy's pupils dilated.

'Put the thing down,' Maggie pleaded.

For just a moment, the hand wavered.

There was a crack. Closely followed by another. Then a third.

The door came crashing in.

'Please?'

Heavy footsteps thundered down the hall.

The hand hung in the air, the object so close now that Maggie could feel her cheek hair singe.

A swarm of police officers in visored helmets filled the small space.

Swiftly, Fatboy turned.

He set the implement down.

# A Moosie's Nest

'Do you understand why you're here?' Brian Burnett leaned towards the small boy.

Lewis darted a sideways look at his mother. 'It's tae dae wi the quine at St Machar.'

'That's right,' Brian replied. 'But before I ask you about that, Lewis, can I just make sure we're talking about the right person?' He slid a photograph towards the boy. 'Can you look at this picture for me? Is this the girl you came across in the kirkyard?'

Head bowed, Lewis studied the photograph. He looked up. 'Aye. Only...' his brow creased, 'she wisna smilin.'

Brian straightened in his seat. 'Yes, well, we'll come back to that. But first, Lewis, can you tell me if anyone was with you when you found the girl?'

'Naw.'

'No one at all?'

'Naw.' Lewis scratched his shaven head. 'No at first, onywye.'

'Go on,' Brian encouraged.

'We wis playin in the den. Ah took the huff, so ah went in the kirkyard tae hiv a nosy. Ah fun the quine. She wis lyin on the grun, deid.'

'I want you to think carefully now, Lewis. What made you think the girl was dead?'

'She wisna movin, like.'

'But...'

Lewis jutted his lower lip. 'Ah kent she wis deid cos Willie said so.'

'How the fuck would that wee shite...?' Lewis's mum broke in. She was a large woman, pendulous breasts meeting the folds of her belly. She was clad in tracksuit bottoms and a T-shirt, dishevelled hair framing a face filled with anger and embarrassment.

'Mrs McHardy,' Brian intervened, 'may I remind you that, in your capacity as appropriate adult, you are not permitted to speak.'

The woman's face seemed to fall in on itself.

Inwardly, Brian sighed. Maybe he'd come on a bit strong. 'OK, Lewis,' he said quietly. 'Carry on. Willie said Lucy was dead. But…' he jotted a note on his pad, 'you've just told me you were on your own.'

'Aye, mister, ah wis. But then the ithers came lookin fur me.'

'Oh, OK. So then what did you do?'

'We did a runner.'

Brian drew a deep breath. Exhaled at length. 'I'll ask you again, Lewis – did you do anything before you left St Machar kirkyard that evening?'

There was a long silence while Lewis inspected each of his chewed fingernails in turn.

'I asked you a question.'

The boy looked up. 'We jist wanted tae mak her comfy.'

'Comfy?' Burnett probed. 'How?'

'Liftin her up, like. Onta one o' they big stanes.'

'Whose idea was that, Lewis?'

'Canna remember.' The boy's eyes slid away.

'Think,' Brian urged. 'This is important.'

Lewis hesitated, then, 'Willie's.'

'And did you help Willie?' he pressed.

Lewis nodded.

'How did you do that?'

'Took an arm and a leg each, the four o us. No Kyle. He's naethin bit a fuckin pain.'

'Lewis!' The lad's mother jabbed him sharply in the ribs.

'So,' Burnett steepled his fingers, 'you admit, Lewis, to having moved Lucy's body.'

Lewis cast a covert glance at the lawyer who sat, expressionless, by his side. 'Aye.'

'Is it OK if I ask you some questions?' This addressed to Lewis by detective constable Susan Strachan, who sat alongside Brian.

Lewis looked to the lawyer for support. Found none. He turned to his mother.

'Dinna look at me,' Morag McHardy ducked away, defeat written all over her face. In her short career, Susan had seen that look on too many women: women worn down by circumstance and kept down by need.

The boy looked at the DC. He nodded.

'After you left the kirkyard – you, Willie, Kieran, Ryan and Kyle – can you tell me what happened then?'

Lewis thrust out his chin. 'We went hame.'

'All of you?'

'Aye. Kyle hud tae be hame by eight o'clock.'

The DC lowered her voice. 'Then can you explain to me, Lewis, why your pals had to come looking for you?"

The boy's leg started to spasm. 'Dunno.'

'Because that's what happened, isn't it?'

'N-no.'

Susan shifted in her seat. 'How would you respond, Lewis, if I said you were telling fibs?'

The boy looked up at the video camera. Looked down at the constable. 'Ah'm no.'

'I need to remind you, Lewis,' she persisted, 'that the reason I'm asking these questions is because the police are investigating a murder here. This is a very serious matter, and the way you answer my questions could have very grave consequences. Do you understand me?'

'Y-yes.'

'Well, then,' she adopted a more conciliatory tone, 'let me ask you again. Did you go back to the kirkyard on your own that evening?'

'Christ almighty!' The boy's mother leapt to her feet.

There was a soft pattering sound. A pool of liquid formed on the floor by the boy's seat.

Not again! Susan sighed inwardly. She turned to her superior officer for guidance.

'Let's take a break,' Brian announced. 'Interview suspended at…' He checked the time on the clock, switched off the tape and rose to his feet.

## X

The red light on the recorder winked. 'Are you all right now, Lewis?' Brian enquired.

The boy nodded.

'Did they get you something to eat?'

His face lit up. 'Coke and a KitKat.'

'Good. Well then, do you remember that before your wee break, you were going to tell us about going back into the kirkyard? Is that what you did, Lewis?'

The lad shuffled in his seat. 'Might have.'

'And just say you did,' Brian smiled encouragement, 'what might you have done? Once you got back there, that is?'

Lewis turned his head away. 'Don't remember.'

Morag McHardy's bulk stirred in its chair. 'Ur we gaun tae sit here aw nicht?'

'Mrs McHardy, you've already been warned…'

'Aye,' she glowered, 'richt.' She turned to her son. 'Ye better tell the man. *If* there's onythin *tae* tell.'

Lewis studied his trainers. He stuck a finger in his mouth, gnawed on it for a few moments, took it out again. 'Ah wanted a keek at the quine's willy. Oh,' he corrected. 'Pussy. Wimmin dinna hae a willy.'

Brian resisted the urge to smile. 'That's right, Lewis. They don't. So correct me if I'm wrong – you wanted to have a look at Lucy's private parts.'

'Aye.'

'And to do that, did you have to pull down her jeans?'

323

The boy nodded again. 'An her breeks.'

'Yah wee…' Morag McHardy's outburst was quelled by a stern look.

'What did you find? Can you tell me that, Lewis?' This from Susan.

Lewis looked to the female detective. 'A wee pussy. It was nice,' the boy had a dreamy look in his eyes. 'Soft. Like a moosie's nest,' he added lamely.

'Have you seen a pussy before, Lewis?' the DC enquired.

'Aye.' The boy's voice was indignant. 'Ah seen them on the internet. Bit they wur nae like…' He broke off sharply. 'Naethin but baldy yins.'

'Lew-is!' Morag McHardy again.

'An oor Michelle's hud a Brazilian. Landing strips, the first time round,' he snickered behind his hand. 'An then she hud it aw aff.'

His mother blushed scarlet. 'How the fuck d'ye ken that?'

'Heard her on the phone tae wan o' her mates.'

'Anything else?' Brian came back in. 'I mean did you do anything after you'd had a look?'

Vigorously, Lewis shook his head.

'All right,' Brian scribbled further notes. 'We can come back to that later. What I want you tell me now, Lewis, is whether Lucy had a mobile phone.'

'Aye. It wis in her jacket pocket.'

'Where is it now – Lucy's phone? Did you take it?'

'Nick it, d'ye mean?' Lewis scratched his head. 'Naw. Ah pit it somewhere safe.'

Bingo! Brian leaned forward. 'And where would that be?'

Lewis cast him a vacant look. 'Dunno.'

'Lew-is,' Morag McHardy again.

The lad whirled to face his mother. 'Ye tell me no tae leave stuff like that lyin aroon.'

'All right,' Burnett intervened. 'We'll return to that. So to recap, Lewis, you went back to the kirkyard. You had a look at Lucy's privates. Did you do anything else? Before you left Lucy, that is.'

'Ah laid the lassie oot. That's whit ye dae wi deid folk. Richt, Mum?' Lewis looked to his mother for approval. Morag McHardy turned her face away. 'That's whit they did tae ma gran. Afore they took her to the crem,' Lewis addressed Brian.

'So you laid the girl out, you say? How did you do that, Lewis?'

'Stretched oot her arms and legs. Nice an tidy, like.'

'As if she was sleeping?'

'Naw. Like a cross.'

'A cross?' Brian pounced on the word.

'Nae a straight up an doon cross. It wis a X-shape ah wis meanin.' His face lit up. 'We got that in Sunday School – how Andrew wis a friend o' Jesus, an he...'

'Button it.' Morag McHardy rolled her eyes.

'So you had a wee keek, Lewis, and then you made the girl tidy?'

'Aye,' he grinned.

'What did you do then? Touch Lucy, maybe?'

'The bugger's nine year old.'

'Even so, Mrs McHardy.'

Brian earned himself another hard look. 'Lewis?'

'She looked that puir, lyin oot in the cold like that,' Lewis turned an apologetic face. 'Ah pit a wee cross on her.'

A shiver ran down Brian's spine. 'Why did you do that?'

The boy shrugged. 'Keep the bad folk away.'

'That's whit ye get fur watchin them fuckin videos.' Morag McHardy's face was livid.

'Would those be videos you were shown by a big boy?'

Lewis gave Brian a sideways look.

'Do you remember? Back in my flat, you told me...'

'Naw,' Mrs McHardy answered for her son. 'It's they fuckin Goth things ye're aye...'

'Never mind about that,' Brian quieted the woman with a look. 'We'll return to the videos later. And when you left Lucy, did you leave her lying outstretched on the big stone with her jeans undone and that wee cross on her body?'

The boy nodded. 'Aye.'

'Let me ask you one more thing.' Brian collected his thoughts. 'All that time you were with Lucy – the first time, when you went into St Machar and found her lying there and the other lads joined you, then when you went back on your own to have another look – in all that time, did Lucy show any sign of life?'

A flicker of alarm crossed the boy's face.

'A small movement, maybe?' Brian prompted.

'No.'

'You sure?'

Lewis nodded.

'Quite sure?' Brian persisted.

For a moment, the lad hesitated.

'Do you remember what you've been told?' Brian continued. 'Your answers will have very serious consequences. Not just for you, but for your mum too.'

Lewis looked to his mother. Morag McHardy squeezed her eyes shut.

'Let me put this to you again. Did you see any sign of life?'

The boy shook his head so hard Brian felt dizzy.

'Lewis,' Brian dropped his voice. Leaned across the table.

'She made a noise.' Lewis's eyes were out on stalks. 'A wee wan. Like she wis snorin.'

There was a stunned silence in the room.

Brian bent forward until his eyes were level with Lewis's own. 'And what did you do?' he asked in a soft voice. Not that it made a difference. According to Alec Gourlay, the girl would have died anyway.

The boy cast around the small room: floor, walls, ceiling. He glanced from one official to another: DS, DC, solicitor.

He eyed his mother. Morag McHardy's eyes remained resolutely shut.

Lewis looked down at his hands. Looked up again. He scanned

the four blank faces. Fixed his eyes on Brian.

'Ah jist wanted the quine tae shut up,' he pleaded. 'Look, ah'll show ye.'

Lewis brought a hand to his face. 'Ah said "wheesht", that's aw.'
He spread five small fingers over his nose and mouth.

# Mindin yer Back

Maggie let herself in. Pulled the door to. For a few moments, she leaned back, exhausted. There wasn't a sound from upstairs. Downstairs either. She tiptoed down the hallway and stuck her head into the dark kitchen. Through the window, a full moon cast long shadows onto gleaming worktops through clouds thready as skeins of wool. Tired as she was, Maggie felt a warm surge of satisfaction. She never went to bed leaving a dirty kitchen. Her mother had trained her too well.

She turned. All she'd been thinking about for the past hour was a hot shower and a clean bed. She retraced her steps. At the foot of the stairs she stopped. She'd look in on Colin, she resolved, before she turned in. One hand on the newel post, Maggie stiffened. She was sure she'd heard a noise. It came from behind, from the direction of the front door. Perhaps she'd been followed. Palpitations thudded in her chest. No, surely not. The street had been deserted when she got out of her car. Still, Fatboy had given her a fright. And hadn't Brian warned her if she persisted in pursuing Gilruth, she'd be dealing with dangerous people?

It came again, a low, guttural sound. Like air being expelled from a tyre. No, not a tyre. A balloon, maybe, or a... She stood stock still. Held her breath for as long as she could manage. Snore.

The sitting-room door stood slightly ajar. Hand flat against the woodwork, Maggie exerted gentle pressure until she could just see in. The sodium streetlights cast an unearthly glow over George's chair, stripping it almost completely of colour. Beyond that, the settee loomed out of the gloom like some great grey pachyderm. As her eyes grew accustomed to the dark, she could make out a figure curled there. On the carpet stood a bottle and an empty glass.

'Wilma?' Maggie bent. Gently, she rocked the slumbering figure.

'Ah-ah-ah-ah…' A series of small snorts issued from Wilma's nose.

'Wilma!' Maggie poked a tentative finger into her neighbour's arm.

The figure turned over, back to her. Maggie jabbed again, more aggressively this time.

'Wha-a-at?' The body jerked. Rolled over. One eye blinked open, followed after an interval by the other.

'What are you doing here?'

Wilma's head jerked upright. 'Ah wis waitin fur you, ya daft bugger.' She rubbed her eyes. 'What the hell time is it?'

'Past midnight.'

Ponderously, Wilma heaved herself to a sitting position. 'How did it go?'

She smothered a yawn. 'Tell you in the morning.'

'*Maggie.*' Wilma was wide awake now.

'Seriously, Wilma, I'm shattered.'

'I'll make you a good strong cup of tea.'

'No, it would only keep me awake.'

'Drink, then. I've a bottle on the go.'

'Oh, all right.' She flopped down onto the settee. 'Just the one.'

Maggie took a mouthful from the generous glass of wine Wilma poured. She swilled it around her mouth, savouring the brambly flavours of the Shiraz, then swallowed, letting the peppery liquid prickle the back of her throat.

'Well?' Impatient voice. 'Did them kids play ball?'

She threw a rueful smile. 'Yes and no. I didn't get much joy on the drugs front, I'm afraid.'

'Oh.' Wilma's face fell. 'Wasn't that the whole point of the exercise?'

'Yes. And I did manage to scare the living daylights out of the lot of them during our wee session down the beach. All except Willie.' Maggie pulled a face. 'He was still protesting his innocence when I left him.'

'Then if you didn't get any joy on the drugs…'

'I got something else. Wee Kyle let on it was them moved Lucy Simmons at St Machar.'

Wilma's eyes popped. 'What did he have to say?'

'It was Kieran that filled in the gaps. And after we got to Brian's…'

'Hang on. Brian Burnett? How does he come into this?'

'I took the kids to his place. Willie Meston was so desperate to avoid any contact with the law, I thought maybe Brian might be able to help. He was pretty shocked…' Maggie yawned, 'when he discovered what the boys had been up to. And to top that, Lewis was able to fill us in on the drug dealer.'

Wilma brightened, 'So you got a result after all?'

'And how? Seems the guy is not only dug in to that flat I've had my eye on – the one Kyle goes to the child minder. But he's had Lewis round to his own place to watch porn movies.'

'What a dick!'

'And as if that wasn't enough, there seem to have been some very odd things going on in Esplanade Court. Anyhow, Brian was a big help. Smoothed the path for us at Queen Street.'

Wilma grinned. 'Didn't I tell you he had the hots for you?'

Maggie grimaced. 'Still, I counted myself lucky to get my statement in without running into that bastard Chisolm.'

'So you all went down there together?'

'Brian took the kids. I followed.'

'Did you now?' Wilma threw her a quizzical look.

She buried her nose in her wine glass.

'Maggie!'

'As a matter of fact,' she raised her head. 'I nipped back to Seaton first. Thought I'd check out that flat.'

'You reckon that was a good idea?'

'We-ell,' Maggie looked hang-dog. Her encounter with Fatboy had frightened the wits out of her.

'The dealer, was he there?'

'Yes. Shouldn't have been, but the child minder had gone missing.'

'So what did the guy have to say for himself?'

'Oh,' she looked away, 'not a lot. And I couldn't have been in there long before the police came crashing in, complete with enforcer, and took the pair of us down to Queen Street.'

'Maggie Laird,' Wilma tittered, 'that's some going.'

Maggie glowered. 'What d'you mean by that?'

'Well, first you've had uniform at your door. Next thing you're being escorted down the nick by the boys in black, visors an all.'

She ignored this. 'What I can't understand is who set that up. I mean, Brian wouldn't have had time, and...'

Wilma's nose twitched.

'It's not funny.'

Her shoulders started to heave.

'Wil-ma!'

She was laughing now, mouth wide, head thrown back.

'Stop it.'

Wilma covered her face with her hands, but her shoulders continued to shake.

'What I can't work out,' Maggie ran on, 'is how the police managed to turn up, complete with search warrant, at the very moment when...?'

'When, what?' Concern was etched on Wilma's face. 'Did something happen in that flat, Maggie?'

She shrugged. 'As I was saying, it couldn't have been Brian, and...' Her eyes met Wilma's. Sharply, Wilma turned her head away.

'It was you, wasn't it?'

She turned back. 'What makes you think that?'

'Because you've got that guilty look on your face. Have you been spying on me, Wilma Harcus?'

'No.'

'Then how did you know they were in black, with visors, the lot that took us away?'

Wilma shrugged. 'That's what a drugs raid looks like.'

'I never said it was a drugs raid.'

'Yes, you did.'

'I did *not*. Wilma, I'll ask you again, have you been spying on me?'

'Not spying. Shadowing, mebbe?' she ventured. Then 'If you must know, I was mindin yer back.'

'Why on earth would you...?'

Wilma cut Maggie short. 'You've had me scared half to death, Maggie Laird. And tonight, when I saw you go in... And then you didn't come out again... I damn near had a heart attack. Oh, Christ,' she banged a hand to her forehead, 'I've put my fuckin foot in it again.'

Maggie drew herself up. 'How long has this been going on?'

'Off and on. Ever since thon night you forgot your phone.'

'You've got a nerve.'

'Aye,' Wilma countered, 'I have. It's one of the reasons we make a good team.' Hastily, she changed the subject. 'What about the kids?'

'I never saw them after they went off with Brian. The police would have had to wait for legal representation before they could be interviewed, I suppose. And get the mothers in.'

'No dads?'

'Not a one to be seen. What d'you think will happen to the kids now?'

'Most likely get taken into care,' Wilma slurred, her eyes heavy with fatigue. 'And once that bunch of bleedin do-gooders from Social Services get involved, there's no telling where those weans will end up.'

'But it's not as if the boys did anything wrong. I mean, Lucy was most likely already dead when they found her. The rest you can put down to... Oh, I don't know, kids do such random things. I suppose they *were* culpable in not ringing the police straight away, but the poor girl could have been lying there for goodness knows how long. Those kids were just in the wrong place at the wrong time.'

'Well,' Wilma covered her friend's free hand with her own, 'that surveillance practice of yours in Seaton fairly paid off. If you hadn't acted on your instincts and chased up the drugs angle, you'd never have found out about the other thing and the police might still be going round in circles. Makes you a proper private investigator now, don't you think?'

Maggie gave a huge yawn. 'If you say so. What about you, though, getting Brannigan to own up to perjury?'

'Christ,' Wilma grinned, 'that was some sport.'

'I can imagine.'

'Don't give me that face.'

'I'm not. You did well, there, Wilma. And we've travelled a fair distance together, you and me. But...' Her face clouded suddenly. 'There's a way to go yet, before I'll get justice for George.'

# No Comment

'Christopher – is it all right if I call you Christopher?'

The lad they called Fatboy leaned back in his seat. 'You can call me anything you like,' he answered with a careless shrug.

Brian pursed his lips. He could see this was going to be a bummer. Chisolm had wanted to put someone else on it, but Brian had argued his corner. He wanted this one for Maggie.

'Well,' he responded smoothly, 'Christopher will do for now. So, Christopher, perhaps you'd care to tell me what you were doing in a seventh-floor flat at Esplanade Court in Seaton?'

Fatboy eyed the detective. 'No comment.'

Inwardly, Brian sighed. 'How would you respond if I told you that a quantity of drugs and a large sum of money were found in that flat?'

'No comment.'

Not to mention the implement Brian had been briefed on. *X marks the spot.* Once again, the words ratcheted through his head. And a mountain of empty Calpol bottles. He wondered if the guy was a kiddie-fiddler and all. 'OK, then,' Brian focused his thoughts. 'Let's go back to the Castlegate. What have you been up to there?'

Heavy sigh. 'No comment.'

Christ, what are they like? Watching too much telly, the lot of them. 'Do I take it you'd prefer to wait until your lawyer gets here?' He threw a meaningful glance at Susan Strachan, whom DI Chisolm had insisted on assigning to the interview for a bit of empathy. 'For the benefit of the tape, the suspect has been cautioned but has declined his right to have a solicitor present.'

Fatboy leaned forward. 'As I've already informed your desk sergeant, my father will see to all that.'

'Your father, eh?'

The big lad sat back. 'James Gilruth. You do know who he is?'

'Oh, yes.' Brian nodded. 'I know who James Gilruth is all right.' He paused for a long moment. 'Only...'

Fatboy cocked his head.

'We've got a wee problem there.'

'A problem?' A flicker of alarm crossed the young man's face.

'Yes.' Brian was beginning to enjoy this. 'He seems to have disappeared.'

Fatboy started. 'How d'you mean disappeared?'

'I mean he can't be reached.'

Gilruth's maybe got himself a bidey-in, Brian mused. He felt a stirring in his crotch. Christ knows when Brian last had sex. He folded his hands in his lap to hide his erection.

'But...'

Brian jerked his head towards his DC.

'We've made repeated attempts to contact Mr Gilruth,' Susan smiled sympathetically, 'but I'm afraid his phone is switched off.'

'That can't be right. He never switches it off.'

She didn't miss a beat. 'Somebody has.'

'Well, my mother...'

'Oh...' Tumescence subsided, Brian clutched a hand dramatically to his head, 'I'm sorry to have to tell you this, Christopher...'

Fatboy eyed Brian. He didn't look nearly so nonchalant now.

'Your mum's in Accident & Emergency. Up at ARI,' he added for good effect.

'But how could she...?'

'What do you mean, Christopher?' Answer a question with a question. If the bastard was hell-bent on going 'no comment', two could play that game.

'I don't understand what...'

'Seems there was a wee altercation."

'An altercation?' Fatboy echoed. 'Who with?'

Brian adopted a po face. 'I'm not at liberty to say.'

'When did this happen? Can you tell me that?'

'Earlier this evening, so I've been informed.'

'Where?'

Brian leaned forward across the table. He lowered his voice. 'At your parents' home. Rubislaw Den, that right?'

Fatboy blanched.

Brian grinned. 'Why don't we start again?'

# I Forgot to Say

'What are you two doing up there?' Maggie shouted up the stairs.

'Nothing.'

'Colin Laird, you've been doing "nothing" for the past two hours. I need Wilma down here to help me with some billing.'

Colin stuck his head round the bedroom door. 'Chill, Mum.'

'I'll "chill" you, you big lump.' Maggie marched up the stairs. 'And take that thing off your head.'

'It's not a thing. It's a beanie, Mum.'

*No!* Maggie's heart skipped a beat. *Please God, no!* When the kids had owned up to moving Lucy's body she'd assumed no one else could have been involved. She made to push past into Colin's room. Dispel for good and all the notion that had been burning a hole in her head.

'Mu-um...' He barred the way. 'You can't come in here.'

*Oh, Lord!* Her chest tightened. 'Why on earth not?'

'Because me'n Wilma are working on a project.'

Her whole body sagged in relief. 'A school project?'

Colin shuffled his feet. 'Not exactly.'

'Well...' Suddenly, Maggie felt the need to sit down. 'If it isn't homework, Wilma needs to come downstairs and give me a hand. We *are* supposed to be running a business.'

'Give us five minutes, Mum.'

'*Colin.*'

'What?'

'I need Wilma *now*.'

X

337

'Well, if it isn't Mrs Harcus.' Maggie looked up from her billing.

'And if it isn't *Missus* Laird.' Wilma responded with a cheeky grin.

Maggie set her chin.

'Oh, come on, don't be so sarky.'

'Sarky? You've got a nerve. I've been wading through this billing for an hour or more while you've been upstairs playing computer games with Colin.'

'Tough titty.'

Maggie winced.

'And we weren't playing computer games.'

'What were you doing, then?'

Wilma threw her a sideways look. 'Research, if you must know.'

'*Research?*' Maggie hooted. '*You?*'

'Just because *I* never went to college.'

'Oh, Wilma,' her expression was crestfallen, 'I didn't mean it like that.'

Wilma laughed. 'Just taking the piss.'

'Well, don't. We've got a mountain of stuff to get through, and enough time's been wasted already.'

'Fine.' Wounded voice. 'If that's what you want.'

'Research, you said?' Maggie moved to make amends.

'Yes. Colin was showing me how you can use a RAT. Remote Access Tool, to you. Enables you to access other folk's computers.'

'Spare me the details. All I want to know is are they legal, these things?'

Wilma deliberated for a moment. 'Depends. The tools themselves are legal.' She flashed a wicked grin. 'It's what you use them for.'

She changed the subject. 'Have you heard any more out of Queen Street?'

'No.' Maggie shuffled envelopes into a neat pile. 'I expect Brian's up to his neck, what with the boys and…'

'It was thon drug dealer I had in mind,' Wilma mused. 'Wonder who he is? Fair gave you a fright, by all accounts.'

'When will tea be ready?' Colin ambled into the dining room.

Maggie looked up from the table. 'Half an hour.'

'*Half an hour*? I'm starving, Mum.'

'Well, if you hadn't kept Wilma upstairs…' She broke off. 'How do you know about these RAT things anyway?'

'Oh,' he shrugged, 'everybody knows about those. Everybody my age, anyway,' he added.

'Kirsty texted. She's coming home in a couple of weeks.'

'Thought she had a summer job.'

'She does.'

'Why's she coming home, then?'

'The project she's been working on is going to finish early. Isn't that great?'

No response.

'Colin.'

'Mmm.'

'Oh, damn and blast!'

'What?'

'I can never get a word out of you.'

Colin looked blank. 'I just said a word.'

'What was that?'

'What!'

'Very funny,' Maggie spat.

'Just kidding.' Colin returned a beatific smile.

Her heart melted. She'd been so hard-pressed since she took on the business, she realised, that she hadn't stopped to count her blessings. Her son had such a sweet nature, and in no time at all she'd have both her children back home. Maggie started mapping out in her head the things the three of them would do together.

**X**

'Mu-um. Are you listening to me?'

'Sorry, Col, what were you saying?'

Wilma had gone home and Maggie and her son were sitting at the dining table.

'I was saying, d'you remember way back, when you went for that what-do-you-call-it?'

'No.'

'The hair thing.'

'Oh,' she chuckled, 'you mean my makeover?'

'Right. Well, you asked me about some guy at Gordon's – Chris something or other.'

'Christopher Gilruth.'

'And I didn't give you an answer.'

'No. Not that that's unusual.'

'Name didn't click at the time.' Colin scraped the last of the food from his plate. 'Chris left over a year ago.'

'That's OK. Doesn't matter now.'

'But, Mum...'

'Mmmm?'

'I remembered right after, only I forgot to say.' He frowned. 'You know how we call one another by our nicknames at school?'

'Ye-es?'

'Well, Christopher Gilruth, the guy you were asking about... His nickname – it was Fatboy.'

# A Result

'Well,' Chisolm fixed his sergeant with a hard stare, 'did you get a result?'

Brian Burnett edged in the door. Dropped onto a chair. 'No, sir. Not to begin with, anyhow. Suspect went "no comment" at the start.'

'Lawyer?'

'Lad was read his rights when he was booked in. Didn't want to know. *My father will see to it*, sez he. Mother was in bits when Drugs broke the news. Looked like she'd already done a couple of rounds in the ring, mind.'

'Domestic?'

'Looks like it.'

'Likely to be pressing charges?'

'In Rubislaw Den? Fat chance.'

'The Den? So what I've heard is correct?'

'On the nail, sir. Got positive identification not long since: one Christopher James Gilruth.'

'Jes-us,' the inspector whistled through his teeth. 'James Gilruth Junior. Who'd ever have believed we'd get one over on Gilruth?'

'Not "over" exactly, sir.'

Chisolm shrugged. 'Near as. Where is he, anyway, our James? From what I've heard of the man, I assumed he'd be in here like a bullet, with a line-up of the legal profession's finest as long as your arm.'

'Can't be reached, sir. So we've been told.'

'Out of town?'

'Not according to the wife. But his phone's switched off.'

'That's not like Gilruth. If ever there was a man who likes to be in control…'

'Mebbe he's got himself a bidey-in.'

The inspector scoffed. 'Why would he do that, Sergeant? I understand he's got a ready supply.'

'All those hairdressers.' Brian rolled his eyes. 'A free massage any time you fancy, never mind a bit of "personal service" when the notion takes you.'

'Enough of that.' Chisolm changed tack. 'At the start, you said? So the suspect didn't manage to keep it up, then, the "no comment"?'

'You have to be joking, sir. Once that wee lassie of yours came on with her sympathy routine, he wanted to tell her his life story.' Brian smirked. 'Still going, last I heard.'

'You haven't left her in there on her own, Burnett? Once James Gilruth gets wind, our man will be down here like the bloody proverbial. Need I remind you that interview room protocol needs to be strictly adhered to? More so since…'

'Understood.' Brian didn't need reminding. Hadn't Maggie Laird's problems sprung from just such a breach? 'Once I've given you the update I'll get back down there pronto. In the meantime I've somebody keeping an eye via the camera link.'

'Good man. The suspect, has he admitted to pushing the drugs? That's what matters.'

'Yes sir. He's owned up to the drugs. All pretty low level, from what he's told us so far. Says he's been using since second year at school. Started supplying to friends. Went from there.'

'So why would a…'

'Arrogant bastard. Said he did it because he was bored.'

'Bored?'

Brian shrugged. 'That's what the fella said.'

'So how come this Christopher Gilruth was running that young boy? Meston, isn't it?'

'Da's in the nick, sir. Kid volunteered, allegedly. Wanted to maintain an income stream for his ma.'

'And this high-rise flat, what was Gilruth doing there?'

'Passing the time, according to him, while his runner did trades elsewhere.'

'So,' Chisolm countered, 'what's stopping our Christopher doing the trades himself, did you manage to establish that?'

'Yes, sir. Fella thinks he's Mister Big.'

'How old did you say this guy was?'

'Nineteen.'

'Way to go. In Aberdeen, anyhow, from what I've heard.'

'You're right there. If the serious players get a handle on him, he'll be mincemeat.'

'Drugs tell me they turned up a load of B-class stuff and a heap of cash when they searched the place.'

'Hadn't got that.'

'They've been watching the place for days. Seems your intel was spot on, Sergeant.'

'Looks like it, sir.' Brian tried not to look smug.

'What about the other stuff?'

'There's usually a bunch of kids in that flat, we've been told.'

'Teenagers?'

'No, sir. Little kids. Three...four...Pre-school, anyhow.'

The DI fingered his stubble. 'I see. And have we managed to establish how the suspect got an intro to the flat in the first place?'

'Through young Meston, sir. One of the boys we're interviewing, Ryan Brebner, the wee brother Kyle goes there. Willie Meston gets sent to pick the child up once in a while.'

'And the woman?'

'Kymberley Ewen. Single parent. Three of the children living at the locus are hers. Apparently she's been child minding on the sly for a couple of years. Drugs got that from the neighbours. Not that she'll be registered,' Brian sniffed. 'History of abuse there too: alcohol, prescription drugs.'

'Do we have Ewen in custody?'

'No, sir. Kym was AWOL when the raid took place. They've put out a shout for her. She'll be steamin fu somewhere. Can't have got far. Apparently Gilruth was in the habit of slipping her a few quid so she could go off and have a bevvy.'

'Leaving him alone in the flat with the kids.' Chisolm frowned. 'Our Christopher a kiddy-fiddler?'

'Says not. By his account, he was just passing the time.'

'In a high rise in Seaton with a bunch of under fives?' He snorted. 'That'll be right.'

Brian scratched his head. 'Suspect told us he was "holding the fort".'

'Who for?'

'The child minder. Alleges he was just "giving Kym a wee break". Then, when she tootles off, he keeps the kids occupied. Plays party games.'

'And you'd swallow that?'

Brian shrugged. 'Probably not.'

'And all the while this happy-clappy's going on upstairs, the Meston kid's off trading round the tower blocks?'

'So it's alleged. Doesn't look good, does it, sir?'

'It certainly does not. Plus, if it was all so fucking *Blue Peter* in there,' Chisolm folded his arms across his chest, 'how come they're running toxicology tests on those kids?'

'The Ewen woman was in the habit of doping them up: huge quantities of Calpol, if the empties are anything to go by. God knows what else. But the suspect maintains his presence there was perfectly innocent. Says he'd fucked up his final year exams at Gordon's. His old man was hell-bent on him getting into uni. Had organised some sort of tutor. All got a bit heavy. Christopher moved out of the family home into a flat. He maintains he went down there – to Kym's place – to get away from it all.'

'Let me get this straight, DS Burnett. You're telling me he went from a pile in Rubislaw Den, via some flat, to a high rise in Seaton "to get away from it all"?'

'That's what he's saying, sir. According to Christopher, he has a pretty fractured relationship with his old man, and the mother's out and about doing her thing. Hardly ever on the scene, so, the way

I see it, the lad's sitting in this pad of his the whole day, looking at God knows what on the internet.'

'Doesn't he have any friends?'

'Only one from what I can gather: Torquil somebody or other. Except he's already gone up to uni and it's Torquil who's the supposed tutor so…'

'Our Christopher has had a bellyful of his mate Torquil.'

'Exactly. And when Willie Meston comes looking, and wangles him into Kym's flat in Seaton, Christopher begins to build up a relationship.'

Chisolm knitted his eyebrows. 'I'm not following you, Burnett.'

'I think the lad was lonely, sir.'

'*Lonely?*'

'Well, maybe not so much lonely,' Brian hesitated, 'so much as isolated. Christopher seems to spend hours on his computer.'

'That's hardly unusual.'

'No, sir. But judging from what he's told us, he lives in a virtual world, as it were. Divorced from his family. And we've already established he has no friends.'

'So?'

'I think Christopher Gilruth saw these kids as a surrogate family.'

'But,' the inspector steepled his fingers, 'I understand Gilruth took that boy…' He broke off. 'The one you and the Laird woman brought in.'

'Kyle, sir?'

'That's the one. I understand Gilruth took that boy into the bedroom on a number of occasions. That would suggest there was some level of sexual activity going on.'

'Christopher insists it was only horsing around.'

'I think he's having you on.'

'According to him, sir, it wasn't like that. He insists there was no sexual assault.'

Chisolm splayed his fingers on the desktop. He'd seen it too

345

often, how something that started off quite innocent suddenly took a darker turn. He'd speculated time and again over what prompted it, that tipping point.

'Speaking of assault…' The inspector spoke from beneath angry brows. 'What's this I hear about some implement?'

'It would seem, sir, that when Christopher Gilruth was apprehended he was in possession of some sort of screwdriver. Only…' Brian rolled his eyes. 'There was this cross on the end.'

*X marks the spot.* Once again, the words ratcheted through his head.

'Continue.'

'Well, sir, it looked suspiciously like a branding iron.'

'A *what*?'

'Sir, I know it sounds sick. But they watch such a lot of sicko stuff, these young guys. Live in such an unreal world. The lines must get blurred sometimes. I think this branding iron, if you could call it that, was just another example of the guy acting out his fantasies.'

'And where does this implement come into the equation?'

'We haven't got to the bottom of it yet, sir.' Brian reddened at the unfortunate pun.

'Do you think the Child Abuse Unit needs to be involved?'

'I don't think so. From what I've observed today, Christopher Gilruth is emotionally immature, but would like to come across as a hard man. I think he looked at Willie Meston, saw how his gang look up to him. Thought he could emulate that. Make these little kids into a kind of club.'

'*Club*?' Chisolm's eyes stood out on his cheeks.

'Sir, I know it sounds far-fetched, but I honestly think Gilruth cares about those children: the wee boy, Kyle, in particular.'

'And this branding iron… Has Gilruth given an indication of where he intended to apply it?'

Sweat stood out on Brian's brow. 'God only knows.'

# What about Justice?

The bell rang, one staccato buzz.

Maggie opened the door.

Allan Chisolm stood on the doorstep. He was wearing a sharp pin-striped suit, plain white shirt, discreet dark red tie.

'Inspector Chisolm.' She determined not to look cowed. She could still remember how angry she'd been that last time he came calling. 'Come in, won't you?'

The inspector followed her through to the sitting room. Maggie took up position facing him. At her back, the big chair spoke George's unseen presence.

'Have a seat.' She made an effort to sound cordial. Behind her unruffled exterior her heart was beating fit to kill.

The DI perched stiffly on the edge of the settee.

She waited for what was coming. The silence between them seemed to last for hours, though it could only have been a few minutes at most. Finally, it was Maggie who spoke.

'I know why you've come,' she began cautiously.

*Take your time.* She'd need to be chary if she were to bring her plan to fruition. Even with Brannigan cornered and a confession on tape, Chisolm might be reluctant to help her get the case reopened. And he might not have forgotten that last time she'd kept him standing in the hall with the rain dripping out of him.

He cut her short. 'Before you say anything, Mrs Laird...' He gazed intently into Maggie's good eye. 'I'd like to apologise.'

*Wow! There's a turn-up for the books.*

'We may not have seen eye to eye...' Colour suffused the DI's face as his faux pas dawned.

'That so?' She responded drily.

'Don't get me wrong...'

Maggie could sense a 'but' coming. *Typical. Not like a man to offer an unqualified apology.*

'I was riled,' I admit, the last time I came here. The investigation into Lucy Simmons' death was running on. Six weeks and we still didn't have a cause of death,' the inspector broke off. 'My team was taking flak from all directions: the press, the parents, not to mention the fifth floor.'

*Oh, yes. Let's not forget the fifth floor.* There was no way Maggie was going to go down that road.

'It was all we needed,' Chisolm continued, 'you getting up Gilruth's nose, stirring it up with the drugs boys. Not to mention other...' He cleared his throat, '...matters that have been brought to my notice. Nonetheless,' the inspector fingered his lapel, 'I feel that perhaps I didn't handle it as I might have – our last meeting.'

Maggie felt her face flush. She hadn't exactly handled it well either. Still... She twisted her wedding ring on her finger. *Get to the point, man.*

'So...'

Why was he always so tongue-tied around this woman, Allan Chisolm wondered? It wasn't as if she was a stunner: some knock-out blonde with pneumatic boobs or legs up to her armpits. He recalled the day he'd first come into contact with Maggie Laird. He'd thought her a funny wee thing: striking enough, he supposed, with that flaming red hair. No, not red. Auburn? Chestnut, maybe? Chisolm wasn't great at that sort of thing. And those quirky eyes, there was something about them: so sleepy, sometimes, they seemed to draw you in. Other times they could cut right through you. The Laird woman had a temper on her too, the DI had discovered since.

'I want to offer my sincere apologies.'

'Thank you.'

Maggie looked into the inspector's face. She took in the dark hair. The straight nose. The square jaw. The slight dimple in the chin. And those deep blue eyes. Perhaps they weren't as dead as she'd first thought.

'Perhaps you would let me explain?' Chisolm exhaled slowly, as if a heavy weight had been lifted off his chest. 'You've been instrumental…in helping us resolve a number of matters.'

She raised a questioning eyebrow.

'A case of fraud.'

'Oh, that?' She threw the inspector a sardonic smile.

'The drugs problem in Seaton.'

She tilted her head in acknowledgement.

'Those young boys… Their involvement in that. And in the tragic death of Lucy Simmons. But I won't pretend that I'm happy to see a private investigator get involved in what is properly police business, far less a major investigation. I'm sure you'll know from your late husband that we detectives guard our own cases somewhat…' the DI deliberated for a moment, '…obsessively.'

She pursed her lips, determined not to smile.

'Nevertheless,' Chisolm cleared his throat, 'your intervention has helped us progress a rather moribund police inquiry.'

*Moribund.* The word made Maggie think suddenly of George. She turned her head away.

'That lad, Meston. He's a hard nut to crack, even at his young age. Happily, the other lads have been able to answer a number of outstanding questions for us.'

'I'm glad.'

Chisolm grimaced. 'The circumstances were rather bizarre.'

'So I understand.'

'But if you hadn't taken your duty of care to those children so seriously, who knows how much longer it would have taken to get to the truth of the matter.'

Maggie assumed this was meant as a compliment.

'Please believe me, Mrs Laird, I do have great sympathy for the predicament you've found yourself in, through no fault of your own.'

She stiffened. Was she to take criticism of George as implicit?

'I should never have questioned your business acumen,' Chisolm went on. 'Your ability to carry on your husband's business. Far less your relationship with DS Burnett.'

Once again, Maggie felt herself colour. She'd taken advantage of Brian Burnett. Sailed close to the wind, the very thing she'd pilloried Jimmy Craigmyle for. She wondered for a moment how much Brian had told his superior officer, how much the inspector really knew.

Chisolm paused. He held her gaze. 'I wanted to express, in person, my appreciation of your efforts in helping North East Division resolve these matters. That's why I've come here today.' He flashed a smile. 'Now I've got that out of the way, what was it you wanted to talk to me about?'

'Just one thing, really.'

The inspector cocked his head.

'My husband... You'll have heard about the trial?'

'It would be hard not to.'

'The informant, Brannigan – he committed perjury, you know. Said my husband and his partner had...'

Chisolm held up a hand. 'Let me stop you there. If you're going to tell me about a tape obtained under, shall we say, dubious circumstances...'

'So,' Maggie bristled, 'Brian told you about that?' She wished now she hadn't confided in Brian Burnett.

Chisolm sprang to his sergeant's defence. 'DS Burnett only did so in the light of recent developments.'

'And they are?'

'The drug dealer we have in custody: lad who goes by the name of Fatboy. But of course, I'm forgetting you were present when he was apprehended.'

'You mean Christopher Gilruth?'

The inspector's eyes widened. 'He told you his name?'

'No,' she glowed with satisfaction, 'I found that out for myself.'

'Mrs Laird, you never cease to surprise me. I'd caution you, still, against dabbling in the affairs of James Gilruth.'

She threw the man a sharp look.

'I say this for your own sake,' the inspector added softly.

Those blue eyes again.

'The recent developments you alluded to?' Maggie enquired.

'They involve Gilruth.'

'In what way?'

'I tell you this in the strictest confidence.'

'Naturally.'

'The drugs this Fatboy was supplying, it seems they came by a roundabout route from one of Gilruth's clubs.'

'Oh.' Her jaw dropped. So Jimmy Craigmyle was right enough?

'So circuitous, in fact,' Chisolm added, 'that his own son was completely in the dark. But to answer the question I think you were about to put to me earlier – the tape. The one that *somebody* – and I won't ask you who – went to such lengths to obtain would not stand up in a court of law since it was obtained, as I understand it, under duress. It would require a substantial body of new evidence to persuade the powers that be to reopen your husband's case, and...'

She cut him short. 'What about justice?'

'Ah.' The inspector looked contemplative all of a sudden. 'Justice.'

Maggie swayed on her feet. She'd come so close. Taken such risks...

'Mrs Laird, are you all right?'

'Yes.' Her eyelids fluttered. 'Go on.'

'As I was saying, the tape on its own would not stand up. However, taken together with the information we've already ascertained from Gilruth junior...'

*Pull yourself together!* 'So you think there's a chance...'

'Of getting the case reopened? There may well be. I understand from DS Burnett that your husband's former partner is willing to testify to turning off the interview recording.'

*Don't ask, don't get!* 'And would you be prepared,' she fixed Allan Chisolm with pleading eyes, 'to go upstairs with that?'

He smiled. 'I would.'

*You've done it!* Maggie's chest felt so tight she thought she'd pass out on the spot. She'd pulled it off! Well, almost.

'What about Fatboy? I mean Christopher. I've been worrying, you see, about those wee boys.'

'I'm afraid,' Chisolm looked down at her, his expression grave, 'you'll have to trust me on that one.'

Maggie gazed into those sharp blue eyes. Beneath the veneer of rectitude there was, she decided, an honourable man.

'Trust you?' she said in a soft voice. 'Oh, yes, I do.'

# Sorted

*Aberdeen Police tonight issued the following statement:*

*A nineteen-year-old man has been charged...*

'Did you hear that?' Maggie caught the end of the newsflash as she came through Wilma's back door.

'Aye.' Wilma killed the TV. 'Watched it earlier.'

'That it sorted, then?'

'Seems like it. Come in about.' Wilma led the way through to the conservatory. 'You look bloody shattered, woman.'

Maggie sank gratefully into one of the big chairs. 'I am.'

'Kids OK?'

'Yup. I put Kirsty on the Dundee Express this afternoon. Colin's got a sleepover after rugby training so I'm off the hook. How about you?'

'Ian's working overtime. Said he'd be late.' Wilma hesitated, 'But haven't we got billing to do?'

Maggie grinned. 'Nope. All up to date.'

'Aren't *you* the kiddie?'

'Not *me*, Wilma. *Us*.'

'Us, then,' Wilma beamed. 'So how's about I crack open a bottle?'

Languidly, Maggie stretched. 'Why not?'

'What a friggin week it's been.' Wilma set a couple of glasses down on the coffee table and poured a generous helping of red wine into them.

'Week? Month, more like.'

'And the rest. Anyhow, here's to you, Maggie.' She raised her glass, took a slurp.

'And you, Wilma.' Maggie swilled a mouthful around her tongue, savouring the sensation of it before she swallowed.

'We've covered a fair bit of ground this last while, don't you think, pal?' Wilma took another slurp.

'Haven't we just? Mugging up on the legals. Building our client base.'

'Then you nailing Craigmyle and Brannigan.'

'Hang on,' Maggie interrupted, 'it was you delivered Brannigan.'

Wilma beamed. 'What a team! But the Seaton drugs investigation was down to you, Maggie. And that poor student's death. Those wee lads on the fringe of it.'

Maggie grimaced. 'Poor soul. But what about all the other stuff?' She took another glug of wine. 'Remember that surveillance job I did? Sat outside half the night and it was the wrong house?'

'And the time I served papers on that fella in the altogether?'

'And the guy that set the Alsatians on me?'

'And that pair up Nigg Point. The car was rockin that hard I thought it was going to lift off.' Wilma topped their glasses up. 'In broad daylight, too. Ah wis fair knocked oot o' ma stotter, ah'll tell you that for nothin.'

'You'd have lifted off if that fella had caught up with you,' Maggie teased. 'You have to admit, Wilma, you *can* be a bit of a loose cannon at times.'

'*You've* got a bloody nerve, Maggie Laird, the way you go head-on at things. What about your run-in with that Fatboy, not to mention the time you went off in high dudgeon to beard James Gilruth?'

'Don't remind me. It was a daft thing to do, going to see him like that. I can only conclude I was still in shock, what with the trial and its aftermath and George dying like that. Seeing conspiracies at every turn,' Maggie's lips formed a bitter smile. 'I was in such a dark place, Wilma, clutching at anything, anything at all, that would help make sense of it. Still,' she sighed, 'I guess it was a good exercise, if nothing else. Helped me cut my teeth as a PI.'

'Still, the fella's fair got his comeuppance.'

'How so?'

Wilma grinned. 'You mebbe haven't squared things with the father yet, but you've fingered the son.'

Maggie sat up straight. 'I don't see it like that. It's a disaster whichever way you look at it: for that boy, Christopher. For the parents, for Kym, for wee Kyle. It hasn't all been a disaster, though, the business – has it, Wilma?'

'No, of course not. Look at the number of corporate clients we've got signed up now.' She took another gulp of wine. 'And the corporate accounts are where the big money is, don't you think? All thon insurance frauds. And they're on the up and up. You only have to look at the billing.'

Maggie took another sip of her wine. 'I suppose.'

'And if this new contract comes up trumps, we'll really be sorted.'

'I know. Who'd have predicted that day you'd to run me to Queen Street, I'd be able to get justice for George *and* build something useful out of the ashes of his career? And it's kept me close to him, in a way.' She looked wistful, all of a sudden. 'We can't be so bad at it, either, can we? *A woman's touch.* Isn't that what they said?'

'Aye. And they're no daft. Folk feel less threatened by a woman, Maggie, so you can get more out o' them. Plus PIs can go places police can't.'

'You're right. Fingers crossed, then.'

Wilma twined her fingers. 'Fingers crossed.'

'We might as well finish it.' She upended the bottle into Maggie's glass.

'Dear Lord, have we drunk all that?'

'Not a problem.' Wilma struggled to her feet. 'Plenty more where that came from.'

Maggie closed her eyes. She couldn't believe how far they'd come in the space of a few months. When she thought back to…

'Here we go,' Wilma emerged from the kitchen brandishing another bottle.

'You're a bad influence on me, Wilma Harcus. I'm fairly getting a taste for this stuff. I never used to drink till I teamed up with you.'

'I remember,' Wilma grinned. 'One wee spritzer and you were out of it. Changed days, huh?'

Maggie couldn't believe how much she'd changed since Wilma Harcus first stood on her doorstep. She might look the same.

Well…she raised a hand to her head. Maybe not the hair. But she wasn't the same. She was tougher. More decisive. More accepting of people as she found them. And more aware, of herself and others. Maggie felt the colour rise in her face as she recalled her reaction to Allan Chisolm.

'Here you go, pal,' Wilma proffered the bottle.

'I can't. Really.'

'Course you can. No billing to do. No kids to get up for in the morning.'

'All the same…'

'Lighten up,' Wilma joshed. 'That's your problem, Maggie Laird, you never let up.'

Maggie stiffened. 'I can't help it.' She thought back to Methlick, to the farm. Her parents had led a hard-working, pretty cheerless existence. And she'd been the product of that: innocent, old-fashioned, her values from another generation. What was it Wilma called her once – a country mouse?

She jolted back to the present. 'Well, if I'd let up, as you call it, we wouldn't have got the results we have.'

'True.' Wilma refilled their glasses. 'So why don't we drink to that?'

'Ah wis thinkin…' Wilma's accent always got broader once she'd had a couple of drinks.

'What were you thinking?'

'We're needin tae think aboot oor USP.'

'I suppose that's another one you got off *The Apprentice*?'

Wilma drew herself up. 'As a matter of fact…'

'Oh, don't be like that.'

'I'm not. Anyhow, it stands for unique something-or-other.' She burped. 'What it is that you're tryin to sell.'

'But we're not trying to sell anything.'

'Yes, we are. Only it's a service, not a product. And the name we got off George…' Hurriedly, Wilma crossed herself. 'God rest his soul. It isn't that great, to be honest.'

'I know.' Maggie threw her friend a rueful smile. 'I mean... Prestige? In a dump like that? Bless him! But I have to agree with you. It *is* a bit clunky.'

'Cack-handed you mean? Like me?'

'No, Wilma, quite the opposite. If you hadn't talked me into this whole thing, we wouldn't be sitting here now. With our very own business. The friendship we've developed.'

'Works two ways.'

'How come?'

'You've turned my life around, Maggie Laird – an ignorant Torry quine like me.'

'You're not.'

'Not any more,' Wilma beamed. 'But I'd have done nothin but low-paid jobs for the rest of my days if I hadn't had this opportunity. And look at the weight I've lost. The fun I've had at the gym. Plus I feel I fit in now among these folk in Mannofield. I never felt *that* before.'

'That right?'

'Aye,' Wilma hiccuped.

'But back to the name... You're right. It's too long, too...'

'Awkward,' Wilma snorted. 'Prest-ige Pri-vate In-vesh-ti-ga-shuns. Pretty fuckin useless when you're pished.'

Maggie giggled. 'And talk about being pished... Have you come up with any names, then, if you've been thinking about all this?'

'Nope.' Wilma shrugged. 'Wouldn't know where to begin.'

'I suppose the USP, as you call it, would be a good enough place to start.'

'Right enough, except...we don't friggin have one.'

'We *must* have one.' Maggie knitted her brow. 'We just have to put our heads together.'

'Have a top-up, then, that'll get the brain cells going.'

She held up her hands. 'No more.'

'Aw, come on. We might as well finish the bottle.'

'We've polished off a whole bottle already. And anyhow, I thought alcohol shrank your brain cells.'

Wilma glugged wine into both their glasses. 'Whatever.'

Maggie sat in contemplation for a few moments, then, 'You *could* say we give a very personal service.'

Wilma snorted. 'Sounds like a fuckin massage parlour.'

'Don't remind me.' Maggie rolled her eyes. 'Except what else do we have to offer? We can't say we're bigger. Better. More professional. We don't want to say we're smaller. Cheaper…' She broke off.

'We could say we're two feal quines,' Wilma chortled, 'like thon adverts on the telly. *Sheila's Wheels.*' She belched loudly. 'Only not.'

'Why don't we use our own names, then: Laird and Harcus?'

'Naw,' Wilma slurred. 'Disna rhyme.'

'Well, of course it doesn't rhyme,' Maggie asserted. 'I mean, Laird has one syllable, Harcus has two. Laird has a hard 'a', Harcus has…'

'There you go again, fuckin Miss Know-It-All.'

Maggie leaned forward in her seat. 'I'm not disagreeing with you, Wilma. You're right, you know. Laird and Harcus *does* sound wrong.'

'Pity,' Wilma hiccuped. 'They sound posh, like, our names. A whole lot better than Prestige Private Investigations, that's for sure.'

'I've got it!' Wilma leapt to her feet. She stood, tumbler in hand, swaying alarmingly.

'What?' Maggie opened one eye.

'Turn the names back to front: Harcus and Laird.'

'Sounds pretty good.'

'*Pretty good*?' Wilma hiccuped once more. 'It's fuckin *amazin*.'

She bent. Drained the last of the bottle. 'How'sh about we drink to that?'

Maggie grasped the arms of her chair.

Hauled herself to her feet.

She stood, unsteady, gripping her glass.

'Harcus and Laird,' she slurred.

Wilma threw her a wolfish grin.

'Harcus and Laird,' she raised a toast.

# Maggie Counts her Blessings

Maggie sat, knees drawn up, in George's chair. She cast a critical eye over her front room. Pulled a face. Compared to Wilma's immaculate home, hers was this side of shabby. Still, it would have to do a while yet. Kirsty had a year of her university course still to complete, four if she took Honours. Then if she opted to remain in law, there would be the Diploma in Legal Practice to obtain before she could get a job. Since the cutting incident, she'd been studying hard. Or so she said. As for Colin, if he settled down... applied himself...there's no reason why he couldn't follow his sister to uni. He might even get a bursary. Maggie closed her eyes. She was mortified now that she'd ever suspected her sweet-natured son of involvement in that poor girl's death. But she'd been at her wit's end, what with losing George so suddenly, the mounting debts, her children's manifestations of distress. And then that guy Gilruth in the middle of it all: the way he'd sent those men after her. No wonder she'd been stretched to breaking point, had imagined so many irrational things.

Kirsty still made the occasional jibe about Wilma. But that was born out of grief. Maggie could hear her daughter's shrill voice still:

*That fat cow...she's just some slag from Torry...landed on her feet from what I can gather...*

Then, later:

*Nobody asked you to take on my dad's business. You say you're doing it for the best. Best for you, maybe. You're trying to be Dad. And you can't be. You never could be.*

George had been the family's rock, there was no two ways about it, and Maggie had been devastated by his death. In the space of a few months, her life had changed radically. Talk about a reversal of fortune! Not only was she a single parent now, but her role as a mother had dwindled. She'd have to accept that her son and

daughter didn't need her any more, not in any meaningful way. Still
– she gave herself a little shake – she should be thankful for her
blessings. Didn't she have two healthy children and a solid roof over
her head? Plus she'd made a good friend in Wilma. The thought
of her comforting presence through the party wall was enough to
bring a smile to Maggie's lips. They'd negotiated a winding path, the
pair of them. And there would be pitfalls ahead. But with every day
that passed, she'd grown in confidence.

And what of the future? Well, it wasn't so bleak. With the reo-
pening of the case, she'd made significant progress in her quest for
justice for George. She'd managed to hang on to her post at Seaton,
a job she enjoyed. The agency was now on a sound footing: the
workload shared, the admin well-organised. Maggie's sorties into
the field had taught her to draw on her inner resources. She'd had a
string of minor successes and, if Allan Chisolm were to be believed,
had made a significant contribution to solving a major police case.
Plus she'd learned to trust her instincts. Grit, though, that's what
her experiences as a private investigator had really brought to the
fore. Reflectively, she stroked the solid arms of the chair. His chair.
George would be proud of her, of that she was sure.

Maggie opened her eyes.

Straightened her spine.

*A country mouse* – wasn't that what Wilma had called her?

Well, Maggie Laird wasn't a mouse any more.

# Acknowledgements

For early reading and advice, I am indebted to Professor Kirsty Gunn, Jenny Brown and Esther Read.

For specialist input, Professor Dame Sue Black, Ronald Manning of Aberdeen Public Mortuary, Sergeant Teresa Clark of Police Scotland and former Detective Sergeant Bill Ogilvie.

For patient and skilful editing, Allan Guthrie, Sheila Reid and Louise Hutcheson.

Thanks go to my publisher, Sara Hunt, for seeing Harcus and Laird's potential.

For support and encouragement, to my family and friends, not least Maggie Laird, to whom my protagonist bears no resemblance whatever.

And to the good folk of Aberdeen, whose Doric tongue I have diluted, my apologies.

The events in this novel are entirely fictional and inaccuracies wholly mine.